TWELVE

A DATE WITH OBSESSION

Alan Reynolds

Fisher King Publishing

Published by
Fisher King Publishing
The Studio
Arthington Lane
Pool in Wharfedale
LS21 1JZ
England

Also by Alan Reynolds

Breaking The Bank

Flying With Kites

Smoke Screen

Taskers End

The Coat

The Sixth Pillar

The Tinker

Valley Of The Serpent

A huge thanks to Rick Armstrong for his
unstinting support, guidance and friendship;
also to Samantha Richardson and
Rachel Topping at Fisher King Publishing,
thank you for your patience and great artwork
and to Lisa Slater at Make Your Copy Count
for editorial and proof-reading support.

Dedicated to my family and friends, and to all
those who have supported me in my writing –
your encouragement has been inspirational.

Much love

Do not seek love; love will find you
Alan Reynolds

Chapter One

"Have a great weekend, Sarah. Are you doing anything special?" said Pete Draper, Head of Procurement. Middle-aged, balding, with evidence of a healthy appetite, he was smartly dressed in a suit, the appropriate corporate wardrobe for his role and status.

Sarah thought for a moment. "No, nothing special, just a few chores. You have a good weekend too." She watched as her boss turned and walked down the corridor towards the lift.

Other colleagues turned off their monitors and began packing their bags. There was always an air of excitement just before leaving time on a Friday afternoon. The office was abuzz; banter flowed freely. It was four-fifty. Sarah checked her outstanding files one more time to make sure there was nothing urgent. She thought about making a phone call to a potential supplier, but it wasn't important and could wait until Monday. She logged off the store website; Huntsman and Darby, known as Huntsman's, the largest department store in town, and the most expensive.

Her screen-saver appeared; a loving family picture. Her brother, Spencer, sister-in-law, Angie, and her gorgeous niece, Amber, taken on holiday on one of the more remote Greek Islands last August. In her darkest moments, she envied him, but she would never begrudge his happiness; she loved him unequivocally. She switched off her computer. Her handbag was under her desk; her office space, not generous but manageable. She had come to view it as her private domain after five years and had grown quite protective of her work area. There were more pictures of her family in frames including one of her mum and dad.

"Goodnight, Sarah," said Michelle Stevens, one of the other

buyers in the department and as close to a friend that Sarah had.

"Goodnight," replied Sarah.

"I'm hoping so," said Michelle, holding up a colourful store carrier-bag festooned with love hearts. "Splashed out in the lingerie department, didn't I? Rhys is in for a treat tonight." She winked dramatically and headed for the exit.

Of course, it was Valentine's Day, Sarah suddenly remembered. No wonder there were more risqué jibes than usual. It had been a long time since she had celebrated Valentine's Day. She sighed but quickly snapped out of it. She had her own plans for tonight.

She picked up her handbag, checking around to make sure she had everything she needed. She noticed a couple of colleagues chatting by the water-cooler at the back of the office and waved. "Goodnight. Have a great weekend."

"You too," they shouted back and carried on their discussion. There were just four staff in procurement; Sarah, the senior buyer, reported directly to Pete Draper; her friend Michelle and the two part-time admin support staff came under her wing. They were an excellent team, and Sarah had enjoyed her time working for the company.

She passed the HR Department, which seemed to be in darkness, and the staff at the Customer Experience Centre who would be staying until the store closed at six o'clock. She could see several people tapping away on their computers; some were on calls. She reached the lift and descended the six levels to the exit. The doors parted, and she was greeted by the bright lights of the Cosmetics section which took up most of the ground floor. She looked around; it was busy, mostly, it seemed, with men searching for a last-minute gift for their partners. Heavily made-up assistants were doing their best to help them choose appropriately.

Sarah waved to a couple of staff she knew by sight and headed for the exit. The evening was dark, and there were spots of rain in the air, but at least it was mild, and there was none of the snow which had caused havoc just after the Christmas break.

It was a well-trodden path to the station, and she followed the pavement with thousands of others, making their way to catch their trains like an army of soldier ants. The station approach was austere and not particularly welcoming, just a functional edifice, as the hordes of commuters piled through the entrance and made their way to the ticket barriers. Sarah checked the platform, there were regular changes, but tonight it was the usual, 3B. She presented her monthly pass to the reader at the gate, and the barrier opened giving her just enough time to go through before it snapped shut, ready for the next passenger.

There were crowds on the platform as the arriving train eased its way down. A surge forward, as everyone tried to jockey for positions by one of the carriage doors. Some were particularly adept at this exercise, displaying a degree of self-satisfaction as the door opened right in front of them. A pause to allow passengers to get off, then a scrimmage as the waiting throng surged through the narrow doors, desperate to find a seat. It was like some perverse version of musical chairs. Sarah never indulged in this free-for-all; she would wait for the crush to subside and get on in her own time. She usually managed to find a seat, but not always, particularly on Friday evenings. Tonight, she would be standing for the twenty-minute journey.

The train left on time; her fellow passengers, with few exceptions, were engaged on their phones, texting, messaging, blogging or whatever. Sarah looked out of the window watching the lights of the drab city gradually disappear behind her and into the darkness of open countryside. She could see her reflection in the carriage window. For some reason, she thought about her beloved parents; she so wished she could pick up her phone and chat with her mum. "How was your day, dear?" she would always say, then she would attentively listen as Sarah shared her news.

The accident had happened four years ago, not long after Sarah had joined the store. It still played on her mind; she blamed herself. If only she hadn't asked her dad to pop over and clear a blocked sink. It was only fifteen minutes away, and Sarah always turned to her dad in a domestic crisis. "I'll come too," said her mother. "We can catch up on the gossip while your dad fixes the sink."

It was only seven o'clock, another Friday, but some idiot thought it was ok to have a few drinks after work before driving home. The winding road from her parents' house was notorious for accidents, but the police said this was one of the worst ones they had seen; head-on, both killed instantly; the other driver, three times over the limit, was eventually jailed for five years.

"Jesus," said Sarah to herself; he would be out now, she realised. It was the first time she had considered this; what injustice. She felt the anger well up inside her.

It had taken Sarah a long time to recover from the shock and only now was she beginning to re-build her life. Her brother had been a rock but, having moved to Scotland two years ago, contact was now confined to phone-calls or the occasional video message.

The train slowed down and came to a halt, and the crush started again in the reverse direction; Sarah just waited for the crowd to disperse and exited back into the chilly night air. One or two had raised their umbrellas as they walked away from the station, but Sarah couldn't be bothered to rummage into the bottom of her bag for hers. It was only spitting.

Five minutes later she was pushing her key into the lock of her front door. It was a bit stiff; another job she would have asked her dad to resolve. She turned on the light and was immediately greeted by her cat, Moses.

"Hello Moses, do you want some food?" she said as if addressing a small child. The cat leapt up onto the arm of the sofa, and Sarah bent down to let it lick her face affectionately.

"Come on then," said Sarah.

The cat jumped down and followed her into the kitchen. She went to the cupboard and took out a fresh pouch of cat food and emptied the contents into a bowl. The cat descended on it as if he hadn't eaten in days.

Sarah left Moses to his meal and went upstairs to her bedroom to change. She loved this time of day, a time when she could shut out the cares of the daily grind and just be herself. With a two-day break, the feeling was amplified. She washed and changed and returned to the kitchen to be greeted by Moses relieving himself in the cat-litter tray.

"Oh, thanks for that," said Sarah to the oblivious moggy.

Sarah was extremely organised and tended to cook meals at the weekend and freeze them for consumption during the week; she rarely felt like preparing a meal after work. Tonight, she chose a tuna bake which revolved slowly in the microwave as she made herself a cup of tea. She put the TV on in the kitchen so that she could catch up with the daily news. The cat had finished its business and was rubbing itself around Sarah's legs, seeking attention. Sarah bent down and gave it a stroke which seemed to suffice. It returned to the lounge and curled up on the sofa.

The house was a two-bedroomed terrace. It was small, but it was warm and cosy, and Sarah loved it. It had been financed by the inheritance from her paternal grandparents, and she had spent some time and money bringing it up to her requirements. There was a small front garden and an area at the rear which was more of a yard, dating back to its early twentieth century origins.

She heard the ping of the microwave and placed her steaming meal on a tray, then went into the lounge and took a seat next to Moses who was now fast asleep. Sarah found the remote control and turned on the larger lounge TV. With neighbours on either side, she was careful with the volume so as not to cause any annoyance. She wished they would reciprocate the courtesy. Frequently, Sarah was disturbed by loud music or noise from a games console. She was not one to complain but had mentioned it from time-to-time. There was little else in the way of communication with her neighbours.

She finished her meal and returned to the kitchen placing her plate in the dishwasher, before taking a banana from the fruit bowl to consume while watching the end of the news. Tonight, her evening was going to be different. There was an air of anticipation; a frisson ran down her spine as she thought about her plans. She opened a bottle of Pinot Grigio and poured herself a large glass, then returned to the lounge, sipping as she went.

She had a small table in the lounge behind her sofa; on it was her personal laptop. Placing the wine glass safely away from the computer, she flipped open the lid and signed in. She had the same screen-saver as the one on her work computer.

She smiled as her brother's family appeared. She would call him over the weekend, but not now; this was her time. She didn't want to be disturbed. She opened her web-browser and clicked on the favourites bar; 'LoveNet.com'.

Just a few weeks ago, on New Year's Eve, she had been sitting on her sofa watching TV when she was hit by the realisation that life seemed to be passing by. She decided to try online dating as a sort of New Year's resolution. She needed to change things and decided that finding a partner was a way forward. Her love-life had been virtually non-existent since her college days. Looking back, it seemed her time at University was just one long party, but since her parents' tragic accident, she had become something of a recluse. After the initial condolences from her friends, contact seemed to wane. She found the sympathy difficult to deal with; she left calls and voice messages unanswered until they stopped altogether.

Then there was the department store where she worked. There had been opportunities; she had been propositioned on several occasions, particularly at staff social functions, but most potential suitors were married or just not her type. She had even gone on a blind date, set up by a well-intentioned girlfriend, which turned out to be a disaster. Online dating was the way forward she had decided; it was safe. There were none of the usual rituals required when meeting in a social context. If she didn't like the profile, she just pressed 'delete'; if only all life's problems could be resolved so easily. She had, surprisingly, found it quite exciting.

She took another sip of wine.

Sarah had been registered with LoveNet.com for three weeks, but so far nobody had met her expectations. She logged in and checked her profile again. Age: Thirty-two. Hair-colour:

brown. Eyes: green. Profession: administrator.

She had decided not to be too forthcoming as she didn't want anyone at work to find out she had joined. The rest of the information was accurate. As part of the registration process, she had to complete a personality profile which, according to the website, would ensure the best chance of finding a compatible match. She also had to post four pictures of herself and a short video via the online app; 'a unique service', said Aphrodite, her online host, as she guided Sarah through the formalities. She found this hard just staring at the screen while talking about herself and it took several goes before she was anywhere near happy with the result.

She clicked on the tab that said 'Find Partners'. A woman's voice whispered seductively from Sarah's laptop speakers, soothing and deep. "Hello Sarah, this is Aphrodite, would you like to see the like-minded singles, selected just for you?" A box appeared with three options 'yes, no, cancel'. She clicked 'yes' and took another sip of wine. "Thank you... remember, love is the answer," said Aphrodite, in her intoxicating tones.

It all sounded a bit naff, but Sarah had paid for three months subscription, so she would stick with it.

It was 'Aphrodite' again. "These are your partners chosen just for you through LoveNet's unique matching software. Your love partner awaits."

"I'll be the judge of that," said Sarah, then laughed at her interaction with the virtual assistant. She finished her wine and went to the kitchen to refill the glass.

Back at her computer, she composed herself; for some reason, she felt nervous.

She negotiated the mouse to her first selection and started to read the profile and view the picture. "Hmm," said Sarah, but not in a favourable way. The prospective date was bald, and despite his stated age as forty-five, he looked twenty years older. Sarah moved to the next; a pimply looking geek, twenty-six; hobbies, Star Wars and computer gaming. "Urgh," said Sarah; this wasn't looking great.

She carefully went through each profile and couldn't hide her frustration and disappointment; there had been a great deal of bottom-of-the-barrel scraping, she thought. There was not one that would be remotely suitable. Maybe she was being too choosy, but then why not? It was her life; she needed to be certain before moving onto the next stage.

The final one of tonight's hopefuls; number twelve.

She read the name; Jeremy Steadman, '*but people call me Jez*,' it said. Then the picture; this was more like it. A professional photograph, designer stubble, quite 'hunky' she thought. He would make it to the video stage. She watched the one-minute clip as she drank the rest of her wine. This was promising, she thought, as Jez extolled the virtues of loving relationships.

"I'm looking for more than a life-partner; I want a soul-mate, someone I can help fulfil all their dreams; someone I can dedicate my life to."

His eyes engaged, and it felt as though he was speaking just to her. Sarah shivered. It was a bit over-the-top, but miles better than all the others, and he was good-looking. Number twelve might be the one. She checked the rest of the profile; Age: thirty-five. Eyes: blue. Occupation: IT Consultant. Enjoys keep-fit, running, Chekov and travelling. "Chekov?" she said out loud, "wow." She couldn't imagine any of the rest of tonight's candidates had even heard of the Russian playwright.

This could be it. She replayed the video and checked the

profile one more time. Her hands were shaking as she clicked on the 'Next' button. It was Aphrodite again. "Would you like to contact this person?" said the virtual assistant. There were different methods of communicating with possible partners; mail, video, or chatroom. Again, the three options appeared. Sarah hesitated; then clicked 'chatroom'.

To maintain anonymity, there was a private 'chatroom' where members could engage with potential partners by text message without disclosing personal contact details.

"Would you like to enter the chatroom?" trilled Aphrodite. Sarah nervously clicked 'yes'.

Sarah was starting to feel territorial about her new match. On the face of it, he was so eligible that she imagined hundreds of women wanting to engage with him. She needed to stake her claim before others got their claws into him. The wine was taking effect.

She checked the instructions; it was straightforward enough. There was a dialogue box which said, *'Chat to Jez?'* She clicked on the box and was trying to think of something to say. She entered the word; *'Hello'*; not particularly original, but it was a start. She clicked 'send'.

There was a green light next to his name which indicated he was 'online'. "Shit," said Sarah to herself; "he'll be chatting to someone else". She may be too late. Then came a note above the dialogue box. *'Jez is typing'*, it said. Sarah took another gulp of wine and waited anxiously for the reply.

'Hello, Sarah, how are you?' came the reply. Confident and polite, thought Sarah.

'Fine thanks, you?'

'Fine too. What are you up to?'

'Just chatting with you,' replied Sarah.

'*I saw your profile and video. You look lovely*,' said Jez.

Sarah was taken aback by the compliment. '*Thank you.*'

'*Tell me something about you that is not on your profile,*' said Jez.

Sarah thought for a moment. '*I have a cat called Moses?*'

'*Ha, ha, that's great. Are you religious?*'

'*No, he came in a basket,*' typed Sarah.

'*You are very funny, I love that,*' said Jez.

'*Thank you,*' said Sarah. '*Your turn.*'

'*Ok,*' There was a pause for a couple of minutes, which seemed a lot longer than it was.

'*Are you there?*' typed Sarah, concerned that the connection had been lost; then thought that she might have appeared a bit too eager. The dialogue box opened again, '*Jez is typing*'.

'*Sorry, was just called away. I keep tropical fish. Not sure if they are classified as pets.*'

'*That's interesting; I've not met anyone who keeps fish before.*'

'*Well, it may not be very sexy, but very rewarding, not to mention relaxing.*'

She noticed the use of the word 'sexy' and wondered if it was deliberate to prompt a response. She would play along.

'*It's fine, I love looking at aquariums, sexy or not,*' texted Sarah.

'*Aquaria,*' texted Jez, followed by a laughing emoji.

'*Yes, sorry, you're right. BRB,*' said Sarah.

'*BRB?*'

'*Sorry, be right back,*' texted Sarah. She needed to relieve the effects of two glasses of wine before it became uncomfortable. It would give her a couple of minutes break and reflect on progress. It seemed to be going well; so far, so good.

Sarah finished her bathroom requirements, then went to the kitchen and emptied the remainder of the wine bottle into her glass before returning to her laptop. She noticed that Jez's green light had gone. 'Oh, no, he's logged off,' she said to herself.

There was a moment's panic. She quickly typed a message in the dialogue box. *'Hi Jez, are you there?'*

There was nothing for a minute, then the green light returned, and the dialogue box indicated that Jez was texting again.

'Hello,' it said.

'Hi, sorry about that, just poured a glass of wine,' said Sarah.

'Red or white?' texted Jez.

'White.'

'Let me guess, Pinot Grigio?'

'That's very clever,' said Sarah. *'How did you guess?'*

'It was easy, Friday night, white wine. It had to be Pinot Grigio or Prosecco. Just a lucky shot.'

'Very good, I'm impressed,' said Sarah. *'What's this about Chekov?'*

'I like his plays,' said Jez. *'Very thought provoking.'*

'I only know Three Sisters,' said Sarah.

'I will have to enlighten you,' said Jez.

'Yes, you will.' She was starting to feel intellectually inferior; she had found Chekov's play hard-going when the local amateur dramatic society produced it. She had been at University in Leicester, studying for her degree in business management, and went with a group of fellow students; it would have been at least ten years ago.

The cat and mouse conversation continued for another twenty-five minutes or so until Sarah had to call a further time out. Moses was becoming a nuisance, jumping onto the table and nudging his face against hers.

'*BRB,*' said Sarah. '*Need to feed Moses; he's driving me mad.*'

'*Five loaves and two fishes?*' said Jez.

'*Ha, ha,*' said Sarah. '*Won't be long.*'

Sarah went to the kitchen and took out another pouch of cat food. Her mind, however, was firmly on her new online acquaintance. He was making a good impression and so far, more than met her expectations.

She got back to the laptop and opened the browser. Jez was still online; the green light was showing.

'*Hi I'm back,*' she said.

'*Hi,*' said Jez. '*I've enjoyed our chat tonight. It's ironic that we connected on Valentine's Day, an omen maybe?*'

'*Enjoyed our chat too. A good omen, I hope,*' replied Sarah.

'*Yes, maybe we should meet, what do you think?*'

Sarah was trying to decide if she was ready for this move, but then suddenly thought of the competition; it was time to be bold.

'*Yes, why not?*' she replied, then realised it wasn't very explicit.

'*You don't seem very sure,*' came the reply; he'd spotted the uncertainty. She finished her third glass of wine.

'*Sorry, I'm new here,*' said Sarah. '*Yes, I would like that.*'

'*I see you live in the UK, could you be a little more precise?*' said Jez.

Sarah was feeling much more confident now. '*Leeds,*' she texted.

'*That's a coincidence, I'm not far away,*' replied Jez.

'*Really? That's handy,*' said Sarah.

There was a brief pause, then a reply. '*Sorry, I need to go.*

Do you want to swap mobile numbers save messing around on here?'

'Ok,' said Sarah, and gave Jez her number. Jez reciprocated.

'Sorry must go, chat tomorrow – I'll message you,' texted Jez; the green light went out.

Sarah looked at the screen and felt flat; she was hoping for more and was disappointed he had not confirmed a date.

She re-read the messages, looking for inference; psychoanalysing each word trying to gauge nuances, hidden feelings between the lines. He appeared genuinely interested, and the text messages suggested a connection, but why did he rush away when it was going so well?

She was logging off her computer when she heard a 'ping' on her phone. It was a text message. *'Chat tomorrow, Jez,'* followed by an emoji indicating a kiss.

She replied with the same emoji. *'Look forward to it,'* she said.

That night, she found it difficult to sleep; she was replaying messages in her mind. She felt a sense of frustration and found herself wanting to speak to Jez again.

Sarah's Saturday morning lie-in was interrupted by Moses nudging her face.

"Oh, Moses, go away," remonstrated Sarah, which did no more than encourage the cat to show even more affection.

She checked the alarm clock on the bedside table, seven forty-two. She sighed. "Come on then, let's get you fed," she said to the purring animal and got out of bed.

The cat raced downstairs to the kitchen and stood patiently by its food bowl, still purring. Sarah went to the cupboard for a sachet of cat food.

Moses was soon scoffing his breakfast with the same urgency of previous feedings. Sarah watched for a moment then made a drink. She preferred tea first thing; it gave her a lift. She checked her phone which she'd left charging overnight on the table. She noticed a message alert and accessed her texts. It wasn't one, but several, all from Jez.

'Hello, couldn't sleep- been thinking about you,' said the first, timed at two thirty-eight.

'Just wanted to say hello. Are you there?' Three fifty-five.

'Good morning, hope you slept well,' Six forty-three.

She typed *'Good morning,'* and pressed 'send'. She took a sip of her tea and waited for a reply. After five minutes without one, she decided to return to bed. Moses had finished eating and was making himself comfortable on the sofa.

It was a grey morning and still quite dark. Sarah was deciding whether to read or doze for a while; there was only housework planned for the morning. She started reading but soon began to feel drowsy and switched off the bedside light; a few minutes more wouldn't hurt. Her phone was lying next to her, just in case.

Within a few moments, she had fallen into a deep sleep.

She was suddenly transported to an old house. She was wearing a white shift-dress, popular in the nineteenth century. She could feel herself wandering up and down corridors trying to find her way out. The windows were barred and when she looked through there was nothing there, just a whiteness. She was becoming more and more anxious; her heart was beating faster and faster. Then she was in water, bobbing up and down; slimy walls prevented her getting a finger hold; her hands grabbed, but there was no grip. She could feel her fingernails scraping down the walls. She was shouting. "Help me, someone, help me!"

The sound of a text message woke her. She lay for a second, panting; then the feeling of relief as she realised it was only a dream. Momentarily disorientated, she flayed her arms around searching for her phone. It had manoeuvred itself underneath her pillow; she peered at the screen. It was a message from Jez.

Trying to get her head together, she hazily keyed in her password.

'Hello, hope I haven't disturbed you,' said the message.

She texted back. *'No, I was just having breakfast. Sorry, didn't hear the phone.'*

She didn't want Jez to think she was idle.

No reply; she stared at the phone in frustration, then the dialogue box came alive.

'How are you?' was the message.

'Good, thanks,' replied Sarah.

'I was thinking about you all night,' said Jez.

Sarah wasn't sure how to reply; on the one hand, she wanted to respond in kind, but she also didn't want to appear too keen.

'That's nice,' she replied followed by an emoji of a smiley face.

'What are you doing today?' said Jez.

'Just housework, it's what a girl has to do at weekends, all the boring stuff.'

'Do you fancy coffee sometime?'

'Today?'

'Yes, I want to take you away from your household drudgery.'

Sarah was now wide awake and, without any thought, texted back. *'Yes ok, where, when?'*

'I can get into Leeds. What about lunch? Any thoughts?' said Jez.

There was a café in the store where she worked, but she didn't want to go there; she was too well known.

'Do you know Donicellos?' she texted.

'The Italian Pizza place?'

'Yes.'

'Ok, what time?'

'One-thirty?'

'Yes, that's fine. See you then, bye for now.' The kiss emoji appeared again.

Sarah felt her heartbeat start to race; any thought of housework had disappeared. First question; what should she wear?

She leapt out of bed and opened her wardrobe. Something smart but casual, in control; sexy but not easy; decisions, decisions.

She picked out some new jeans which had been deliberately distressed. The fabric was torn at the knee and thigh with discreet slashes; they were the height of fashion apparently, which meant they had cost almost twice what she would normally pay for a pair of jeans. She looked outside. The weather was brighter, but it was still cold. A blouse and jumper, and her leather jacket would work.

Sarah put her outfit on the bed then headed for the kitchen to get some breakfast, although she didn't feel hungry; her stomach was in knots.

She went back upstairs; some serious pampering was going to be required. She checked her hair; she would have preferred to have gone to the hairdressers, but there wasn't time. She would manage. After a long bath, she did her nails and hair, then returned downstairs for a coffee. The cat greeted her but was just seeking attention; there was plenty of food in his bowl.

She picked up her phone and re-read the messages from Jez. She could feel the excitement mounting.

Sarah checked the times of the trains; she didn't usually travel on Saturday morning. There was one at twelve-fifty which would get into Leeds station at one-fifteen. She put her railcard in her handbag, so that she wouldn't forget it; her mind was all over the place. She couldn't remember feeling like this before, not for a date anyway, and she couldn't understand why. She was only meeting someone for lunch, in a crowded restaurant so she would be quite safe, but she couldn't help herself.

By twelve-thirty, Sarah was ready. She checked her watch for the umpteenth time. Moses was wrapping himself around her legs again, wanting more attention. Twelve thirty-five, she put on her jacket and studied herself in the mirror for the last time; it would have to do.

It was only a five-minute walk to the station if she cut through the snicket; the shortcut which would avoid the main road. She crossed the bridge to the platform for the Leeds train and waited. The electronic destination board stated the train would be on time, just five minutes to go. The platform was busy; Saturday morning was a popular time with shoppers going into the city.

Then came the voice on the tannoy announcing the train's pending arrival. Within a minute, she was joining the others jostling for position at the doors. She found a seat next to a youth who was totally immersed in his mobile phone. Sarah stared out of the window; it was a scene she knew well but, somehow, today it seemed different.

The train arrived on time, and the station was packed, almost resembling the rush-hour. Sarah queued at the ticket barrier, but for a moment, doubts started to creep into her mind. Maybe she should have waited a bit longer, got to know him more before agreeing to meet. But here she was and, taking a deep breath, she headed for the restaurant. Outside the station, the sun was shining. It was still cold, but daffodils were starting to appear in the ornamental flower-beds; not yet in flower, but a sign that spring was not far away.

Donicellos was at the top of the main city-centre complex and was a popular meeting place. She had been there a few times for lunch with clients. She could see the neon sign 'Donicellos Pizza House' glowing just beyond the entrance to the small mall. Sarah breathed in as she took the escalator to the entrance on the second level.

A waiter with a white tea-towel over his shoulder greeted her. 'Buon Giorno signora... have you a reservation?'

'I'm waiting for a friend,' said Sarah.

Then she heard a voice. 'Sarah, is that you?'

Chapter Two

Sarah turned around and recognised him straight away. She waved.

Jez had also dressed for the weather; jeans, a large Aran woollen sweater, an expensive windcheater jacket which was unzipped, a scarf, and black ankle boots. It was as though he'd walked off the pages of a fashion magazine and he would not have looked out of place in a café-bar in Paris.

The waiter escorted Sarah to the table, Jez stepped towards her as she approached. He seemed to hesitate, not knowing what to do, and then, rather awkwardly he kissed her cheek as a fond friend might do.

"You look nice," said Jez as the waiter was making sure she was seated comfortably. It was a small table, set for two, but big enough to ensure there was no invasion of personal space.

"Would you like to see the wine list?" said the waiter before Sarah had time to respond to Jez's compliment.

"Can you give us a minute?" said Jez, sharply and the waiter skulked away to his front of house duties. The rudeness slightly unnerved Sarah.

She decided to ignore it and slipped off her jacket, placing it on the back of the chair; Jez did the same.

"You really do look lovely," said Jez, whose eyes seemed to be scanning the top half of her body.

"Thank you," said Sarah.

"So, how are you?" said Jez.

"I'm fine thanks, have you been waiting long?"

"No, only a couple of minutes, never been in here before."

"I come here quite often; I work not far away," said Sarah.

"Whereabouts?" said Jez.

"Huntsman's."

"Really? It's one of my favourites stores," said Jez.

"Glad to hear it," said Sarah.

"What do you do there?"

"I'm head buyer. Been there about five years," said Sarah.

"That must be very handy; I bet you get a good discount," said Jez.

"Twenty percent," said Sarah. "Not bad, but I don't buy a lot from there, even with twenty percent, it's pretty pricey."

"Ha, I'm glad you don't do my advertising," said Jez mockingly.

"So, what about you?"

"Computers," said Jez.

They were interrupted by a waitress who had come to take their order.

"What do you fancy?" said Jez. "My treat."

The menus were in a small metal stepped-rack in the middle of the table. Sarah took one out and opened it. "Thanks, just a pizza will be fine. I usually have a Margarita here; they're delicious."

Jez looked at the waitress. "Two Pizza Margarita's and a bottle of Pinot Grigio, please," said Jez. "You ok with that?" said Jez, looking at Sarah.

"Yes. That's great." Her eyes locked on his momentarily, but she quickly looked down unable to keep the gaze.

Sarah was considering the early encounters. He was certainly someone who knew his own mind, assertive and confident. He spoke well, in what she would call a 'refined' Yorkshire accent. He sounded his 'aitches' and used the short 'a' sound so 'bath' and 'castle' would be pronounced in the same way as 'café'. He had a similar accent to her boss, Pete.

The waitress made a note and walked away towards the kitchen with the order. Before they could resume the conversation, another waiter arrived with a bottle of wine which he presented to Jez with due ceremony. Jez studied the bottle with interest. "Alto Adige."

"Sorry," said Sarah, not picking up the context.

"It's a winemaking area, Northern Italy, not bad," said Jez.

"I get mine from Aldi," she replied and started to laugh nervously; she still felt tense.

Jez smiled and nodded to the waiter who unscrewed the top and poured a thimble-full in his glass. Jez took a sip and swished it around his mouth.

"Could be a little colder," said Jez. "But it will do."

The waiter poured a measure in Sarah's glass then returned to Jez's and filled it half-full.

"Where did you say it was from?" said Sarah.

"Alto Adige," said Jez. "It's up in the North, the South Tyrol area, beautiful countryside. Have you been?"

"No," said Sarah. "Are you an expert then… on wines?"

"Not really, no, but I do have a reasonable cellar," said Jez.

"A cellar?" said Sarah. "That sounds impressive."

"No, no," he back-tracked; "just a few bottles I've collected over the years. It was my father who was the expert."

"Your father?"

"Yes, he's dead now, died three years ago, unfortunately. It's just me and my mother now. Do you have parents; alive I mean?"

"No, they were both killed in a car accident just over four years ago."

"Oh, I'm sorry to hear that. Any other relatives?" said Jez.

"Just my brother, he lives up in Scotland. I don't see much

of him these days, but we do keep in touch regularly. What about you?"

"No, I'm an only child, just me and my mother," said Jez.

"You must have a large house," said Sarah. "To have a cellar, I mean."

"Hmm, I don't know about that, it's ok, but it's not mine; it belongs to my mother."

"And you work from home? You mentioned computers," said Sarah.

"Yes, my mother likes me to be around. She doesn't get out much," replied Jez.

"What is it you do, then?" asked Sarah.

"Whatever the client needs; software programming, designing websites, among other things. I can do most things from home, just the occasional customer visit."

"How long have you been doing that?"

"About three years."

"And before that?" asked Sarah.

"Worked for a software company."

"Locally?"

"No, down in London. I was only there a couple of years, didn't like it that much to tell you the truth. I moved back when my father became ill. After he died, my mother couldn't cope, so I stayed and set up my own business."

"A big decision," said Sarah.

"Yes, I guess, but I think family is important. It's turned out ok."

They were again disturbed by the wine-waiter carrying an ice bucket. He picked up the half bottle of wine from the table and buried it in the cubes.

Jez glared at the man, irritated by the interruption, but he said nothing. The waiter walked away, muttering something in Italian which probably wasn't complimentary.

Sarah took a sip from her glass; she was pacing herself; she didn't normally indulge in lunchtime drinking.

"So, whereabouts is this big house of yours?" asked Sarah.

"It's not mine, it's mother's," said Jez.

It seemed like a sharp response, but before Sarah could react the food arrived.

"This looks good," said Jez, seeing the large plate of pizza. There was a cutting device by the side of the plate together with a knife and fork. He looked at Sarah. "A good choice, I can see you have great taste."

"Thanks," said Sarah.

They both started to cut their pizzas into slices. Jez picked up his first slice with his fingers and started eating. Sarah cut hers with her knife and fork and consumed the first mouthful.

"Tastes good," said Jez.

"Yes, the food here is excellent," said Sarah.

"Deighton," said Jez.

"Deighton?" asked Sarah, not following the thread.

"It's where I live, Deighton Hall."

"That's up near Skipton, isn't it?"

"Yes, the other side, towards Colne, about five or six miles," said Jez.

"You live in a hall? Wow, that sounds impressive."

"I don't know about that," said Jez. "I was born there, so I don't know anything else."

"You came in by train?" asked Sarah.

"Yes, it's a lot easier. Parking in Leeds is a nightmare," said Jez. "It's only fifteen, twenty minutes to the station in Skipton."

"I would love to hear more about it; it sounds fascinating," said Sarah as she was consuming another slice of pizza.

"Well, my father bought the house. He was an entrepreneur, a very successful one too, in advertising." Jez was wrestling with a piece of pizza that left a trail of melted mozzarella down his chin. He wiped it away with his napkin. The waiter reappeared and refilled the wine glasses.

"Thanks," said Sarah, making eye-contact with the waiter. Jez did not acknowledge him.

"What was I saying?"

"You were telling me about your father."

"Oh, yes; you were asking about the house. Hmm, as I was saying, he sold out in the mid-seventies and used some of the proceeds to buy the Hall. The rest he invested and moved into property development. He did that until he died."

"I see," said Sarah. "And it's just you and your mum?"

"Yes, although there are staff."

"Staff?"

"Well, I say staff… the gardener and the daily. Mother finds housework difficult."

"Yes, I can understand," said Sarah. "It's not easy in a two-bed terrace when you work full-time."

"No, I guess not," said Jez.

Sarah had finished half her pizza but was starting to struggle. She folded her knife and fork to indicate she had finished. "Can't eat anymore, I'm stuffed. Might ask for a doggy-bag."

"I'll ask," said Jez, who had also finished eating. He had one slice left, but he too had put down his cutlery.

"Would you like a dessert, or coffee perhaps?" said Jez.

"Just coffee," said Sarah. Jez raised his arm and clicked his fingers to attract the attention of a passing waiter.

The waiter hovered examining the unfinished food. "It was

lovely," said Sarah. "But I couldn't eat anymore. Can I take the rest home?"

"Si, si, certo… er, of course… nessun problema," said the waiter. Sarah looked at Jez and smiled as the waiter cleared the dishes. 'You would like a dessert menu?'

"Just two coffees," said Jez.

"Si, Americano… Cappuccino?" said the waiter.

Sarah looked at the waiter. "Can I have a latte, please?"

"And an Americano, with milk," said Jez.

Sarah finished her wine and Jez went to pour the remainder of the bottle in her glass, but she placed her hand over the top. "No, no more for me, thanks."

"Would you like to take the rest home?" said Jez.

"No, it's fine," said Sarah, not picking up the hint of sarcasm.

The waiter reappeared with the coffees and a box containing the unfinished pizza which he presented to Sarah.

"Thanks," said Sarah, then realised she would have to carry it. On second thoughts, a doggy-bag was not such a good idea.

"Nice coffee," said Sarah after she took her first sip.

"Not bad," said Jez, which sounded like damning by faint praise.

Sarah took another sip of coffee and looked at Jez, with her cup still at her lips. "What do you think of LoveNet.Com, then?"

"Don't think much of their website, definitely in need of upgrading. Looks a bit dated," said Jez.

"Ha, ha, very funny."

Jez hadn't registered the humour. "Oh, yes, I see, ha, ha."

"Have you been on many dates?" Sarah wasn't sure why she had asked the question.

"No, you're the first one… You?"

"No, same here."

Sarah noticed Jez looking at his watch. "Sorry, I'm not keeping you, am I?"

"Oh, no, not at all; I was just checking the time. I told my mother I would be back by five; there's a train at five-past four. She worries if I'm late; you know what they're like."

Sarah checked her watch. "You have an hour; you'll be ok."

"Yes, it's fine. Do you want to go anywhere else?" said Jez.

"There's a bar just down the road if you like?"

"Yes, ok, I'll just go and pay."

Sarah watched him as he made his way to the pay-desk, trying to weigh him up. He was physically attractive; he'd passed that test, and the affection he had for his mother suggested he was a caring person, all positive signs.

She stood up and put on her jacket and joined Jez as the receptionist was giving him his credit card receipt. He had put on his windcheater but not done it up; his scarf hung down casually from his neck.

They walked to the glass exit door where the front-of-house was in attendance. "Grazie, addio... see you soon," said the man.

"Thank you," said Sarah as Jez allowed her to go through. She was carrying her 'doggy-bag', but as soon as they were out of sight of the restaurant, she found the nearest waste-bin and deposited it.

"I didn't think that through, and I can't see me eating it," she explained to a confused Jez.

The bar was in the public area of one of the hotels at the entrance to the mall. Sarah led the way; it was almost empty. People were checking in at the adjacent hotel reception desk.

Sarah went to the seating area in the corner which had some privacy.

"What would you like, I'll bring them over?" said Jez.

"Just a lemon and lime please," said Sarah.

While Jez went to the bar and made the order, Sarah chose a two-seater leather settee, which she thought would be more conducive to conversation. She had undone her leather jacket but not taken it off.

Jez returned from the bar and sat next to her, close. Sarah didn't feel uncomfortable and responded as he held her hand.

"They're bringing the drinks over," he said.

He looked into her eyes. This time Sarah did not move her gaze. "I've really enjoyed today."

"Yes, me too," said Sarah.

"I hope we can do this again, meet up I mean," said Jez.

"Yes, I'd like that," said Sarah.

Jez went to kiss her, only to be interrupted by an attendant with a tray. "One lime and lemon and an orange juice," she said in a Polish accent and placed the drinks on the table in front of them.

Sarah squeezed Jez's hand, and they resumed; this time a connection was made. They were totally oblivious to their surroundings as they kissed slowly and tenderly, not particularly passionate, but nice thought Sarah. She began to realise how much she had missed this level of intimacy, the closeness of another human being.

"We need to be careful, there're cameras everywhere," said Jez.

"I don't care," said Sarah and they resumed their kissing.

Sarah was beginning to feel warm and took off her coat; Jez was still in his windcheater. They both took a breather and a drink.

"I wish you didn't have to go," said Sarah, checking her watch.

"Yes, me too… but we can meet up again soon; I'll message you. Tell you what, we can have a video call if you like. Have you got a camera on your computer?" said Jez.

"Yes, I use it when I speak to Spence… my brother," she clarified.

"That's great, I'll call you later," Jez checked his watch, three forty-seven.

"I better make a move… Are you going to the station?" said Jez as he knocked back his drink.

"Yes," said Sarah and did the same.

They both stood up and headed for the door which Jez held open for Sarah to pass through.

Ten minutes later they were on the station concourse checking their departures.

"What platform?" said Jez.

"Usual, 3B."

"I'm on 1A" Jez leaned across and kissed Sarah again. "I'll call you tonight."

"Yes, ok," said Sarah as Jez hurried off towards his platform.

Sarah had another ten minutes before her train left and wandered towards platform 3B; her head was in a whirl. She felt a sense of frustration, unfulfillment and disappointed that he had to leave just when things were progressing so well. She wondered, in different circumstances, whether the kissing could have led to even more intimate contact.

The train arrived, and as she sat in her compartment and looked out of the window, she reflected on the hotel bar and imagined Jez walking towards her with the drinks saying,

"I've just booked a room." How would she have reacted, she wondered. She shuddered at the thought; deep inside, it's what she wanted him to say.

Back home, Sarah was warmly greeted by Moses as she walked through the door. She made a fuss of the cat and replenished his food. Her concentration, however, was not on her beloved feline; she was still absorbed by her recent encounter. She found herself looking forward to her call this evening.

Jez checked his watch. The train was on time and would get into Skipton around four thirty-five; just enough time to make his five o'clock deadline if the traffic was amenable. Then he realised, with the train terminating at his home station, all the passengers would be getting off at the same time. Damn, there would be a queue at the gates and to get out of the car park.

"We will shortly be arriving into Skipton, where this train terminates. Be sure to take all your belongings with you before you leave the train." The helpful electronic message from the tannoy reverberated around the compartment.

On hearing this, Jez left his seat. As they pulled into the platform he made sure he was by the doors, so he could beat the crowd.

He waited impatiently for the guard to release the doors. "Come on, come on," he said under his breath.

There was a loud ping and Jez pressed the illuminated green button; there were about ten people behind him with the same idea, but he was first. He leapt from the train and broke into a fast walk; a jog was not appropriate. He reached the barrier and inserted his ticket into the slot. He watched impatiently as other barriers seemed to open; oh no, not faulty, he suddenly thought, but then it opened, and Jez jostled through the station entrance and into the large car park fronting the building.

There was still some daylight, but the cloud and intermittent drizzle made it gloomy; the lights from the cars shone brightly in the murk.

He reached his ten-year-old Land Rover and climbed in. He could see other passengers reversing from their parking slots. He turned the ignition key; the engine coughed, then stalled. "Come on," shouted Jez. The car dutifully obeyed. He selected reverse and started to back out, but other passengers were walking past which prevented him from exiting. He hit his horn and kept going causing them to wait. Another driver honked at him, angry at Jez's discourtesy. Road-rage was rising. He eventually reached the queue trying to join the main road; he counted six cars in front. He checked his watch, four forty-five. "Shit, shit, shit, come on," he said under his breath. Five minutes later he was on the main road leading out of town.

Traffic was light as he headed west towards the village of Deighton. The term 'village' was relative; it was more of a hamlet. There were only a few scattered houses and a pub on the main road; no shops or anything to define it as a separate community.

He eventually reached the turn signposted, 'Deighton Hall', and made a left. Just off the main road, there was the start of a large wood; horse-chestnut, beech, ash, elm, deciduous trees which in summer provided an impenetrable screen surrounding the Hall. It was part of the estate but had been left to fend for itself, providing a natural barrier.

Once in the trees, the tarmac gave way to a black cinder surface. Jez drove the half-mile through the forest bouncing along the undulating track, pot-holed with puddles. Water splashed into the margins as Jez negotiated the snaking road. A couple of minutes later, he reached the eight-foot-high boundary wall. The headlights of the Land Rover picked out the ochre colour of the local stone which encased the entrance gate. His father had commissioned the build, not just to deter intruders; it also kept out deer which would cause considerable damage to the grounds. The gate was activated by a key fob and Jez aimed the device at the gate; it opened slowly. "Come on, come on," he shouted. As soon as it was open wide enough, he drove through; it was supposed to close automatically but did have a tendency to stick.

It was less than two hundred yards to the house which rose majestically in front of him. There was a large pebble parking area, and there was a crunching noise as he screamed to a halt. He checked his watch, five-fifteen. "Bugger," he said.

Deighton Hall was by no means a stately home, but it was nevertheless a substantial property with six bedrooms, two bathrooms, drawing room, hall, living room, study and kitchen. It dated back to the eighteenth century and initially served as the residence of the Lord of the Manor with strong connections to the local farming community. The original resident owned most of the land in the vicinity, but that had long since been sold with only the surrounding three acres belonging to the Steadmans.

Jez locked the Land Rover and walked towards the house. There were lights on downstairs and in the kitchen at the end; the upstairs rooms were in darkness. He reached the large oak front door and pushed it open. He walked through the portico and into the entrance hall. His mother appeared from the kitchen area.

"Jeremy, you're late, you said you would be back at five,"

she said, not hiding her annoyance.

"Don't go on, mother, it's only quarter-past; the traffic was bad at the station."

"I don't know why you had to go traipsing all the way into Leeds. Why couldn't you have met these clients in Skipton like you usually do?"

"I told you, mother, I needed to visit their offices."

"On a Saturday? Seems a bit strange to me. Factories and offices don't usually open on Saturdays."

"Well, these do," said Jez.

"Who did you say you were seeing; the company?"

"I didn't," said Jez. "I'm going to get changed."

"Well, don't be long; your dinner will be ready in five minutes, and you don't want it going cold."

Jez's mother didn't do the cooking. Mrs Dawson, the daily, would prepare meals most days so that they just needed heating; on her days off, it was a salad.

Jez walked through to the stairway in the 'great hall' which led to the first floor and the bedrooms. It was freezing upstairs; his mother only allowed the heating on in certain rooms and his bedroom wasn't one of them, although he had an electric fan heater which he used if it was really cold. He changed into a pair of old jeans and a sweatshirt and returned to the dining area of the kitchen.

His mother was heating the latest offering in the microwave.

"Oh, there you are," she said as Jez entered the room. "Sit down; I'll dish up."

She retrieved the steaming plate from the microwave and placed it in front of Jez.

"Don't know what it's like. Mrs Dawson made it yesterday, some sort of stew. There's a jacket potato as well, but don't go smothering it with butter," said mother.

Jez sat at the old oak table which had been in the kitchen for as long as he could remember. There were cuts and marks evidencing the years of faithful service it had provided for the family. The table was set for two with hessian placemats. He was presented with his food but waited for his mother to sit down.

"Looks like Goulash," said Jez; he took a mouthful. "Tastes ok."

After the lunchtime pizza, Jez wasn't feeling particularly hungry but continued eating.

"I suppose you'll be on that computer until all hours again," said mother.

"It's my job," said Jez.

"But you know how much electricity it uses; think of the cost."

"Don't worry, mother, I'll pay for it." Jez took another mouthful of stew. "I don't know why you insist on staying in this place, anyway. It's ridiculous, the upkeep; Dad's money's not going to last forever."

"This is my home; I live here, and don't speak with your mouth full."

"Yes, but we don't need a house this size. We could move into one of the others when they become vacant," said Jez.

"I like living here," reiterated his mother.

It was a discussion they had had many times, and she was not for shifting; as long as the money held out, she wasn't moving.

She continued her dinner in silence, the atmosphere tense. Jez looked at her; her light-auburn hair and the make-up she insisted on wearing, were immaculate as usual. In case a tradesman called, she would say.

Martha Steadman was looking her sixty-three years, but despite her frugalness around the house, continued her daily regime of personal pampering. She visited her hairdresser in Skipton once a week, and the cabinet in her en-suite was full of pills, potions and creams, designed to hold back the ageing process. Her make-up was garish with bright red lipstick, vampish-looking on someone half her age; her eyebrows plucked and replaced by a black pencil line. Jez always remembered her as pretty, but now she looked more like Bette Davis in 'The Nanny'.

Jez finished his meal and looked impatiently at his mother who was still picking at hers, morsel by morsel, deliberately chewing every piece rigorously before taking the next mouthful. Jez was certain she was doing this on purpose. He was desperate to get to his computer and resume his chat with Sarah. Martha could tell by his demeanour that he was anxious to leave the kitchen; tapping his fingers on the table and fidgeting in his chair as a young child might do, and she reacted accordingly; she would make him wait.

Jez couldn't stop thinking about his new acquaintance, but if he was to pursue his relationship with Sarah further, convincing his mother was going be a major hurdle; she didn't like women. "Manipulative creatures, only after one thing," she would say at any mention of girlfriends.

He knew the reason for her anger; his father was a philanderer, but, despite her numerous verbal attacks on him, Martha always blamed the women. "They're only after your money," she would scream, among the abuse. Jez, in many ways, could understand his father's behaviour; living with his mother was not an easy proposition. Jez would recall the numerous rows between his parents, bitter, hateful exchanges which, while he was growing up, he would try to block out by putting his hands over his ears. Years later, the mutual abuse had never left him. He would often wake in the middle of the night and believe he could hear two people shouting in anger. It was as though the hate had been absorbed into the fabric of the old house waiting for some sort of absolution, an exorcism that would make it stop.

Occasionally it was real; his mother's nightmares would awaken him. He could hear her calling out from her room down the corridor; the same rhetoric from his childhood reverberating around the old house. "You bastard! You bastard!"

As he grew into adulthood, Martha continued to warn Jez about the dangers that women posed, often with outbursts of temper, "Don't go getting yourself involved if you have any sense, they'll only let you down," she would shout at the very mention of any interest in girls. Even while he was away living in London, Jez had found it difficult. Having been let off the leash, he'd taken out girls, several times, but had rarely got past the first meeting. Although he had the outward appearance of an attractive guy, he lacked confidence with women and had no idea how to act. Somehow, he had found Sarah different. For the first time, he felt he had formed a connection.

Eventually, Martha finished her stew.

"There's no dessert," she said as she collected their plates and placed them in the dishwasher. Mrs Dawson would clean up on Monday.

"It's ok; I'll have some fruit later. I'm not that hungry."

Martha looked at him. "You're not sickening for anything are you?"

"No, of course not, I had something to eat at lunchtime with the client, that's all."

"Yes, well, I've told you before about eating big lunches."

"It's fine, mother."

"Yes, well, we can't waste food the price it is these days."

Jez got up and poured himself a drink of water from the tap.

He was going to try a different approach; if he could get his mother out of the house a bit more, it could change things. He sat down opposite his mother who was peeling an apple with a small paring knife.

"I was thinking today on the train; I think you need to go out more, you know, join a club, or a society or something; there are lots in town. You never know, you may meet someone."

"I don't think so!" she said in a derogatory fashion. "Why on earth would I want to do that? I had enough problems with your father; I'm not going to go through all that again."

"It's not good for you to be cooped up in this place all the time."

"I'm fine, and I certainly don't need anybody else, so don't mention it again."

"No, ok, just thinking about you," said Jez.

"No, you're not, you never think about me. What's going on? Are you trying to get me out of the way?"

"Don't be silly, mother, of course not. I was just thinking about it on the train, that's all. You never seem to go out, except for the hairdressers, I just think you are missing out on things."

"Yes, well, I don't think I'm missing out on anything."

"Ok. ok, you've made your point. I'm going to my room."

"Well, don't stay up all night," said Martha. "And don't put that fire on full, you know how much electricity it costs."

Jez walked away and went upstairs. Leaving his mother to finish in the kitchen.

Next to Jez's bedroom was his office, a separate room with extensive gadgetry on display; it was where he spent most of his time. There were three separate computer systems with linked monitor screens and high-end speakers; wires snaked everywhere. He also had a TV, which he rarely watched, and two laptops; in the corner was his aquarium. The room was big with a high ceiling requiring plenty of heat to reach a comfortable temperature. He switched the fan-heater to full power.

His fish-tank lit up the corner and had its own heating system. It was about eighty gallons, quite big by domestic aquarium sizes; Jez pulled up a chair and watched his water-world for a moment; he found it relaxing. Filter pumps sent a cascade of bubbles upwards creating a playground for angel and zebrafish as they glided gracefully around their glass prison. He had twelve in all, living happily together, playing among the plants and aquatic ornaments; he felt he knew them individually; he'd even given them names. There was a scale model of a shipwreck as a centrepiece which seemed to be a favourite hiding place. He checked the temperature – seventy-eight degrees, just right.

He went back to his office chair in front of his monitors and turned on one of the computers; he needed to check something.

Over the years, Jez had acquired a great deal of knowledge in the dark art of computer skills; some were more sinister than others. His fingers skated over the keyboard, pecking the keys; he typed in his interest, Sarah Gooding, Facebook profile.

"Hmm, let's see what we have here," he said to himself.

Chapter Three

Jez accessed Sarah's photos; none recent, some old pictures of her parents and some of her brother and family; nothing to suggest any past relationships. Next, he looked at her list of 'friends', taking a special interest in males, where they worked, any special connections.

There were only about twenty contacts, and she didn't appear to be posting much; her timeline hadn't been used for at least a month. There were several people from work, her brother and his wife, Spencer and Angie Gooding, some miscellaneous girlfriends, possible former University colleagues. There appeared to be no 'distant' male friends; ones picked up purely through social media. That was a good sign.

He checked who was 'liking' her posts. He checked her most recent, a short video showing cavorting cats, shared on 15th January. There was one comment that read, *'Really hilarious, Sarah xx'*. Jez checked the originator, Pete Draper, and viewed his profile. 'Hmm,' Jez said to himself as he read the narrative; Pete Draper, Head of Procurement, Huntsman's. Sarah had replied. *'Thought you would appreciate it, Pete x'*. Now that was a bit worrying.

Jez continued his searches and found her LinkedIn account; everyone in the business world seemed to have a presence, and Sarah was no exception. He read her profile; Educational history, 2:1 degree in business management from the University of Leicester. Work History, a graduate trainee position with an events company before joining Huntsman's five years ago. There were fifty 'contacts' but no recent posts that he could find, nothing that would concern him.

Sarah was completely unaware of this intrusion. Back in her house, having enjoyed the larger-than-usual lunch, she had made herself a sandwich for tea and watched the news on TV. She found concentration difficult; she was still thinking about her lunch date. She cleared up and fed Moses. By the time she had completed her chores, it was seven o'clock. She kept checking her phone for messages, despite having sound notifications switched on; she would be alerted by a ringtone if she received a message. Then she remembered there had been some talk about a video chat. She would need her laptop which she had taken upstairs.

Her spare room had become a bit of a dumping ground for bits and pieces. It was not large, but light and sunny. She had installed a small TV on a bookshelf on the wall which she could watch while doing her ironing. Her washing would air on a clotheshorse before she transferred it to the airing cupboard. There was also a small desk, where she could work or just surf; it was where she usually spoke to Spencer. Her laptop was on the desk. She opened it, logged on and accessed her Skype account. There was no request from Jez.

She sat for a moment and wondered whether she should text him, but for some reason, she didn't want to initiate the calling. She looked at the screen and wondered if she should call Spencer, then remembered he would be out. He and Angie were going to the pictures, he had said; they had managed to get a babysitter.

She was feeling restless.

She went downstairs to the kitchen and poured a glass of wine, then returned to her spare room. She logged onto Facebook and checked her timeline. She hadn't been on there for a while, and she checked what her friends had been doing;

there were plenty of posts and pictures from various Valentine's Day events. She logged out, closed her laptop and returned to the lounge to watch TV with her phone next to her.

Jez finished his investigation into Sarah's private world and opened his phone. It was eight o'clock and mother would be engrossed in her TV programmes in the sitting room.

'Hi,' he texted.

Sarah was sitting on the settee with Moses curled up on her lap; the alert made her jump. She opened her phone and replied.

'Hi.'

'Hope you're ok,' messaged Jez.

'Yes thanks, enjoyed the lunch, thank you for treating me.'

'My pleasure. Are you doing anything tomorrow?'

'Nothing special,' said Sarah.

'How do fancy going into the Dales, Pateley Bridge perhaps? There are a few nice coffee shops.'

Sarah couldn't help herself. *'Yes, that would be lovely. What time?'*

'Can you get to Skipton for about 12.00?'

Sarah had to think; she would need to drive, going by rail would mean a change of trains, and with a Sunday timetable there would be a lot of waiting around.

'Yes, where?' she replied.

'Station car park is £2 all day on Sunday. You can park there if you're driving, and I'll take you in mine – or will you be coming by train?'

'I'll drive over,' replied Sarah.

'Would you like to Skype? It might be easier,' typed Jez.

'Yes, send me a friend request; I'm SarahG30.'

Sarah unceremoniously lifted the cat from her lap; it clearly resented the disturbance and appeared to growl. Sarah went back upstairs, turned on her laptop and opened her Skype account. A friend request was waiting from Jez293. She took a sip of wine then put the glass down next to her within easy reach. Sarah accepted the request and straight away the familiar video sound rang out from her laptop. She clicked 'accept' and the picture buffered for five seconds before Jez's face filled the screen. He mouthed some words which Sarah couldn't hear; she realised she had the settings on mute. She enabled the mic and could hear Jez's voice loud and clear.

"Hello, can you hear me?" said Jez.

"I can now; I hadn't turned on the mic."

"Yes, it does help," said Jez and smiled at the screen.

For some reason, Sarah thought he looked even better on camera. Jez had set up his lighting which gave prominence to his face. Sarah had freshened her make-up and changed into a V-neck sweater; Jez wasn't disappointed.

"You look lovely."

"Thanks," said Sarah.

The pair continued chatting, then just before nine o'clock, Sarah could hear a voice calling. "Jeremy… who are you talking to?"

"Sorry, got to go, I'll message you later," said Jez and the call dropped.

Sarah felt disappointed; they seemed to be getting on so well. She wondered who the voice she had heard belonged to; presumably, it was his mother. She didn't much like the sound of her.

Jez switched off the computer. "Who was that you were talking to?" repeated Martha as she walked into Jez's room. "It sounded like a girl."

"Just someone I was chatting to online, just a friend that's all," said Jez.

"Well, you be careful, you know what I told you. You get all sorts on the internet, don't go getting yourself involved; you listen to what I'm saying."

"Leave it, mother, and mind your own business. I can speak to anyone I like," said Jez.

"You're getting just like your father; he was just the same, never listened. Well, you better listen, mark my words, they are trouble, the lot of them. I'm going to bed; you do what the hell you want."

Martha left the room, slamming the door behind her. Jez could feel the anger swelling inside him; he had never answered back before, but there was a line, and she had crossed it this time. He went back to his phone and messaged Sarah. *'Sorry about that, do you want to Skype again?'*

Sarah didn't think she would hear from him again and had changed into her dressing gown. She heard the 'ping' of a text message and checked the screen; it was Jez.

She logged into the phone and replied. *'Hi, I wasn't expecting to hear from you. I'm in my dressing gown.'*

'Even better,' came the reply. Jez was suddenly concerned he had gone too far. *'Sorry, didn't mean that.'*

Sarah saw the funny side. *'It's ok, give me five minutes.'*

She went back upstairs, took off her dressing gown and put on a sweatshirt. She would feel more comfortable.

Sarah opened her laptop and logged on, then opened Skype and sent a video request to Jez.

It was answered straight away, and there he was smiling at her.

"Hello again, sorry about earlier, mother was just going to bed."

"That's ok; you obviously look after her well."

"I'm her main carer."

"That must be a responsibility."

"Not really, she's mobile and lucid; I think she just misses the company, she's been like this since my father died."

"Are you ok to talk?" asked Sarah.

"Yes, of course, she's in bed now. She'll watch TV for a while then go to sleep. Are you still ok for tomorrow?"

"Yes, looking forward to it," said Sarah.

Jez looked at her. "I thought you said you were in your dressing gown."

"I was, but I put this top on it's more comfortable. Why? Did you want to see me in my dressing gown?"

Sarah wasn't sure why she said that, recognising the connotations.

"Mmm, now, there's an offer," said Jez.

"Hang on," said Sarah and she went next door to her bedroom, took off her sweatshirt and returned to the laptop wearing her dressing gown.

"That looks nice," said Jez. "I wish I could hold you right now."

Sarah felt a shiver run down her body. Here she was, chatting with someone on the internet she had only met today, but there was something about him she found alluring.

"Yes, that would be nice," replied Sarah.

"I love looking at you," said Jez.

"Really," said Sarah, slightly taken aback.

"Yes… I think you're beautiful."

Sarah started playing unconsciously with the top of her

dressing gown. Her hands went behind her head and slid them slowly down the front. She was only wearing panties underneath. She opened the dressing gown slightly to see his reaction. It's amazing how liberated you can be after three glasses of wine.

His face was a picture. He was staring at her.

"Don't stop now," he pleaded.

Sarah pulled open her dressing gown a little more, just so the tops of her breasts were visible.

"Wow," said Jez, "You're amazing."

"You like it?"

"God, yes. I love it. I wish I could hold you."

"Mmm, I would like that," said Sarah, and she meant it. Suddenly, she wanted Jez's hands over her body. She would have to make do with his eyes. She dropped the dressing gown further, stopping at her nipples.

Jez was becoming very aroused. "Wow you are amazing," he kept repeating.

Sarah let go of her dressing gown, and it slid to her waist. She was topless, exposed to Jez's eyes, and it felt so good.

Jez was captivated, completely under her spell. Sarah started rubbing her breasts.

"I want to do that," said Jez.

Sarah also wanted him to do just that; she felt herself becoming aroused.

After a few moments, she pulled up her dressing gown, as if she had come to her senses.

"I need to go now, the cat needs feeding, and I need an early night if we're meeting up tomorrow."

"Oh, yes, fine, ok, of course," said Jez. "I can't wait to see you tomorrow."

"Yes, me too," said Sarah. "Goodnight," and she dropped the call.

Now it was Jez's turn to feel frustrated; he was smitten by his new acquaintance.

Sarah found difficulty in sleeping, but when she did eventually drop-off, the dream returned. She was back walking corridors searching for a way out; the feeling of being trapped was overwhelming. She woke with a start; her heart was pounding. Slightly disorientated, she turned on the bedside table lamp. Moses was fast asleep at the bottom of the bed, dead to the world. Sarah got up and went downstairs to the kitchen for a drink of water; the clock on the wall said two twenty-eight.

The next time she woke or, more correctly, was roused by a hungry Moses, it was ten-to-eight; she felt heady from her fitful sleep. Then, another sensation took over, one of excitement and anticipation, the same she would have as a child with the expectation of Christmas Day. She couldn't remember experiencing this before; meeting Jez had turned her world upside down. She got up and went downstairs to feed the cat and make a cup of tea, gradually becoming compos mentis. She took a first sip of the steaming brew then picked up her phone to check her messages. There were five, all from Jez, at various intervals during the night; the last one at seven-thirty.

'Good morning Sarah, hope you slept well. Looking forward to seeing you later Jez xx'.

She replied straight away.

'Good morning, yes me too, see you at twelve o'clock at the station xx'.

A few minutes later there was a reply of a 'smiley face'

emoji.

Sarah managed to force down a bowl of cereal for breakfast with a cup of tea. She thought back to her last video session with Jez and her impromptu striptease. It had been worth it to see the effect it had on him. She'd always had a wild side; while at college, she would not be averse to dancing on the tables after a few beers, but that spark seemed to have been extinguished over recent years. Jez had somehow brought her back to life.

While Sarah was luxuriating in the shower and choosing what to wear; Jez was in Deighton trying to think of an excuse for his liaison that would not alert his mother. There was a problem, Sunday was the weekly trip into town; it had become something of a routine. Jez would drive his mother to the large supermarket; they would go to the coffee shop and then embark on replenishing the provisions. He couldn't remember the last time they had missed one, probably before Christmas when mother was under the weather.

Martha was still in her dressing gown making tea when Jez walked into the kitchen.

"I won't be able to go into town today, some urgent work's come up," he said, hoping that being assertive was the right approach.

His mother turned around from her boiling kettle. "What do you mean some work's come up? It's Sunday; I need to get the shopping. Can't it wait?"

"No, that's why it's urgent. One of my client's internet has crashed; I have to go and fix it."

"So, you have to drop everything and go running, is that it? Why can't it wait until Monday?"

"Because it's a client and I have a service contract. I can

pick up anything that's urgent on the way back. Make a list; I can call in."

"So, where is this client?" said Martha, pouring her tea into a mug.

"Settle," said Jez, without thinking, referring to the small market-town about twenty miles north of Skipton.

"Well, why don't you drop me off at the supermarket, then you can pick me up on the way back. I can always walk around town and look at the shops; you never know I might find some bargains?"

"No, I don't know how long I'll be."

"Well, we could go and have a coffee, and then you could go and see your client. I don't mind waiting until you come back."

Jez could feel the frustration building.

"No, mother, no, how many more times? I'm going out, and I don't know what time I'll be back."

Martha looked at Jez; she was drinking her tea, quite calmly.

"Who is this client? I don't remember you saying you had a client in Settle. I would have remembered."

"It's a new one," said Jez, who was ready to explode.

"Hmm, really? You never mentioned them. Well, I don't mind going to Settle, it's nice there. I haven't been for ages. Actually, come to think of it, that's a great idea. I wonder if the farmers' market is on. Oh, I do hope so, they have so many nice things, and the vegetables always taste better I think, don't you? We could get the meat from there too. I'm sure there's a butcher's stall; if not, I expect there will be a supermarket… Yes, it will be lovely. Can you look on your internet thing and find out; about the market I mean?"

"No, mother, you are not listening. *We* are not going to Settle. *I* am going to Settle. I'm going to see my client, and then I'll come home when I'm ready."

Martha put her mug down on the draining board with her tea only half-finished and walked out of the kitchen. She stared at Jez with a look filled with hate. "You're just like your father. I'm going to my room; you do what you like, just like you always do. Just think of yourself, never mind me."

It was the guilt trip, played so many times before, but this time he was determined not to give way.

Jez made some toast and coffee, then returned to his den and opened his laptop. He could hear his mother crying in her bedroom; she had made a point of leaving her door open to make sure Jez was aware of her distress. Dramatic sobs echoed through the corridor.

After ten minutes, Jez had had enough; he walked down the corridor and into his mother's room.

"Stop making a fuss, mother; it won't hurt missing one week. If you're that desperate to go to Settle, I can take you one day in the week when I have no appointments."

Martha looked at him, her eyes swollen. "Well, if you're sure you can fit me into your busy schedule, then I suppose it will have to do, but you will need to get some shopping."

She stopped crying like turning off a tap; she'd made her point.

"You could always get a taxi," offered Jez as a possible solution.

"I'm not paying for a taxi, they cost a fortune, and I'm sure they put up their prices when they come to the Hall."

"Ok, well, make a list, and I'll call in on the way back."

Martha seemed calmer; Jez was allowed to make his visit to Settle to see his mysterious client, but under sufferance.

"What will you do while I'm away?" said Jez.

"There's a Columbo on this afternoon; I'll watch that."

Since having their satellite installed, Martha had access to hundreds of TV channels and had become addicted to reruns of old TV shows that she used to watch in the sixties and seventies. 'Columbo', the American detective series was her favourite.

"You must have seen them all a dozen times," said Jez.

"I enjoy them," said Martha.

Seeing his mother had calmed down, Jez went back to his den and opened his laptop. He accessed Sarah's Facebook page again to see if she had been adding any posts, but there was nothing. He noticed the message from Pete Draper again; the kisses concerned him. He suddenly started sweating; his hands were clammy; his heart-rate had increased alarmingly. Was she seeing him, he wondered; perhaps a secret affair. There was a pencil on top of his mouse mat which he picked up. He was holding it in both hands, staring at the screen gradually bending the utensil; then it snapped, and the two pieces flew across the desk. Jez picked up the bits and threw them into his wastepaper basket.

It was almost eleven, and he started closing down his systems. His fan-heater was still on full-blast; it was another chilly morning. He returned to his bedroom and chose his outfit for the meeting with Sarah; then walked along the corridor and shouted to his mother, "I'm off now."

She was still in her bedroom; Jez could hear the TV turned up loud. He shouted louder, still no reply. He pushed open the door; his mother, seated in her armchair next to the window, was watching the TV. She noticed him but didn't initially acknowledge his presence. She paused her programme. "I thought you would have left by now; I thought you said it was urgent."

"Yes, it is I'm meeting them at twelve; they're opening the office for me."

"Seems a bit strange to me, but you go on and do what you have to. What time will you be back?"

"Don't know, depends on how long it takes."

"Well, don't forget the supermarket closes at four today. You'll need to be back by then."

"It depends, I can get what you want in Settle. Have you got the list?"

"It's on the dressing-table."

Jez saw the scrap of paper with half-a-dozen items on it and put it in his pocket.

"Get yourself something for tea. I've got mine in the fridge."

"Ok, mother, see you later," and he walked over to her and kissed her on the cheek which she barely acknowledged. He walked downstairs and out of the house and breathed a sigh of relief. It was eleven-thirty as he made his way out of the estate and on the road heading towards Skipton.

Sarah, meanwhile, had already set off for her liaison in her four-year-old Renault Clio; it would take around forty-five minutes to reach Skipton and then navigate the traffic to the station. It was a crisp winter's day, but sunny; daffodils were starting to make their presence felt, although not yet in full bloom. Sarah was feeling a mix of emotions, excitement and a little nervous, but a sense of anticipation and it felt good; she found herself singing along to the radio.

She had left earlier than was probably necessary; she wanted to be on time and had reached the outskirts of Skipton by eleven-forty. The traffic was slow, but by ten-to-twelve she was approaching the station car park. It was busy, with few parking slots, but she managed to find a place adjacent to the fence that separated the area from the railway tracks. She looked up as a train went by.

She opened her purse and found the two-pound coin she was going to need, then went to find a meter; she'd made sure she had change before leaving. She looked around to see if she could see him but didn't know what he was driving, so she collected her ticket and went back to her car. She sat in the driver's seat and checked her make-up again in the mirror on the sun-visor, then picked up her handbag and left the car. Given the temperature was only just above freezing, she was dressed for the weather in jeans and sweater, with her ankle boots and leather jacket keeping the chilly air from penetrating her.

The nerves were mounting as she reached the station entrance and she stood there for a few minutes watching the cars come and go. She was playing a game with herself trying to guess what car he would be driving. Her best guess was a BMW, five series, probably; then she changed her mind; a Range Rover would be more in keeping with the gentry.

It was a surprise then, when a ten-year-old, rather battered grey-green Land Rover pulled up. With the sun shining directly in her eyes she didn't recognise the driver at first, and then she heard him call from the open driver's window.

"Sarah, it's me, sorry I'm late."

Sarah made the recognition. "Oh, hi," she called and walked around the car. She tried the passenger door, but it appeared to be locked. Jez leaned across and opened the handle from the inside. "Sorry, it gets stuck sometimes."

Sarah made herself comfortable, put her handbag in the space next to her feet and clipped on her seatbelt. She thought he might lean across and kiss her; she wanted him to, but Jez started the engine with hardly a sideways glance; the exhaust pipe rattled as the car pulled away. They reached the main road and Jez negotiated the junction. She looked around the car's interior; it had certainly seen better days. The seats were worn, and the leather faded; the footwell was muddy from soiled shoes, and there were scratches in the wooden fascia.

"I thought we could go up to Settle, how does that sound?"

"Yes, fine, I thought you said Pateley Bridge," said Sarah.

"Yes, sorry, change of plan. I need to get some stuff for Mother. She likes the farmers' market there."

"Oh, right, fine, no problem," said Sarah, feeling slightly let down.

Jez's apparent rudeness was not a deliberate snub, but an indication of his anxiety. As he headed out of Skipton, he started to relax and looked across at Sarah.

"You look beautiful."

Sarah returned the gaze. "Thank you," she said and rubbed his arm affectionately.

"So, how have you been?" she asked, trying to engage Jez in conversation.

"Fine, thanks; lovely morning," replied Jez.

"Yes, a bit chilly, I'll be glad when Spring arrives; I hate the cold," replied Sarah.

"It will be good to get some sun; the daffodils haven't started to flower yet."

"I bet you have a lot of those... at the Hall, I mean."

"Yes, the woods look nice in the spring. We've got Bluebells too; it's like a carpet at the end of April."

"Oh, I would love to see that," said Sarah.

"Yes," said Jez. "It's lovely." He had not picked up on the hint. The visit was not going to happen anytime soon.

Despite the car's age, the heater was in working order, and Sarah undid her jacket which Jez noticed straight away. His eyes strayed from the road for a second, drawn to the contours of her body, as the memories from the previous evening went through his mind.

"You looked great in your dressing gown," he said, not the subtlest of comments.

"Thank you, glad you liked it."

"Yes, very much. I had trouble sleeping."

Sarah giggled.

She watched the countryside go by, not at its best yet, but there were new lambs in the fields, and the tops of the hills were still glowing white reflecting the lying snow in the late-winter sunshine. The road was quite busy with tourists, mainly walkers, taking advantage of a fine Sunday morning.

The journey to Settle took another twenty minutes and with the market in full swing, finding a parking space would be the next challenge. However, Jez found a free parking spot just off the main street; it was after twelve forty-five.

"How about a coffee?" said Sarah, as Jez locked up the Land Rover.

"Good idea," said Jez and Sarah took his hand. Jez looked at her and smiled.

There were no shortages of coffee shops, busy at this time of day catering for the visitors, and the pair entered the first one they encountered that was not too hectic. It was a very traditional establishment with wooden tables, chairs and china crockery.

They found a vacant table and sat down. Sarah took off her jacket and wrapped it around the back of her chair. Jez unzipped his jacket; he stared at Sarah in her woollen sweater and jeans and caught his breath. Sarah noticed the reaction and smiled.

"They do sandwiches," said Jez, who had picked up the menu from the table.

"Great, I'm feeling a bit peckish," said Sarah who was now, too, scanning the choices.

A waitress dressed in a traditional Victorian teashop outfit, complete with white apron, approached the table and the pair ordered their lunch and drinks.

"It's nice here," said Sarah as she scanned the café. It was busy, with only one vacant table out of the twenty or so covers, and, judging by the clientele and decor, it looked more up-market than some they had passed.

They were sat opposite each other. Jez was looking and feeling more relaxed, and Sarah could detect the change. She reached out across the table and held his hand.

"I'm glad you suggested going out today; it beats housework."

"Yes," said Jez. "I'm glad you could come."

"I hope it didn't cause any problems with your mother."

"No, she'll get over it. I wasn't going to let her spoil our day."

Sarah thought about the reply for a moment but let it go.

"So, back to Huntsman's tomorrow?"

"Yes, afraid so; the mortgage won't pay itself," said Sarah.

"No, I guess not. How big's your department?"

"Oh, it's not very big, just three of us and the boss."

"I see, and what's he like. I assume it's a 'he'?" he added quickly.

"Pete? Yes, he's great, one of the best I've had. If it wasn't for him, I might have left before now."

This did nothing to allay his fears about a possible

relationship; he could feel a well of jealousy starting to surface.

Further interrogation was interrupted by the arrival of their order, and the waitress assembled the sandwiches, plates and drinks on the table from a gold-coloured trolley.

"Look they've even cut the crusts off," said Sarah. "Makes your hair curl, my mum used to say."

The waitress heard the comment and smiled. Jez hadn't registered the remark, still thinking about Sarah's work situation.

The waitress left with the empty trolley and Jez and Sarah started eating.

"What about your work?" said Sarah "Tell me some more about what *you* do."

Jez looked at her. "Not very interesting; I construct websites and deal with general IT queries from my clients."

"Sounds impressive, I wouldn't know where to start," said Sarah. "I'll have to get you to have a look at my laptop; it's so slow."

"Yes, ok I can fix that for you," said Jez.

They finished their lunch and Jez once again insisted on paying.

"Where do you want to go now?" asked Sarah as they left the café.

"I need to get some bits and pieces for mother from the market," replied Jez.

"Ok, lead the way, I've not been here before."

"Just up here," and Jez led the way to the myriad of stalls that were crammed into the market square.

Sarah was happy to tag along with Jez, and as her feelings for him were starting to grow, physical needs were beginning to surface. She watched him as he bought some vegetables at one of the stalls and her mind started to drift. He was tall, good-looking and appeared to have a good physique, although that was difficult to tell under his jacket. She was dying to find out.

After thirty minutes, Jez was loaded with produce in three plastic carrier bags.

"Why don't you drop those off at the car and we can have a wander. I'd like to have a look around."

"What's the time?"

Sarah looked up at the clock on the church. "Half-past two, according to the town clock."

"Yes, ok, the car's not far."

With Jez carrying the bags in both hands, Sarah linked her arm in his but was almost running to keep up with him.

"Hey, slow down, I can't run in these boots," she said.

"Sorry," said Jez, and he slowed to a more leisurely pace.

It took five minutes to reach the Land Rover, and Jez opened the back and deposited the shopping.

"I'll need to get those in the fridge pretty soon," said Jez.

"I don't think anything's going to go off in this weather," said Sarah. "It's freezing."

Jez looked at her. "No, you're right... so, where would you like to go?"

"I don't know, let's just wander around and see what we find; maybe an antiques' shop or something."

Jez checked his watch again, but this time, Sarah did not notice. There would be probably an inquest if he was not back by four. Just then there was a tinny ring-tone coming from his jacket pocket.

"You better get that," said Sarah. Jez looked at the caller.

"It's mother," he said.

"Hello," he said with one finger in his ear to blot out any

extraneous noise. He listened.

"No, mother, I'm still working, I can't come home now. What's the matter? Well, it will just have to wait. You can watch the TV downstairs… no, I can't come now. I'll see you later." Jez dropped the call.

"Everything alright?" asked Sarah with a look of concern.

"Yes, it's fine. She says her TV's not working in her room. I'm not surprised the hammering it gets."

"Do you have to go?"

"No, I'm ok for a while."

Chapter Four

They walked back hand-in-hand to the town square; Sarah felt happy and content. For Jez, today was also a special time. It had been a long time since he had experienced closeness with anyone. In recent times, emotionally, he had become virtually self-sufficient through necessity, but now he felt himself becoming more and more drawn to Sarah. He was not going to allow anything to jeopardise his blossoming relationship; she belonged to him now.

They spent another half-an-hour looking around the shops and market. It was Sarah's first visit, and she fell in love with the place with its quaint seventeenth-century buildings. The surrounding hills seemed to look on with approval as they explored the town.

They reached the Museum. "What about having a look in here," said Sarah.

Jez noticed there was a line of people waiting to get in.

"Let's make it another time; we don't want to be stuck in a queue for ages," said Jez.

"Oh, ok," said Sarah and they walked by.

They climbed the cobbled streets and hill at the back of the Market Place. From the top there were sweeping views across the town; in the distance, they could see St Alkelda's Church in nearby Giggleswick. Sarah took out her phone from her handbag.

Jez was stood against a dry-stone wall a few feet away in a world of his own; he appeared to be admiring the view. He was deep in thought.

"Come on, it's selfie time," said Sarah waving her phone in Jez's direction.

"What, oh, yes," said Jez, and they put their heads together and looked into the phone. Sarah clicked and checked the results. "Hey this looks alright," she said and passed the phone for Jez's approval.

"Yeah, looks great, can you send me a copy?"

"Of course," said Sarah, and proceeded to send Jez a text with the photograph attached.

As they walked back towards the town, Sarah spotted a narrow alleyway. "Let's go down here," she said.

Jez looked confused; it didn't seem to lead anywhere, just a backyard. As they entered the passage out of sight from passers-by, Sarah stopped and leant against the wall. Jez held her, and suddenly she grabbed his neck and they were locked in a kiss. For Jez, it was instinctive and arousing, and Sarah could feel him, hard against her thigh. She was longing to hold it but now was not the time. Then, a distant clock struck four bells, which seemed to break the spell. Jez pulled away.

"I need to get going," he said.

Sarah tried to hide her disappointment. "Yes, ok. That's a pity; I was enjoying that."

"Yes, me too," said Jez. "But I'm not sure about the parking around here… I don't want to get a ticket."

"Oh, ok," said Sarah, and the pair exited the alleyway and headed back to the Land Rover.

There was no parking ticket; Jez got in and opened the door again for Sarah from the inside. She took off her jacket and placed it on the back seat before getting in.

With the familiar rattle of the exhaust, Jez turned the car around and set off back to Skipton. With the exertion of the walk and the heater in the car, it soon became warm. Sarah felt sleepy and content.

Jez looked across at her. "You really are beautiful, you know."

She looked at him and placed her hand on his thigh. "Thanks," she said. "It's been a special day."

"Yes, it has," replied Jez.

"Are you doing anything Tuesday evening?"

Jez thought for a moment; he hadn't considered an evening meeting; it would cause problems.

"No, I'm pretty sure I'm free," he replied, but inside he was running through all kinds of scenarios.

"Would you like to come over to mine, I'll cook us dinner? I've booked Wednesday off work; I need to take my holiday before the end of March, or I'll lose it."

"Yes, ok, I'll need to check with mother, but it should be fine."

"You can let me know," said Sarah, who was getting impatient with Jez's mother's unseen intervention.

"Yes, I'll message you later. We can do Skype again if you like," said Jez.

"Yeah, ok, but I need to do a few chores; work tomorrow, remember."

It was Sarah's turn to play hardball; she wasn't going to be taken for granted. He was going to have to make a choice sooner or later.

It was nearly five o'clock before Jez pulled into the station car park. Sarah leant across the seat to kiss him. She was expecting more than just the merest of pecks, but it was brief and hurried as though Jez needed to be somewhere else. "Chat later, yeah?"

"Yes, ok, I'll message you," said Jez, and Sarah got out.

Jez pulled away and accelerated towards the exit, the Land Rover kicking up debris and mud behind it.

Sarah walked back to her car; now she was deep in thought; it was her first hint of doubt about him.

It was gone five-thirty as Jez pulled up outside the Hall. He picked up the shopping and walked in; he could hear the TV in the lounge blaring out.

He took off his jacket and dropped the carrier bags on the kitchen table, then walked towards the noise. His mother appeared at the doorway before he could enter.

"So, you've decided to come home then, after leaving me on my own all day," she said with a face like thunder.

"Yes, it took longer than I thought. Do you want me to have a look at the TV?"

"No, I managed to sort it out myself… no thanks to you."

"What was the problem?"

"I don't know, I just turned it off, and when I turned it back on again, it was working."

"That's good… I'm going up to my room," said Jez.

"Aren't you going to keep me company? You've been out all day."

"I'm not competing with the TV… they can probably hear the noise in the village."

"It's ok, I'll turn it off," said Martha, and she disappeared into the lounge. There was a deathly hush as the TV was shut down.

Martha reappeared and went to the kitchen; Jez followed.

"I expect you've eaten with your clients."

"Just a sandwich," said Jez.

"So, you expect me to cook something?"

"No, I'll get myself something. The shopping you wanted is on the table; it will need to go in the fridge soon, it's been in the car."

"I'll see to it," she said and started emptying the contents of the carriers onto the table.

She looked at the name on the bag. 'James Elcock and Sons. Family butchers', it said.

"Never heard of them, hope it's ok… Some of the meat I've had before from the market's been tough."

"But, mother, you said… no, never mind. Do you want some tea? I'm making myself a cup."

"Yes, if it's not too much bother," she said and started putting the perishables into the fridge.

Jez was looking over her shoulder. "Is there any more of that cottage-pie left?"

"I don't know; you can have a look when I'm done."

Jez went back to the kettle and made the tea while his mother finished in the fridge.

"So, did you sort out this mystery client, then?"

"Yes, thanks."

"A woman was it?"

"What's that got to do anything?"

"I can smell perfume on you… cheap, too, it smells like."

Jez was not about to be drawn in. "It was only a greeting, they do that nowadays, you know hugging and all that."

"Hmmm, well I hope you know what you're doing."

"Yes, mother, it's fine."

Jez could smell Sarah's perfume. It reminded him of her; it was on his scarf. He would take it up to his room.

After his mother had finished in the fridge, Jez extracted the cottage-pie and heated it in the microwave. There were some frozen peas in the freezer which he added; his Sunday dinner was complete.

Martha made herself a salad from the market produce, and they sat down to eat together at the kitchen table. There was an uneasy silence, just the clacking of knives and forks. Then Jez dropped his bombshell.

"I'm going into Leeds on Tuesday evening."

"What do you mean, going into Leeds? Why do you need to go there? It's a long way; what if you break down?"

"It's a meeting, and it's not that far, thirty miles at the most."

"Yes, but why go out there? It'll be dark. You don't like driving in the dark; you're always telling me."

"No, I'm not. I've never said anything of the sort."

"What time will you be back?"

"Late I expect."

"What sort of meeting is it?"

"A business meeting, computers and stuff. Some of my clients will be there."

"I see; including the trollop you were with today, I suppose?"

"No, it doesn't, and she's not a trollop. It'll be mostly men, I expect. I don't have an attendance list."

Jez had given up on his cottage-pie which was now cold and unappetising.

"Don't worry, I'll be here during the day, you won't be on your own all the time."

"What about locking up? You know I don't like being on my own at night."

"I'll see to that before I go out, don't worry. I'm sure there'll be something on TV to keep you amused."

Martha stood up, took Jez's plate away and emptied the leftovers into the waste-bin, her face and behaviour showing her all-too-familiar displeasure.

"There's no dessert," she said.

"It's ok; I'll have some fruit."

Jez went up to his room, leaving his mother watching TV. He spent a few minutes watching his fish in the aquarium, so peaceful, a great way to de-stress after the altercation. He logged-on to his computer system, holding his scarf to his face; Sarah's perfume lingered and gave him all manner of thoughts. He pictured the dressing-gown incident and re-played it in his mind. He must mean a lot to her for her to be so forward, he reasoned; nobody had ever done that before.

He opened his phone, accessed the selfie from Settle and stared at it; they looked so good together, just like a real couple. He forwarded the image to his email address and saved it to the 'Sarah' folder that he had already created. He opened the picture, enhanced it to his liking, then printed a six-by-four copy for his wallet and an A4 version which he would put on his wall.

His next port of call was Sarah's Facebook page; he wanted to see if she had posted anything about their visit to Settle; maybe she had posted the selfie. He checked her timeline; there was no mention of their trip, but she had been online. There was a post she had shared; fairly innocuous, a short video-clip of a two-year-old baby mimicking a dance on a TV, very cute. *'This had me in hysterics'*, she had posted.

Jez checked the responses from her 'friends', just three 'likes' and one 'comment'. He read the comment. *'Adorable xx'*. He noticed the name of the originator, Pete Draper. He wondered, again, why her boss would put kisses; either he was a very liberal boss, or they were too close. Either way, he didn't like it; he would give it some serious thought. Pete was encroaching on Jez's territory, and that wasn't allowed.

A hungry Moses greeted Sarah as she opened the door to her house. She'd been thinking about Jez on the drive back; she had enjoyed the day and wanted to see him in a more intimate setting; she hoped he would be more relaxed on Tuesday. There was something, though, she had noticed. When it came to any romantic expression he seemed almost shy; that was the only description she could come up with. She thought he was a good-looking guy who most women would find attractive; Sarah certainly did. However, his kissing was uncertain, and not particularly passionate; it reminded her of her teenage experiences. Was he gay, she suddenly thought, but quickly discounted that idea. Why would he use a 'straight' dating service if that was the case; there are plenty catering to same-sex relationships. Perhaps he was just shy.

She fed the cat and started to prepare some food for herself; she was feeling peckish. Tonight, she would need to spend a couple of hours washing and tidying before she could settle down for the evening.

Jez was in his den considering Sarah's boss, Pete Draper. There was definitely something going on; he was convinced. The thought of Sarah being with someone else had Jez almost hyperventilating. It was as if someone had flicked a switch. He thought about the restaurant. Perhaps it was a favourite haunt for her trysts. Maybe her boss had entertained her there, or vice-versa. Jez was breathing heavily; he felt strange, a mix of anger and, not just jealousy, but extreme hatred. Sarah was not to be shared, with anyone.

The boss, he thought again, was probably married; that was it, they needed to keep it a secret. Jez formulated a plan. It took him less than forty-five minutes to set his trap.

He checked the time; he would see if Sarah was online and wondered if she would be in her pyjamas again. He hoped so. It was nine o'clock, and she was offline. He sent a text.

'Hello, I expect you're still busy. Thank you for today, I really enjoyed it. I'm free if you want to chat.'

Jez waited, but there was no reply.

Sarah had seen the message but was ironing the clothes she would need for work and didn't want to be interrupted. At ten o'clock, she finished her chores, fed the cat and took a shower. She changed into her dressing gown and texted Jez. There were two other messages from him, seeing if she was ok.

'Hi, sorry, had to get my ironing out of the way.'

Straightaway a reply. *'Hi that's ok, do you want to Skype?'*

Sarah replied. *'Ok, but I can't stay long. I need my beauty sleep.'*

Seconds later the familiar sound rang from Sarah's laptop; she accepted the call.

The picture buffered for a moment and then Jez's face appeared.

"Hi," he said.

"Hi," replied Sarah. "Sorry I couldn't get here sooner."

"That's ok, did you get your chores done?"

"Yes, all done."

"Thanks for today, it was great," said Jez.

"Yes, I enjoyed it. Do you want to come over on Tuesday, or do you need to stay with your mother?"

"No, it's fine. My mother can go to hell. I can do whatever

I like."

"Oh, ok." Sarah was shocked by the forcefulness of his expression; there was real anger behind it. She looked at him; his eyes seemed to be staring; he was looking directly into the camera, not at the screen. When she spoke to her brother, the eye-contact never seemed to be so intense; she found it a bit unnerving.

"You look beautiful," he said.

"Oh, thanks, although I don't feel it; I just got out of the shower."

"Hmm, that's sounds good."

She detected a change in him; his demeanour seemed different.

Jez was different; he felt different; it was a confidence thing. Sarah was his, and he was not going to share her with anyone.

Jez was hoping for another flash of breasts from Sarah, but he was going to be disappointed.

"Anyway, I need to go," said Sarah. "Early start tomorrow and Mondays are always hectic."

"Oh… ok," said Jez, unable to hide his disappointment.

"We can chat longer tomorrow," said Sarah, detecting his demeanour.

"Ok," said Jez. "Have a great day."

He mouthed a kiss at the screen.

"You too. Goodnight," said Sarah.

"Bye," said Jez, and Sarah disconnected the call. She shut down her laptop and went to her bedroom where Moses was already asleep on an old jumper at the bottom of the bed.

Jez was feeling frustrated and wondered if Sarah's interest was already starting to wane. Perhaps she was thinking of Pete, her boss; she was going to be in for a surprise. He would try harder; there was no way he was going to lose her.

On Monday morning, the inbound commute was as bad as ever. It was dull and drizzly. There were no seats when the train pulled in, and Sarah had to stand. As always, the passengers on the train were locked in their own worlds, reading the free newspaper, on their phones or tablets. There was minimal conversation, just the rattling of the carriages as it ferried them to their destination. Sarah found it quite depressing. The train arrived on time and ejected its several hundred passengers onto the concourse; there was the usual crush at the automated barrier to exit the station.

Sarah made the short walk to the store; the cold air was as reviving as the numerous coffee hits she would be taking later. She was at her desk for eight-thirty. A voice disturbed her as she was checking her emails.

"Morning Sarah."

It was her boss, Pete Draper, passing her workstation on the way to his office. "How was your weekend? Did you do anything special?" He stopped to hear the response.

"I went to Settle, yesterday; I've not been before; it's really nice."

"Settle? Hmm, not been there for years. Must go again, it is nice."

"What about you?" asked Sarah, returning the courtesy.

"We had a few friends over for drinks on Saturday; it was Tony's birthday… so it was quite late by the time we got to bed. Had a bit of a lie-in yesterday, nothing special. Anyway, catch up later, best get on." He continued to his office.

The morning was as hectic as predicted and it was gone eleven before Sarah had dealt with the incoming email queries and quotes from tenders. She took her break and went to the kitchen to make a coffee; she had her own stash in her desk drawer. There would be milk in the fridge provided by the store.

There were two or three other colleagues also on a break, and she spent a few minutes catching up on the gossip when the concierge from the storefront, dressed in his customary morning suit, put his head around the door.

"Sarah Gooding in here?" Then he spotted her. "Hi Sarah, delivery for you," he said and produced a huge bunch of flowers.

"Wow, thanks Clarke".

She took the bouquet from him, and her coffee-colleagues quickly surrounded her.

"Hey what's this, a secret admirer?" said Moira from Accounts.

Sarah opened the card that was attached. *'Thought these might brighten up a dismal Monday… Love Jez xx'.*

Others were trying to peer over her shoulder at the card.

"Come on, who are they from?" said Tracy from HR.

"Mind your own business," said Sarah with a smile, and put the note in her pocket.

"You need to put those in water," said Moira. "I think there's a jug in the cupboard," and she went off in search of a suitable vessel. "How about this?" she said pulling a ceramic jug from one of the shelves.

"Thanks," said Sarah and she filled up the jug with water and added the flowers.

"I'm going to have to decide how to get them home," she said, admiring the blooms.

"Put some wet kitchen roll around the stems and put them in a plastic carrier-bag; they'll be fine," said Tracy.

"Yes, good idea. I'll sort them out later."

Sarah took another glance at them and went back to her desk.

She opened her phone and sent a text. *'Thanks for the flowers, they are lovely, catch up tonight x.'*

Jez was in his office when the message came through. He was pleased with the response; it had apparently had the desired effect. He liked the 'x'.

For a while, Sarah found it difficult to concentrate; it had been a long time since anyone had sent her flowers. It was a lovely gesture, and she suddenly felt a bit guilty; maybe she had been a bit hard on him the previous evening.

Sarah started to pack away her work about quarter-to-five, ready for the usual rush to the station. She collected her bouquet from the jug; the carrier bag was firmly wrapped around the stems so that any water wouldn't drip onto her coat.

Loaded up with her bag and flowers, she received plenty of attention as she walked through the store to get her train.

The journey was busy as usual. Sarah was careful that the flowers were not damaged in the crush, and within half-an-hour, she was at her kitchen table arranging the blooms into a glass vase. Moses took a keen interest, and she had to pick him up a couple of times when he had jumped up to see what she was doing.

Satisfied with her arrangement, she put them on the table in the lounge, then returned to the kitchen to make a cup of tea. She checked her phone; there were three messages from Jez.

'Glad you liked the flowers.'

'Hope you're ok.'

'Thinking about you.'

She texted back. *'Hi Jez, just got in, flowers look lovely, chat later, Sarah x'.*

She was relaxing on the sofa, with Moses on her lap around eight o'clock, when her mobile phone rang.

She picked it up, thinking it might be Jez. She didn't recognise the caller but accepted the call.

'Hello.'

'Hi, is that Sarah?'

'Yes.'

"Oh, hi, it's Tony Chambers; Pete's partner."

"Oh, hi Tony, how are you?"

"I don't know… something terrible's happening. The police have been here all evening on Pete's laptop. They say he's been distributing kiddy-porn, which is absolute nonsense; he wouldn't do that. I know him."

Sarah could hear sobbing on the phone.

"Oh Tony, that's terrible. Is he ok?"

"They've just taken him away. They said they're going to charge him."

"But that's ridiculous. Have you got a solicitor?"

"Yes, I've called our friend Jacob. He's going to meet Pete at the police station in Lion Street. I hope they believe him. It's just nonsense. He's such a wonderful man, so kind; he'd do anything for anyone. He would never be mixed up in anything like this." Tony was sobbing.

"Yes, I'm so sorry; I don't know what to say."

"Well, it's obvious someone's hacked into his computer, somehow; there's no other explanation. What I don't understand is why anyone would pick on Pete."

"Maybe they didn't; maybe it was just random."

"But that's just evil. It destroys people's lives."

"Is there anything I can do?" asked Sarah.

"Pete asked if you could cover for him at work… say he's

gone down with a virus or something."

"Yes, of course. Will the police want to check his work computer?"

"I don't know; they didn't say."

"Ok, well, ring me tomorrow and let me know what's happening," said Sarah.

"Yes, of course," said Tony, and he rang off.

Sarah was in deep thought. She'd known Pete since she started at the store. He was, as Tony had described him, a lovely man; everybody at work liked him. He was easy to talk to and a great boss. She didn't believe for one second that he would be involved in child pornography. A wave of sadness swept over her.

She picked up her phone; she had an idea.

"Hi," said Jez. "I wasn't expecting to speak to you till later. I thought I'd let you settle in and get your chores done."

"No, that's fine, I need to ask you a question," said Sarah.

"Of course," said Jez.

"You know about computers?"

"Yes, it's my job. Why, has yours crashed?"

"No, no, nothing like that… It's just a good friend of mine has been visited by the police for downloading kiddy-porn."

"Really, how awful. You can't trust anyone these days. You think you know someone and then something like this comes out of the blue."

"No, no, Pete's not like that at all."

"We all have dark secrets," said Jez.

"I don't," said Sarah.

Jez back-tracked, realising the implications. "No, no, I didn't mean that. I was just saying you never can tell with people."

"Hmm, well, I know Pete. Tony was in bits when he called me."

"Tony?"

"Yes, his partner, they're devoted to each other."

"This friend is gay?"

"Yes, Tony is Pete's civil partner."

It went quiet.

"Jez? Are you there?"

"What, oh sorry, mother just called me, wanted to know who I was talking to."

"Do you need to go?"

"No, it's ok. So, what do you want to know?"

"Is it possible his computer could have been hacked?"

Jez didn't answer immediately; he wanted to give the impression he was thinking.

"Hmm, well, it's possible I suppose, but not likely."

"Won't the police be able to tell?"

"They might; it depends how good they are... the technical people, I mean."

"Well, I would presume they would be good," said Sarah.

"Hmm, not always, I've met one or two at conferences, and I don't rate them that much at all."

"Well, I hope they can find out, I don't know how Pete must be feeling; he'll be devastated."

"Was there anything else I can help with?" said Jez.

"No, that's all, I'll text you later," said Sarah and rang off.

Sarah was pensive, trying to take in the events. There was no way Pete could be a paedophile, just no way.

She tried watching the TV, but her concentration levels had fallen. She decided to do something constructive to take her mind off the events, so she started cleaning out the kitchen cupboards.

At nine-thirty, curiosity had got the better of her, and she phoned Tony back; she needed to know what was happening.

"Oh, hi Sarah. Pete has just got back. I'll put him on for you."

"Hi Sarah, it's Pete. I'm sorry you've been caught up in all this."

"It's ok; I've been so worried. What's happened?"

"Well, as they say, I'm out on bail."

"What…? Does that mean they don't believe you?"

"They say they have evidence that I've been distributing child-porn and they're investigating."

"But, what I don't understand is, why have they picked on you?"

"I honestly don't know; they said they'd had a tip-off. One of my friends had an email from me with an attachment which he opened and contacted the police."

"Hmm, some friend, why didn't they just call you?"

"I don't know, that's what I can't understand. They could have just deleted it. Any of my friends would know it's nothing to do with me."

"What about work?"

"I'll take tomorrow off and speak to Sir Basil in the morning. I have no idea what he'll say."

"But you're innocent; surely he'll support you?"

"I hope so, but you know what they say, mud sticks."

"Hmm."

"Please don't say anything for now."

"No, of course not," said Sarah.

Back at Deighton, Jez was feeling a bit guilty about his hasty actions. Setting the scam had not been difficult. His internet set-up was linked to a VPN, a virtual personal network, which would render his internet activity entirely untraceable. He had access to the 'dark web', the shady area of the internet frequented by drug-dealers, hackers, gun-runners and paedophiles. Finding illegal photographs was not a problem; then he infected Pete's computer with a virus which would move the pictures to his laptop; fairly straightforward stuff with Jez's knowledge.

He shrugged his shoulders; he would not dwell on it; what's done, is done.

The situation, however, was weighing heavily with Sarah; the question in her mind was, why. There was nothing in Pete's behaviour that she had ever found improper; he was always a model of professionalism. Over and over, Sarah questioned the events; maybe he did have a dark side like Jez had said. She was not convinced.

The event had taken the shine off the evening and by the time Sarah was ready for bed, she didn't feel like Skype and texted Jez. *'Sorry, going to have an early night, this business with Pete is just too upsetting. I'll call you in the morning. If you are still ok for dinner tomorrow, can you be here for seven? I assume you are not a vegetarian.'*

Jez texted back straightaway. *'That's a pity; I was looking forward to seeing you. Never mind, I will be with you at seven tomorrow, and no, I'm not a vegetarian.'*

He re-read the message; no 'xx', and quite cold. His earlier actions had created a situation he had not envisaged. He could feel himself getting angrier and angrier. He went over to his aquarium and watched the fish to help him calm down.

The next morning, Sarah was at her desk at eight-thirty as usual; she hadn't slept well. She'd considered calling off her dinner-date but didn't want to disappoint Jez. She had already cancelled the Skype call the previous evening.

Once the rest of the staff had arrived, she called them together for a team meeting and explained that Pete wasn't feeling well and wouldn't be in. One of the girls went to the stationery department and bought a 'get-well-soon' card which they all signed.

At eleven o'clock, Sarah had a call on her internal phone. "Hi Sarah, this is Cressida Bolton, Sir Basil's PA, he would like you to come up and see him."

Sarah knew who Cressida was; she always announced herself as Sir Basil's PA; "Hi Cressida, yes, what time?"

"Now," replied the PA and the phone was disconnected.

Sarah looked at the receiver. "Supercilious bitch," she muttered under her breath.

It was like a call from royalty; Sarah left her desk and walked up the flight of stairs to the seventh floor and the Directors' suite, wondering what she had done wrong; it was a rare occurrence to get a summons from the Chairman.

It was so quiet as she walked down to the Chairman's office, you could hear a pin drop. The PA was sitting at her computer in a small room next to Sir Basil Huntsman's suite; he didn't like the term office, which did not, in any case, aptly describe the residence.

"Hi, Sarah. Go in; Sir Basil's waiting for you."

Sarah looked at her in her business suit and airs and graces; the eye-contact was brief, and Cressida went back to her work without any further formality or courtesy.

Somewhat anxiously, Sarah knocked on the door. "Come,"

bellowed a voice from within.

"Ah, hello Sarah, come in, shut the door, will you?"

Sarah entered the inner sanctum that was Sir Basil's suite, beautifully decorated with fine art prints and walnut furniture, it took up almost half of the seventh floor and had extensive views across the city. There was a conference-table where board meetings were held and an area in the corner with four armchairs and a coffee table in the middle. Sir Basil was behind his 'executive' desk; there was a single chair in front.

"Sit down," said the Chairman as Sarah approached.

Sir Basil Huntsman Bt was an austere man, Sarah hadn't met him that often, but Pete always called him a 'cold fish'. Having inherited the business, and the Baronet title, on the death of his father, he ruled the store in a style more appropriate to the 1930's, but it had served the business well.

He got straight to the point. "I've had a telephone conversation with Mr Draper who tells me you are aware of the rather delicate situation he finds himself in."

"Yes, Sir Basil," replied Sarah.

"Terrible business, terrible business."

"Yes, Sir Basil," repeated Sarah, uncertain of what else to say.

"I've spoken to Human Resources about it and, on their recommendation, I have suspended Mr Draper with immediate effect until we are clearer on the outcome."

Sarah felt devastated for her boss.

Sir Basil continued; "I want you to take over, for the time being, just temporary, you understand. You'll need to speak to HR about your salary; they tell me you'll be entitled to an increase while you are covering. Any questions?"

Sarah had loads, but for a moment her brain failed to

function correctly.

"What do you want me to tell the rest of the team?"

"Hmm, yes, good point, just tell them that Mr Draper has taken some extended leave and you are covering, that should do it."

"Yes, of course, Sir Basil."

"Was there anything else?"

"No, Sir Basil."

"Then that will be all Sarah; I'll see you at the next senior managers' meeting."

"Thank you, Sir Basil."

Sarah got up and walked out of the room, then breathed a sigh of relief as the tension drained from her body. She walked past the PA's cubicle without acknowledgement; first stop, the ladies' toilet.

Before returning to her desk, she called in at the HR Department, and they gave her a letter confirming her appointment as 'temporary' Head of Procurement, reporting directly to the Operations Director, and her salary while she was in the role; it was a substantial increase.

Sarah was still trying to take in the events. There was clearly an expectation that Pete would not be returning to work anytime soon. She felt sad about his situation and angry that the company was not being more supportive. She would call him later and see how he was.

As she sat down, she realised something else. There would be no way she could take time off tomorrow; she would need to message Jez and cancel the proposed dinner engagement.

Chapter Five

Sarah picked up her mobile phone and sent Jez a text.

'Hi, sorry, I have to cancel tonight, something's come up at work, and I can't take tomorrow off. Maybe we can do something at the weekend if you're free.'

The reply came back almost straight away. *'That's a shame. I was really looking forward to seeing you.'*

Sarah responded. *'Me too, I'll call you later and explain'.*

Jez was angry; really angry. He'd arranged everything with his mother, and now he would have to start all over again, but there was nothing he could do.

Sarah had spent the rest of the day in Pete's office. She had been given his internet authority, and his emails would automatically be diverted to her internal email account; she could now sign 'Sarah Gooding, Acting Head of Procurement'. She wished her parents could see her; they would be so proud.

It was after five-thirty before she could get away from the office. She would have liked to have stayed longer but was concerned about Moses who would need feeding.

It was another hour before she was opening the front door; Moses was at her feet in seconds, nuzzling against her legs. She put her bags on the table and fed the cat, then checked her phone. A call had come through while she was on the train, but she did not take it; she hated people chatting on their phones on the train and refused to be drawn into the habit. There were three messages from Jez, which she ignored, checking her 'missed calls' instead. She recognised Tony's number and called him back.

"Oh hi, Tony, it's Sarah, sorry I missed your call, I was on the train."

"Hi Sarah, thanks for calling back, I wanted to let you know we have some news. They're not charging Pete."

"Oh, Tony, that's great news, what happened?"

"Their tech guys found the hack. Apparently, it was quite sophisticated; they hadn't seen this particular scam before."

"Oh, I'm so glad," said Sarah.

"Unfortunately, there's some bad news too, Pete's in hospital."

"Hospital…? Why, what's happened?"

"He got back this afternoon, Jacob drove him from the police station. He'd only been home a few minutes, and he suddenly went very pale and then just collapsed. I was going frantic. He wasn't breathing at first, so I did CPR, then called 999. They say he's had a heart attack."

"Oh, I'm so sorry, Tony. How is he?"

"He's in intensive care; they say he's 'stable', whatever that means. I've just popped home to collect a few bits and grab something to eat; then I'm going back."

"Is there anything I can do?"

"No, I don't think so. Oh, you could tell Sir Basil and let him know."

"Yes, of course, and I'll come and see him tomorrow night if he's up to having visitors."

"Thanks, Sarah, I'll keep in touch and let you know."

Sarah rang off and was in deep contemplation as she made her dinner. Her thoughts were disturbed by a text alert. It was Jez. *'Hello, are you ok, I was beginning to worry'*.

She texted back. *'Sorry I have just had some bad news, I'll call you later'*.

She didn't feel like talking to anyone at the moment.

By eight-thirty, she had done her chores and was beginning to relax. She called Jez.

"Hi, it's me," she said as the call was answered.

"Oh, am I glad to hear from you, I was getting worried; what's wrong?"

"You know my boss that the police had been questioning about downloading child-porn?"

"Yes,"

"Well, this morning he was suspended from work, and I've temporarily been put in charge of procurement. That's why I had to cancel tonight."

"It's ok, can't be helped."

"That's not the end of the story. Pete was released without charge this afternoon, the police have confirmed it was a scam."

"Well, that's good news, isn't it?" There was a degree of indifference in his voice that Sarah detected.

"Yes, it is, but when he got back home, he had a heart attack, and now he's in intensive care."

"Oh dear, that's terrible," said Jez.

"I know. If I could get my hands on those evil bastards who do these scams; well, I don't know what I would do, but killing is too good for them."

"Yes," said Jez. "It's terrible."

"I can't stop thinking about it."

"I wish I could take your mind off it in some way."

"Thanks, I'll be ok; it's just been a difficult day."

"What about I take you out for a meal again, something a bit more special? That might cheer you up."

"When were you thinking? Only it won't be this week, I've got too much on, and I want to go to the hospital to see Pete tomorrow if he's allowed visitors. Anyway, it's my turn. I think I owe you a meal after cancelling tonight. What about Saturday, you can come here, and I'll cook you something?"

Jez was thinking; he would need to do battle with his mother again and think of another excuse.

"Er… hmm, yes, ok, that would be great," said Jez, but not as enthusiastically as he should have done.

"Don't worry if it's not convenient," said Sarah.

"No, no, it's fine, I would love to," said Jez. "You'll have to give me directions."

"Yes, of course, it's easy enough to find. Anyway, I need to go, Moses is feeling left out; I was late home tonight."

Jez was thinking the cat was not the only one feeling neglected, but he didn't say anything.

"Yes, of course," said Jez. "We can catch up tomorrow."

Sarah rang off and, after feeding the cat, spent an hour catching up on some TV before going to bed.

Jez, meanwhile, opened the drawer to his desk and picked up his scarf. He pressed it to his nose and sniffed. There were still traces of Sarah's perfume. He looked at her pictures on his wall; pride of place was the Settle selfie. "See you Saturday," he said.

The following day, Sarah had spoken to Tony, and it was good news, Pete was out of intensive care and looking much better. After work, she took a bus to the hospital to visit him. She took a get-well-soon card from all the team; even Sir Basil had signed it. Sarah spoke to the head of HR and updated her. In light of the information, Pete's suspension was rescinded, and he could return to work as soon as he was fit. Sarah had the letter with her to deliver.

It took Sarah twenty minutes to get to the hospital and another ten to find the ward. She walked down the row of beds and to a side ward in the corner where Pete was. Tony was sitting next to the bed, and Pete was connected to an array of monitors. She stood at the door.

"Hello, is it ok to come in?" said Sarah. Tony looked as if he was asleep; his head was resting on his elbow. "I hope I'm not disturbing you."

"Hi, Sarah," said Tony, drowsily. There was a significant shadow around his chin; he had clearly not shaved for some time.

"Hello Sarah, thank you for coming; That's so good of you," Pete rasped.

"That's ok, how are you feeling?"

"A bit better, thanks, they've pumped me full of drugs, so I've been sleeping quite a bit. They've put in a stent, and I'm going to be on Warfarin for life."

"Oh dear, it sounds awful," said Sarah. She held his hand and squeezed it. "I've bought you some grapes." They both laughed.

"Yes, they do a good selection in the food-hall," said Pete and laughed again, and then started coughing.

Tony looked at him with some concern. "Are you alright, dear?"

"Yes, I'm ok. So, what's the news?" said Pete.

"Oh, nothing for you to worry about, I've got it all under control," said Sarah.

"I never doubted that for one minute," said Pete and Sarah squeezed his hand again.

"Oh, I've got you this as well," and she produced the rather large card.

Tony opened it for Pete so that he could read the comments.

"Sir Basil's signed it as well, you *are* honoured," said Sarah.

"That's good of him, thank you, that's very kind," said Pete.

"I've also brought you this," and Sarah handed Pete the letter. "It's from HR, rescinding your suspension."

"I should think so too," said Tony.

"It's ok, Tony, they were only doing their job," said Pete. He started coughing again.

"Are you ok?" asked Tony. "Shall I get a nurse?"

"No, it's ok, it's just my throat where they stuck the tubes down; it's very sore."

Sarah didn't stay too long, partly due to Pete's condition, but also because she needed to get back to feed Moses.

There was a bus-stop directly outside the hospital that stopped close to the station. Although she had left work early for the visit, it was after six o'clock before Sarah reached the train, and another thirty minutes before Moses got his food.

Sarah had received several text messages from Jez during the day, some of which she responded to, others she ignored while she was busy. She realised he was feeling side-lined because of recent events. She would try to make it up to him at the weekend.

Back in Deighton, Jez was becoming increasingly frustrated with Sarah's lack of contact. She had ignored several text messages, and he felt angry and helpless. He was beginning to regret his hasty intervention with her boss; it had become a significant distraction. A question of rage, blind to the consequences.

The atmosphere in the house was terrible; he and his mother were hardly on speaking terms. He had found it difficult to concentrate on his work and had started to make mistakes which had proved costly in re-work time. The cancellation of his 'meeting' the previous evening had also created problems; his mother was becoming suspicious.

It was after dinner; his mother was putting the dishes in the dishwasher ready for Mrs Dawson, the daily help.

This time he decided to play hardball.

"I'm going out on Saturday night," he announced.

She looked at him. "Again?"

"Yes, I have a date."

"A date… ah, it all makes sense now, all these meetings. You're just like your father; lies, lies, lies. So, who is this trollop?"

"She's not a trollop!" shouted Jez.

"Of course she is; they all are," said Martha.

Jez was ready to explode, but he restrained himself. "I'm not arguing with you; I'm going to my room."

He could hear his mother banging the crockery to emphasise her annoyance. He heard a plate smash followed by cursing.

Jez opened up his computer and accessed his music files; some Deep Purple would ease the frustration. Then he opened 'Sarah's folder' and stared at the pictures of her.

The night-time chats with Jez had become part of Sarah's routine over recent days; she found a certain catharsis in sharing her news, and he seemed a willing listener. That evening, she recounted her trip to the hospital and progress in her new role at the store. It was just a voice call, she didn't feel like making the effort for a video, despite Jez's suggestion. She had an important conference the following morning, and she needed an early night.

For the next two days, Sarah was pre-occupied with her new role in the company. She was already signing letters to suppliers as 'Acting Head of Procurement' and had attended her first Leadership Team meeting on Thursday morning, chaired by Sir Basil. In keeping with the company's culture, it was all very formal which Sarah had initially found daunting, but the other team members were extremely generous in supporting her, and she soon felt at ease.

That evening, after work, she again called in to visit Pete at the hospital. There was some good news; he was making a better-than-expected recovery and was hoping to be allowed home over the weekend. She noticed he looked much better and had lost the grey pallor he had presented on her earlier visit. There was some additional news; doctors had told him he was going to be off work for at least three months. Sarah had mixed emotions; she wanted Pete to get well but found herself wishing she could have his job permanently. She berated herself for feeling that way; she was not normally like that.

Riding the train home Friday evening, she thought again of her parents and wished she could talk to them; she had so much to tell them. Tonight though, she was feeling different from usual Fridays. Usually, she would be drained and exhausted, but tonight the adrenaline was still pumping with the excitement of her new position. She would have stayed longer had it not been the need to feed Moses.

Jez was not in her mind, and she ignored the numerous text messages she had received. Unusually for a Friday, she had managed to get a seat and, like the majority of her fellow passengers, took out her phone. She accessed her messages; there was another one from Jez, sent fifteen minutes earlier. '*Just checking you are ok. I thought you might be on the way home. Jez xx'*

Sarah replied. *'Sorry I've been a bit elusive today; I've been up to my eyes in work. I'm on the train now, chat later. Sarah x'*

Jez looked at the message in frustration and wondered what he could do about it. He was beginning to become concerned she might cancel the dinner-date; she had not mentioned it in her messages.

He texted back. *'Great, are we still ok for tomorrow?'*

Sarah hadn't forgotten but had not given it a great deal of thought. She replied.

'Yes of course, do you have any preferences or allergies I need to know about?'

'No, I'll eat most things, what time?'

Sarah re-focussed from the work issues crisscrossing around in her head. It would be good to switch off; she needed some downtime.

'7 pm?'

'Great, chat later, Jez xx'.

Sarah started making a list of what she needed to do. Cleaning the house was a priority; washing, which she had put off during the week; then there was the shopping and food she would need to get, and that was before she had started the cooking. She was beginning to wish she hadn't suggested the dinner-date; she had enough stress on her hands.

The week had certainly taken some of the gloss off her relationship with Jez. It wasn't that she had lost feelings for him; just, she had become preoccupied by other priorities.

That evening after dinner, she started the chores, and it was after ten before she sat down on the sofa with a glass of wine to watch some TV. She was exhausted; the week's anxieties were beginning to wash over her. With the warm glow of the gas fire adding a comforting ambience, and Moses curled up on her lap, she felt herself drifting off to sleep. The ping of a text message startled her.

She knew it would be from Jez; she had promised to call him but hadn't had the time.

'Hi, just checking you are ok, I thought you were going to call.'

She replied. *'Sorry, I have been on the go all night doing the washing, just sat down with a glass of wine.'*

'Wish I could join you,' replied Jez.

'You can tomorrow,' replied Sarah.

'Can't wait. Would you like to Skype?'

'Do you mind if we don't? I'm so tired, and I need to go to bed.'

'Of course, I'll text you in the morning. Sleep well xx,' replied Jez.

Back in Deighton, Jez was livid. He had been incredibly patient with Sarah and was hoping for another Skype session; it was Friday after all. He was trying to be philosophical, but it was difficult. It was only the thought of his dinner-date that was keeping him going.

It hadn't helped that his relationship with his mother had got even worse. She had virtually ignored him for two days; meals had been eaten in silence, and he was left to sort out his own washing for the daily help.

He was in his den; he could hear his mother's TV on in her bedroom almost at full volume, deliberately trying to break Jez's concentration. Jez knew the game and was determined not to let her win. He had put two pillows at the bottom of the door to absorb the sound. He was trying to think of ways he could win Sarah 'back' and had the germ of an idea. He would see how Saturday night went before taking it further.

Saturday morning and there would be no lie-in for Sarah; she was up before eight o'clock. She checked her messages. The last had been delivered at seven thirty-two.

'Hi, hope you slept ok; can't wait to see you again tonight. Jez xx'

She replied. *'Hi, yes. I'll text later x.'*

She needed to get going and didn't want to get caught up in a text conversation that would delay her.

Sarah was not one to do a great deal of entertaining. This was the first time she'd invited a man to her house in over five years of living there, so there was a certain amount of pressure to make it a success. She also wanted to reconnect with Jez; her work commitments had taken the edge off her emotional needs. She still hadn't decided what to cook; a search of the supermarket shelves would provide some inspiration. She started making a list of basic ingredients while she ate her breakfast; something simple which would not take too long to prepare and cook.

She had finished her washing the previous evening, but there was the ironing to do; that would be after lunch, she decided. To save time, she would visit the supermarket as soon as she had eaten; it would not be too busy.

She was back before ten o'clock with her produce. She decided on a chicken dish; something she had made before when she visited her brother in Scotland.

Back in Deighton, tensions were building; it started over breakfast. Jez was reading the newspaper at the kitchen table with two rounds of toast and a jar of Marmite.

"So what time are you seeing this trollop tonight?"

It was the first attempt at a discussion for almost two days.

"I'll be leaving just after six," replied Jez.

"What about the shopping?"

"That's tomorrow."

"Yes, but I assume you will be sleeping with her, why else would you be going?"

"Don't be crude, mother, Sarah's not like that," said Jez, indignantly.

"Of course she is; that's what they all want these days."

Jez ignored the comment and continued eating his toast and reading the newspaper.

"Sarah. So that's her name is it, this trollop? And you're going all the way to Leeds just to say hello. I find that hard to believe."

"I'm not discussing it, mother, but I'll be back to do the shopping tomorrow, don't worry."

"Oh, I'm not worried. It's you that won't have any food on the table if we don't go to the supermarket."

Martha got up and went to the sink. Jez could hear the rough clunking of crockery as his mother washed her mug and plate. Everything else went into the dishwasher.

That was the end of the discussion. Jez had decided to ignore his mother's remarks; he didn't want anything to spoil his date. In truth, he was in a great mood and was feeling a twinge of excitement at the thought of seeing Sarah again. He got up from the table, leaving his plate and mug, and took his coat from behind the door.

"Where are you going?" asked Martha with some surprise.

"Just into the village to pick up a few things. Is there

anything you want while I'm out?"

"No, nothing that can't wait until tomorrow. Why are you going out? Surely it can wait until we go shopping."

"No, it can't. Won't be long."

Jez left the house and headed down the long drive to the main road in his trusty Land Rover. He would normally turn right towards Skipton, but instead, he turned left towards the village.

About half-a-mile down the main road, there was a petrol-station which included a mini-market where you could buy the essentials. Jez had used it many times when they had run out of milk or bread; it saved making a trip to Skipton. He pulled into the forecourt and filled up with diesel. Outside there was a good display of flowers arranged in buckets. He chose the largest bunch and went inside. There was a reasonably-stocked off-license, and he scanned the shelves looking for something suitable to take with him for dinner. On the top shelf were the expensive items; decent quality reds and just two bottles of Champagne. He looked at the prices and frowned; they cost far more than in the supermarket in Skipton, but they would have to do. Ignoring the top-shelf stock, he took a bottle of Australian red and went to the counter to pay.

Armed with his contribution for the evening, he returned to the Hall. He left the wine in the car but had to take the flowers into the house; they would need to be kept in water.

Martha heard Jez return and was waiting by the door; as he walked in, she immediately saw the flowers.

"Flowers? For me? What's this, a peace offering? Well, I should think so, causing your mother so much grief."

Jez looked at her. "They're not for you."

Martha glared at him, then turned and walked away without

saying a word.

By six o'clock, Sarah was almost ready for her dinner guest; her chores were complete, and the place looked tidy. She'd received several texts from Jez, but they were beginning to interfere with her schedule; she ignored the last one.

She prepared her ingredients for the meal and then took a shower. It had been a hectic day and what she needed was a nap, just a few minutes to recharge her batteries, but there wasn't time. She dried her hair and chose her outfit for the evening. The previous day she had bought a red baroque-print chiffon top from the store which she liked and, although more expensive than she would normally choose, with her staff discount it did not break the bank. She tried it on, initially without a bra, but, with the gaping front, realised straight away that it would give off the wrong signals. Even with a bra, the result was still 'sexy'. Then she thought, why not? It was about time she had some fun. Jez was the first man in a long time that she found remotely attractive in that way. Her outfit was completed by a pair of jeans and a comfortable pair of flat shoes.

By twenty-to-seven she was back in the kitchen pouring herself a large glass of wine; she started to feel anxious.

Back in Deighton, Jez was going through a similar routine, but found himself being continually harangued by his mother; it was stretching his patience to breaking point. He was in his bedroom getting ready; he could hear her pacing up and down in the corridor outside. He checked himself in the mirror; new shirt, jeans, his brown leather jacket and a pair of casual loafers. He sent a final text to Sarah.

'Just leaving, looking forward to seeing you soon. Be there

at seven. Jez xx'

The reply came almost immediately. *'Ok, see you soon S x.'*

He felt a twinge of excitement, but that would not last. He left his bedroom and was immediately confronted by his mother.

"Ooo, look at you all dolled up like a dog's dinner. I hope you remembered the condoms when you went to the garage. You don't want to be bringing anything nasty back home. That reminds me, I must remember to tell Mrs Dawson to disinfect the toilets thoroughly."

"That's disgusting, mother," shouted Jez.

"Well, you can't be too careful these days. I was always reminding your father when he went out galivanting with his trollops."

"Well, do you know what?" said Jez. "Right now, I have every sympathy with him. No wonder he went astray, having to put up with you."

There was silence; Martha was lost for words. Jez walked away and started to descend the stairs to the hallway; his mother followed. She grabbed his arm.

"No, Jeremy, don't say that. I'm sorry, I didn't mean what I said."

"Get off me, mother, you're embarrassing," said Jez.

He pulled his arm away, causing Martha to stumble. She missed a step and started to fall forward. Jez caught her before she could completely over balance. She grasped the bannister rail and held on, steadying herself.

Jez left her and went into the kitchen to collect the flowers which he'd left on the table in a large vase of water. He couldn't believe his eyes. All the flowers' heads had been cut off and were lying forlornly on the table next to the bare stems.

"Mother!" he screamed.

Martha appeared at the kitchen door. "I'm sorry, I was angry," she whimpered.

"Why did you do that?" said Jez, searching for the right words. In truth, he wanted to kill her.

"I don't know; I was angry like I said."

"That's no excuse. I'm entitled to some happiness in my life. Why do you want to spoil it?"

"But you're happy here, just the two of us, like it's always been."

"No, not anymore. I hate living here, and I hate you!"

"Don't say that. You're not yourself; I understand that. This trollop's turned your head. You'll see; it'll be all right. You'll soon get over her; you just need to let her go."

"I'm not letting her go, let's get that straight," said Jez. "Right now, she's the only thing that matters in my life."

Martha's rage was starting again.

"Go on then, clear off. You're just like your father and look what happened to him."

Jez ignored her remark and put on his jacket; it was only six o'clock, but he couldn't stay any longer; he needed to get out. He was beginning to wish she had fallen down the stairs. He checked his keys and headed for the front door.

"What time will you be back?" said Martha.

"Later," said Jez.

"Well, make sure you close the bottom gate when you leave, I don't want any intruders."

Jez ignored her and slammed the front door; at least it would have slammed if it wasn't so heavy.

He locked the door from the outside; his mother had keys if she needed them.

As he walked towards the Land Rover, the security system was immediately activated, bathing the front of the Hall in bright light.

It was starting to get dark; sunset was half-an-hour earlier, and it had rained heavily during the afternoon. The significant moisture in the air had created a rolling mist. The weather made it feel more like November than February.

He sat in the car and just breathed deeply for a moment. He needed to re-focus and calm down. The security lights switched off on their timer; the area was in complete darkness. He started the car; the familiar exhaust-rattle accompanied the Land Rover as it slowly navigated the pot-holes down the drive. The headlights picked out the trees in the adjacent woods, and, with the swirling mist, it gave an ethereal look to the surroundings. He reached the gate in the boundary wall, aimed the fob, and it opened. He drove through. It would close itself if it didn't stick; which it was inclined to do from time-to-time.

He had some time to kill; he didn't want to arrive too early, so he stopped off at the supermarket in Skipton to buy some more flowers to replace those mutilated by his mother. It was on his way. He berated himself for not thinking about this earlier; he could have saved a lot of money on the wine. The selection of flowers was, as expected, much larger than the garage and this time he chose a bunch of red roses, which happened to be the most expensive items on display.

He paid for the roses and went back to the car. He rattled out of the car park and took the turning to Leeds. After about ten minutes he heard his phone ringing; it continued until the answer-phone kicked in; then dropped. Not having a hands-free kit, Jez found a layby. He thought it might be Sarah. He put on the internal light and checked his missed calls. He might have known; it was his mother. He was in two minds whether to call back or not, but he decided he had better.

He keyed in the number and waited for the answer.

"Jeremy?"

"Yes, mother, what did you want?"

"I just wanted to make sure you closed the bottom gate. You know I don't like being here on my own."

"It's fine, mother, go and watch TV. Was there anything else; I've got to go?"

"No, that was all. What time will you be back?"

"Later, mother. Just leave me alone," said Jez and rang off.

He was starting to feel angry again at the intrusion; his mother was just game-playing, and he knew it.

It was six-thirty, and he was about fifteen miles from Sarah's house; he would be punctual.

Sarah meanwhile, was slightly nervous waiting for her dinner-guest, but at least she had managed to switch off from work; she was ready to enjoy herself. She had poured herself a second glass of red wine while she was finalising the meal which was now cooking slowly in the oven; it was just the rice to do which would not take long. She checked her watch, not for the first time; then went to her music system and plugged in her iPod. She put the player in 'shuffle' mode and adjusted the volume to ambient.

It was two minutes to seven when she heard the rattling Land Rover pull up outside. Sarah didn't have a garage; her Clio was parked outside the house. There was a parking space immediately in front. Sarah went to the window and watched Jez reverse into the bay. She returned to the sofa and waited for the doorbell to ring.

Chapter Six

Jez gathered up his gifts and walked to the front door; he could feel the excitement mounting.

There was a small concrete frontage, behind a three-feet tall hedge. Several flowerpots, containing spring primulas not yet in bloom, were placed, ready to bring some colour in a few weeks. Jez walked up a couple of steps and rang the bell.

He could hear a door opening; a light appeared, and then there she was, looking incredible.

"Hi," said Jez. "Glad I got the right house."

"Hi, yes, come in," said Sarah, and stood to one side so he could pass.

There was a small vestibule, then a door leading to the lounge. Jez went in and waited for Sarah to lock the front door. He presented her with the flowers.

"Oh, thank you; what lovely roses," she said, and kissed him on the cheek. "I'll just go and pop these in some water."

"I've bought this as well," said Jez and handed over the bottle of wine.

"Thanks, that's great; you didn't have to," said Sarah.

"I wanted to, to say thank you for inviting me, you've gone to a lot of trouble," said Jez looking at the table. She had set it for two, and there was a small candle in the middle.

"That's ok; I've quite enjoyed it really. It's given me a bit of a break from work. Sit down, dinner won't be long," said Sarah.

Jez sat on the sofa; Moses was fast asleep in his cat basket next to the gas fire.

"Would you like a drink?" said Sarah.

"A glass of wine would be fine, thanks," replied Jez and

Sarah disappeared into the kitchen.

"So, how has your day been?" said Sarah as she returned with the drinks.

"It's been ok, but not got much work done; been looking forward to coming to see you if I'm honest," said Jez, taking his first sip.

"Yes, me too," said Sarah taking the first taste of her third glass of wine. Whether it was the drink or the fact that Sarah was just relaxing, she was beginning to reconnect with him. He still had that rugged look that attracted her on the website, and he had lost the stare that seemed to unnerve her on Skype; maybe it was just the computer.

Jez looked at her. "You look stunning. I love that top."

"Thank you, it's new, from the store."

"I must shop there more often," said Jez.

There was still a mixture of uncertainty and anxiety which made the conversation stilted; both were experiencing similar emotions.

"I love your house," said Jez, looking around the room. "How long have you lived here?"

"I moved in just before my parents died, over five years now," replied Sarah. "My Dad did the decoration."

"He did an excellent job," said Jez.

"Yes," said Sarah. "Make yourself at home; I'll just check on the dinner."

Sarah got up and returned to the kitchen. Jez noticed that Moses was beginning to stir, and he watched as the cat left its basket, stretched, as cats do, and headed towards him. It reached Jez's legs and started nuzzling against them. Jez was not anti-cats, he just didn't like them, or dogs for that matter. He pushed Moses away with his leg but that seemed to encourage him further, and the cat made a grab for Jez's foot, biting it in an affectionate, not aggressive way. This time Jez was not so gentle. He lifted his foot, the momentum propelling Moses off the floor and about three feet across the room. The cat went scurrying into the kitchen. Jez could hear Sarah talking to it.

Sarah returned to the lounge. "Dinner won't be long. I see you've met Moses."

"Yes," said Jez. "What a lovely cat, very playful. Must be good company for you."

"Ha, ha. All he does is eat and sleep, oh, and crap. When I die, I want to come back as a cat."

"You believe in reincarnation?" said Jez as he sipped his wine.

"No, not really, just a joke," said Sarah. "Do you want to sit at the table? The dinner will be ready shortly. I hope you like it."

"I'm sure I will," said Jez and he moved from the sofa to one of the chairs. "Does it matter which chair?" asked Jez. Sarah was back in the kitchen.

"No, it doesn't matter which."

Jez sat on the chair facing the kitchen, his back to the front door. Moses was nowhere to be seen, A couple of minutes later, Sarah appeared with two plates; she presented one to Jez and placed the other at the vacant setting. "Careful, the plates are hot," she said as she sat down.

"This looks delicious," said Jez as he started cutting into his chicken.

"It's chicken with a white wine sauce, mushrooms and onions. I've done rice rather than pasta; I thought it would be lighter."

"It's great, thank you."

There was a break in conversation as the pair started eating. It was Jez who opened the discourse.

"So, tell me about this new job of yours; it sounds exciting."

"Mmm, yes, it is. I'm really enjoying it."

"Acting Head of Procurement. What does it mean?" said Jez as he negotiated another mouthful of chicken.

"I look after all the buying for the store. Well, I say 'me', I have a small team to manage."

"Wow, a big responsibility."

"Yes, it is, although I've been in Procurement for a while, and I know most of the big suppliers, so that's fairly routine."

"Are you responsible for negotiating prices?"

"Yes, although we have a pricing policy that we use as guidelines, so there's not a lot of negotiation."

"So, it's take it or leave it?"

"No, not exactly; not quite as blunt as that, but we do have a certain buying power which helps."

"Hmm, interesting, and this pricing policy, do you share it with your suppliers?"

"Good grief, no. It's top secret. It would be extremely valuable to our competitors."

"Yes, I guess it would, I hadn't thought of that... This chicken is great," said Jez, wanting to move the discussion away from work.

Sarah took another sip of wine; this was her third glass, and she was starting to feel very relaxed. Jez looked at her top and her very visible bra; he had visions of the dressing-gown moment.

"You look terrific," he said.

Sarah noticed his gaze. "Thanks," she said. "It's getting quite warm in here. The fire gives off a good heat." She started wafting her top to circulate air. Jez almost choked on his last piece of chicken. Sarah smiled.

Sarah put her knife and fork down. "That's me stuffed," she said, not a word she would normally use but after three glasses of wine, inhibitions were beginning to disappear. She gazed at Jez and moved her hand to his and squeezed. Jez got up. He was stood over her and leaned down to kiss her. She responded immediately. It was long and more passionate than the one in the Settle alleyway.

"Mmm, save that for later. I have some dessert."

"I thought that was dessert," said Jez, and laughed.

He sat back down and watched Sarah clear the dishes and go into the kitchen. There was the ping of the microwave. She returned a few minutes later with two steaming bowls of sticky toffee pudding.

Just then Jez's ring tone sounded from his jacket pocket.

"Sorry about that, I meant to turn it off," said Jez.

"Don't you want to see who it is?" said Sarah.

"No, it won't be important," said Jez, and he started to tackle the sickly pudding. "This is great."

"Supermarket, I'm afraid," said Sarah, enjoying the dessert.

"That was delicious," said Jez, having cleared his dish. "Thank you."

"Do you want some more to drink or a coffee?"

"Just a coffee, I need to drive later."

"Oh, yes, of course." There was disappointment in Sarah's voice; she had planned to invite Jez to stay over if everything went well.

"Mother doesn't like being left on her own. It's one of the trials of being a carer," said Jez, to lessen any negative connotations.

"It's ok; I'll get the coffee."

Jez sat back on the sofa. There was no sign of the cat, who had gone upstairs, according to Sarah.

The atmosphere was tranquil; the room was warm from the glow of the gas fire. Jez noticed the music for the first time; not his preferred taste but seemed to enhance the occasion.

Jez could hear the clattering of dishes in the kitchen. He got up and went to see if he could assist. Sarah was stacking a dishwasher in the corner of the kitchen under the worktop.

"Can I help?" said Jez.

"No, it's fine, it won't take a minute; go and sit down, and I'll bring the coffees."

Jez watched as she stacked the plates. "Ok, but let me know if I can help."

Jez seemed to be in a trance when Sarah returned with the coffees. He had heard her go upstairs, presumably for a comfort break, and could tell she had refreshed her make-up and perfume.

She pulled up a small coffee table from beside the sofa and placed the coffees on it. Then sat next to Jez on the settee. He noticed another change; Sarah had removed her bra.

Jez could feel a pain in the pit of his stomach; he was becoming aroused.

"Wow, you look incredible," said Jez.

Any thoughts of coffee had disappeared as their desire consumed them. The kissing resumed with growing urgency. Jez wasted no time in exploring the delights on offer. He had imagined this moment ever since the Skype flash, wondering what it would feel like to actually hold what had been shown him.

Jez started teasing her nipples with his fingers which caused

Sarah to moan gently. He could feel her hands pulling at the button on the top of his jeans. It gave way, and slowly she eased the zip downwards. He was now licking Sara's nipples, the sensation causing them to harden. He could feel her long fingers searching for the gap in his boxer shorts, and his erection bounced free from its confinement, strong and proud. She held it in her right hand and started to pump it up and down.

Jez let out a gasp and a moan; then an expletive. "Shit!"

Sarah could feel warm liquid running down her fingers.

"Bugger," said Jez.

Sarah broke from his grasp and looked at the back of her hand which was covered in goo.

"I'm so sorry," said Jez, acutely embarrassed.

"It's ok, let me get some tissues," said Sarah, and she went upstairs.

Jez was mortified; how could this happen? It was something he had not experienced before. He looked around and could see the sofa had not escaped the ejaculation. "Shit," he said again and started wiping the stain with his handkerchief, hoping that Sarah wouldn't notice.

Sarah returned with a roll of toilet paper and handed it to Jez who proceeded to clean himself off.

"I'm so sorry," repeated Jez.

"It's ok," said Sarah. "I mean, I should take it as a compliment, I suppose."

"There's some on the sofa, I'm afraid."

"Oh, ok, I'll get a cloth."

She went to fetch a kitchen cloth and some fabric cleaner.

"I'm so sorry," said Jez. "I'll pay for any cleaning."

"Don't be silly; it'll be fine when it dries. It shouldn't leave a mark. You'll need to get those jeans washed," she said pointing to the damp mark around his zip.

"Yes," said Jez, seeing the discolouration.

"I'm so sorry," said Jez again. "It's been such a long time."

"Stop apologising, it happens; it's not the end of the world," said Sarah, who had poured herself another glass of wine. She was beginning to see the funny side of it.

"I tell you what, now you've emptied the tank, so to speak, what say we try again? Somewhere more comfortable."

Jez looked at her. "Are you sure?"

She took his hand and led him upstairs. "The bathroom's just there," she said pointing to the first door at the top of the stairs. "I'll be waiting in here," and she walked through to her bedroom.

Jez cleaned himself off and relieved himself, then joined Sarah.

He had fantasised about making love to Sarah; it had dominated his thoughts in recent days, and it was everything he had imagined. For Sarah, though, the experience was like her first couplings at University, and she felt far from fulfilled.

"It's a pity you can't stay," said Sarah, although deep down she was not really that disappointed if it meant more frantic fumbling.

"Yes, but I said I'd be back tonight, and she'll only worry."

"Yes, it's ok; I understand," said Sarah.

"Maybe next time, if I'm not being too presumptuous," said Jez,

"Yes, ok," said Sarah, but not with too much enthusiasm. Jez did not pick up the indifference.

"I know; maybe we can go away for a couple of days," said Jez.

"What about your mother?"

"Don't worry, we'll work something out," said Jez.

"Well, it's something to think about, but I couldn't at the moment, what with work and everything."

"Yes, it's ok, I understand," he said. Inside, though, he was far from happy that Sarah's work continued to impinge on their lives. For the moment, he would say nothing; he didn't want to jeopardise any future get-togethers.

He looked at his watch. "Oh, is that the time? I'd better go; it's almost midnight."

"Yes, ok."

Ten minutes later, Jez was in his Land Rover; the noise as he started the engine reverberated around the terrace. It would have woken at least one neighbour. Sarah waved him off with a mix of emotions, and she was recounting the evening as she finished tidying the kitchen.

The night hadn't been the sparks and fireworks she had hoped for, certainly not on the physical side; he'd definitely not lived up to her expectations as a lover. It was as though it was his first time, although she was sure that it wasn't. His mother was also becoming a problem; she seemed to cast a shadow over everything. She realised that Jez had responsibilities which he could not relinquish just because she was in his life and she respected that. Nevertheless, a man in his thirties having to be back in case his mother fretted, was a concern.

Jez was in turmoil as he headed back to Deighton. He was furious with himself at his earlier 'embarrassment', but Sarah had been understanding. He wasn't sure if other girls would have been so accommodating. Needless to say, his feelings for Sarah had increased even further; if that were possible. He worshipped her and resented the fact that he couldn't stay the night as they both had wanted. His hatred for his mother had increased exponentially. He just wanted to return to Sarah and hold her again.

He was out of Leeds and into the open countryside; there were no streetlights. In the darkness, Sarah was dominating his very being. Then, without warning, an image jolted him. Suddenly, from nowhere, he was visualising Sarah making love to someone else, an ex; several exes, maybe. The thoughts seemed to consume him, eating at his brain and he couldn't seem to shift them; raging jealousy was taking over that he couldn't control. Hands were pawing her, hard penises thrusting into her; her fingernails digging into someone's back and buttocks in the heat of passion. He banged his fist on the steering wheel in anger.

He tried breathing deeply; the thoughts gradually dissipated. Then he remembered the missed call he'd had earlier. He guessed it would be his mother and his mind shifted to the altercation that almost certainly lay ahead; ironically, he calmed down.

He reached the gate of the estate; it had stuck halfway again, and he had to open and close it manually; he would need to get it fixed. He continued up to the Hall and was greeted by the security lights illuminating the front of the building. The mist and rain had gone, just a hazy moon as he exited the Land Rover.

He noticed the lights were still on downstairs. He was not surprised; this was the first time in over three years that he had stayed out this late. He assumed his mother had either forgotten or left them on for some comfort.

He unlocked the front door, locked it behind him and walked into the hallway. He could hear the TV blaring out in the lounge. He was ready to remonstrate with his mother, but when he walked in, she was slumped in the chair. For a moment he thought she was dead, but as he reached her, she stirred and squinted at him.

"So, you've finally come home then," she said, opening her eyes and focusing on her son.

Jez turned off the TV.

"You've been drinking," said Jez, smelling alcohol on her breath.

"So what? What do you care? Why didn't you call me back? I left you a message? There was a prowler outside, the lights went on, and I heard him. I was so frightened."

"It was probably a deer," said Jez.

"No, it wasn't a deer; it was a prowler. I know it was."

"Well, there's nobody out there now. Why don't you go to bed?"

Martha staggered out of the chair, clearly unstable on her feet. She looked at him with hate in her eyes. "So, did you get laid? That's the expression they use nowadays isn't it?"

"I'm not talking to you, mother; I'm going to bed," said Jez.

Having consumed a lot of wine and with the exertions of the day, Sarah dropped into an alcohol-induced sleep but woke up about an hour later wide awake. She felt thirsty from the excess alcohol and would need to hydrate to avoid a headache in the morning. She checked the clock it was two twenty-three. Moses was at the bottom of the bed on his blanket; he stirred as Sarah put the light on and went to the bathroom. She replenished her glass of water and went back to bed.

Her thoughts returned to work, and she was now desperate for sleep as she would need her mind fresh for Monday. That only made matters worse; she tossed and turned for another hour before exhaustion took over, and she drifted off. It was not a restful sleep, however, and she experienced nightmares again. They were like the ones she had had before, a feeling of being trapped and unable to breathe. At five o'clock she woke with a start, breathing heavily. Moses was now also awake; seeing Sarah sat up in bed, he started meowing. She went down to the kitchen to feed him.

The next time she woke, it was nine-thirty, and there were two text messages from Jez that she had not heard. She would reply later; she needed a shower.

Sunday morning and Jez was awake at seven o'clock also suffering from a hangover, but not associated with excess alcohol. He checked his phone hoping for a message from Sarah but was disappointed. He started to text.

'Hello, I just wanted to say thanks for last night. It was the most amazing experience of my life. Chat soon? Love you, Jez xx'.

He could see that Sarah was not online but hoped she would reply quickly. He couldn't wait to talk to her again, but more than anything he wanted to be as close to her as he had been the previous evening.

He rechecked his messages at eight o'clock, but there was nothing. He sent another.

'I hope you're ok this morning; I can't stop thinking about you. Text me when you can, all my love Jez xx'.

Martha was still in bed, and Jez was pleased about that. He got dressed and went downstairs to get something to eat and make some tea. He would let his mother sleep; he couldn't stand another confrontation.

While the kettle was boiling, he decided to look around outside to see if there was any evidence to justify his mother's concerns. He opened the front door and took in a reviving breath of fresh air. It was chilly but bright; a touch of frost had left a white tinge on the lawns. He stepped onto the gravel forecourt and checked the front perimeter of the Hall; then went around the back. He was looking for anything that might indicate the presence of an intruder. There was nothing; then he spotted some footprints; well not feet exactly, cloven hooves; a half-eaten shrub and tell-tale droppings. Jez's earlier assessment was confirmed; it was a deer.

It could have got in through the open gate, but, more likely, reached the house via the woods. The security lights would normally have scared it off. It was rare for them to come this close to the Hall since Jez had had the them installed.

Satisfied with his investigative work, he went back into the Hall and made his breakfast. By ten o'clock, he still hadn't heard from Sarah and was beginning to worry. He sent another text.

'Hi, are you ok? Please let me know. Love Jez xx'.

Ten minutes later there was a reply.

'Sorry, had a lie-in. Chat later when I've finished my housework. S x'.

Jez was desperate to speak to her; he replied.

'Yes great, maybe Skype, it will be so good to see you xx'.

Sarah was now feeling the effects of too much alcohol and sleep deprivation. She was not inclined to put on make-up and wash her hair for a Skype chat; she would make an excuse.

'Will pass on the Skype chat, another time. I'll call you after lunch.'

Jez felt a tinge rejected; he thought after what they had shared the previous night, she would have been keen to talk.

He made himself a coffee and was seated at the breakfast

bar when his mother walked in. She ignored Jez and went to the sink to fill the kettle.

"I remember when you used to make me a cup of tea," she said.

"Thought you might want a lie-in," replied Jez.

"Thinking about your trollop, more like. I hope you're still taking me to the supermarket this morning; I need some things."

"Yes, as soon as you're ready… if it hasn't closed by then."

"I'll be ready by eleven-ish," said Martha.

"Hmm, yeah?" he said sarcastically. "Oh, by the way, that intruder last night?" Martha looked up from her tea-making. "It had four legs, so there was nothing for you to worry about."

"What do you mean?" said Martha.

"It was a deer like I said. Probably came through the woods. It's eaten one of the shrubs."

"No, it was a man, definitely a man."

"You saw him?"

"No, but I heard him; it was definitely a prowler."

"Well, he's got four legs and ate one of the shrubs, so tell me if you see him again because we'll make a fortune posting the pictures on Twitter. Let me know when you're ready. I'll be in my room."

Martha just looked at him, angry that she had been proved wrong.

Jez got up and went to his den; he had one or two bits and pieces to do. He was feeling restless; he just wanted to be with Sarah.

Sarah was starting to feel more awake by midday; two mugs of coffee had helped. She was thinking about work. She had a busy week ahead and was about to start to make a list of things she needed to do when she remembered she had promised to phone Jez.

It was almost midday by the time Martha had finished getting ready. Jez looked at her as she collected the shopping bags together; she would never pay the charge for carrier bags in the store. It was not an eco-thing; she hated the thought of giving the government more money.

Her over-powdered face and garish red lipstick, which had become her trademark, made her look like a hideous mannequin. Jez always found it embarrassing walking beside her in the supermarket; she seemed to attract a great deal of attention, although she was totally oblivious to the stares.

They had reached the town and were heading towards the supermarket when Jez's ringtone sounded. He thought it might be Sarah and instinctively removed the handset from his jacket pocket to check the caller. Sure enough, it was Sarah. His eyes were off the road for just a second.

"Look out!" shouted his mother.

Jez slammed on the brakes and dropped the phone. It was a zebra crossing, and a line of people were starting to cross. The woman in the middle of the road, holding the hand of a four-year-old, screamed abuse at Jez as he stopped a few inches from them.

He waved apologetically at the couple and could see one or two other pedestrians looking and pointing in his direction.

Martha couldn't resist the dig. "Why don't you look where you're going? You could have killed someone. Too interested in talking to your trollop, never mind other people."

"Shut up, mother!" he shouted.

"Don't you tell me to shut up, you should be concentrating

on the road, not trying to answer your phone."

Jez could feel his heart beating quickly as people continued to cross. The car behind was becoming impatient and started to hoot his horn. Jez looked around and remonstrated with suitable expletives, but the driver would never have heard. Eventually, there was a break in the flow of pedestrians, and he was able to proceed to the supermarket.

The town was busy with shoppers and a few tourists; the coffee shops were doing a brisk trade, and there were queues outside the more popular ones. The store car park was almost full by the time they arrived, and Jez had to drive up and down the rows of cars several times before he found a suitable space.

He had calmed down after his near miss, but his mother continued the tirade. "That'll teach you to keep your eyes on the road instead of chatting to your trollop," was the latest comment.

Jez's phone had dropped into the well of the car and was now somewhere under the driver's seat. His mother had got out but continued the haranguing as he searched for the missing handset. "Hurry up; the café will be full if we're not careful."

"You go on in, mother and get a seat. I won't be a minute."

Martha picked up the empty bags from the back seat and slammed the door shut, causing Jez to jump and hit his head on the steering column. "Shit!" he exclaimed.

He found his phone and switched it on. There was a message from Sarah.

'Did try to call but there was no reply. S x'.

Jez was in a dilemma. He wanted to call her back, but would no doubt face the wrath of his mother.

"Sod it," he said to himself and redialled.

"Hi," said Sarah on the fourth ring.

"Hi, sorry I missed your call; I was driving."

"That's ok; I said I would call. How are you today?"

"I'm fine; keep thinking about last night."

"Yes," said Sarah without expanding.

"I wish I was with you now."

"Ha, you wouldn't if you saw me. I've got my old slops on; no make-up and my hair needs washing."

"Wow, sounds wonderful," said Jez. "Look, can I call you back later? I'm just at the supermarket with my mother, and she will only get agitated if I don't help her with the shopping."

"Yeah, sure, I'm not going out."

'Thanks, I'll call when I get back, about three-ish I expect.'

'It's ok, no problem, I'll be here,' said Sarah and Jez dropped the call, frustrated that he couldn't chat longer.

He went through the main entrance of the supermarket and turned left for the coffee shop. It was heaving with people enjoying a break from the shopping or having some lunch before embarking on the chore.

He saw his mother who beckoned him angrily.

"Where have you been? I can't hold this chair forever; people keep asking me if it's taken."

"It's fine, mother, what do you want to drink?"

"Just a cup of tea and a tea-cake, I didn't have any breakfast, thanks to you."

"How was that my fault?" said Jez.

"Never mind. There's a bit of a queue; I should hurry up if you want to get served."

Jez made his way to the counter with his tray and food; he had chosen a pack of sandwiches.

His mother was right; it took at least fifteen minutes to get the lunch and pay. He looked across to his mother a couple of times, and she appeared to be scowling at him.

It was gone three o'clock before Jez returned to the Hall following the shopping expedition and he was shattered. The late-night activities were starting to tell. He and his mother had hardly spoken apart from the odd snide comment.

"I hope you're not going to kill us on the way home," she said on leaving the supermarket.

Jez carried in the shopping then went to his room and sat by his fish for a few minutes to relax. He took out his phone and called Sarah.

"Hi," he said when she answered.

"Hi, have you finished the shopping?"

"Yes," replied Jez. "I'm glad that's over for another week; it's a nightmare."

"Bad as that?"

"Worse, but there you go. What have you been doing?"

"Housework, washing. Been doing some prep for tomorrow. I'm just watching some TV with a cup of tea."

"Sounds wonderful, wish I was with you," said Jez.

"Yes," said Sarah.

Jez didn't respond; she could hear shouting in the background.

"Is that someone shouting?" said Sarah.

"It's just mother carrying on; it's ok," said Jez.

"Well, I better go anyway. I've just had an email from work, Sir Basil's called a meeting of the senior leaders for eight o'clock tomorrow morning, so it looks like an early night. I'll need to be up for six-thirty."

"That's a pity; I was hoping we could Skype again."

"Better not, maybe later in the week."

"Ok, will you be able to chat later?"

"No, it's ok, I better sort out this email and get myself prepared for tomorrow."

"Oh, ok, tomorrow then?"

"Yes, I'll call you when I get home tomorrow night sometime."

"Ok, that's fine, sleep well, and I hope everything goes ok tomorrow."

"Thanks, you too," said Sarah and she dropped the call.

Sarah went back to the computer and re-read the email. It was going to be a strategy meeting to discuss the latest trading figures. Sir Basil wanted all heads of department to bring ideas for income generation and cost savings for each area of operation.

Sarah took out a pen and pad and started jotting ideas. She was still working on her pitch at nine-thirty, but her concentration levels were now non-existent. She closed her laptop and started getting ready for bed.

Jez couldn't understand how someone could switch off their emotions so quickly. He thought about the previous evening and making love to Sarah. He kept saying to himself; "this time last night, this time last night", and re-running the events in chronological order. He could see her body, smell her perfume and taste the wine on her lips; an intoxicating mix. Somehow, he had to refocus Sarah's mind, away from work. He wasn't sure how yet.

Chapter Seven

It was Monday morning. Sarah had not slept as well as she had hoped, the eight o' clock meeting dominated her thoughts; a lot was riding on it. Expectations and scrutiny would be high. This would be an opportunity to show Sir Basil what she was capable of and prove he had made the right decision appointing her. The more she tried to relax, the more restless she became. Despite her early night, sleep eluded her for lengthy periods; when the six o'clock alarm woke her, it took her several minutes to get her head together.

On the train, she took out her notes and read through them; she was confident that she had fulfilled the brief. She was in her office by seven-thirty and made herself a coffee; it would not be the last of the morning.

The boardroom was on the seventh floor, just along the corridor from the Chairman's office; it too enjoyed panoramic views of the city. There was a large table in the middle with twelve seats. Three water jugs and six drinking glasses were positioned at intervals. There was a long sideboard against the wall opposite the window; on top of it, was a large flask of coffee, along with several cups and saucers. Cressida Bolton, Sir Basil's PA, was flitting in and out, fussing around, checking the projector, making sure everything was ready.

Sarah was the last to arrive, just after ten-to-eight, and her five colleagues were helping themselves to the coffee and a plate of chocolate biscuits. There was not a lot of conversation, merely polite greetings and enquiries about the weekend. Five minutes later, the team were starting to take their places at the table. You could hear a pin drop.

Sir Basil liked to keep his audience waiting and, ensuring

everyone was present; he walked in just after the allotted time. Everyone stood up and waited for him to be seated.

"Good morning," he said, looking around the room at the six senior managers attending. They represented the critical functions of the store; operations, finance, procurement, sales & marketing, HR, and the quaintly-named, 'customer experience' department. Their job-titles were all 'heads of'; there were no internal directors; all the company directors were members of the Huntsman family and would not be attending today's meeting.

"Good morning," the six replied. Sarah was feeling slightly nervous; this was only her second senior-leadership meeting.

"I have been going through January's sales figures, and I wanted to share some of my thoughts," said Sir Basil. "Mr Freeman, would you do the honours?"

Austin Freeman was Head of Finance, and he opened a PowerPoint slideshow from his laptop. Everybody focused on the screen.

"As Sir Basil has said, we have the January sales figures, and it's clear we are facing significant challenges." The slide showed a row of figures. "This is the third year in a row we have seen a fall in like-for-like sales across the post-Christmas period, but this year has seen the biggest drop, almost thirty percent. I haven't got February's figures in yet, but the first two weeks does reflect a similar trend."

There were looks of concern among the gathering. Sir Basil looked on gravely.

"Some of this we can put down to the weather; we had that awful cold spell in week two which depressed sales considerably, but we have to face some difficult truths. The impact of online shopping is starting to have a major effect on our business."

Sir Basil looked at the Head of Operations. "Mr Matthews, have you got a handle on this?"

"Yes, Sir Basil," Ryan Matthews, Head of Operations, responded. "We have seen an increase in our own online shopping activity, but we do need to spend some money on the website. We have seen occasional crashes through sheer volume, and it's looking dated compared to some of our competitors. That's one of my recommendations," he added.

"Ok, thanks, we'll come on to that later," said Sir Basil.

Sarah was busy copying down figures as Austin Freeman continued his tale of doom and gloom. Then, each manager was asked to come up with recommendations and viable solutions. "Our very existence may depend on this," said Sir Basil, dramatically.

It was Sarah's turn; she stood up. She hadn't prepared a PowerPoint presentation as the others had done, and initially, Sir Basil looked disapprovingly.

She spoke more confidently than she was feeling. "As I see it, we need to ask some serious questions about what sort of store we want to be and then ask, is this what our customers want?"

There were some nods around the table; Sir Basil was unmoved. "Go on," he said.

"Well, I did some research on womenswear and menswear stock levels, and it is clear to me that the traditional high mark-up, designer labels are becoming less popular and, of course, there's the competition with online retailers. At the moment, we have to sell a large portion of clothing merchandise at significant discounts to clear the shop-floor for the spring ranges; and that's after the January reductions. I have spoken to the sales staff as they are key to this; they know what customers are demanding. Good quality, reasonably-priced clothes. I am not convinced that all our lines are in keeping with this. In fact, looking across the store more broadly, it seems the only department that's moving merchandise in line with expectations is electrical and computing. Our prices are on a par with specialist retailers, but shoppers need expert advice, which is where we add value."

There were looks of approval from the team.

"Furnishings and cosmetics are fairly flat, although we did have a good run up to Valentine's Day with some of the new perfume ranges. I don't have the precise figures yet, but I'm sure Austin will confirm that."

This was a conversation that many wanted but had never dared to raise. She was marginally exceeding her remit, treading on the toes of 'Sales and Marketing'.

"What are you recommending then, Sarah?" asked Sir Basil.

"Two things. I'm looking at the existing contracts with our suppliers and reviewing any that are coming up for renewal. I'll check with Howard to make sure we're getting the expected level of return; if not, I will cancel further orders. The second thing is looking closely at existing mark-ups; I will again liaise with Howard and make sure that the sale prices match our mark-up policy. My concern is, although we price items correctly, we're not selling them at those prices and end up discounting which makes a nonsense of our mark-up policy."

Sir Basil looked at Howard Taylor, Head of Sales. "Is this correct, Mr Taylor?"

"Hmm, partly; there are certainly some slow-movers that we've had to discount, but they tend to be the exception, not the rule."

"Do you talk to procurement to make sure we are buying the

right lines?" said Sir Basil.

"Of course, I used to have regular meetings with Pete, and I'm sure I will have meetings with Sarah, once she's settled in."

"By the way, how is Mr Draper, do we know?" asked Sir Basil and looked around the room.

Sarah interjected. "I spoke to Tony, his partner yesterday, and he seems to be making good progress, but it's too early to say when he'll be back."

"Thank you, Sarah," said Sir Basil.

"Mr Taylor, you were saying about the meetings with procurement, with Mr Draper. Did you discuss sales strategy or just ask procurement to place an order?" clarified Sir Basil.

"Well, as I have responsibility for sales, I would tell Pete what I wanted, and he would try to get the best price; or, at least, I assume he did."

Sarah was dying to intervene but waited for the exchange to finish.

"I see, well I think you need to talk to Sarah as a matter of urgency and make sure we are all on the same page."

"Yes, Sir Basil." Howard sat down and looked at Sarah, not in a friendly way.

The meeting went on for the rest of the morning with a great deal of discussion on cost-saving strategy. Wendy Phillips, Head of HR was told that there would be a moratorium on recruitment until further notice, and Sir Basil asked her for a full review of the pay structure across the store. He would hold a full staff meeting in the next few days, he said.

At one o'clock, Sir Basil called a halt to the meeting, and Cressida walked in with a trolley laden with sandwiches and six small plastic bottles of orange juice.

Sarah wanted to get back to her office but, as no-one else

had left, she took a couple of sandwiches and moved to the corner of the room to eat them. Everyone was stood up, and Sir Basil circulated the group. He eventually approached Sarah who was drinking her orange juice straight from the plastic bottle. He was carrying a plate of sandwiches.

"So, Sarah, how are you settling in?" he asked.

"Yes, good thanks," Sarah replied.

"I was impressed with your presentation, I must say; it made a lot of sense. Can you do some more digging for me this week and speak to Cressida to set up a meeting with me, say Thursday or Friday. I want to hear your conclusions?"

"Yes, of course," said Sarah, and Sir Basil moved on to engage another manager.

By one forty-five the group were dispersing; Sir Basil had already left, and Sarah was about to leave when Howard confronted her.

"I know you're new to the role, but I just thought I'd mention that we don't try and drop our colleagues in it at these meetings."

"What do you mean?" said Sarah.

"You were implying that there was no proper discussion between sales and procurement," said Howard sharply.

"That's not true; I was just giving my observations, that's all. I had no intention of criticising anyone."

"Hmm, I'm not sure the others saw it that way," said Howard.

"Well, that's too bad, I have enough to do, without trying to appease people's sensitivities. We both know the store's in trouble and if tough things need to be said, then so be it."

Howard was taken aback by this response; the culture at the top was generally one of compliance and servitude; managers tended to tell Sir Basil what he wanted to hear.

"Hmm, you have a lot to learn, Sarah."

"Yes, maybe so, but in the meantime, I want to do all I can to make a difference."

"Hmm, anyway, I've said what I needed to say, I suppose we'd better set up a meeting," said Howard.

"Yes, ok send me an email," she said frostily and walked away and out of the boardroom.

She reached her desk and, after taking a moment to calm down from her altercation with Howard Taylor, checked her emails; there were dozens. There was a knock on the door; Sarah looked up. "Have you got a minute, Sarah?"

It was Geraldine Masters, one of her part-time staff.

"Yes, what is it, Geraldine?"

"I need to give you this," she said, handing Sarah an envelope.

"It's my resignation; I've decided to leave."

"You better close the door and sit down," said Sarah.

Geraldine complied as Sarah opened the letter and read it.

"So, what are you going to do?"

"I've got a job with North Shires Building Society, in their head office. It's handier for me, and it pays better."

"I see," said Sarah.

"When do you start?"

"They will take me at the end of my month's notice," replied Geraldine.

"Ok, thanks for letting me know. I'll get this up to HR."

Geraldine was still sitting in front of Sarah.

"Was there anything else?"

"No," said Geraldine, who was expecting an attempt to make

her stay with the store, or, at least, more enquiry. Her manager seemed disinterested which made her decision to leave after seven years even more acceptable. She got up and left.

Sarah sighed, put the letter on her 'to do' pile and continued going through her emails.

At three o'clock, having been caught up with more supplier enquiries, she picked up her phone to speak to HR.

"Hi, Wendy, it's Sarah, from procurement, have you got a minute I need to discuss an issue with you?"

Sarah left her office and walked down the corridor. The admin centre was stretched across the whole of the sixth floor and, having the customer experience department on the same level, meant that one or two customers were milling about. The HR department was in a separate area accessed by a secure door with a keypad. Sarah used her key-card; there was a click as the door lock was released. Wendy Phillips' office was the first door on the left; it was open.

"Hi Wendy," said Sarah. The Head of HR looked up.

"Come in, Sarah, take a seat... What did you think of the meeting this morning?"

"Interesting," said Sarah. "I think I've upset Howard Taylor, though."

"I wouldn't worry about him; he's a bit of an old woman. I think what you said made a lot of sense."

"Thanks," said Sarah, who appeared to have found an ally.

"What can I do for you?" asked Wendy.

Sarah passed her Geraldine's letter of resignation.

"Oh, that's a pity; she's been here for some time," said Wendy.

"Yes, seven years, I think," said Sarah. "It's going to leave me a bit short in the department; we're starting to get backlogs which I need to avoid in the present climate."

"Yes, I can understand that," said Wendy. "But, as you heard this morning, we're not going to be able to recruit a replacement."

"Yes, I know. I wondered if there was anyone else you could move across, someone bright and flexible, ideally full-time? I'll soon train them up."

"Hmm, I can't increase your headcount, that's for certain, and the other departments are clinging onto experienced staff, they're like gold dust. We're suffering a bit of a turnover problem at the moment," said Wendy. "I'll speak to one or two people and see what I can do."

"Thanks," said Sarah.

"What's the news on Pete, when do you think he'll be back?"

Sarah wasn't sure whether this was a veiled criticism or a genuine enquiry.

"I don't know; Tony said he was recovering slowly, but it won't be in the short term."

"Hmm, it looks like you'll be in the hot seat for a while," said Wendy.

"Could be," said Sarah.

"Well, I hope so; it's about time someone had the balls to shake things up," said Wendy which Sarah recognised was a big compliment.

"Thanks," said Sarah. "Will you let me know if you can find someone?"

"Yeah, sure," said Wendy, and Sarah went back to her office.

Sarah made another cup of coffee; it was almost four o'clock, and she decided to take a breather for a moment before tackling the next headache. She picked up her mobile phone and turned it on. There were five messages from Jez; each more desperate than the last. '*Just let me know you are ok*', said the last.

Sarah hadn't given Jez a moment's thought. She quickly sent back a text. '*Very busy, chat later. S x*'.

Back in Deighton, Jez was furious. She hadn't replied to his messages and seemed to have completely ignored his suggestion of a few days away.

It had been a tough time with his mother. She had moved from being obdurate to being downright aggressive, and Jez was finding it hard to control his anger. It had started with him raising the topic of a couple of days away.

It was just after breakfast; Jez was still suffering from a 'love' hangover after the weekend. He just wanted to be with Sarah. He posed the bombshell.

"I'm thinking of going away for a couple of days," he said as his mother put the crockery in the dishwasher; Mrs Dawson was due at ten o'clock.

"What do you mean going away?"

"As in a holiday. I haven't had a break in ages."

"Oh, I get it, with this trollop of yours, I take it."

"She's not a trollop; stop calling her that."

"They all are. I told you, only after one thing, and it's not sex. You mark my words she'll screw you for every penny she can get and then walk away."

"That's rubbish; you don't know her, she's beautiful, kind and hardworking."

"Oh yes, just because she's opened her legs for you."

"Don't be so crude, mother; that's a terrible thing to say. She's not like that at all. Anyway, I'm going, and you can't stop me."

"And what about me? What do I do while you're cavorting with this trollop?"

"You can do what you like. Mrs Dawson will be around during the day; you won't be on your own."

"What about locking up at night?"

"You can ask Mrs Dawson to do that as she leaves. I mean, you won't be going out, will you?"

"But what about in an emergency?"

"You can call an ambulance or get a taxi. You're just being bloody awkward."

"No, I'm not, and don't swear."

Before the conversation degenerated further, Mrs Dawson's car pulled up at the front of the house.

"I'm going to my office to do some work," said Jez.

His mother just stood there ready to burst with rage.

As soon as he had reached his room, he took out his phone and texted Sarah.

'Hi, looking good for a few days away, I can't wait. What days suit you? Love Jez xx'.

He was hoping for an immediate response, but after fifteen minutes, he switched off his phone and tried to concentrate on some work.

Jez had several projects on the go, including a new website he was developing for a client. He'd sent several versions of the design, and the customer seemed pleased with the way it was progressing. It would only take a couple of hours to finish; then he could send the final version and raise an invoice.

He ran his own limited company and website, Deighton Securities Ltd. He had some regular clients who were happy to pay monthly premiums to ensure immediate service in case of a breakdown. Over recent months he had also picked up several design commissions; business was going well.

He found it hard to find any motivation towards his unfinished web-design, but by midday, he had more-or-less completed the project. He made a call to the client and sent through the finished result, then sent another text to Sarah.

'Hi, hope you are ok, it will be great to hear from you. Love Jez xx'.

Again, the message went unanswered, and Jez was becoming frustrated at the lack of response. After ten minutes he sent another, but still, nothing. He was starting to imagine things; perhaps she was ill, but then he remembered her precious meeting. She had obviously been distracted; he needed to do something about it. But first, he needed to see what he was up against; he had an idea.

It was after four o'clock when he received the 'chat later' text, and there was no mention of the days away. He hoped that Sarah would be more amenable after she had finished work.

Jez was to be disappointed.

At half-past five, Sarah left her office with her work laptop and a load of issues she needed to resolve. Following Geraldine's resignation, she would be an experienced member of staff down with no certainty of a replacement; she would need to consider re-allocating workloads which wouldn't be well-received. She was also thinking about the task that Sir Basil had set her; she would do more investigations tomorrow and made a note on her pad before leaving to speak to Howard Taylor. She hoped he had calmed down after his outburst at lunchtime. So much to do; so much to think about.

She arrived home around six-thirty and made a fuss of the cat; it was another demand, but a welcome one. It gave her some comfort. She didn't feel particularly hungry but made herself an omelette; she had some eggs that needed using before their sell-by date.

She was just opening her laptop to start some work when a message came through on her phone; she had a feeling it would be from Jez.

'Hi, hope your meeting went well, are you ok to chat xx?'.

Sarah exhaled deeply. *'I'll call you later, just a bit tied up at the moment.'*

'Tied up? I like the sound of that; I'll be right over.'

Sarah was not in the mood for boyish humour.

'Chat later,' she replied and turned off her phone.

It was nine-thirty before sheer fatigue, and lack of concentration forced her to shut down her laptop. She went to the kitchen and made a coffee, then checked her phone. There were two messages from Jez, checking on her well-being, and one from her brother. She read it.

'Hi Sis, how are you; not heard from you for a while. Do you want to arrange a Skype call sometime and we can catch up? Amber is dying to see you. Let me know when you can. Love Spence x.'

She started feeling guilty; she and her brother were close, and it had been a couple of weeks since they had a chance to chat. She sent a reply.

'Yes, sorry just taken over a new job at work and it's been manic. Can I call you over the weekend?'

A couple of minutes later there was a 'smiley' emoji reply followed by 'xx'.

Sarah started drinking her coffee and smiled. She had missed Spence and was cross with herself for neglecting her brother.

Then started thinking about someone else she had neglected. This time she made a call.

'Hi, it's me."

"Hi, it's so good to hear from you; I've missed you," said Jez.

"Yes, I'm sorry I've not been in touch; I've just been so busy. How are you?" replied Sarah.

"Fine, fine thanks. I thought you'd been busy when I didn't get a reply to my messages."

"Yeah, sorry about that, not had a minute. I've even had to bring some stuff home."

"Hmm, that's not good."

"No, but I'm sure it will ease off once I get my feet under the table."

"I thought it was only going to be temporary?"

"Well, when I spoke to Tony yesterday, he said that Pete was feeling a bit better, but I got the impression he might ask for early retirement. Tony doesn't think he can stand the stress. I've not said anything to work yet though."

"So, you might be in this role permanently?"

"That's my hope. I want to get as far as I can, which is why I am a bit preoccupied at the moment. I need to make a good impression."

"Yes, that makes sense. What about going away?" said Jez, raising the question he was dying to ask.

"What do you mean?"

"We talked about going away."

"Oh, did we? Hmm, well, I can't at the moment, not until things calm down a bit."

"Oh, ok," said Jez, utterly crestfallen.

Sarah could immediately sense Jez's disappointment.

"Don't worry; I will make it up to you. I just need to get through the next couple of weeks."

It was not what Jez was hoping for. "Yes, of course, I understand, just tell me so I can arrange cover for my mother."

"How is your mother?"

"Oh, you know,"

Sarah didn't know but wasn't going to pursue it further.

"Anyway, I must get my beauty sleep. Chat again tomorrow, yeah?"

"Yes, ok," said Jez, and Sarah rang off.

Tuesday morning and the atmosphere at the store was decidedly downbeat; you could sense it on the shop-floor where the usual buzz seemed to be missing. Word had got out about the trading situation, and there had been a short item on the local TV news the previous evening. It had been reported that sales performance at the Leeds 'flag-ship' department store, Huntsman and Darby, was 'lower than expected' for the post-Christmas period. Ryan Matthews, Head of Operations, was interviewed, following claims that the store was 'in difficulty'. He was, upbeat in his assessment of the present situation; "slightly below expectations, but in line with what other retail outlets had been experiencing, and the bad weather had also contributed", he said. He explained that plans were already in place to overhaul and improve its customer 'offering'.

Sir Basil was expected to do the interview but had asked the Head of Operations to comment on his behalf. The chairman was under a great deal of pressure from the other board members to do something about it; there were concerns that the usual annual dividend was in jeopardy.

Sarah had arrived at her desk at seven-thirty and had not

seen the broadcast. She was clearing some outstanding emails when her assistant, Michelle, knocked on her door. "Can I have a word?"

Sarah turned from her laptop.

"Yes, of course, have a seat."

Michelle sat down. "Did you see the TV last night?"

"No, I was working."

"So, you didn't see Ryan on the news about the falling sales?"

"No, I didn't," said Sarah.

Michelle gave Sarah a brief rundown of the content, but Sarah was concerned that she hadn't been warned about the news item.

"What do you think it means?" asked Michelle.

"Well, there are going to be some changes; I haven't got any details yet, but I will tell you as soon as I have any news."

"Thanks, but what about the department, now Geraldine is leaving? I can't cope on my own."

"No, I appreciate that. I've already discussed the situation with Wendy Phillips, and I'll let you know as soon as I hear anything. Is that all?"

Michelle was not particularly happy but recognised that Sarah seemed busy.

"That's all," said Michelle and she got up and left Sarah to her emails.

The interruption meant Sarah had lost her train of thought; she heard a text 'ping' on her phone which was on the desk. She glanced at it; it was from Jez. She switched off her phone and went back to her emails. She continued down the 'unread' list and noticed one from Cressida, Sir Basil's PA. It was timed at four fifty-five the previous evening. She read the content. It said there would be a press announcement in response to the latest sales position and an interview with Ryan Matthews on the local news.

Sarah berated herself for having missed it. There was more. Sir Basil would be arranging individual discussions with all heads of department, Tuesday morning.

Sarah was in a panic; she had no idea what it was about and had not prepared anything. She had intended to arrange a meeting with Howard from Sales and Marketing later that morning in line with Sir Basil's suggestion. She picked up the internal phone and dialled Howard's number.

"Taylor," was the reply, which not only sounded unfriendly, it was downright aggressive; not his usual greeting.

"Howard? It's Sarah from Procurement," she said. "We need to arrange a meeting. Are you free, later this morning?"

"I don't think it will be necessary."

"Why?"

"I've been asked to take early retirement."

"What?"

"Sir Basil's looking for a scapegoat for the decline in sales, and it's me; no thanks to you."

"What do you mean by that?" said Sarah.

"That little outburst yesterday, sealed my fate I reckon."

"That's not fair," said Sarah. "I wasn't blaming you."

"That's not how Sir Basil sees it, but I don't want to discuss it; it's done." Howard hung up the phone.

Sarah looked at the receiver in astonishment; she couldn't understand why he would blame her for his departure.

A few minutes later, Sarah was interrupted again, this time by Sir Basil's PA.

"Oh, hi Sarah, it's Cressida, Sir Basil's PA, he would like to see you at ten o'clock."

There was no discussion on convenience; it was a summons.

"Right, ok, I'll be there," said Sarah, starting to worry. Maybe she was being moved out too.

It was with some anxiety that Sarah walked up the stairs to the seventh floor. Cressida was on her computer in her cubicle. She looked up. "Oh, hi, Sarah, take a seat, I'll let Sir Basil know you're here."

Sarah sat on one of the two chairs outside the chairman's office while Cressida made the call.

"He won't be a minute," she shouted across to Sarah and went back to whatever she was doing. Sarah could feel her hands getting sweaty and was trying to dry them on her skirt.

The door opened, and Sir Basil beckoned her in. "Come in Sarah, sit down," he said as he made his way around his desk and sat down without further formality. He got straight to the point.

"As you probably know, things have moved on since the meeting yesterday morning. I expect you'll have seen the press release I issued."

"Yes," said Sarah, which wasn't true, but she guessed Sir Basil would not have been pleased if she was not abreast of the wider picture.

"I had a call from the BBC about the trading figures, yesterday afternoon, wanting a reaction; I have no idea who leaked those, but they were pretty accurate. So, it was necessary to issue a defensive response. Did you manage to see Ryan Matthews interview?"

"No, I didn't watch any TV last night."

"Pity, he did a good job."

"Yes, I heard that."

Sir Basil put on a serious expression. "Sarah, I've been discussing the situation with the other directors; there was an emergency board meeting last night, and there are going to be some changes. You might have heard, Mr Taylor is taking early retirement and I'll be bringing in someone with a bit more flair. As you rightly pointed out yesterday, some of our product lines are just too staid, and customers are not buying them."

Sarah wasn't entirely sure how to respond but decided to say what she felt. "Yes, I think that will be a step in the right direction."

"Well, I was impressed with your presentation yesterday; it is that sort of plain-speaking I need in this store; people do not always feel able to speak out; I don't know why. It's not been helpful to forward-thinking."

"Thank you," said Sarah.

"But, that's not why you're here, not directly, anyway; there's another thing. I had a call from Mr Draper this morning, and he's confirmed that he does not intend to return. He wants to take early retirement. So, I would like you to continue as Head of Procurement on a permanent basis with immediate effect."

"Thank you," said Sarah. "That's fantastic, thank you. I don't know what to say," she repeated. She wanted to jump off the chair in celebration.

Sarah decided to raise an issue while the momentum was in her favour. "That does leave me with a problem, Sir Basil. Geraldine Masters handed in her resignation yesterday which, with Pete's departure, means our team is one and a half people short. I know about the moratorium on recruitment, but I can't manage the department with just Michelle and Amanda; it would collapse. Can I have your permission to fill my old position if I'm taking over Pete's? I can manage the department on that. It will give us a significant saving."

Sir Basil looked at her. "Yes, I don't see why not, speak to HR on my authority. Will you need to recruit externally?"

"Not if I can find the right person in store. I'll speak to Wendy."

"There are some good people in sales who may like a change."

"Yes, thank you, Sir Basil, I'll check on that."

"Right, that's all. We will meet again on Friday, yes?"

"Yes," said Sarah and left the Chairman's office with a myriad of thoughts. Jez wasn't one of them.

Chapter Eight

Sarah walked down the stairs to the sixth floor; her mind in a whirl; only now was the enormity of the situation beginning to sink in. Head of Procurement was her dream job. She thought about her parents again, and how proud they would be. She wished they were here to celebrate with her.

She made a detour on the way back to her office to see the Head of HR. She was seated at her desk as Sarah put her head around the door.

"Hi Wendy, have you got a minute?"

"Hi Sarah, yes, of course. I hear congratulations are in order."

"Thanks, yes, I've just had a meeting with Sir Basil."

"It's great news, one up for diversity, eh?"

"Yes, there is that," said Sarah.

"What can I do for you?"

"It's about the issue we talked about yesterday, now that Pete's retirement has been confirmed, I really do need to find a replacement; I can't function on half a team. Sir Basil said I can recruit externally, but I want to avoid that if possible; it will take months. There's a girl on womenswear I was chatting to last week who seemed really switched on."

"I don't know what Howard will say," replied Wendy.

"Well, I hear he's leaving, so he might not be too worried."

"Hmm, I'm not sure he'll be that amenable if I tell him it's for Procurement."

"What do you mean?"

"Let's just say, you are not his favourite person at the moment."

"Why, what's he been saying?"

"I think he blames you for him being pushed out; welcome to office politics."

"But that's ridiculous."

"Yes, I know. Do you know the name of the sales assistant?"

"I think her name is Moira, but I don't know her second name."

"Oh, yes, I know who you mean, Moira Tunny. Yes, she's on the fast-track Graduate scheme. That might give me some leverage. Leave it with me."

"Thanks, Wendy, you're a star."

Sarah grabbed another coffee and returned to her office.

Back in Deighton, Jez was in a different place entirely. He'd been viewing Sarah's Social Media pages again. There was not much on Facebook; Sarah had not posted anything for some time, but there was much more traffic on LinkedIn, the business community website. There were people from all over the country and beyond congratulating her on her position as 'Acting Head of Procurement'; the information was, of course, now out of date. He read the comments and her replies. All very professional, but, nevertheless, invading Jez's domain; she was his. The more he read, the more irritated he became. In the end, he logged off, unable to view anymore.

He returned to his latest project. After a few taps on his keyboard, his main monitor sprang to life with the pages of the Huntsman and Darby intranet site. This was the 'secure' internal web-pages, purely available to Huntsman's staff, with individual log-in access. Parts of the site were restricted to designated people, such as Finance and the HR department, which had details of all the staff files, including names, addresses, salary, last performance reviews and so on.

He searched for Sarah's file and read it with interest; she had done well. Last year's bonus was in the higher band, recognising her contribution. Pete, her line manager, was effusive in his praise; 'someone with potential', he had said. Her new salary following her promotion was also generous.

He checked the 'Directors area'. This had taken him some time to access but had been worth the effort. Finding the sales information was a real bonus. He wasn't an expert in Finance but knew enough to see that the store was in difficulties. Maybe, just maybe, he could push things along a little. He reasoned that if the store was to close, Sarah would be out of a job and would not be so distracted.

He found the confidential January sales figures; then copied and pasted them on to his laptop, complete with the comments from the Chairman to the Head of Finance, which would undoubtedly give the information provenance.

He then attached the files to an email and sent it to the local BBC. It would come from 'a source from within the company', who would prefer to remain anonymous but who was concerned about the potential job losses. It would not be traceable. He hoped the local media would take the matter seriously which would provoke adverse publicity for the store.

Back at the store, Ryan Matthews, Head of Operations was waiting outside Sir Basil's office ready for his audience. Matthews had responsibility for all the operational functions of the business, including the Intranet and the company website. After about ten minutes, he was called in,

"Thank you again for stepping up for the media coverage yesterday; the other directors were impressed."

"Thank you," said Matthews.

"As you are no doubt aware, we had an emergency board meeting last night. It was a long night, as you can imagine."

"Yes," said Matthews.

"The other directors want to know how the sales figures came to be leaked to the press. I have spoken to Mr Freeman, and he's adamant it did not come from his department; in fact, only a handful of people had access to the information."

"What did the BBC say?"

"What do you mean?"

"When they asked you for comment, yesterday."

"They didn't; they just said they had information. They wouldn't say where it had come from."

"Well, it could be someone with a grudge," said Matthews.

"Yes, that's possible, but they would have needed to get the figures from someone, or somewhere."

"Yes, that's true."

"Mr Freeman wondered if we might have been hacked, what do you think? Could someone have got hold of the information by getting into the website?"

"Well, I'm not sure, if I'm honest. It wouldn't be easy."

"Well, you're Head of Operations, how secure are we?"

"Good question. As I said yesterday, the whole IT structure needs an overhaul… the website, intranet, the lot; it's nearly seven-years-old, which is ancient in IT terms. I've asked for a project budget, but I've been turned down, time and time again, as you know."

Sir Basil was feeling uncomfortable, as chair of the finance committee, he was aware of the constraints that had been placed on operations in previous years.

"Yes, quite so," said Sir Basil. "Is there any way you can find out?"

"Not really, hackers usually demand a ransom, but we've had nothing on that score. My guess it's come from within. I can get the security team to look into it."

"Yes, do that, and let me have an update on Friday."

Ryan Matthews was dismissed.

Back in Deighton, Jez was considering his next move. He was grateful that his mother was in her bedroom; she was feeling under the weather, she had said. Jez could hear Mrs Dawson's vacuum cleaner downstairs.

By late morning, he had sent Sarah three texts which had gone unanswered; he wasn't expecting a reply but thought he would try again, just to let her know he was thinking about her. He thought it might give her a boost during her stressful day. Her phone was switched off.

Sarah managed to grab a quick sandwich in the staff canteen. Although it was not deliberately segregated, there was a section by the window which was where managers would normally sit, and so other staff avoided it. As Sarah was queueing to pay for her food, she saw Howard Taylor chatting with other managers; they seemed to be glancing in her direction. She ignored them, paid for the sandwich and returned to her office.

The afternoon continued with more paperwork flooding her desk. She had prioritised everything in order of importance. Top of the pile was the research that Sir Basil had asked her to do. She was studying the pricing guidelines which the store used in negotiations. This ensured there was some consistency in the way the store worked with suppliers. It was based on an arithmetical formula linked to the required return. This was then reflected in the marked-up price in store. The information was competitor sensitive and required an additional password to access; only the Heads of Department and Sir Basil had the necessary authority.

Sarah did some calculations, and it was clear that there were some anomalies. Some lines were not giving anything like the necessary returns; not just on the shop-floor mark-up but in the price paid to the suppliers. It seemed the store was breaching its own pricing policy and was paying more than it should for certain popular items. Sarah was desperate to speak to Pete to find out why, but that was not possible. She would collate as much information as she could and hand it to Sir Basil.

At four o'clock, she received a call from Wendy in HR with some good news. She had managed to arrange a transfer of Moira Tunny to Procurement, starting next Monday. Sarah arranged to see Moira at eight-thirty Wednesday morning to discuss the role. She got up and went to the kitchen for more coffee. While she waited for the kettle to boil, she checked her phone; more texts from Jez. She decided to respond.

'Hi Jez, sorry for not replying to your texts. I'll call you tonight around eight. I have some news for you. S xx'.

Jez heard the alert on his phone and read the message. The news would be about the days away; it had to be. His spirits suddenly lifted.

Sarah left the office around five-thirty and went for her train. As she left the lift on the ground floor, she looked around the cosmetics department in front of her. It seemed deserted; bored sales assistants were chatting or playing with their phones. She was sure they were banned on the shop-floor. Perhaps, with the news that Howard was leaving, discipline was slipping. She would mention it. She headed for the exit and the concierge, dressed in his best morning suit, opened the door and doffed his hat.

"Goodnight Sarah," he said. "Enjoy your evening."

"Thank you, Clarke," said Sarah.

She thought about the man as she walked towards the station. Everybody called him 'Clarke'; she had no idea what his full name was. He'd been with the store for over twenty-five years. She admired his dedication; it summed up everything that was good about Huntsman's.

Sarah arrived home and was greeted by Moses, who followed her as she went upstairs to change from her work attire. She fed him and poured herself a glass of wine; she deserved it.

After dinner, she opened her laptop and logged on. She would work for an hour, then relax in front of the TV.

At nine o'clock, she heard the ping of a text message on her phone.

"Shit," she said to herself, realising she had forgotten to call Jez.

She opened the message; *'Are you ok? I thought you were ringing me x.'*

She keyed in Jez's number, and he answered straight away.

"Hi," said Sarah. "Sorry, I got stuck in some work and lost track of time. How are you?"

"Ok, thanks, missing you, though."

"Yes, sorry, it's manic at the moment, but I do have some great news."

Jez had spent some time earlier searching for possible locations for their trip away. He wanted it to be romantic and had found some beautiful hotels which he was sure she would like. It had given him some much-needed motivation.

"Yes, you said in your text. I'm dying to hear," said Jez, quite upbeat.

"Well, I was called to Sir Basil's office this morning, and guess what? You remember Pete, my boss, well, he's taking early retirement, and I've been promoted on a permanent basis."

There was silence.

"Hello," said Sarah. "Did you hear?"

"Hmm, yes, sorry. That's great news. I'm pleased for you."

"Yes, I've got so many ideas and, I'm working on a big project for Sir Basil. Keep this to yourself, but I've found a problem with our pricing policy, which I think Pete may have been covering up. Come to think of it; I bet that didn't help his heart problems." Sarah was speaking quickly with excitement. "I don't know what Sir Basil will do when he hears about it."

"So, what *is* the problem? If you can say. Don't worry if you can't."

"No, it's ok; it's good to be able to talk to someone."

Sarah explained the pricing policy and how certain orders had been procured without meeting the required margins.

"It's a shambles; it's supposed to be rigidly applied across all our suppliers, but it's not. I found some lines where we're paying way more than we should and not adding the normal mark-up. Then of course, if we need to discount those items in the sale, we're not making any money, or at least, not what we should."

"Hmm, yes I can see that, but why?"

"Online shopping's part of the problem. Some of the suppliers are selling stuff on the internet at the same price, or a little more than they are selling to us. We can't compete with that. It's clothing where the main issues are, Food and furnishings seem to be ok, and electrical, that seems to be doing quite well. I don't know why Pete, or Howard, for that matter didn't flag it up. Howard's in charge of Sales and Marketing. He's leaving soon, too."

"Hmm, quite a shakeup by the sound of it."

"Yes, but it will be for the best. There're lots of things happening which is why I haven't been able to call. Sorry about that."

"So, you won't be able to get away then?"

"What? Oh, no, no, not until I've sorted everything out at work, I'm afraid," Sarah could sense Jez's disappointment and started feeling guilty. "Look, I've got an idea, why don't you come over again on Saturday? We could get a takeaway which will save me cooking. You can stay over if you like."

Suddenly Jez's spirits were lifted. "Yes, ok, great. Hey, I've got a better idea. Let me take you out for a meal to celebrate your promotion. There must be some nice restaurants near you. What do you think?"

"Yes, ok. There's a great Italian in the village; I haven't been for ages, but the food's very good. What about your mother?"

"Don't worry, I'll sort her out; she'll be fine."

After a couple of minutes catching up, Sarah called a halt; she needed to get some sleep.

As he put his mobile phone down on his office desk, Jez had mixed emotions. He was ecstatic at the thought of staying over with Sarah, but on the other hand, it would be another four days before he saw her again. It wouldn't be so bad, but his messages were being ignored and their conversations in the evening were becoming shorter and shorter. He'd not dared to mention a Skype call; that would be a waste of time.

He thumped his fist down on the desk; his keyboard jumped up, and his computer mouse fell onto the floor; he caught his phone just as that was about to go the same way. He could feel the frustration; it was like cancer eating away at his brain. Sarah's work at the store was taking over her thoughts, and he was being pushed to one side; he couldn't allow that, he just couldn't.

He went over to his aquarium and watched the fish; it calmed him and helped him think. He pondered Sarah's 'problem' with the procurement issue.

He could hear the television blaring out from his mother's bedroom; the Saturday overnight was going to be another problem he would need to resolve.

Despite her early night, Sarah had had difficulty sleeping again, mostly trying to wrestle with work issues. There was a client meeting due which was not going to be straightforward; she was working on a strategy.

She had also been thinking about Jez. She was aware that she was not giving him the attention he deserved. She thought for a moment that he might return to the dating site and try his luck elsewhere; she couldn't blame him. She'd felt cornered into suggesting he called again on Saturday, but, with no chance of her getting away anytime soon, she hoped the offer of an overnight stay would make things right.

She was back at her desk by seven-thirty the next day.

Jez was also up early, thinking of ways he could redirect Sarah's attention to him. He would be back on Huntsman's Intranet site later. In the meantime, there was a more pressing issue, his mother. He was finishing his breakfast when he heard steps coming down the stairs. She appeared in the doorway looking worse for wear; her hair was wild and uncombed. With no make-up, the lines on her face were more noticeable, and she looked pale and drawn. Her dressing gown seemed to hang on her frame.

"Where's my tea?" she said, shuffling into the kitchen.

"I didn't know whether you were getting up or not today," replied Jez,

"I need to; it's my hairdresser's appointment today. Will you take me?"

"I'm a bit busy, what time?"

"You're always too busy these days. It's that trollop; she's filling your head. No time for anyone else."

"That's nonsense," replied Jez. "I have clients."

"Hmm, well, my appointment is at eleven, but if you're too busy to take me, then I suppose I'll have to get a taxi."

"No, no, it's fine, I don't have anything urgent," said Jez. He needed to raise Saturday's overnight stay; maybe this would smooth the way a bit.

"Are you sure? Only I'd hate to put you out or anything," she said sarcastically.

"I said, it's fine," retorted Jez, sharply. "Do you want some tea?"

"If it's not too much trouble," said Martha.

Jez filled the kettle while his mother sat at the table and picked up the newspaper that Jez had been reading.

He made the tea and took a mug to the table; he placed it in front of his mother who was digesting the inside pages. There was no acknowledgement.

"Just so you know, I'm seeing Sarah on Saturday. She's invited me to stay over."

This had Martha's attention; she looked up with her face twisted with anger. "Oh. My. God. You've really got your feet under the table now, haven't you? So, what am I supposed to do while you're out all night fucking your trollop?"

Jez was taken aback. He had not heard his mother use the 'f' word since the altercations with his father when the arguments had degenerated into personal abuse.

"I'll ignore that remark," said Jez. "You'll be alright. Don't worry; I'll be back in time for the supermarket on Sunday."

There was an uneasy silence. Martha was deep in thought; she couldn't find the right words. She stood up, took her tea and left the kitchen. "We'll need to leave at half-ten," she said and went back upstairs.

Jez knew he hadn't heard the last of it.

Sarah checked her diary; the client meeting she had been concerned about was a lunch appointment with a Bruno Čapek. She had not met him before; he was one of Pete's important clients, and he'd always dealt with him. His company, ZTP Textiles, supplied many of the upmarket garments stocked by the store. It was one of the companies she had identified as over-priced.

She was working through her emails when there was a knock on her door. She looked up; it was Moira. Sarah checked her watch.

"Oh, sorry, Moira," said Sarah. "I lost track of time. Come in; take a seat. Let me just send this email."

Sarah went back to her screen and completed her message. She pressed 'send' and exited the screen.

"Sorry about that, it's all been a bit hectic at the moment, as you can imagine," said Sarah.

Moira had her full attention; her dark hair was perfectly groomed, and she wore a smart business suit; she had clearly made an effort to impress her new boss. "Congratulations, by the way, on your appointment," she said.

"Thank you," said Sarah. The favourable impression was enhanced.

The discussion lasted about twenty minutes; Sarah explained the role she wanted Moira to fulfil and did most of the talking. "You can work alongside Michelle for the first couple of days, you'll soon get the hang of it," said Sarah before dismissing her new team member. "See you on Monday," was her parting comment. Sarah returned to preparing for her lunchtime appointment.

In Deighton, Jez was back on his computer thinking of ways to encourage Sarah to be more attentive. Access to Huntsman's Intranet may give him some ideas.

Just before ten-thirty, his mother knocked on his door. "Are you ready to go, Jeremy?" she said in a contrite way. Jez was on his guard.

"Just finishing something."

"Don't be long; I don't want to be late."

A couple of minutes later, Jez left his room and was putting on his jacket as he went down the stairs. His mother was waiting at the front door.

The journey to the hairdressers in Skipton was made in silence. Jez was thinking about Sarah; Martha was wondering how she could distract her son from his obsession. The constant abuse was having no effect and created considerable stress. She would have to try another tactic.

There was a loading bay in front of a small parade of shops which housed the hairdressers; Jez pulled in just before eleven.

"Would you be able to pick me up about two, dear? It will

save me getting a taxi."

Martha looked at Jez in a way that was difficult for him to decline the request.

"Yes, ok, mother, I'll see you about two o'clock," said Jez and drove away into the traffic.

Sarah spent the morning looking through Pete's files getting more background on ZTP Textiles; past orders, prices, delivery times, and so on. According to the notes, the company was based in the Czech Republic and, over the last five years, they had averaged well over two hundred and fifty thousand pounds worth of stock a year. Deliveries were always on time, and quality levels were excellent; there were very few returns. Their prices, however, had risen quite sharply according to her calculations. Pete had justified the increases on the grounds of exchange rates, and a growth in labour costs. They charged significantly more than the store's pricing formula allowed.

She would need to speak to Sales to check the stock turnover, but she had thought from her own observations that the garments sold well; very few lines were discounted in the six-monthly sales. Unfortunately, with Howard Taylor now on 'gardening leave', there would be no-one in charge for her to discuss the contract; she was on her own.

At twenty-past twelve, Sarah received a call to say her clients had arrived. 'Clients?' She was expecting only one. She had decided to conduct the meeting in her office and then go to the canteen for lunch; she had reserved a table in an area sectioned off for entertaining. She quickly positioned another chair in front of her desk.

She took the lift to the ground floor and could see two gentlemen were waiting; they appeared to be watching the sales staff. Both were carrying briefcases

The elder one turned and saw Sarah approaching. "Miss Gooding?"

"Yes, you must be…"

"Bruno Čapek, Managing Director, ZTP Textiles, pleased to meet you. This is my colleague, Petr Hlavka, Head of Sales."

The other man shook hands with Sarah.

She did a quick assessment. Both were immaculately dressed in expensive lounge suits, white shirts, ties and black shoes. The Managing Director was shorter than his colleague and a few years older, but probably not much over forty. Facially, distinctively Slavic in appearance, the younger man sported a fashionable well-trimmed beard.

"My office is on the sixth floor if you would like to follow me," said Sarah and led them to the lift.

As the doors closed, there was that uneasy silence that you get in elevators; all three stared at the illuminated display as it counted floors. Sarah was stood behind them and noticed the edge of a tattoo on the back of the sales manager's neck.

"This way," Sarah said as the doors opened, and she led them along the corridor to her office.

"Would you like something to drink?" asked Sarah.

The men looked at each other.

"Tea, please," said Bruno.

"Coffee," said Petr.

As they passed the admin office, Sarah ordered the drinks and led the men into her office.

"Please take a seat," said Sarah.

"Thank you," said Bruno, and the pair made themselves comfortable. "We were sorry to hear about Mr Peter. We have done business with him for many years, but we look forward to doing business with you."

"Yes, thank you, it's been an interesting time," euphemised Sarah. "How was your journey?"

"Fine, thank you, we arrived yesterday afternoon, in Manchester," said Bruno.

His English, like his appearance, was excellent, with just a hint of an Eastern European accent.

"So, are you staying in Manchester?" said Sarah

"No, we are in Leeds tonight, at the Corillium."

"Ah, yes, the new one. I've not been, but I've heard it's nice," said Sarah, just as the drinks were delivered.

"Yes, it's very comfortable."

The sales manager still hadn't said anything, but Sarah could feel his eyes assessing her and not in a comfortable way.

Drinks dispensed, Sarah brought the meeting to order.

"As I understand from your email to my predecessor, this is simply a pricing review?"

"Yes, but we also have details of some exciting new lines which Petr will show you."

"Ok, that's fine, I'll need to involve Sales and Marketing, but, unfortunately, we've also lost our Head of Sales, Howard Taylor. Did you ever meet him?"

Bruno looked at his associate. "Yes, we have met him," he said.

The ZTP team appeared slightly wary, trying to get the measure of the new Head of Procurement. In previous years these meetings had been almost a 'tick-box' exercise, with little or no actual negotiation.

Bruno reached down and lifted his briefcase onto his lap

and opened it. He produced a file with the name 'Huntsman's' written on it in felt-tip pen. He produced a schedule of garments and prices and handed it to Sarah.

"We have done much research, and these are the prices we will need to charge for this year's items. They are the best prices."

Sarah was scanning the clothing on the list. She was well-prepared and had her own list of prices, including a note of last year's costs and what she would need for this.

"But these are much higher than last year," observed Sarah.

"There are some small increases, we have new machinery and more people to pay, but overall it is still a very good price for such quality."

"Hmm," said Sarah, doing some mental arithmetic. "I'm sorry, but there is no way we can pay these prices in the present economic conditions. If we add our normal mark-up, no-one will buy them."

The M.D. looked at his associate gravely. "That is a great shame; we have many exciting lines which will go very quickly. We have customers in London, in Oxford Street, and they sell, how you say? Like the hot cakes, yes?"

"But we are not in London, and we can't sell at London prices," countered Sarah.

"So, what is your proposal?"

Sarah gave them her figures. The two men went down the list. "But, the prices are less than last year," said Bruno.

"Yes, because you overcharged us last year."

"Mr Peter was happy. He always respected our clothing. You still make good profit, I think."

"Not when you add in the administration costs. We are

just about breaking even by my estimates."

"Then you charge too little," said Bruno.

"We charge what the market can stand; clothing is very competitive, as you're no doubt aware," retorted Sarah.

Just when Sarah thought the negotiations were going to become adversarial. Bruno looked at his figures again. "Let me speak with Petr, please excuse us if we speak in Czech."

"Of course," said Sarah.

The pair spoke animatedly for several minutes. Sarah was trying to follow the conversation by watching body language and tone of voice, but she was not able to gain any comprehension.

"Sorry about that," said Bruno. "I want to ask a question. Would it help if we… erm… included an incentive? Would that help the situation?"

Sarah was stopped in her tracks. "What do you mean?"

"The arrangement we had with Mr Peter, we could continue with you," said Bruno, hesitantly, as if testing the water.

"You mean a backhander?"

"I do not know this word, 'backhander'. It is commission, that is all. We pay to you instead of Petr here. It is ok; he has good pay; he will not mind."

Petr was smiling. "It is good, yes?"

"You paid commission to Mr Peter?" asked Sarah, deliberately using the same phraseology, just for clarification.

"Yes, good commission, very good commission. We do good business, yes?" said Bruno.

Sarah was deep in thought still trying to take in the ramifications. Bruno could see Sarah was concerned.

"Look, do not say anything now. Please check the figures

again. I think when you have had a chance to check them in more detail, I am sure they will be ok for you." Bruno looked at Sarah, not menacingly but in a way that made her feel uncomfortable.

"I have an idea. You must join us for dinner tonight, I insist. Mr Peter always came with us for dinner. It will be nice, we will have, how you say? A good relationship, yes?"

This threw Sarah completely; it was something she had not envisaged.

"It will be good to discuss things somewhere more comfortable."

Sarah thought for a moment. Sir Basil was always talking about getting close to clients and customers. "It's the way we should be doing business," he would say. Sarah was keen to make a good impression; this was, after all, her first client negotiation. She looked at the men. They both smiled at her.

"Yes, ok, what time?"

Chapter Nine

Jez returned to Deighton around eleven-thirty; he couldn't settle into his work. He was already getting messages from clients asking when their websites would be finished, or laptops repaired.

He texted Sarah again, just to let her know he was thinking about her and hoped her day was going well. She was entertaining Czech businessmen and would not be able to return the message.

Back at Huntsman's, after some deliberation, Sarah had arranged to meet Bruno and Petr for dinner at eight o'clock at the hotel. They had agreed to shelve any further discussions on orders and pricing to give Sarah more time to consider their proposals so, at one-thirty, Sarah took the men to the canteen for lunch. Over sandwiches, provided by the store, Bruno gave more details about their business.

There was no doubt it was a substantial enterprise, with clients across Europe, especially Germany which made up sixty percent of the turnover. Most of their UK customers were in London, but they also had business with a major store in Manchester where they were due to return tomorrow, before flying back to Prague.

As the discussions continued, Sarah was beginning to feel more comfortable and confident with the clients. She found the men charming and courteous and had no concerns about her dinner invitation later. Nevertheless, she wished she were not on her own, just for moral support.

By two-thirty she was escorting the men back to the ground floor. They shook hands outside the lift.

"Thank you for your hospitality," said Bruno. "We will see you at the hotel tonight at eight o'clock."

"My pleasure," said Sarah. "Yes, I'm looking forward to it, and I'll spend some time going through your prices this afternoon so that we can discuss them again tonight."

As she rode the lift back to the sixth floor, Sarah was recounting the morning's events. She was incredulous at the suggestion that Pete would take any sort of bribe however it was dressed up, but she had no reason to doubt her visitors' account. She had no idea what to do with the information; she needed to speak to someone.

It took another half-an-hour to clear up the waiting emails and answer some queries from her assistant.

"While I've got you," said Michelle. "Is there any news about your old job?"

Sarah had delayed addressing the question of her successor as Senior Buyer. Michelle was the obvious choice as the most experienced of the team, but Sarah had decided to take her time before making an announcement.

"I need to discuss it with Sir Basil, but I hope to be able to say something on Monday."

Michelle seemed satisfied with this response and went back to her workstation.

The topic of Pete's backhanders was hindering Sarah's concentration. Part of her wanted to forget about it; she had enough on her plate without being involved with any subsequent investigation which was bound to ensue. She needed a second opinion. She picked up the phone and dialled an internal number.

"Ryan? It's Sarah. Have you got a minute? I could do with

your advice. Great, I'll see you in the canteen in five minutes."

Sarah logged off her computer and walked to the canteen.

She was queuing to pay for her drink when the Head of Operations walked in.

"What would you like," said Sarah. "My shout."

They took their drinks and walked over to the 'management' section which was empty.

"So, how can I help?" asked Ryan, as he released two chocolate digestives from their cellophane packaging. He took one and passed the other to Sarah.

"Thanks, I could do with a sugar hit," she said, taking a bite. She swilled the first mouthful down with a sip of coffee and cleared her throat. "I had a meeting with two suppliers this morning from the Czech Republic. It was just a routine pricing meeting, but the prices they were quoting were way outside our policy guidelines. When I explained that they were not acceptable... sorry, this is difficult."

"Go on," encouraged Ryan.

"Well, to put it bluntly, they offered me an 'incentive'." She made inverted comma signs with her fingers.

"You mean, a bribe?"

"Basically, yes, but that's not the worrying part. They said they had been paying Pete 'commission', that's what they called it; for some time."

Ryan thought about this information. Sarah looked at him, tall, smart and good-looking and only a couple of years older than her. She had always been attracted to him, but he had a wife and two young children, so she had never been tempted to take their professional relationship any further.

"I don't think you have a great deal of options, you must report it," said Ryan.

"Yes, you're right. It's just with Pete's heart condition and everything, maybe it should be just left alone; you know, water under the bridge."

"Hmm, I take your point."

"The other thing is, it will be difficult to prove, I mean, if Pete denies it; which I'm sure he will, and I can't see the Czechs admitting anything untoward."

"Fair point. What are you going to do?"

"Well, I was hoping you could give me some guidance; compliance does come under your remit."

Ryan was now in a tricky situation; Sarah had ostensibly passed the hot potato to him.

"What we don't know, of course, is how many more there are out there; this could be just the tip of the iceberg, for all we know, and it's no use looking at the contracts; everything will be off-book. But it could explain why so many of the contracts are outside the store's pricing policy," she added.

"I'll have a word with Adam Fowler. Have you met him?" said Ryan. Adam Fowler was the senior compliance officer.

"No, I don't think so," replied Sarah.

"He's fairly new, only joined us in December. Very bright and certainly knows his stuff."

"Yes, ok, great, ask him to call me and set up a meeting."

The discussion concluded, and Sarah felt relieved that she had shared her problem; the feeling of isolation had been lifted.

Before returning to her office, she decided to call in at the Womenswear department; she needed to buy a new outfit for the business dinner.

With the pending meeting, Sarah needed to leave early to

get ready. She walked through to her team and gave Michelle an update and some work. She explained about the dinner meeting but said nothing about the alleged bribery investigation.

As she travelled home on the four-thirty train, Sarah suddenly remembered her phone; she had not checked her messages. As expected, there were several from Jez; she was starting to find them irritating. There was an air of desperation about them which seemed to be adding to her stress levels.

She texted back. *'Hi, sorry I've not replied to your messages but been very busy. I'm going out tonight to meet some clients, so I won't be able to chat. S x.'*

There was an immediate response.

'Out? Where to?'

'Just Leeds.'

'Where?'

'The Corillium.'

'The new one?'

'Yes.'

'Oh ok, have a good evening. Hope we can chat tomorrow. Looking forward to Saturday, can't wait to see you again.'

'Yes, ok. Chat tomorrow.'

The impact on Jez was devastating; he was filled with fury. He was in his office and could feel it building; he wanted to hit out at something. He went to his fish, but his only thought was to lift up the aquarium and throw it somewhere. He went to his bedroom and lay on the bed trying to calm down, but it was difficult. How could she?

He was convinced it was an excuse; the same one he had used with his mother; client meeting? No way. He had no idea what he was going to do, but there was only one way to find out. He would go to Leeds and wait for her.

He went downstairs; his mother was in the kitchen, looking better for her trip to the hairdressers. She had also benefitted from chatting to other people. The pampering was just what she needed. Jez, rather reluctantly, had picked her up from the salon at two o'clock but declined the request to take her to the supermarket for a cup of tea.

"I'm going out later," said Jez as he walked into the room.

"Out? Where are you going?"

"Leeds."

"Leeds? Oh, I see, out with your trollop again. Is that it?"

"No, not this time, I'm meeting a client. And it's Sarah, mother. Please show some respect."

"What time will you be back?"

"I don't know, depends on how long the meeting takes."

Martha looked far from happy.

"Don't worry, I'll lock up before I leave," said Jez.

Martha's mood quickly changed. "I'm going to my room," she said and went upstairs. Jez could hear the TV blasting out.

With everything going on, Jez's clients were going to be further delayed in delivery. There would be some unhappy customers.

Sarah arrived home and hung her new clothes up to get rid of any creases, then spent a few minutes playing with the cat; Moses had also suffered from lack of attention.

As she showered and got ready, she thought about the meeting. She was not going to give way on pricing and certainly was not interested in any 'incentives'.

In negotiations, she remembered, there was always a need to have a back-up plan in case there was no agreement. Her only back-up plan would be to look for new suppliers which was not going to be easy and also had its own risk. Choosing a new range of stock from another provider would be a big gamble. They could, in fact, lose more money if the lines did not sell. It all added to the tension she was starting to feel.

She caught the train back into Leeds at seven-fifteen to be in good time for the meeting. She spent most of the journey catching up with the news on her phone. A couple of times she checked her messages. There were no more from Jez which was surprising, but she didn't feel like initiating any conversation with him. She would text him tomorrow.

The Corillium was less than ten minutes' walk from the station. It was one of the many new hotels that were starting to emerge in the city centre, reflecting the growth in the local economy. As a four-star hotel, it was one of the best in town, and Sarah was looking forward to seeing the inside.

The hotel frontage was predominantly glass, giving it an 'airy' feel, and there was a good view of the inside. Sarah could see it was busy with queues at the reception desks. The front entrance comprised of swing-doors and, adjacent, automatic access for those with luggage or wheelchairs. There were two employees on hand in corporate livery to help with baggage; a large gold-chrome luggage trolley was parked to one side.

One of the employees acknowledged her. "Good evening ma'am," he said and touched his hat.

Sarah looked at him. "Hello," she replied and went through the swing doors.

It was ten-to-eight. There was a large meeting area, slightly raised in the atrium with several armchairs and sofas all in a matching dark pink colour; coordinating well with the rest of the décor. It was quite busy, and a waitress was moving about checking for refreshment orders. Sarah took it all in; she was interested in corporate presentation, and her first impressions were very favourable.

There were three lifts on the far side; she watched the comings and goings as guests were ferried to their rooms. At two minutes to eight, the middle elevator opened, and her two hosts walked out. Dressed smart but casually, they looked quite different from this morning. Sarah was pleased she had made an effort, her new skirt and top were certainly in keeping with the hotel clientele.

Bruno saw her straight away and walked up to her; he was carrying the same leather briefcase from this morning's meeting.

"Sarah, you look beautiful, if I may say. And wearing one of our lines if I am not mistaken?"

"Hello, Bruno, Petr. Yes, thank you."

She shook hands with the pair. Petr acknowledged the greeting.

"Lovely hotel," she said as the men accompanied her to the lift.

"Yes, we like it. Please, come; the table will be ready. We are in the 'Starlight' restaurant on the seventh floor. It is better than the one on the ground floor or at the bar," explained Bruno.

The elevator reached the top floor and opened; the smell of food permeated the air. They turned left to the restaurant entrance. The maître d' was stood in the doorway; he greeted them warmly, checked his reservation list, then escorted them to their table. It was next to the window, and there were extensive views across the city. The lights shone brightly, and Sarah could see the top of the store in the distance.

"This is nice," said Sarah.

"Yes, we have stayed here once before, the last time we met

Mr Peter," said Bruno. "Would you like a drink, some wine perhaps?"

Petr was examining the menu with interest.

"Yes, please," replied Sarah and Bruno handed her the wine menu.

The wine-waiter took the order and, after a few minutes, the food too. Sarah was feeling tense, but confident and in control. She looked around the restaurant; it was less than half-full, and there was a low buzz of conversation. Some unidentifiable music was audible in the background.

Bruno leaned back slightly in his seat. Petr was next to him, and Sarah felt she was about to undergo an interrogation.

"So, since our meeting this morning, have you had chance to consider our prices for this year?"

She made eye-contact with Bruno; her body language, assertive.

"Yes, I have. I'm sorry, but we just can't accept your new prices. I did some calculations, and the average increase is around ten percent and on some of the lines, even higher."

Bruno looked at Petr. "Excuse us, please," and the pair started talking in Czech.

She watched them; the body language was different from the morning's exchange, less confrontational. There seemed to be a touch of humour as the hint of a smile appeared on Petr's face.

The conversation was interrupted by the wine-waiter who presented Bruno with a bottle of red. Bruno examined the label. "Yes, it is fine, please just pour."

The waiter half-filled Sarah's glass and followed with Petr's and Bruno's.

Sarah took a sip.

"I hope you like it," said Bruno

"Yes, thank you, it's fine," said Sarah.

"Excuse, again please," said Bruno and he and Petr continued their discussion for a few more minutes.

"Pardon, our rudeness, but it is easier for us to speak in our language."

"Of, course; no problem," said Sarah.

"You are new in your job, yes?"

"Yes, but I've been in Procurement for over five years," she said, slightly defensively.

"Excellent, excellent, you will learn perhaps the ways of business. It is not just percentages and prices. It is the way we do business. You will find cheaper suppliers; you can do that, of course. If I take my phone out now, I will find you six or seven companies, and then I will tell you why they are cheaper. Many, they do not have good quality fabrics; many don't have the expert workers, but all of them will not pay the workers. Have you heard of the 'Partnership for Sustainable Textiles'?"

Sarah looked blank. "No, I don't think so," she said.

"It is from Germany, it says how we should treat our workers, how much we pay. We have signed up for this, which is why we have to charge more. It means you can say your clothes are from very good people."

Sarah was deep in thought. This brought a new perspective to the negotiations, and she could see straight away the possible marketing possibilities around ethical sourcing.

Bruno watched as she digested the information,

"Petr and I have discussed the prices you gave us this morning, but we cannot afford them, they are too low, we make no money. But, we do wish to keep our business with Huntsman's; you are important customers. So, we have a new proposal; no increases for one year, and we will discuss again then. That is our best offer."

"So, let me just get this straight, you are offering to continue the existing contract prices for a further year?"

"Yes, and, with inflation, that means it is less, yes?"

Sarah wanted to give the impression that she was thinking about it, but, realistically, this was her only fall-back position. The other alternative was to walk away, and she had already decided that would be a last resort.

She picked up her glass and took a sip.

"Hmm, I think we may be able to agree on that; yes, ok; present contract and prices extended for a further year with a review at that time."

"Ok, that is good, then we shake hands, yes?"

Sarah offered her hand, and the deal was done.

"I will send you an email to confirm in the morning, and let marketing know for their pricing and promotions," said Sarah.

"That is good, now we can enjoy our food, yes?" said Bruno. He put his hand in his pocket and produced a gift-wrapped box.

"This is for you, to say thank you for your understanding."

"What is it?" said Sarah.

"Why don't you open it. It is a gift, that is all."

Sarah undid the bow and took off the paper, then opened the gift box.

"Oh, that's beautiful," said Sarah. "But I can't accept it."

"But you must, it is our custom. It is, how you say? To seal the deal. Yes?"

Sarah was deep in thought.

"It is just a small token; it is not expensive. Please, you will do us the honour."

They were interrupted by the waiter bringing the first

courses.

Sarah looked again at the bracelet. It certainly seemed more than a trinket, and the designer name on the box confirmed it.

"Please try it on," said Bruno, and Sarah wrapped the jewellery around her wrist and examined it, rolling her wrists to get a better angle as the light reflected in the gemstones.

"It suits you," said Bruno. He was right.

"Well, what can I say?" said Sarah. "Thank you, very much; I am very grateful."

"No, thank you for your courtesy and understanding," said Bruno. "It has been a pleasure doing business with you."

It was just after ten o'clock when the group finally finished the meal and coffees.

"Would you like a liquor?" asked Bruno.

Sarah checked her watch.

"No, I have a train at ten-thirty, I need to go in a minute."

"You are walking to the station?"

"Yes, it's not far."

"Yes, I know, but you cannot walk on your own at this time of night. Petr will walk with you, see you are safe."

"No, you don't have to, it's fine."

"I insist," said Bruno. "It will be no problem."

The two men got up.

"Ok, if you insist," said Sarah. "Thank you."

The waiter saw the three prepare to leave and brought Sarah's jacket. Bruno took it and helped her put it on, then escorted her to the lift.

They reached the ground floor, and Sarah shook hands with Bruno, then Petr led her to the exit.

Earlier, Jez was still trying to come to terms with Sarah's

apparent betrayal. Part of him wanted to hit out; part of him wanted to curl up in a ball and cry. His concentration levels were nil. With Martha also in an obstreperous mood, there had been no dinner. Jez had not considered making anything; he was not hungry. He was trying to work out the timings of his journey to Leeds; he had forgotten to ask what time Sarah would be going out. He estimated it would be between seven-thirty and eight o'clock.

He checked the time; six-forty. With the traffic, it would take at least forty-five minutes to get to Leeds; then he would have to find somewhere to park.

He picked up his keys and jacket, then went upstairs. He knocked on his mother's door, then pushed it open. Martha was asleep. Jez switched off the TV.

"Mother; wake up. I'm going now."

"Eh… what?" said Martha, groggily.

"I said, I'm off now. I'll be back later."

"Oh, ok dear, what time? Do you know?"

"No, it depends on how long the meeting lasts," replied Jez. "I'll lock the bottom gate."

Jez left his mother to recover and left the house.

It took over an hour to reach the hotel; traffic had been dreadful getting into Leeds. It was not an area of the city he knew that well and, without satellite navigation, he was using some notes he had made from the internet giving him directions. The hotel car park was down a side street. There were double yellow lines on both sides, so he would need to use the hotel's facility. He drove up to the barrier, and the ticket machine flashed. He pulled out the ticket, then suddenly noticed the price. "How much!?" he said out loud to the ticket machine, but it remained inanimate and made no reply; ten pounds for three or four hours, daylight robbery.

As he found a parking bay, he suddenly had an awful thought. What if she was staying the night with this 'client'? He couldn't handle that; he tried desperately to remove that idea from his mind, but it was still there, taunting him. He locked his car and followed the signs to the reception. His original plan was to park up and observe the hotel from a distance, but with parking restrictions in the city centre, that would be impossible.

He was in a quandary. He had no idea whereabouts in the hotel she was or even if she had arrived. He had assumed she was there, as it was now gone quarter-past eight. He came out of the car park entrance into a corridor leading to the reception foyer. He stopped at the end of the corridor and peered into the lobby trying to be as inconspicuous as possible. He surreptitiously scanned the reception area. He couldn't afford to be seen; that would cause all kinds of problems. He could see the lifts and a bar from which he would have a vantage point. Keeping to the edge of the area, he skirted around until he had reached the bar. Of course, she could be in there, having a drink before they went elsewhere; to his room, perhaps. The thought made him shake.

A waiter gave him a strange look. "Can I help you, sir?"

The dialogue shook him for a moment.

"Oh, er, yes. Half a lager, please."

"Certainly, if you would like to take a seat, I'll bring it over to you."

Jez continued looking at the clientele. It wasn't packed by any means, but there were still many people about.

Satisfied she wasn't in the bar, he found a seat from where he could view the lifts. A few minutes later, the waiter appeared with his drink and handed him the tab. "How much!?" Jez gave the man a five-pound note.

"Keep the change," said Jez, although the fifty pence would not go very far.

Now he would wait.

It was a boring evening. He managed to make his lager last, despite several visits from the ever-attentive waiter who continued to eye Jez up with some suspicion. Jez spent most of the evening just staring at the lifts. He checked his watch, not for the first time, and started wondering how long he should keep the vigil. He was thinking of leaving when he suddenly saw Sarah exiting the lift. Several people were queuing for the elevator and, in the melee, he didn't notice Bruno, just Petr shepherding her towards the swing-doors.

Instinctively, he left his seat, walked quickly through the lobby and out of the hotel. He looked right, then left, and spotted them about a hundred yards away. They weren't holding hands or anything, Jez noticed; maybe he was married, and they were being discreet. They turned the corner to the right and Jez ran to the bottom of the road; he didn't want to lose sight of them. He watched as they crossed over the main road which was busy with buses and taxis at this time of night. They made another turn towards the station. He kept them in sight as they walked towards the station entrance, but as they reached the doorway, they shook hands. The man turned and walked towards Jez.

Jez turned and headed back to the hotel, deep in thought.

Ten minutes later he was winding through the late evening traffic on the road to Skipton.

Back on the train, Sarah was feeling pleased with the way the meeting had gone. The carriage was almost empty as she looked out of the window at the lights of the city. After a few minutes, seeing no one was around, she took the bracelet from her handbag and examined it more closely; it was beautiful. Any misgivings she had had in accepting it were quickly put to one side. It was customary, they had said, and she was not about to break with tradition.

She put the gift back in its box and returned it to her handbag, then took out her phone and checked her messages. There was one from her brother, just a catch-up, but, surprisingly, none from Jez.

She felt a sense of relief; she was beginning to find his constant messaging irksome. His behaviour was becoming almost obsessive, but she felt a pang of guilt and decided she would text him; she was after all 'seeing him'.

'Hope you're ok, just on my way home. I'll tell you all tomorrow S xx', she texted.

Jez had left Leeds and was in the countryside. There were no street lights and his headlights reflected in the cats-eyes of the single carriageway shining like a beacon keeping him on the correct side of the road. He felt a vibration in his pocket as a text message came through to his phone; it must be from Sarah.

His emotions were still all over the place; confusion replaced anger. He was running through everything he had seen in his mind. The walk from the hotel to the station did not seem to be the conduct of two lovers. There was no hand-holding or any other sign of affection. Maybe she was telling the truth; perhaps it was a business meeting after all. Part of him wanted to believe that; the thought of Sarah being with another man kept playing in his head, eating at his brain.

He needed to check the text.

His phone was in the pocket of his jeans where he always kept it. He fumbled with his left hand, but with his seated position, and tight jeans, it was not easy extracting it. He berated himself for not putting it on the console in between the seats alongside him; he hadn't thought at the time. He was shifting in his seat, trying to give himself more room, and gradually he managed to negotiate it to the pocket entrance. Unfortunately, as it reached the opening, the added pressure of the fabric caused it to shoot out with some momentum, and it landed in the footwell.

"Damn," Jez shouted to himself.

He leaned down trying to steer one-handed and keep his eye on the road; he flayed around with his left hand, but he could only just about reach the floor. Then he felt it. He looked down to try to see if he could get a better purchase with his fingers. Suddenly, the Land Rover lit up as an oncoming car flashed urgently.

Jez was on the wrong side of the road; he yanked his steering wheel to the left to return to the carriageway. Unfortunately, the sudden turn was far too sharp for the ancient vehicle, and Jez lost control. The back end was fish-tailing as he wrestled with the steering wheel, but it was too late; the Land Rover spun off the road. It hit the bank at fifty miles an hour which was enough to flip the car over. It rolled again and stopped on the other side of the road on its roof.

It was on a blind bend and without warning, a second car came around the corner from the opposite direction and hit the inverted vehicle a glancing blow which sent it spinning further.

Jez was still strapped in his seatbelt. He was disorientated, but conscious and, as far as he could tell, not seriously injured. He could feel his legs and arms. He could hear noises outside and could smell diesel fumes. He needed to get out.

A voice shouted. "Quick, get him out. It's on fire!"

The door opened, and Jez could feel someone trying to unbuckle his seatbelt. He was still dazed and tried to find the release button.

"Has anybody got a knife?" asked another voice.

Jez could smell burning, and he started to panic; his movements became more frantic.

"Keep still mate, I've got you," said someone else from the passenger side. The door opened, and there was more fumbling; then suddenly Jez fell backwards, released from the confines of the restraints. He was dragged unceremoniously from the vehicle across the upturned passenger seat onto the ground. Flames were now beginning to lap around the front of the car, under the bonnet. Black smoke was starting to billow from the sides.

"Are you ok, mate?" said the rescuer, as Jez tried to get to his feet.

"Yes. I think so. Where's my phone, I've got to get my phone."

"Don't be daft, you can't go back in there; we've got to move away; it could blow."

Jez made a grab for the door, but he was held back by two people.

"Come on, mate; leave it," said the man, and Jez watched as the flames took hold and edged towards the battered leather seating.

There were a few people about now; three cars had stopped on the outgoing carriageway, and someone was warning traffic the other side of the bend to prevent further collisions. The flames were now engulfing most of the vehicle but had not yet reached the diesel supply.

Jez's rescuer had taken charge of the scene and moved

everybody back. There were several small explosions, just bangs and crackles, as flames consumed the car's innards. Then a larger boom as the fuel tank exploded. The on-lookers ducked down, but there was little in the way of flying debris. A few minutes later, the sound of sirens could be heard in the distance.

Chapter Ten

For a while, it was a major incident. Police had to close a main trunk road while the fire-brigade extinguished what was left of the conflagration; it had, by this time, almost burnt itself out. There was a long wait while a breakdown truck towed the carcass of Jez's Land Rover to a compound. It took three hours to re-open the road, and the diversions were lengthy.

Jez was taken away in an ambulance but had been able to able to give the officers his details and a version of events as he'd remembered them. He was intentionally vague.

"I remember a rabbit; it came out of nowhere," he said. "And I just swerved. It was pure instinct. The next thing I know, I'm rolling over," he managed to stutter. The police were very understanding and said they would call at the Hall to take a statement the next day. Luckily for Jez, the car that had flashed its headlights had failed to stop; so there was nobody to contradict his story.

It was after midnight before Jez was being checked over by the medical team at the large hospital on the outskirts of Skipton. The Consultant said he had been extremely fortunate; he had no serious injuries. His shoulder hurt as a result of the tension from the seatbelt, but it was not broken or dislocated. There were just a few bumps and bruises to show for his near-death experience.

Jez was more concerned about what he was going to say to Sarah; it was all he could think about in the ambulance. His car was a write-off, and so was his phone; he had no means of contacting her. His mother would also be asking questions. He could imagine the conversation; it was his own fault for being out that time of night.

By two o'clock, he had been discharged and immediately had a problem; his wallet was in the dashboard of the now burnt-out Land Rover. The fire brigade had left, and the wreckage had been cleared to a breaker's yard somewhere.

He came out of the treatment room and into the waiting area where ten or twelve people were sat patiently. He went to the reception desk and explained the circumstances.

"Is there any way I can get home?" he said. "I can't walk, in my condition; it's a long way."

The lady looked at him. "Are you on benefits at all, dear?" she asked.

"Benefits? No, why?"

"I could get you a taxi; the Trust would pay for it."

"No, what about tax-payers?" retorted Jez,

"Sorry, you'll have to make your own arrangements. Have you got any friends you can call?"

"What? It's two o'clock in the morning."

"Sorry," said the woman. "I don't make the rules. The phone over there is free if you're calling a taxi," she said, pointing to a handset on an adjacent wall "They may be able to do something for you."

Jez walked away wondering what to do. He reached the phone; the area immediately around it was dark and discoloured, evidencing regular usage. He thought about the number of greasy heads that had leant against the wall at that point. He picked up the receiver and stood back as far away from the headset as the cable would allow. It automatically dialled and was quickly answered by a voice with a sub-continental accent. Jez explained the problem.

"I will have to go into the house and get the cash. Will that be ok?"

He was told that it would be fine; a driver would be with him in ten minutes.

The taxi arrived, and Jez explained his situation again to the driver, who seemed happy enough.

On the journey back to Deighton, the enormity of what had happened started to sink in; it was delayed shock. He began shaking.

"Are you ok?" the driver asked.

"Yes, I'm ok," said Jez and he gradually settled.

They arrived at the gate to the grounds, and Jez got out and unlocked it with the fob. Luckily his house keys were in his pocket; otherwise, he would have been in real difficulties.

They reached the house and Jez could see a light on in the kitchen. A nice gesture from his mother, he thought, ensuring the place was not in total darkness for him when he returned.

He opened the front door and went in; the taxi was waiting with the engine idling.

Jez went straight to the kitchen to where his mother kept some cash for emergencies.

"Oh, you've decided to come home, then," came a voice that made him jump.

"Oh… Hi mother, where's the emergency cash? I need to pay the taxi," said Jez, ignoring the remark.

"In the tin on the first shelf," replied his mother. "What's happened? Where's the car?"

"I've had an accident; I'll tell you in a second, I need to pay the taxi."

Jez took a twenty-pound note from the tin and headed back out the door to pay the driver. He watched as the car turned around and headed back to the road. The gate would be left open; he was not going all the way down to the perimeter.

Martha was at the door when he returned to the house.

"Accident? What accident? What's happened? Are you alright?"

She could see a red mark on his forehead which was beginning to turn into a bruise. She held his head up to the light. "Hmm, you're going to have a black eye, if I'm not mistaken. Looks like you've been in a fight or something. Sit down; I'll make some tea."

"Thanks." Jez started shaking again.

Martha went into the kitchen and put the kettle on.

"Come on then; what happened?" she said as Jez sat down.

He explained his version of events; swerved to miss a rabbit, the car caught fire, lost his phone and wallet.

"What are we going to do about shopping on Sunday?"

"Don't worry, mother. I'm sure we'll manage."

Martha made the tea and handed him a mug.

"Steady," she said. "Here, I'll put it on the table; your hands are shaking."

They were uncontrollable. Jez put his hands to his head.

"What did they say at the hospital?" said his mother.

"I'm ok, just a few bumps and bruises; I was lucky."

"Well, if you're no better tomorrow you must call the doctor. I don't know why you had to go out at that time of night. I told you not to go."

"Yes, mother, you did," retorted Jez. He took a swig of his tea and returned the mug to the table.

He got off the chair and stood up; his legs nearly gave way.

"Where are you going?" said Martha.

"I need to go to bed," replied Jez, and shuffled out of the room. Martha just watched him, then washed the mugs under the tap.

Thursday morning, Sarah was on the commute by seven o'clock; early travel routines were becoming the norm. She checked her phone and was surprised to see no messages from Jez; he had not even replied to the one she had sent from the train the previous evening. She considered this for a few minutes and wondered if he had cooled his interest. She sent him another text.

'Hello, on the train, hope you're ok; I haven't heard from you S x'.

She started reading the free newspaper until she reached the terminus in Leeds.

In the office, she started dealing with her emails and sent a confirmation to Bruno detailing the agreement reached at the hotel. She felt pleased with the outcome of her first high-level client meeting; it had gone well. She thought about the bracelet which was safely in her jewellery box in her bedroom; it would be worn for special occasions. It was a nice gesture from the client and any unease she had had about accepting it was long gone.

She checked her appointments; there was one she was not particularly looking forward to with the senior compliance officer, scheduled for ten-fifteen.

Michelle joined her around nine o'clock for an update. "I see you're meeting Adam Fowler this morning; nothing wrong is there?"

"What? Oh, no, nothing. I just wanted to discuss some thoughts about compliance, haven't had a chance since I took over."

"Lucky you, I could be very compliant with him; he's hot. Half the admin team are lusting after him."

Sarah looked up in surprise. "Really? I can't say I'd noticed," she said and laughed.

Michelle left the office, and Sarah was trying to remember what the new compliance officer looked like; she couldn't place him.

At nine-thirty, Sarah was starting her third coffee of the morning when her phone rang.

"Hello, Sarah?"

"Yes,"

"It's Adam Fowler. Look, I'm really sorry about this, but I was wondering if we could put our meeting back a couple of hours; something urgent has cropped up."

"Yes, of course," said Sarah. "When were you thinking?"

"Twelve, twelve-thirty? We could meet over lunch; my shout since I'm the one changing things."

"Yes, ok. At the canteen?"

"Yes, or we could pop to La Boulangerie, it would be more private. Ryan mentioned you have an issue to discuss."

"Er… Yes ok, good idea. Let's say twelve-thirty. I'll meet you in cosmetics, by the lifts."

"Great, see you then."

Adam rang off, and Sarah reflected on the conversation, not the content, but his voice, no trace of a Yorkshire accent, and smooth, like chocolate almost. She shivered momentarily then went back to her computer.

Just before twelve-thirty, Sarah went to the rest-room and freshened up, applying new lipstick and perfume. She checked herself in the mirror then made her way to the ground floor.

Adam was waiting.

"Adam?" said Sarah, half-recognising him.

"Hi, Sarah, how are things; are you finding your feet?" That voice again.

"Ha, sort of, they haven't touched the ground yet."

Now that she had a good view of him, she could understand why the girls in admin were after him.

Adam led the way from the store, and they walked for two minutes to the eatery. They queued for a few minutes, then managed to get a table in the corner at the back which would ensure some privacy.

"I'll get some cutlery," said Adam, putting his sandwiches opposite Sarah and going back to the counter.

He handed Sarah a knife and then took a sip of his coffee.

"Coffee's great in here; I'm a sucker for anything French," said Adam.

Sarah looked at him. Dark-blue eyes, dark wavy hair, 'designer' stubble leaning towards a beard, slim; he looked like the male models that you see in the clothes catalogues lying around in Menswear, but rugged, dangerous even.

Sarah cut a piece of her baguette and took a bite.

"So, Ryan says you've got a compliance issue you want to discuss," said Adam, opening the discussion.

"Yes, did he give you any background?"

"No, not any detail, said something about a backhander."

"Hmm, yes," said Sarah, and she outlined the full circumstances. "I have no idea how much is involved, or how long it's been going on, and I don't know how many other clients might be implicated. The Czechs aren't the only ones where the pricings are outside the guide formulas."

"Hmm, that's disturbing."

"The problem is, I have no idea how we're going to prove it. I can't see Pete admitting anything and the clients certainly won't. It's not in their interest; they just want the business."

"Well, with Pete now gone, I can't see any point in going for a prosecution; it would be counter-productive and wouldn't look good from a P.R. perspective. Any court case at this moment in time would not be welcome for Sir Basil, on top of the negative press we've been getting recently."

"Yes, that's my thought, exactly," said Sarah. "Which is why I need some guidance."

"Well, my view would be to draw a line under everything. Now we have a change in senior management in Procurement, and in Sales, we can start looking at compliance in a different way. I've been working on a Code of Conduct for supervisors and senior managers which I'm going to issue shortly. I'll include something on 'Incentives'. How does that sound?"

"Yes, that's fine by me, thank you, very pragmatic."

Adam looked at Sarah, and something seemed to happen; she found it difficult holding his gaze.

"So, come on, tell me about yourself, how long have you been with Huntsman's? Ryan said only a short time," said Sarah. "I've seen you about the store, but nobody's introduced you."

"Ha, no, not got 'round to procurement yet. Yes, beginning of December. What would you like to know?"

"Where you're from; it's not Yorkshire, that's for sure."

"Ha, ha, you can tell? I was brought up in Salisbury, went to University in London. I wanted to be a Bio-chemist but ended up in Compliance. What about you?"

Sarah gave him a potted history.

"You've done really well, most of the senior management here are in their sixties, apart from Ryan," said Adam, who had finished his sandwiches and was consuming the last dregs of coffee.

"Thank you. What about outside work?"

"Rugby, mostly. I used to be semi-professional when I was at Uni, played for Saraquins."

"Wow. Do you still play?"

"Yes, most Saturdays, you should come and watch. I play for Meanwood."

"Yes, that would be good. I'd like that," said Sarah, without thinking.

His eyes met hers. They were, what one of her friends called 'bedroom-eyes'. She never understood the phrase, but, now she knew exactly what she meant.

"I'll let you know when the next home game's on. It's not this week; we're away down in Wakefield; maybe the following Saturday?"

"Yes, thanks; that would be great, looking forward to it."

"Would you like my mobile number?" said Adam and took out his phone.

"Yes, it could come in handy," Sarah heard herself say. "You'd better have mine, too."

The hour just seemed to fly by, but with a pile of work on her desk, Sarah called time around one forty-five. "Better get back," she said.

"Would you like to do lunch again tomorrow? It's Friday," said Adam.

"Goodness, so it is; where has this week gone? Yes, ok, that would be nice. Same time?"

"Yes, suits me, nothing in the diary," said Adam, and the pair made their way out of the café.

Back in her office, Sarah checked her phone again, still no messages from Jez, but this time she was not particularly bothered. She found herself thinking about a week on Saturday and the rugby match; she was really looking forward to that. Then there was lunch tomorrow.

In Deighton, things were different.

Jez had hardly slept; various aches and pains from the accident were starting to surface. His shoulder had stiffened; he couldn't raise his arm above it and getting dressed was a slow business. A look in the mirror revealed a red mark on the side of his face which was starting to turn orange. He looked like he had been a few rounds with a heavy-weight boxer. He groaned.

His instinctive reaction was to go back to bed and stay there, but there was too much to do; he desperately needed to regain contact with Sarah. He had already thought of a plausible story which would satisfy any curiosity about why he had gone out.

He went downstairs; he could hear his mother moving around in the kitchen. She looked up from the range where she was boiling an egg.

"Didn't think I'd be seeing you up this early," her greeting.

"Lots to do," said Jez and started to boil the kettle.

"You're going to have a right shiner by the look of you," said Martha looking at Jez's face. "What about the rest of you, any problems? Only they can surface later, you know."

"I'm ok, just a few bruises."

After breakfast, Jez took a shower and examined himself more closely. There were more bruises on his hip, his legs and his shoulder but otherwise, he had gotten off extremely lightly from his trauma. The shock of what might have happened had dissipated, and he was starting to focus on what he needed to do. He made a mental list; insurance, bank, car, phone; not necessarily in that order.

Thirty minutes later, he was using the house phone to make

his calls. He thought about calling Sarah but realised she would be busy. He would text her later from his new phone. The good news was, the insurers would cover car rental for up to fourteen days while he replaced his vehicle. The bad news was that they would only pay the market value of a ten-year-old Land Rover; two thousand five hundred pounds. He would not be getting much for that; except maybe a ten-year-old Land Rover.

At ten o' clock, he called a taxi; he would need to go to Skipton to complete his business. Mrs Dawson arrived and let herself in; Martha was in the bathroom. Jez went to greet the daily.

"You been fighting?" she said looking at Jez.

"No, I was in an accident last night."

"Sorry to hear that. I thought it was strange, your car not being there."

"No, it's a write-off; I need to go to Skipton and get a hire-car."

"Well, you go steady, young Jeremy, you don't look too good."

"Yes, Mrs D; just waiting for the taxi."

By ten-thirty Jez was being dropped off at the station car park; Amber Car Hire had an office adjacent to the booking hall. Without his driver's licence or credit card; it took longer than usual, and it required a call to his insurers before they would release a vehicle. Fortunately, Jez had remembered a utility bill and the insurance case number. It took an hour before Jez was driving away in a silver Nissan Primera.

He left the station car park rather gingerly as he familiarised himself with the new controls. He parked in the market square, then walked to the phone shop. It was where he had got his original phone from, and he recognised the assistant. His account was checked, and, having taken out insurance cover when he bought his previous phone, it would be replaced free of charge, more good news. After another forty-minutes of form-filling, he left the shop with his new phone.

It was approaching midday, and before going to the bank, he stopped for a coffee. He still had some change from the twenty pounds he had taken from his mother's biscuit tin. He would replace it later.

He took the phone from its box and started to set it up; he was desperate to contact Sarah. The charge indicator said eighteen percent, which would be more than enough. Then he had a problem. He had lost all his contacts; well, not lost exactly, they were backed up on his computer at home. Having always called or texted Sarah on speed-dial, he couldn't remember her number; it would have to wait until later. He cursed at his stupidity.

After finishing his coffee, he headed to the bank where there was another lengthy delay while he ordered new bank cards and withdrew some cash to keep him going.

It was after two-thirty before he eventually arrived back at the Hall. Mrs Dawson had seen the car pull up and opened the door for Jez who was carrying the carrier bag containing his phone.

"Like the new car," said the daily as Jez walked in.

"Is mother about?" said Jez, sharply.

"She's gone to bed, said she had a headache," replied Mrs Dawson.

"Oh, ok; I'm going to my room, I need to charge up my phone."

His peace was disturbed a few minutes later by the arrival of a police car.

"The police are here," shouted Mrs Dawson.

Jez went down and let them in, he ushered them into the kitchen and offered them some tea.

The formalities took less than twenty minutes; Jez signed his statement, and they left, seemingly happy with his story regarding the accident.

Sarah was feeling productive following her lunch meeting with the senior compliance officer, and for the first time since she took over the role, she was beginning to feel on top of things. At four o'clock, she went to the coffee machine for her final hit of the day and checked her phone. There were two messages. She read the first one.

'Enjoyed your company, look forward to lunch tomorrow, Adam'.

She read it again and noticed her heart rate had increased; she could feel her cheeks begin to flush.

She opened the second message.

'Hi sorry I have not been in touch, I was in a terrible accident last night. Went to see a client and on the way back, I swerved to miss a rabbit and rolled the Land Rover. It caught fire. Luckily, I wasn't hurt; just a few bruises, but I lost my phone and wallet, and the car's a write-off. I've missed you so much. Love you Jez xxx".

For some reason, Sarah felt guilty and quickly texted back.

'Sorry to hear, glad you're ok, you must tell me all later, S x'.

Later that evening, Sarah was at home finishing off some work when her phone pinged. She had a feeling it would be from Jez.

'Hi, you ok to chat?'

Sarah sighed, then texted back. *'Give me five minutes,'* she replied.

Four minutes fifty-eight seconds later her phone rang.

"Hi," said Sarah. "You ok?"

"Hi, yes, a few bruises and a headache but ok; I was very lucky, I could have died."

"Hmm, that sounds terrible."

"Yes, it was; that'll teach me to swerve for a rabbit."

"Well, it's good for the rabbit at least."

"Yes, I guess."

"You managed to get your phone replaced quickly," said Sarah.

"Yes, and the insurance people have arranged a car hire. I'm running around in a Nissan Primera, nice car but it's not my Land Rover. Quite sad really, I bought that the day after I moved back to Deighton, over three years ago now. I thought it would be more in keeping with the area than the three series. It only had thirty-thousand miles on the clock, too."

"You had a BMW?" said Sarah.

"Yes, when I lived in London, it was what everybody in IT seemed to drive, apart from the managers; they all had five series."

"I see," said Sarah.

"How did your meeting go at the Corillium?" asked Jez.

"Yes, it went fine, I managed to get the deal we wanted."

"So, were you late finishing?"

"No, not particularly; I caught the ten-thirty. One of the clients walked me to the station which I thought was very chivalrous of them."

Jez started to realise that Sarah was probably telling the

truth after all. If only he had trusted her, he would not have had the accident and suffered from the subsequent fallout.

"Anyway, I better go, I've some bits and pieces to finish off here before I go to bed," said Sarah. "Chat tomorrow?"

"Yes, ok. Have you thought any more about going away somewhere?"

"Hmm, sorry, no I haven't, but it won't be this month. Are you still coming over on Saturday?"

"Yes, I can't wait, I've missed you so much," said Jez.

Sarah hadn't missed Jez at all.

"Yes, ok. Well, we'll chat tomorrow. Goodnight," and before Jez could reply there was the discordant noise of a dropped call.

As Sarah put her phone in her handbag ready for the morning, she was thinking about Saturday night and wished she hadn't agreed to an overnight. She wasn't sure if she could cope with Jez's growing neediness. She thought about cancelling, but she had made a promise and would stick with it.

Jez sensed that Sarah had cooled towards him; he put it down to work pressures and would win back her attention on Saturday. He wanted to make it a night she would never forget.

On Friday morning Sarah had that end-of-the-week feeling as she rode the train into Leeds. It had been a productive week, and she felt a strong sense of motivation; she couldn't wait to get stuck into her work. She had a planned meeting with Sir Basil at ten, and then her lunch appointment with Adam. She smiled at the thought; he had been on her mind a great deal.

After the usual morning routines, Sarah collected everything she would need for her meeting with Sir Basil and walked up to the seventh floor. Cressida was her usual officious self and made Sarah sit on the chair outside the chairman's office like a naughty schoolgirl waiting to see the headteacher. Five minutes later, Cressida's phone rang, and she picked it up. She looked across at Sarah. "Sir Basil will see you now," she said.

Sarah tried hard to contain her anger; this was a part of the store's culture she would love to change.

"Ah, come in Sarah, take a seat. I'll get Cressida to get us some coffee."

Sarah's mood changed as she visualised the fawning PA making coffee for them.

"How are things?" asked the chairman.

"Good, thank you Sir Basil, starting to find my feet."

"Yes, Ryan was saying good things. So, what have you got for me?"

Over coffee, Sarah outlined some of her findings and her plans to resolve some of the pricing issues; she did not mention the backhanders; that was water under the bridge. Then she wanted to float her new idea; she had prepared well.

"I had my first client meeting on Wednesday, and I've found something out which I think will be of interest."

"Go on," said Sir Basil as he sipped his coffee.

"Have you heard of the 'Partnership for Sustainable Textiles'?"

Sir Basil looked at Sarah as if this was some sort of challenge.

"No, I can't say I have," he said somewhat defensively.

"I don't know if you remember that incident in Bangladesh about four years ago; a big factory collapsed, nearly twelve hundred died?"

"Hmm, yes, I do, vaguely."

"It was a sweatshop, a huge garment factory where they made tee-shirts and other clothes in appalling conditions. I did some research around it."

"Hmm, I see," said Sir Basil.

"The Partnership I mentioned was set up in Germany by one of their ministers after the Bangladeshi disaster. The aim was to try and improve working conditions and pay across the world. There was an attempt to get it accepted by the EU, but that hasn't worked."

"What's this got to do with Huntsman's?"

"Ethical sourcing. The clients I met were from the Czech Republic, and they've signed up to the Partnership. It occurred to me we could use this as a marketing tool."

Sir Basil looked at his empty coffee cup and placed it on the table. "Hmm, I can see your point, but I have had this discussion before with your predecessor. Mr Taylor looked into it from a marketing perspective, but the impact on pricing was just too much."

"I think there's a different climate now in the marketplace; people are much more aware of ethics in retailing."

"You could be right but, in my experience, everybody is ethical until they're asked to pay higher prices and then they'll just head for the cheapest option. Look at the competition from the Swedish and German discount supermarkets."

"Yes, that's true."

"Look, I'm not against the idea, and I can see the possible marketing opportunities. Why don't we wait until the new Head of Sales and Marketing is appointed, then we can agree on a coordinated approach?"

"Yes, ok," said Sarah, slightly crestfallen that her idea had not been more enthusiastically endorsed. "Is there any news on an appointment?" she added.

"I was speaking to HR earlier, and they think they've found someone. I am seeing them on Monday."

The meeting continued for another twenty-five minutes before Sarah was dismissed.

Despite the push-back on her ethical sourcing idea, overall, she was happy with the way the meeting had gone. Sir Basil seemed pleased with the progress she had made on the pricing issues. She reached her desk and checked her phone; there were six messages from Jez. She sighed and put her phone back in her handbag. It was almost midday, and she had four client calls waiting for her that she needed to respond to before her lunch appointment.

By twenty-five past twelve, Sarah just had time to refresh her make-up before taking the lift to the ground floor. She had a strange feeling, one of anticipation; like a first date. She kept reminding herself it was just a business colleague but, somehow, it seemed more than that.

Earlier, Jez was struggling to get out of bed; he'd had another restless night and was using pain-killers to enable him to sleep. He checked himself in the mirror; the bruise on his face didn't look so angry, but his shoulder was still sore.

He hobbled downstairs to the kitchen; his mother was sat at the table reading the paper and glanced up at him.

"You don't look too good. Why don't you go to the doctors?"

"I'm fine mother, don't fuss," replied Jez and went to make some tea.

"Are you still intending to stay the night with your trollop on Saturday?"

Martha had hardly been able to think about anything else since Jez mentioned it.

"Yes, and it's Sarah, I keep telling you."

"Well, you're not going to be much good to her in your

state, are you? You can hardly move, let alone anything else."

"I'll be fine, and stop being crude. I told you before; she's not like that."

"Of course she is. The sight of a bit of money and down come the knickers faster than you can say 'pound notes'," Martha's anger was starting to rise again. "Your father was just as bad; he couldn't resist it; anything in a bit of skirt. I told him it would be the death of him and it was."

"What are you talking about?"

"I never told you about your father. How he died."

"You did. You said it was a heart attack."

"Yes, it was, but I didn't tell you the circumstances," Martha was at the sink washing up a mug, looking out of the kitchen window, unable to look Jez in the eye. "Well, it's about time you knew."

"Knew what?"

She turned and looked at him; her face was a snarl.

"What really happened; how he got his heart attack."

Jez returned the gaze but didn't say anything.

"He was shagging one of the girls in the village; old enough to be his daughter. I found out later he was showering her with gifts. Even bought her a car for fuck's sake."

Jez was trying to take it all in.

"They were in a hotel in the Dales somewhere, and he collapsed on top of her; right in the middle of it. I almost felt sorry for her, but it serves her right for what she did."

"You're making it up."

"No, I'm not, why would I? You can check in the local paper; it was quite a scandal at the time. Why do you think I don't go into the village?"

Jez was incredulous.

"I can't discuss this, mother; I'm going for a shower."

He went back upstairs reflecting on his mother's exposé. He thought the world of his father and looked up to him. If it wasn't for him, they would not be enjoying their current lifestyle. He certainly couldn't blame him for cheating on his mother. She would try the patience of a saint. It was just so sad. It did give Jez a better understanding of his mother's reaction to Sarah., but she would come around once she had met her. He was sure of that. It was something he wanted to raise with Sarah on Saturday, tea with mother; now that would be a challenge.

He suddenly felt a twinge of excitement. He picked up his phone and sent another text to Sarah. *'Hope you're ok, bruises are looking better, less resemble a boxer today, ha, ha. Can't wait to see you tomorrow. Love Jez xxx."*

He thought back to the chat the previous evening and Sarah's preoccupation with work; he needed her to re-focus. Tomorrow he would give Sarah some real attention.

By ten-thirty, he was feeling much better; his mood further lifted by the thought of what lay in store for him tomorrow night. He needed to go into town; he had an idea.

Chapter Eleven

Sarah reached the ground floor, and Adam was waiting for her in the same spot as the previous day.

"Hi," he said, as she walked towards him, he had a big smile. She heard his voice, and she wanted to melt.

"Hi, how's it going?" she replied.

"Yeah, good thanks."

It was a dry chilly morning, and both were wearing short coats. Adam stood to one side to allow Sarah to exit. Clarke was on duty and doffed his hat as they passed. They turned left and headed for the café just a short walk away.

"What's your commute like?" asked Adam.

"Not bad, fifteen-twenty minutes on the train. What about you?"

"It's a drive, unfortunately. I've got a flat in Roundhay, near the Park, takes about forty minutes, but I do have a parking slot which makes it easier."

"Wow, you're honoured."

There was an underground lot in the store basement that could accommodate around fifteen cars. You were very privileged indeed to be allocated a space.

"Yes, I didn't know that at the time, they just offered it when I joined," said Adam.

They ordered their lunches and found a seat at the back of the café.

"So, how was your meeting with Sir Basil?" asked Adam, when they had made themselves comfortable.

"It was ok. I mentioned my idea of ethical sourcing, but he didn't seem that keen," said Sarah.

"Hmm, pricing, I guess."

"Yes, unfortunately, but I'm going to keep pushing, I do think it's the way forward. He's interviewing someone on Monday for the Sales and Marketing job."

"That will be a good role for somebody," said Adam.

"Or a poisoned chalice. Sales are still a big problem, according to finance."

"Yes, it'll be tough, that's for sure, but if they get it right, there'll be a lot of kudos. It'll certainly look good on their LinkedIn profile."

"Yes, now there's a thought," Sarah took a bite of her baguette; Adam was consuming a French Roll.

She continued her update. "I've been working my way through the contracts, the big ones anyway; there are more than half over the pricing formula. The problem is, having paid it once, it'll be difficult to get a reduction in the light of the present trading climate; everybody's struggling with margins. Our only option is to increase our prices on the shop-floor, and you've seen the problems with that strategy."

"Well, let me know if there's anything I can do. Even if it's just to bounce ideas."

"That's really kind," said Sarah.

"Anyway, enough of work; what are you doing next Friday night?" said Adam.

Sarah thought for a moment. "Hmm, washing my hair," she smiled. "Why?"

"There's a do on at the rugby club; I wondered if you fancied going. There'll be a disco."

Sarah was taken by surprise.

"Er… yes. I'd love to. Yes, that would be great; what time?"

"About seven-thirty, but it won't get going until nine, finishes at midnight; we can't get the license."

"Ha, midnight's good for me; you'll have to give me directions."

"Yes, of course, how far away are you?"

"Minton, about twenty-five minutes, I suppose."

"Yes, that'll be about right."

Sarah smiled. "It's been ages since I went to a disco. What do they wear these days?"

"Just about anything," said Adam and started to laugh.

"Hmm, I'll have to think about that. We'll need to be careful; Sir Basil frowns on in-store relationships."

"We'll need to make sure he doesn't find out then," said Adam, and reached his hand across to Sarah's. She looked around to see if anyone else from the store was in the vicinity but couldn't recognise anyone. She took his hand and held it; for the second time, she felt like a naughty schoolgirl. She looked into his eyes and suddenly wanted to be very naughty.

"I've wanted to do this since I first set eyes on you," said Adam.

"Really?" said Sarah.

"Yes, I think you are the most gorgeous woman I've ever seen. Sorry if that's not a very professional thing to say."

"I'll forgive you," said Sarah. She was smitten; her heart was pounding, her stomach had butterflies, and her mind was in freefall.

He squeezed her hand.

"Woah, steady on, I need to get some work done this afternoon."

"Yes, me too; what a shame," said Adam.

"Mmm, yes," said Sarah. She needed to change the subject she was starting to feel warm.

"So, where were you, before you joined the store?" she

asked. Adam was still holding her hand.

"What? Sorry, I was distracted. Before I joined?"

"Yes."

"I was with the Standard Bank of South America in Canary Wharfe, in compliance."

"That must have been a challenge."

"You can say that again."

"So, what brought you up to Leeds? I mean it's a bit of a come-down after the City, and I bet the salary was nowhere near?"

"Yes, that's true, but I was beginning to hate the rat-race, the commuting, the back-stabbing, all of that. I needed to get away, and I've always liked Leeds; my sister went to Uni here. I used to visit her regularly; the parties were amazing. I also have a mate I was at Uni with who plays rugby at Meanwood. He introduced me to the club."

"I see," said Sarah; she hadn't taken her eyes off him.

"And, when I saw the job advertised, I thought 'why not?' I'd had enough of London."

"Yes, I don't think I could live there now; I couldn't afford it for a start. I don't know how people get on the property ladder," said Sarah.

"Most of them don't; everybody's renting, or at least everyone I knew."

"You're renting the place in Roundhay, then?"

"Yes, for the moment, I want to see how things work out before committing to a mortgage," said Adam.

"That makes sense," said Sarah, and checked her watch. "Sorry, gonna have to go, I've got a pile of stuff to finish off before I leave tonight."

"Yes, you're right," said Adam.

With reluctance, they both got up and walked towards the café exit. Adam was behind Sarah, so close she could smell his aftershave.

They returned to the store, and Sarah pressed the button for the lift. They got in, and immediately Adam pressed the button for the sixth floor before anyone else could enter. With the lift empty, Adam leaned across to Sarah and kissed her. With only ten seconds between floors; it was the briefest of encounters. The fun was spoiled by one of the admin team getting in on the third floor.

"Hi Maisie," said Sarah. "Been shopping?"

"Yes," said the girl, holding up a carrier bag. "Mum's birthday tomorrow."

Sarah looked at Adam, and he smiled; there was a significant amount of unfinished business.

Back at Deighton, Jez was blissfully unaware of events elsewhere and was considering his dinner-date with Sarah. It was all he could think about.

His mother was in the sitting room; the sound of Mrs Dawson's vacuum working on the upstairs landing had driven her from the bedroom.

Jez looked around the door. "I'm going into town, won't be long."

Martha looked at him. "What are you going into town for; you were only there yesterday."

"Just a couple of bits and I need to call at the bank. See you later."

Jez drove down the drive to the main road. He was hardly able to conceal his excitement; despite his aches and pains, he felt like singing. Even his mother hadn't annoyed him today.

The roadside verges were awash with emerging daffodils, their yellow flowers seemingly at odds with the grey morning, bringing colour to a drab day. Just like Sarah; she was the brightness in Jez's grey world. He loved the analogy; it fitted perfectly.

He parked in the market square and made his way to the bank. He would not receive his new bank card until Tuesday at the earliest, and he needed to make a purchase; Sarah needed spoiling. He drew out five hundred pounds and walked the short distance to a jeweller on the corner of the High Street. He'd seen the necklace when he was in town earlier; he was sure she would love it.

He had the item gift-wrapped, and it was presented in a smart mini carrier-bag with the name of the jewellers on the side. He walked back to the car; there was another job he needed to do, but that would have to wait until he reached home. He had promised to take Sarah out for a meal, and he needed book a table at a restaurant. He hoped he hadn't left it too late, but part of him wanted all of them to be fully booked so they could stay at Sarah's house with a takeaway. He didn't want to share her with any strangers in a restaurant. There would be more time for themselves.

As he was passing the only department store in town, he noticed a shirt in the menswear window; it looked great. He checked the price; it would mean another call at the bank. Any other time the detour would have been a vexation, but not today. So, it was back to the bank to draw out more cash and then back to the store to make the purchase before continuing to the car park.

It was lunchtime when he arrived back at the Hall; Mrs Dawson had made some sandwiches and she and Martha were sat at the kitchen table eating them.

"Mrs Dawson's made you some sandwiches; they're in the refrigerator; I didn't know what time you were coming back, so we didn't wait. Did you manage to get what you wanted?"

"Yes, thanks," said Jez. He was holding the carrier bag containing his shirt.

"Been splashing out, I see."

"Just a shirt," said Jez. The necklace was in the bag with the shirt; he didn't want his mother to see that. "I'll just take it upstairs."

"Let's have a look at it," said Mrs Dawson.

Jez opened the carrier-bag and lifted the shirt half-out.

"Let's see it properly," said Martha.

As Jez took out the shirt, the bag containing Sarah's gift caught in the wrapping and fell out of the carrier onto the floor.

"My, my," said Martha, seeing the jewellers name. "We've really been splashing out; haven't we?"

Jez put the gift and shirt back in the bag and went upstairs.

Martha looked at Mrs Dawson. "Got a new girlfriend" Mrs Dawson smiled. "It won't last," Martha added which sounded more like a threat than an observation.

Jez heard the comment, but he would prove her wrong. He had found his life-partner; he was certain of that.

He took out his phone and sent a text message to Sarah.

'Hi, just seeing if you're ok, I'll book a table for us at Il Travatore; it has great reviews. Is 7.30 ok?'

Sarah was on the train when she checked her messages. She read the most recent from Jez but didn't know what to do. For whatever reason, Cupid's arrow had bounced off and flown in another direction. She really wanted to spend the night with

Adam instead.

It was on her mind as she went about her early evening chores. At seven-thirty there was another message from Jez.

'Hi just seeing if you are ok to chat. I've booked a table at the Italian, counting down the hours. Love you, Jez xx'.

Sarah was in a quandary; she texted back. *'Just catching up with some chores will call you later S x'.*

It gave her some breathing space; she couldn't cope with all the emotion right now.

She had to make a decision; it was unfair on Jez if she were to lead him on further. She needed to find a way to let him down gently. There was no way she could spend the night with him, not now.

She was washing up the dinner dishes when she heard the 'ping' alert on her phone. She thought it would be Jez again, and picked up the phone in exasperation.

She saw the name and opened the message straight away.

'Hi Sarah, don't know about you but I can't seem to settle, wondered if you fancied meeting for a drink? Adam.'

She thought for a moment. She couldn't think of anything she would like to do more, but after a hectic week, she just needed to crash out.

'I would love to, but I'm up to my knees in washing. Call me; we can chat instead.'

Sarah left the pots to drain. Her mobile rang.

"Hi," said Adam in that wonderful creamy, dreamy voice,

"Hi," said Sarah, unconsciously dropping her voice half an octave to match Adam; it was not deliberate, just an instinctive reaction.

"I was thinking about you," said Adam.

"Yes, I was thinking about you too," said Sarah.

"I hope you didn't mind me asking about going out for a drink; I just wanted to see you again. I did think it might be a bit short notice."

"No problem. As I said, I would love to, but I've only just taken my Marigolds off."

"Now steady on, that conjures up all kinds of images."

Sarah laughed; it was the first time in a while. Her mood had lifted significantly; she felt different.

They continued chatting for another hour. Sarah's evening plans had gone out of the window, but she didn't care.

"I better go," said Sarah, eventually. It was nine-thirty.

"Yes, glad we could chat. What about tomorrow or Sunday for that drink?"

"Can't tomorrow, but possibly Sunday. Text me; I'll let you know."

They signed off, and Sarah was just about to return to the kitchen when her phone rang again. She knew who it would be.

"Hi, I thought you were going to ring."

"Yes, just finishing off."

"I tried you a few times, but your phone was busy. Who were you talking to?"

"Excuse me?" said Sarah.

Jez backtracked quickly. "You were a long time that was all. I was waiting for you."

She ignored the question. "So, are we still going for this meal tomorrow night?"

"Yes, of course, didn't you see my message? The table's booked for seven-thirty."

"Ok, are we meeting at the restaurant?"

Jez was concerned at her coldness; it was almost aggressive. "Are you ok? I'm sorry if I've upset you in some way."

"No. It's ok; it's been a long day. So, what are the arrangements then? Shall I meet you at the restaurant?"

"I thought I could come to yours and pick you up."

"No, it's ok; it's out of your way. I'll meet you there at seven-thirty."

"Ok." Jez was confused; the signals had completely changed, and he had no idea why. "Are you ok; you sound very distant?"

"Yes, I'm fine, just a bit tired that's all. Look, I'll see you tomorrow at the restaurant, ok?"

"Yes, ok; sleep well. Lots of love."

"Yes, you too," said Sarah and dropped the call. She let out a big sigh.

Jez hardly slept a wink. He kept replaying the phone call in his head. There was no mention of him staying over, and he didn't sense it was right to mention it; Sarah did not seem particularly receptive. It was the pressures of work; it had to be, and he wasn't sure yet what he was going to do about it.

He went to the bathroom. He didn't immediately recognise the image that stared back at him from the shaving mirror. The side of his face was an orange-purple colour, and the cuts on the top of his forehead were now large scabs. His once designer-stubble looked more like tramp's whiskers, not an attractive prospect for his first overnight stay with Sarah. He groaned as he tried to put on his shirt; his shoulder was still very painful.

Downstairs, his mother was in the kitchen eating her breakfast. She had a mug of coffee in her hand.

"So what time are you off on this jaunt of yours tonight?" she said before he could sit down.

"I'll be leaving here about six-thirty," replied Jez as he

made some more tea.

"I hope you've got plenty of condoms; I don't want you bringing anything nasty back here."

"I'll ignore that remark," said Jez, but she had a point. He would stop at the garage on the way out.

After breakfast, he went back to his office to try and finish some work. He was starting to get some serious grief from his clients. One had already cancelled some work he had been asked to do. He couldn't think about that just now; his sole focus was Sarah. He sent his first text of the day.

'Hi, hope you're feeling better this morning. Can't wait to see you later, not long now. Love you, Jez xxx'.

Sarah heard the 'ping' while she was starting a load of washing; she hadn't had time to do it the previous evening. She opened the message and just deleted it.

She got another message around ten o'clock; this one she did respond to.

'Hi, been thinking about you all night. I hope you are free for a drink tomorrow night.'

'I would love to go for a drink. Where and what time?'

'I can come over to Minton, save you a drive. Seven-ish?'

'Yes, that'll be fine. The Station's not bad; it's only a five-minute walk. Do you know it?'

'Don't worry, I'll find it, see you then, I'll call you later if you're free.'

'I should be, but I'll be out from about seven, just meeting a friend.'

'Ok, I'll try and call you around five xx.'

'Great xx.'

Sarah thought again about whether to cancel the dinner, but having promised Jez, she felt obliged to honour the date. She would not be inviting him back after the meal; she was sure of that. How he would react, she wasn't sure.

She sat on the sofa and Moses immediately leapt up beside her craving some affection. She stroked him. She would have to finish with Jez, it was the only fair thing to do, but not tonight; she couldn't face the drama.

Adam called just after five, as Sarah finished her shower; her hair was wrapped in a towel, and she was wearing her dressing gown.

"Hi," said Adam. "You ok?"

"Yes, fine thanks, just got out of the shower."

"Mmm, that sounds nice," said Adam. Sarah suddenly imagined him applying the soap.

"What have you been doing?" said Sarah, quickly changing the topic.

"Just about to leave Wakefield."

"Of course, the rugby. How did you get on?"

"We won, twenty-eight, seventeen," said Adam. "It was a tough game."

"Really? Glad you won, what are you going to do now?"

"Heading home, then chill, I think. A couple of the lads are going to the club for a drink; I might join them later or might just catch up on some TV. I'll see how I feel. Looking forward to seeing you tomorrow."

"Yes, me too," said Sarah.

"Anyway, enjoy your evening, and I'll call you tomorrow."

"Yes, thanks, ok, chat tomorrow."

Sarah dropped the call and was faced with a range of emotions, mainly involving Adam. She had no idea why she felt this way, but it felt good.

Back in Deighton, it was different. Jez had chosen his apparel for the evening, his new shirt, some grey chinos and casual leather shoes. He would put his leather jacket on the back seat; he would need it later. He was carrying a small rucksack containing his overnight things and the gift he had bought for Sarah.

His mother was in a strange mood, and he was trying to avoid any contact. He had finished getting ready by six-fifteen and went downstairs. His mother was in the sitting room watching TV. The sound reverberated around the ground floor. Rather than face any further abuse; he put his head around the door and shouted over the noise from the TV.

"I'm off now. See you in the morning."

His mother turned her head briefly and glared at him. Then turned back and continued watching her programme.

Jez felt wretched; all the joy and anticipation of the evening was falling apart. He still hadn't heard from Sarah; his last text had gone unanswered, and he wasn't sure if she would even show.

He left the house and put his stuff in the boot of the Nissan, then headed out of the Estate. He hadn't been to the restaurant before but had studied the map on the website and was confident he could find it without difficulty. He couldn't be bothered to work out the Nissan's Sat-Nav system.

He was correct, and by twenty-past seven, he was outside the Italian. He followed the signs to the parking area around the back. It seemed to be doing a good trade; the car-park was almost full, but he was able to find one of the few remaining spaces. He looked around and couldn't see Sarah's car. As he exited the Nissan, he was hit by the cold night air and the smell of garlic. He picked up his jacket from the back seat and put it on, then went to the boot and took out Sarah's necklace from the rucksack.

He walked along the service road passed the kitchens to the front entrance. There was a small window open; the sound of rattling pans and waiters and chefs shouting in Italian was audible. There seemed to be a lot of stress.

The frontage was more welcoming; the neon sign, 'Il Travatore', cut through the chilly evening, welcoming customers.

Jez pushed open the entrance door. There was a marked difference in temperature. A small waiting area greeted him with a bar to the left. A row of seats was positioned opposite, and a party of four were consuming drinks and studying menus. A man in a smart suit approached carrying a clipboard.

"Buonasera, signori. Have you a reservation?"

"Yes. Steadman," replied Jez. The man checked his manifest.

"For two?"

"Yes," said Jez,

"Una momento, per favore."

The instruction wasn't stretching Jez's linguistic skills too much.

"Please; sit here."

The waiter pointed to a vacant seat next to the chattering foursome.

"You want a drink?"

"Later," said Jez.

"Si, si, bueno," said the man.

He beckoned to a dark-haired young girl who was wearing a tight white top, black skirt and tights. She approached Jez with two menus. The noise from the adjacent party was increasing; it was somebody's birthday.

"Would you like to see the wine list?" said the waitress who appeared to have mastered English far better than the Maître d'.

"Thank you," said Jez, who was now feeling nervous; the uncertainty of their first meeting had returned.

He ordered half a pint of lager and checked his watch; it was seven thirty-five. He looked anxiously through the glass front door to see if he could see her car. Five minutes later, he saw her drive by and down the side towards the car park. Jez gave a sigh of relief.

A few moments later, Sarah was at the front door, and Jez stood to greet her. The two couples from the adjacent chairs had been led into the eating area, and it was now much quieter.

"Hi," he said and went to kiss her; She turned her head, so it became a cheek kiss.

"You look great. Are you ok?" said Jez.

She looked beautiful, he thought; smart jacket, top and jeans.

"Yes, fine, you?" she replied.

"Yes, ok, thanks. What would you like to drink?" said Jez. "I've got a couple of menus," and he handed her one.

"Just a tonic water," said Sarah. The waitress had seen the new arrival and took the order.

"Are you ok?" repeated Jez. "Only you hadn't replied to my messages, and I was concerned in case you weren't well or something."

"No, I had my phone switched off; I had a lot to do today. Shall we order?"

Jez called the waitress over.

"What are you having?"

"Just a main course; I couldn't eat a starter as well."

"Yes, ok. I'll do the same. Maybe have a dessert instead?"

"Yes," said Sarah. She looked at the waitress. "I'll have the chicken and prosciutto with white wine and mushrooms."

The waitress looked at Jez who was still studying the dishes.

"I'll have the Pollo Al Limone, Miele e Rosemarino," said Jez in the best Italian accent he could muster. He thought it might impress Sarah.

"That sounds good," said Sarah.

"It's very good," said the waitress. "Your table is ready if you'd like to go through."

Jez and Sarah picked up their drinks and followed the girl. It was a large area with about fifty covers. Jez could hear the birthday party; the noise levels had increased again. All the seats appeared to be taken. In one of the alcoves there was a table for two; in the middle was a candle and a small glass vase containing flowers. There were real cloth napkins and sparkling cutlery. Two wine glasses and two water goblets were placed next to the settings.

"Can I take your coats?" asked the waitress. They both took off their jackets and handed them to the girl, then sat down. Sarah found it difficult to make eye-contact. Jez wanted to break the ice and handed her the gift which he had removed from his jacket pocket.

"What's this?" she said.

"Open it and see," said Jez.

As she was opening it, Jez noticed the bracelet on her wrist but didn't say anything.

"I hope you like it."

She took out the necklace. "Oh, this is lovely, but I can't accept it."

"Of course you can. You have been working too hard, and you need spoiling,"

Sarah started to feel guilty and was in a quandary.

"Thank you; it's lovely.

Jez took it from her. "Let me put it on for you."

He got up, stood behind her, gently looped the gold chain around her neck and fastened the clasp. There was a heart on the chain which nestled nicely in the throat area of her neck.

"It suits you," said Jez.

"Yes, it's beautiful. You shouldn't have."

"As I said, you need some T.L.C. You haven't been yourself over the last couple of days. I was worried about you."

"I'm fine," said Sarah, her tone dispassionate. "Work's been a bit full on, that's all; busy, busy, busy."

She looked around the restaurant for no apparent reason, and then took a sip of her tonic water, before making eye-contact again. She noticed Jez's bruised face and scabs on his forehead.

"What about you, are you ok after the accident?"

"Yes, fine thanks; my shoulder is a bit stiff, and there are one or two bruises, but I'll be as right as rain in a couple of weeks."

"That's good news; thank goodness it wasn't any worse."

"Yes, it could have been," said Jez.

The waitress returned to the table with some breadsticks and olives.

"What would you like another drink?" she asked.

"I'm fine, thanks," said Sarah, holding up her half-filled glass.

"Me too," said Jez, and the waitress returned to other tables.

The conversation was strained, just like their first meeting. It was almost thirty-five minutes before their meals arrived. Sarah gave short answers to Jez's questions.

"How are things at work?"

"Ok."

"Have you sorted out the issues you mentioned with the pricing policy?"

"Yes. It's fine now."

Sarah was thinking about her gift; she couldn't accept it, but she didn't want to upset Jez further; he was already in for a big disappointment.

The dinner was duly consumed; although, in Sarah's case, she had left a good portion.

"Are you sure you're ok?" said Jez, seeing the half-eaten food.

"Actually, I'm not feeling that well. I almost phoned and cancelled, but I knew how much you were looking forward to it."

Jez looked concerned. "Do you want to call a doctor? We could find a pharmacist if you like; I'm sure there'll be one open around here."

"No, it's fine. I just need to go home and have an early night. You don't mind, do you? I'm sorry to disappoint you, but I don't think I would be much company."

"No, I understand. Do you want me to get the bill?" said Jez.

"If you don't mind. Thank you."

Jez summoned the waitress who came to the table and started clearing the plates.

"Was the food ok?" she said looking at the remains on Sarah's plate.

"Yes, I'm sorry; I wasn't very hungry."

"You want coffee or a dessert?" said the waitress.

"No, if you can just let me have the bill, please," said Jez.

Suddenly, the noise levels increased as three waiters, one carrying a cake with a lighted sparkler on top, walked towards the two couples who had been in the foyer earlier. The whole restaurant started singing 'Happy Birthday'. There was an uproar from the table.

"Can we have the bill please?" said Jez a little more forcefully.

"One minute," said the girl. "Are you paying with a card?"

"No. Cash," said Jez. He was still waiting for his replacement bank card.

The waitress returned with the tab and Jez took out three twenty-pound notes from his wallet and paid. "Keep the change," he said.

She escorted the couple out of the eating area and stopped at the bar to give the money to the Maître d'.

"You have coats?" she said, and Jez pointed out the two garments.

He helped Sarah with her jacket and then put on his own before opening the door for her.

"Thank you," said the waitress as the pair left. "I hope we will see you again."

"Where's your car?" said Jez.

"Over there," said Sarah, pointing to the far end of the car park.

Jez walked alongside her not really knowing what to say. All his hopes and plans had come crashing down. He felt empty as he watched her car pull away.

Chapter Twelve

Sarah was home within five minutes and was immediately greeted by Moses nuzzling up to her legs.

"Do you want some food? Come on then," and the cat followed Sarah into the kitchen. She took out a pouch of cat food from the cupboard; Moses watched her every move and let out a 'meow' as she put the bowl of food on the plastic mat next to the fridge. Sarah went to the wine-rack and picked up a bottle of red and unscrewed the top. There was an empty glass on the draining board, and she poured herself a large measure. She took an almighty gulp, then another. The glass was half-empty.

She felt wretched about the way she had treated Jez; it was not her usual character. Sometimes you have to be cruel to be kind, she told herself. She looked at the clock on the kitchen wall; ten-past nine. She went back into the lounge and turned on the TV, then picked up her phone. There was a message from Adam. *'Thinking about you,'* was all it said.

She texted back. *'Hi'.*

The reply was immediate. *'Hello, how are you?'*

'Ok, just got back.'

'I was thinking about you.'

'I was thinking about you, too. What have you been doing?' replied Sarah.

'Nothing, just watching TV. What are you doing?'

'Nothing, I was thinking of going to bed.' Sarah replied and took another gulp of wine; the glass was empty.

'Would you like some company? I can be with you in fifteen minutes.'

'Really?'

'Yes, if you would like.'

'Yes. I would like that a lot.'

'You better give me your address.'

Sarah gave Adam her address. *'Will you find it ok?'*

'Yes. I have a Sat-Nav. See you soon xxx'.

Sarah's mood changed totally. She couldn't believe what she had just done. She went upstairs and had a quick shower, dried off and applied her favourite body lotion. She searched the drawers in the dressing table. There was only one reason Adam was calling. She found her only negligee and put it on; it was pink and floaty with matching transparent panties. She put on her dressing gown over the top.

She went downstairs and poured another glass of wine. She was beginning to feel light-headed. Five minutes later she heard the throaty roar of a car engine. She opened the curtains and could see the shape of a BMW parking a few doors up.

She watched him get out of the car and took a deep breath. There was a discreet rap on the door; Sarah opened it.

"Hi, come in."

Adam closed the door behind him and walked into the lounge.

"Here, let me take your jacket," said Sarah. "Would you like a drink? I've opened a bottle of red?" She spoke quickly, partly due to nerves.

"Yes, great, thanks."

"Have a seat; I won't be a minute," said Sarah and went into the kitchen. Moses was fast asleep in his basket.

She poured Adam a drink and returned to the lounge. Adam stood up, took the glass from her and took a sip. "You look incredible," he said. She could feel his eyes on her.

She took the drink from him and put the glass on the coffee table next to hers. In a nano-second, they were locked in a kiss that seemed to go on and on. Sarah was in ecstasy; she could feel his hands on her breasts, then lower. He pushed her dressing gown onto the floor. She unzipped his jeans and could feel him inside his shorts. She thought she was going to faint.

"Let's go to bed," said Sarah and grabbed Adam's hand.

Nothing was said as she led him upstairs into her bedroom. She took off her negligee top and lay on the bed as Adam took off his clothes.

For the next hour, Adam took Sarah to heaven and back. He was a master in the craft of love-making. Not for one moment did Sarah wonder where he had acquired this expertise; she didn't care. Tonight, he was all hers.

"Do you want to stay?" said Sarah, later.

"Yes, that would be great," said Adam; and it was.

Around three o'clock, Sarah was awake and sensed Adam's presence. It felt strange to have someone lying next to her. She turned over and cuddled him, her hands moving down his body. She could feel it, so strong. She pulled the duvet off and gently lowered herself onto him. Adam started moaning softly.

It was eight o'clock before Sarah woke again; she could hear Moses scratching at the door. She looked at Adam who was still sound asleep.

She gently got out of bed so as not to disturb him, and she put on her dressing gown. She opened the bedroom door, and the cat meowed.

"Shh," said Sarah and went downstairs followed by Moses.

A few minutes later, with the cat fed, she made some tea. She drank two glasses of water to rehydrate after the alcohol from the previous evening. She felt surprisingly alert, no headache, but more than that, she felt content; it was the only way she could describe it.

Before going upstairs, she checked her phone; there were already five messages from Jez sent at various intervals through the night. She sighed and switched off the phone.

She took the two mugs to the bedroom. Adam was still asleep. She put one mug on the bedside table on her side; then went around the other. "Adam, I've made some tea."

"Eh, what? Oh, thanks," he replied, still very drowsy.

"I didn't know if you took sugar or not."

"No, it's fine, thanks."

Adam lifted himself up to a seating position, and Sarah handed him the mug.

"Careful, it's hot."

She returned to her side of the bed, took off her dressing gown and got in.

"Hmm, thanks it's just what I needed," said Adam. "You look incredible."

"Thank you," said Sara, sipping her tea.

"Mmm, thanks," said Adam after he'd finished. He put the mug on the bedside table and turned over.

"I can't keep my hands off you," he said as once more he began to stroke Sarah's body.

"Me neither," said Sarah as her hands explored Adam's chest hairs and moved lower. "You have an amazing physique."

"Thank you, I have to keep fit, or I couldn't play rugby."

He could feel her hands stroking him. They started kissing.

Sunday mornings were never like this.

Back in Deighton, Jez was in a bad way. The previous evening, he had arrived back at Deighton at nine-thirty. The downstairs light was still on, so his mother was up. He knew he was going to face some abuse; he was not going to be disappointed. He could hear the TV in the sitting room as he let himself in, although it was not as loud as it was when he had left. He went into the room, and his mother turned toward him. His presence had made her jump; she hadn't heard him arrive over the noise of the TV.

"God, you gave me such a fright. What are you doing here? I thought you said it was going to be an all-night job or did she kick you out."

"I don't want to talk about it," said Jez.

Martha pointed the remote control at the TV and switched it off.

"Come on, what happened? Tell me."

"Nothing, she wasn't feeling very well that was all."

"Hmm, that girl is no good, believe me, nothing but trouble the lot of them."

"I'm going to bed," said Jez and went upstairs.

He was in a mess; all his hopes and dreams had been shattered. He tried to rationalise the situation; it wasn't all bad. She did say there would be other times. Maybe when she was better, she would want him to stay over. He would hold onto that thought.

He tried to shut it out but closing his eyes didn't ease the feeling. If only he hadn't been so hasty in trying to discredit her boss, Sarah wouldn't be under all this pressure. He needed to find a way of getting her to focus on him, away from the work distraction. He had hoped the necklace would work, but she didn't seem to appreciate it.

All these thoughts were going through his mind as he tried to sleep. He did eventually drop off but was awake again by seven o'clock.

He gingerly pulled himself out of bed; his shoulder was

still painful, another reason for his fitful sleep. He went to the kitchen and started making some tea. While the kettle was boiling, he took two painkillers to deaden the throbbing.

He walked back upstairs carrying his tea and could hear his mother's footsteps in her bedroom. She was awake. Jez did not want to see her; there was sure to be another confrontation.

He was at the top of the stairs as his mother trudged down the corridor towards him. Too late. He stopped as she approached.

"Where's my tea?"

"I didn't want to wake you," said Jez.

"I'm already awake. Why are you up? You've been mithering about that trollop of yours, haven't you?"

"I told you, mother, she's not a trollop, stop calling her that."

"Well, she certainly blew you out yesterday, didn't she?"

"She was ill; I told you."

"Yes, you said. Probably took one look at you and couldn't bear you near her."

"You can say what you like, but one day I'm going to marry her."

"Ha, ha, ha, of course you are, dear; of course you are."

He could feel the rage boiling inside. His hands were shaking causing his tea to spill dripping on the carpet. Martha was now at the end of the corridor at the top of the stairs; Jez was alongside her.

"Get out of my way," he said and pushed her aside causing her to stumble.

Martha put out a hand to stop herself but missed the bannister. The momentum took her forward and she over-balanced. There was nothing to stop her, and she fell headlong down the stairs. It was a curved staircase, not steep, but wide with at least thirty steps. Jez watched in horror as she rolled over and over, hitting her head several times. She landed on the floor at the bottom.

"Mother!" shouted Jez. "Are you alright? Mother; I'm sorry; I didn't mean it. Mother!"

He put his mug on the floor and rushed down the stairs to Martha. Her head was hanging at a strange angle. Jez ran back upstairs and grabbed his phone. He keyed in the emergency number.

"Ambulance, quick, my mother's fallen down the stairs. She's unconscious."

Jez went back down the staircase and checked his mother's condition. There was no sign of life; she didn't appear to be breathing. He cradled her head in his arms. "Mother, wake up, wake up, Mother, I'm sorry, I'm sorry. Please forgive me, I didn't mean it." There was no response.

His mind was racing. He left her and went up to the top of the stairs and checked around. There was nothing to incriminate him. He picked up his mug and went back downstairs and into the kitchen, leaving his mother lying where she had landed. He was in total turmoil.

Twenty minutes later, Jez could hear the sirens; he opened the front door. The ambulance stopped, and the paramedics rushed toward him.

"Ok," said the lead medic. "What have we got?"

"It's my mother; she's had a fall."

He led them inside to the bottom of the stairs. "What's her name?"

"Mother," said Jez. "Sorry, Martha."

"And you are?"

"Jez, her son."

"Hello, Martha, can you hear me? My name's Tom; I'm a

paramedic. This is Ronnie," he said introducing his colleague.

"Martha? Can you hear me?"

Ronnie checked Martha's pulse, looked at her partner and shook her head.

"Sorry, Jez but she's gone. There's nothing we can do for her," said Tom.

"What? No, she can't be."

"I'm sorry. We need to call the police."

"What? Why?"

"Unexplained death, it's the law," replied Tom.

"But I told you, she fell down the stairs."

"It's ok; it's just a formality," said Tom. "Nothing to worry about."

Ronnie was trying to look after Jez who had gone white. He was worried.

An hour later, the place was a hive of activity as the police arrived to assess the scene.

"Hi, I'm Detective Sergeant Mayfield, can you tell us what happened?" said the lead police officer. Two other constables were looking around.

Jez was almost in a trance. "I just came out of the kitchen; I was going to take mother a cup of tea when I heard this bumping noise. I rushed out and found her lying there."

He pointed to his mother's body which was being wrapped in a body bag.

"And that's all you can tell us?"

"Yes, I was in the kitchen when it happened."

"Did she have any medical conditions that you know of?"

"No, although she's not been as sprightly on her feet lately. I noticed she was shuffling about yesterday. You know, not walking as well as normal. She said one of her legs was hurting when I asked her."

"Did you say anything to her?"

"I said if it didn't get any better by Monday, I would take her to the doctor."

Jez put his head in his hands. "If only I'd listened."

Jez was very convincing, and the officer had no reason to doubt his version of events. Photographs were taken of the stairs and surrounds.

Jez was in the kitchen being consoled by the paramedic who had made him another cup of tea.

"Here, I've put some sugar in it; it will help with the shock. Is there anyone I can call, any relatives?"

"No, it's just the two of us, since my father died," said Jez and put his head in his hands. "What am I going to do?"

"I'll get one of the support people from Social Services to visit you tomorrow; they'll be able to help." It didn't really register with Jez.

At the foot of the stairs, Mayfield was surveying the scene.

"Do you want me to call in forensics?" asked one of the team.

"No, I don't think that's necessary," said the D.S. "It looks like an accident. We'll wait for the P.M."

In Minton, by nine-thirty, Sarah was in her dressing gown serving scrambled eggs on toast for her and Adam; she couldn't remember being this happy. It was domestic bliss.

Adam left around ten o'clock. He picked up his jacket from the back of the chair where he had left it the previous evening. Sarah was still in her dressing gown. They embraced, then kissed.

"You better go before I drag you back to bed," said Sarah.

"You're not making it easy," replied Adam who was sliding his hand up the back of her dressing gown and holding her bare bottom.

"No, but I have so much to do today."

"Do you still want to meet up for a drink tonight?"

"Yes, if you don't mind coming over."

"No, that's fine. About seven?"

"Yes, that'll be fine, but I can't offer a stop-over; I need to catch up on my sleep."

"That's ok; I'll need a week to recover," said Adam.

"I hope not that long," said Sarah. She smiled as she opened the door.

It was a grey day, but dry. Sarah watched as Adam got into his car, a metallic-blue BMW, M3. The throaty roar echoed around the terraced houses as he pulled away. He waved to Sarah as he drove by. Sarah was impressed with his choice of vehicle. Although not a total petrol-head, she was interested in cars through her father who was a keen enthusiast; they regularly used to watch Top Gear together. An M3 was very expensive. She thought no more about it and went back inside; she really did have a lot to do.

She showered and changed, cleaned the bathroom, and by eleven-thirty, was ready for a coffee. She took her phone from her bag expecting more messages from Jez; there were no new ones since she last looked. Given the situation, she thought that a bit strange.

She sipped her coffee and considered the right way to tell Jez that it was over. She couldn't do it face-to-face as that would mean him visiting; even a phone call would be traumatic. She considered writing a letter, but he wouldn't receive it until

Tuesday, and she wanted this over and done with as soon as possible. The alternative was text or email.

She opened her laptop and composed an email.

'Dear Jez,

Sorry about last night and thank you for your understanding. I have been doing a great deal of thinking about our relationship, and I feel that we both want different things. I'm not looking for any long-term commitment, and I think it's best that we finish before it gets too serious. Please don't contact me anymore. Thank you for your kindness and the gift you gave me last night which I will, of course, return.

Sarah.'

She was about to press the 'send' button when she heard the "ping" of a text message on her phone. She saw it was from Jez and was in two minds whether to open it or not. Curiosity got the better of her.

'My darling Sarah, sorry I have not been in touch with you this morning. I wanted to see if you were feeling better, but I have some bad news, Mother died this morning. She fell down the stairs. I'm in such a mess I don't know what to do. I wish you could come over; I really need you right now. All my love Jez.'

The message stopped Sarah in her tracks. She was in a quandary. She finished her coffee and sat stroking the cat who was beside her on the sofa.

She suddenly felt desperately sorry for Jez. He'd done nothing wrong; maybe tried too hard, but nothing else. However, she had no romantic feelings towards him anymore; he was just a friend, that's all. She thought about Jez and his neediness; Sarah had no desire to replace his mother. She made a decision.

It was callous, but it had to be done; Jez's day was about to get worse.

She went back to the laptop on the table and clicked 'send'. She expected the fallout shortly.

It started very quickly; first a reply email.

'Dear Sarah,

I've just received your email. I can't believe you mean what you're saying. We have something so special; surely you know that? It must be the pressure of work, and I understand that. I am sure once things settle down, everything will be fine.

I love you with all my heart.

Jez xx'.

Sarah decided to ignore him for now; she had things to do.

Later that afternoon, she checked her emails; there were no new ones. Then she opened her phone. She couldn't believe what she was seeing; twenty-three text messages, all from Jez. She read the first. *'Please don't break my heart.'*

That was enough. She deleted the rest and put a block on all messages and calls from Jez's number. It was going to have to be tough love.

She opened her emails and composed another.

'Dear Jez,

I am sorry that things haven't worked out between us but please do not text me again; I have blocked your number. The truth is I have started seeing someone else. I didn't want to tell you as I knew you would be upset but it's time to move on.

Sarah.'

She pressed 'send'.

The impact of this email on Jez had to be seen to be believed. The physical signs were hyperventilating; then he was sick in the kitchen sink. He lost his balance and had to sit down. He couldn't take it in, but there it was. He read the email again.

Next came anger. He screamed at the top of his voice; the sound echoed around the great hall and up the stairs where his mother had died earlier. He hadn't given her a thought. He walked around the empty house screaming, first just a scream, then abuse. He started talking to himself; "Mother was right, you are a trollop. TROLLOP," he yelled at the top of his voice.

What should he do about it? That was the question. His mother was dead; that was all her fault. "MURDERER," he screamed. Then he just broke down. The sobs were relentless convulsions which shook his body. They went on for over an hour.

Sarah was ready for her date with Adam by six forty-five. She had been surprisingly productive and was feeling upbeat. She found herself singing along to the radio as she completed her housework.

It was only a ten-minute walk to the pub. It was a cold night, so she dressed warmly; jeans, a jumper, a leather jacket and flat shoes. It was a traditional pub close to the railway station; Sarah passed it every day. She walked in and went into the bar area. It was quiet; there was a group of young men in the corner adjacent to a TV screen that was showing re-runs of football matches. She ordered a glass of wine and chose a seat away from the group.

A couple of minutes later, Adam walked in and looked around.

"Over here," called Sarah, and Adam walked over to her.

"Sorry I'm late," he said.

"You're not, I'm just a bit early."

"I'll just get a drink. Don't go away."

"I won't," Sarah replied. She didn't want to be anywhere

else.

Adam returned to the table with a small glass of lager and sat next to Sarah. He turned and kissed her.

"Missed you," he said.

"Missed you too."

"Thanks for last night, it was pretty special," said Adam.

"It certainly was," said Sarah.

They continued chatting, holding hands. A couple of times, Adam leant over and kissed her when no-one was looking.

"I like your car," said Sarah. "How long have you had that?"

"Not long, about four or five months… just before I left the bank."

"Really? They must have been paying you well to afford an M3."

"Not really, I do a spot of investing from time to time; I started when I was down in London. I've got some good contacts. I thought I would treat myself, so I traded in my Nine-Eleven."

"You traded in a Porsche for an M3?"

"Yes, it was ten-years-old."

"Hmm, even still."

"I see you're well up on cars."

"Not really, my Dad was a real F1 fan, some of it rubbed off I guess."

They continued chatting until ten o'clock when Sarah called a halt. "I need to get some sleep, busy day tomorrow."

"Yes, me too, do you fancy lunch tomorrow?"

"I'll text you about eleven and let you know," replied Sarah.

They walked arm in arm to Adam's car.

"This is nice," she said.

"The car?" said Adam

"No; this," and she hugged his arm. He turned and kissed her, and they were locked together for what seemed an eternity.

"Wish I was lying next to you tonight," said Adam

"Yes, so do I but we wouldn't get any sleep."

"That's true."

He got in the car, and Sarah watched him drive out of the car park. She walked back to her house as if she were floating on air.

Jez was up at six o'clock on Monday morning. He sat in the kitchen, hardly aware of his surroundings. Clinicians would say he had Post-Traumatic Stress Disorder, a deep depression that was eating away inside. He had lost his energy and had very little mental capacity; it was as though he was in a fog. He made some tea, but the actions were robotic.

He was looking out of the window. He hadn't bothered to shut the boundary gate after the last of the emergency services had left, and now there was a deer was on the lawn. Normally, he would have chased it away, but instead, he just watched as it mooched around the grass looking for edible treats, so graceful, so innocent.

He eventually went upstairs to change; he hadn't bothered to shower or shave; what was the point?

At eight-thirty, there was a caller. Jez was in his office staring at the fish in the aquarium. The bell in the great hall rang for the second time. As he descended the staircase, he could visualise his mother rolling down in front of him and her body crumpled at the bottom. He shivered momentarily before the third ring of the bell made him re-focus, and he went to the front door.

He squinted in the pale daylight; there was no recognition.

"Jez Steadman?"

"Yes," said Jez.

"I've called for my laptop; you've had it over three weeks, and you've ignored my calls and emails. I've found a more reliable technician."

"Oh, I see. What name is it?"

"Lever, Shaun Lever."

"Wait here," said Jez and closed the door leaving the man on the doorstep.

Jez trudged upstairs into his office and looked through the pile of laptops and computer towers awaiting attention. They were all labelled, usually in alphabetical order with the date received and date completed on them. His filing system had failed in recent days. "Lever, Lever, Lever," Jez repeated as if trying to process the information. "Ah, here it is. One crap laptop, Mr Lever."

Jez shuffled back down the stairs opened the front door and threw the laptop at the waiting client. The man moved to one side, more by instinct, and the computer crashed onto the pebbled drive. Jez shut the door.

There were more frantic rings of the doorbell, but Jez ignored them and went back to his den and his fish.

At ten o'clock, another car parked in front of the house. It was Mrs Dawson. She let herself in and called out. "Jeremy? Are you here?"

Mrs Dawson went into the kitchen and came out again. Jez stood at the top of the stairs. She physically jumped with shock.

"Holy Mother of God, Jeremy, you gave me such a shock. What are you doing? Are you alright? Come down; I'll make us a coffee."

Mrs Dawson went back into the kitchen and started to boil

the kettle.

Jez appeared in the doorway and looked like a zombie.

"Jeremy, are you alright? Here; come and sit down. I heard about your mother; it's all around the village. I am so sorry. Is there anything I can get you?"

"No, no I'm ok, thanks."

"Well, you don't look ok. Have you eaten anything?"

"I'm not hungry," said Jez.

"Look, I know it must have been a shock, but you must look after yourself. Would you like me to make you an omelette or something?"

"No, I'm fine," said Jez.

Mrs Dawson made the coffee, handed Jez a mug then sat down opposite him at the kitchen table.

"So, come on, tell me what happened?"

"Eh?"

"Your mother, they say she fell down the stairs."

"Oh. Yes, it was awful; she just went over and over and over, like somersaults, you know?"

"Really? Then what happened?"

"I went to see if she was ok, but she was all limp; her head was hanging to one side."

"How awful."

"Yes, it was terrible."

"What did you do?"

"I just held her; then I called the ambulance."

Jez was in a trance-like state. Mrs Dawson was watching with growing concern.

"I think you should see a doctor Jeremy; the shock's upset you."

"I'm ok, I'm ok," said Jez.

Another ring echoed around the hall. Mrs Dawson got up from her chair. "I'll get it; you stay here."

The daily opened the door. It was a matronly figure in a coat and glasses. A Fiat Punto was parked next to Mrs Dawson's car.

"Hello, I'm looking for Jeremy Steadman. I'm Jessica Slater, Social Services." She produced ID; the photograph was at least ten-years-old and bore little resemblance to the presenter.

"You better come in," said Mrs Dawson.

She whispered as they walked through the hall towards the kitchen. "Am I glad to see you, I'm really worried about Jeremy. Come through; we're in the kitchen. Would you like a coffee?"

"Yes, please," said the visitor.

Jez was still at the kitchen table with his head in his hands.

"Jeremy, this lady is from Social Services," said Mrs Dawson.

"Hello Jeremy, my name's Jessica, I understand you had a bereavement yesterday. I'm from Social Services, and I'm here to help."

"I don't need any help. I'm fine," retorted Jez. "I just want to be left alone."

"Yes, I know you do, but there are some formalities we need to see to, and I can help you. You probably don't feel like it. I can understand that."

Jez looked at the woman and started sobbing.

"It's ok; it's fine to feel like this when you've lost a loved one. It was just you and your Mum, was it?"

"Yes," said Jez, who had buried his head in his hands again.

"Ok, now here's what we're going to do. The lady here… sorry I don't know your name…"

"Mrs Dawson; Ivy Dawson."

"Ivy will make us a nice strong cup of tea with some sugar. I want you to drink that while I explain what you need to do."

Jez looked at the woman; practical, straightforward, just what he needed to get him out of the free-fall of moroseness.

She left him for a moment and went to talk to the daily. "He's in a bad way," she whispered. "It's the shock. I'm going to talk to him, but we may need to call a doctor."

"Yes, ok," said Mrs Dawson and continued the tea-making.

"It's a lovely house. How long have you lived here?"

Jez looked at the woman, he spoke slowly. "I was born here… I moved out when I went to University; then I worked in London for a while... then I came back when my father died."

"So, you've been looking after your mum since?"

"More his mum looking after him, eh, Jeremy," chirped Mrs Dawson, still attending the kettle, trying to bring some levity to the situation.

Jez looked at her and smiled. "Yeah, that's probably right."

"Now, there are some things you will need to do. Did your mum make a will?"

"Yeah… I can't remember… I think so… It will be with the solicitor."

"Good, do you know the name?" said Jessica.

"Yeah… It's… Hugo Burton… he's in Skipton, er… Blunt Smythe." Jez was slurring his words as if he were drunk. His head was now in his hands and he was speaking through his fingers.

"Ok, I will call him for you in a minute. What about registering the death?"

"Eh…? I don't know; I have no idea… They said something about a post-mortem."

"Who said?"

"The police… Who do you think?"

"No need to be rude, Jeremy, she's only trying to help," said Mrs Dawson as she brought over the tea.

"It's ok, I'll speak to them and see what's happening. Don't worry Jeremy, I'll see to it."

Jez looked at the woman. "Sorry… Thank you," he said.

"Look, why don't you take a shower and tidy yourself up a bit; you'll feel much better, then we can work out what needs to be done. I'll call your solicitor."

Jez finished his tea; he seemed more alert following the social worker's intervention. "Yeah, ok, thanks," he said and limped upstairs. The pain in his shoulder had returned; in fact, he ached all over.

"Hmm, I don't like the look of him; he looks like he's still in shock," said Ms Slater. "I think he should see a doctor in any event."

"I don't think he's right to drive," said Mrs Dawson.

"No, you're probably right. Do you know which surgery they use?"

"Well, Mrs Steadman always went to the one in the village. Don't know about Jeremy."

"I'll give them a call. Do you know the number by any chance?"

"Yes, it's the one I use, but I don't think they do house calls."

"Oh, yes they will," said the woman. "I can be very persuasive."

Chapter Thirteen

Sure enough, the social worker's influencing skills did the job, and a doctor would call after morning surgery.

Jez came downstairs feeling slightly more refreshed but looking dreadful.

"Do you want another drink, Jeremy? I think you should eat something too. Let me do you some toast."

"Yes, ok," said Jez.

"How are you feeling?" asked Jessica.

"Tired," replied Jez.

"Well, I've asked the doctor to call and check you over; I think you're still suffering from shock."

"You didn't have to do that; I'm fine, honest."

"It won't hurt to get you checked over. He'll give you something to help you. Don't worry; I see it all the time. Kids dying is the worst, tragic some of them. Just last week…"

"I think we can dispense with the details, thank you," interrupted Mrs Dawson.

"Oh, right, yes, of course," said Ms Slater. "I've just spoken to Mr Burton, your solicitor; what a nice man, he said he would call this afternoon about four-thirty."

"Thank you," said Jez.

"Here you are," said Mrs Dawson, presenting Jez with a plate of toast. "Here's some Marmite, too. I know you like that," she added, passing him the jar.

"Well, I'll be off then," said the social worker. "I'll call again tomorrow, see how you're getting on… I'll leave my card; it's got my mobile number on it. You can call me any time."

"Thank you," said Jez.

Mrs Dawson saw Jessica to the door. "Are you staying for a

while?" asked Jessica.

"Yes, I don't finish until four."

"Good; I don't think he should be left on his own at the moment."

"No, I agree, although he'll be on his own after I've left."

"Hopefully the doctor will give him something to sleep."

"I'll leave him a meal before I go, that'll help."

"Yes, I'm sure it will. He's lucky to have you."

"I've been with the family a long time. I still can't get over it. Mrs Steadman seemed right as rain Friday when I left."

"Well, these things happen."

"Suppose," said Mrs Dawson, and the woman left.

"Thanks for the toast, Mrs D. I think I'm going to have a lie-down," said Jez as the daily returned to the kitchen

"Right you are, Jeremy. I'll get on; I won't disturb you."

An hour later, there was another ring on the doorbell. Mrs Dawson answered.

"Hello. I'm D.S. Mayfield, North Yorkshire Police. Can I speak to Mr Steadman, please?"

"You better come in," said Mrs Dawson. "Come through, would you like a drink; tea, coffee?"

"No, I'm fine thanks."

"Jeremy's asleep; he's still in shock, you should see the state of him. We've had to call the doctor."

"Sorry to hear that; and you are?"

"Mrs Dawson, Ivy, the housekeeper."

"I see, do you mind if I ask you a few questions?" He took out a notebook.

"No, of course not; have a seat. Are you sure I can't get you a drink?"

"No, I'm fine thanks."

They both sat down at the kitchen table.

"So, how long have you worked for the Steadmans?"

"Twenty years, going on."

"I see; so you would have a good idea about the relationships in the house?"

"Oh, I'd say. The stories I could tell you," she said, before realising what she had said.

"Go on," encouraged the officer.

"Well, Mrs Steadman and Mr Steadman senior were always rowing; when he was here, that is, which wasn't very often."

"And he's dead I understand?"

"Yes, must be three years since; heart attack, poor thing. Mind you; he was a one for the ladies. It was his downfall in the end."

"Oh? In what way?"

"Died on the job, if you know what I'm saying, according to the rumours anyway."

"I see. What about Jeremy? How long has he lived here?"

"He was born here, then worked away, and then he came back just after his dad died to look after his mother, or so he said. Mind you; I think it was the other way around. I was just telling the social worker."

"What was their relationship like?"

"Hmm, a bit up and down. He's got a new girlfriend, and his mum wasn't happy. They argued about it."

"What, recently?"

"Yes, the last week or so I suppose. She didn't approve."

"I see." The officer was writing everything in his notebook.

"What about yesterday? Did Jeremy say what happened?"

"Only that she fell down the stairs. Sounded terrible, did

somersaults she did, so he said."

"Somersaults? Are you sure? He told you she did somersaults?"

"That's what he said this morning. Mind you; he was in a right bad way; didn't know half of what he was saying. It's hit him hard; I've not seen him like this before. He's a bright lad, and usually very polite."

"I would like to speak to him again. When would be a good time?"

"Hmm, I don't know. The doctor's supposed to be here around twelve; not sure what he'll say. Why don't you pop by tomorrow?"

"Yes, ok; I'll do that," said the officer and he got up and left.

Sarah had arrived at her desk at seven-thirty as usual, buzzing with energy and ideas, blissfully unaware of the problems in Deighton. She had checked her emails and messages on the train; there were none from Jez. It seemed her 'tough-love' approach had worked. There was one from Adam that read, *'Miss you, xx'*, and she sighed. She replied, *'Me too xx'*.

As she tried to manage her emails and correspondence, her mind kept returning to Saturday night which she would never forget as long as she lived. Today was the start of a new chapter in her life; she was convinced. She checked her diary; there was a team meeting at nine, and she was seeing clients at eleven. It was another busy day. Before that though, she needed to speak to Michelle to confirm her appointment as a senior buyer.

Michelle was over the moon. "I must buy some cakes," she said when told the news.

At ten-thirty, Sarah checked her messages, and there was another from Adam. *'Free for lunch?'*.

Sarah replied. *'Can we make it 1? - have clients this morning'*.

'Perfect, see you at 1', came the reply.

Sarah was putting her phone away in her handbag when Michelle knocked on her door and presented her with a chocolate profiterole and a paper tissue. "Gets a bit messy," said Michelle.

"Bang goes the diet," said Sarah and took a bite. "Can we have a chat tomorrow morning; there are one or two issues I need to discuss with you?"

"Yes, what time?"

"Eight o'clock?"

"Yes, right, ok." Michelle was not usually in before eight-thirty, and her body language reflected her annoyance. Sarah detected it straight away.

"Welcome to senior management," said Sarah and smiled.

Sarah's excursions at lunchtime had not gone unnoticed by her team; she was not usually one for taking a full lunch break, but it was becoming a regular event over the last few days. Michelle often interrupted Sarah's break with queries.

Adam was waiting for Sarah on the ground floor.

"Hi, you look great," he said as she exited the lift.

"Thanks. Better not stand too close; you don't know who's watching."

As it happened, someone was watching, but not deliberately. Michelle just happened to be walking towards the lift. The couple's body language as they walked from the store was a giveaway. That was going to rev-up the gossip machine; it would be all over the Admin department by the end of the day. Cressida Bolton would take a particular interest.

Over lunch, Sarah and Adam swapped stories of the morning

and surreptitiously held hands.

"Can't wait until Friday," said Adam.

"No, me neither."

"Do you want to stay at mine?"

Sarah replied, without hesitation. "Yes, I'd love to, I'll need to get back on Saturday morning to feed the cat though."

"That's fine, no problem. I can set the alarm."

"Not that early!" They both laughed.

"How did your meeting go?"

"Yes, it was fine. Had a client meeting this morning, it was another outside the policy formula, but I managed to negotiate a reduction. Still not quite in line, but better than it was."

"Well done, Sir Basil will be pleased."

"Hmm, there's a long way to go yet. Have you heard anything about the new Sales and Marketing person? They were interviewing today."

"No, although I did see someone waiting outside Sir Basil's office, looked as though she was going to a party the way she was dressed."

"Really? Now that's interesting," said Sarah.

They continued chatting over their sandwiches, then reluctantly walked back to the store together at just before two.

Later that afternoon, Sarah received a call from Cressida. "Hi Sarah, Sir Basil would like to see you."

"Oh, hi Cressida, what time?"

"Now," replied the PA.

"Ok, I'll be there in a couple of minutes."

Sarah took the stairs to the seventh floor. Cressida was waiting for her. "Take a seat; he won't be a moment," she said in her usual officious manner.

Cressida looked around to make sure nobody was in hearing

range.

"What's this about you and the hunk?"

"What do you mean?"

"You and Adam Fowler. Don't worry; your secret's safe with me."

"I don't know what you mean?"

"Oh, don't play all innocent. Your lunchtime trysts, you were seen."

"Trysts, what are you talking about? That's complete nonsense; we've been discussing compliance issues away from the office."

"Hmm, well that's not the rumour."

"Well, that's tough," said Sarah, and she took the seat looking suitably affronted.

Cressida's telephone extension rang.

"Sir Basil will see you now," she said with an even greater air of superiority.

Sarah opened the door and walked to the seat in front of the Chairman's desk.

"Ah, Sarah, please sit down. Just wanted to tell you we've appointed the new Head of Sales and Marketing."

"Oh, that's great news; when are they starting?"

"Wednesday, all being well. She's been on a sabbatical, so she doesn't have to work any notice."

"I look forward to meeting her," said Sarah. "What's her name?"

"Tilly," He looked down on a notepad. "Er... Wiseman. Bright girl, she'll bring a new look to the position that's for sure. How are things on the procurement side?"

"Good; I've managed to renegotiate several existing contracts, and over the year we should start seeing better margins."

"Very good, very good," said Sir Basil. "Right, that's all."

"Thank you, Sir Basil," said Sarah. She got up and left. As she walked past Cressida, she gave her a suitable scowl.

Back at her desk, she texted Adam.

'Gossip's started. May have to reconsider lunchtime arrangements. We were spotted.'

The reply came back almost immediately.

'Why should we? Let them talk, got nothing to hide'.

'Yes, you're right, sod them!'

'Ha, ha'.

Later, over her afternoon coffee, Sarah checked LinkedIn to get more information on the new Head of Sales and Marketing. It made impressive reading; her last appointment was as Sales Director with a well-known store chain in London. She left six months ago and had been on a sabbatical since.

Back in Deighton, Jez was up around midday, but he was still far from well.

"Hello, Jeremy, are you feeling a bit better after your sleep?" said Mrs Dawson.

"I'm ok. Who were you talking to earlier? I thought I heard voices."

"It was the police; they wanted to ask you a few questions."

"What did you say to them?" His tone was aggressive.

"What? Nothing. I said you were asleep. They're calling back tomorrow."

"Oh, right, ok," said Jez, more contrite.

"Would you like some tea or coffee. I'll do some lunch after the doctor's been."

"Just a coffee, thanks."

Jez was in the sitting room when the doctor called at around twelve-thirty.

"Ah, Doctor Davies," said Mrs Dawson as she answered the door. "I'm so glad you were able to call. It's Jeremy."

"Yes, I understand there's been a bereavement."

"Yes, Mrs Steadman; she died yesterday. An accident; fell down the stairs. He's taken it quite badly. They were very close, you know."

"Yes, I recall. Where is he?"

"I'll take you through; he's in the sitting room."

"Can I get you a drink, doctor?" asked Mrs Dawson, as they walked through the hall.

"No, thanks, had one before I left the surgery. I'll just have a look at Jeremy."

The doctor was carrying a Gladstone bag with the bits and pieces he would need for a house call. He entered the sitting room.

Jez was seated in one of the armchairs, staring out of the window seemingly oblivious to the new arrival.

"Jeremy, it's Doctor Davies. He's here to see if you're ok," said the daily. She turned to the doctor. "I'll leave you to it, then," she said and went upstairs to clean the bedrooms.

"Hello, Jeremy, sorry to hear about your mother."

"Thanks," said Jez. His eyes were glazed.

"Right; let's have a look at you."

The medic examined Jez for twenty minutes then gave his verdict.

"I think you're severely depressed, Jeremy. I'm going to prescribe some tablets which will calm things down, and a spot of counselling wouldn't hurt too. Mrs Dawson tells me Social Services have sent someone?"

"Yes. She was very helpful."

"Have you got someone to stay with you?" asked the doctor.

"No, my girlfriend's away at the moment," said Jez.

"I see. What about relatives? Is there anyone you can call?"

"No, there's nobody," said Jez.

"Well, once you start taking the tablets you'll start to feel much better. I'll go and speak to Mrs Dawson."

The housekeeper was vacuuming the carpet at the top of the stairs and saw the doctor leave the sitting room. She turned off the machine and went downstairs.

"I'm off now," said the doctor. "But I'll call again tomorrow; he's clearly very fragile."

"Thank you, doctor," said Mrs Dawson.

"I'll leave a prescription. Is there anyone who can pick it up for him? I don't think he should drive just yet."

"Yes, I'll pop out after lunch," said Mrs Dawson.

"Thank you, and if he deteriorates any further, ring an ambulance."

"Oh, right. You think it's that bad?"

"No, I don't think so, but people deal with bereavement in different ways. Just keep an eye on him, I'll call again the same time tomorrow."

"Right, thank you," said Mrs Dawson and walked the doctor to the door. He handed her the prescription for the drugs.

"He mentioned that his girlfriend's away at the moment. Is there any way of contacting her?"

"I don't know," said Mrs Dawson. "He's not said anything about her to me. She's not been to the house as far as I know."

"Oh, ok," said the doctor and left.

Mrs Dawson went back to the sitting room where Jez was still looking out of the window.

"I'll do a sandwich now and then get your prescription." Jez didn't respond. "Did you hear me, Jeremy?"

He turned and looked at her. "Yes, ok."

Mrs Dawson duly collected the prescription, and under her watchful eye, Jez took two tablets. It was three o'clock, and Jez was back in his room sleeping when there was another caller.

"Is Mr Steadman here?"

"He's asleep," said Mrs Dawson. She could see the police car parked next to hers.

"I'm P.C. Greenwood, I understand there was an altercation earlier. We've had a complaint about an alleged assault."

"Oh, I wouldn't think so for one minute. He's not like that."

"Something about a laptop computer?"

"I don't know anything about that. His mother died yesterday, so he's not in a good way. The doctor's just been and given him some drugs. One of your people was here earlier; Sergeant Mayfield, I think, a detective."

"Yes, I know him."

"I'm sure he'll sort things out. I don't want to disturb Jeremy at the moment."

"Ok, can you tell him I called…? I may call back tomorrow."

"Yes, I will," said Mrs Dawson. The officer returned to his car, made some notes and left.

Later, Mrs Dawson took Jez a cup of tea. She tapped on his bedroom door.

"Jeremy, I've bought you some tea. Your solicitor will be here shortly; only I need to get back and put Ronald's dinner on."

There was a noise from the bedroom, then footsteps. He appeared at the door looking pale and drawn.

"Thanks, I'll just wash my face. I'll be down in a minute."

After freshening up, he went to the kitchen where Mrs Dawson was finishing off.

"I've put your tea on the table, and there's some dinner for you in the fridge; it'll only need heating up."

Jez ran his hands down his face trying to get the blood flowing. "Thanks for that, and for everything you've done today."

"That's ok. We'll soon have you back to your old self. Your Mum wouldn't have wanted you moping about. Anyway, I'd better go, my hubby will be wondering where I am. Oh, I nearly forgot, another policeman called; something about an assault. He said he might call back again."

Jez put his head in his hands. "Hmm, don't worry; I'll sort it."

He escorted the daily to the front door. "Now, you take care of yourself, Jeremy. I'll be here at the usual time tomorrow, but if you need anything fetching from the village, leave me a message, and I'll pick it up for you."

"Thanks," said Jez and watched Mrs Dawson drive away.

He felt more refreshed after his rest and was starting to think more clearly. He checked the time; nearly four-thirty. He wondered what Sarah was doing now; another hour and she would be leaving work.

At North Yorkshire Police Headquarters, D.S. Mayfield was having a case meeting with his boss, Superintendent Joe Phillips.

"I've got an update on that death in Deighton, yesterday," said Mayfield. "Preliminary Post Mortem's in, and there's nothing suspicious. Injuries 'consistent with a fall', the cause of death is a broken neck."

"An accident then?" said Phillips.

"Yeah, looks like it. Although, I had a chat with the housekeeper this morning and she said something rather strange. Apparently, the son told her that his mother was doing somersaults as she came down the stairs."

"Well, if she fell from the top that would be more than likely," said the Superintendent.

"Yes, but he told me yesterday he was in the kitchen and didn't see her fall. Just seemed a bit odd, that's all."

"Hmm, well with no forensics and nothing from the P.M. I don't think it's worth pursuing unless you feel strongly about it."

"No, not really. He was certainly in a bad way when I saw him."

"Guilt?"

"Possibly. I guess we'll never know. Anyway, I'll close the case, no point in dragging it out; we'll go with an accident. I'll speak to the coroner's office tomorrow and let them know we're not pursuing it."

There was a crunching of gravel at Deighton Hall just after four-thirty, heralding the arrival of Hugo Burton of Blunt Smythe solicitors. Jez was in the sitting room, staring out of the window when he saw the Audi Q7 coming up the drive. He went to the front door and greeted the man before he could ring the bell.

Jez sort of recognised him; he vaguely remembered the solicitor being around about the time his father died; he had called on a couple of occasions. A tall, slim man, greying dark hair, dressed in a smart suit and carrying a briefcase; he was in his fifties but looked older.

"Jeremy, good to see you again. Very sorry about the circumstances, my condolences on your loss," said the man and extended his hand.

"Thanks," said Jez. "You'd better come in. Would you like some tea?"

Jez was functioning much better after his rest and the first dose of drugs; not, by any means, back to his usual self but at least able to converse more coherently.

"Yes, tea would be nice; two sugars please."

Jez led the man to the kitchen and started making the tea.

"I was so sad to hear about your mother, and in such tragic circumstances too," said the solicitor, making himself comfortable at the kitchen table.

"Yes," said Jez. "I was in the kitchen and heard a noise; when I came out, there she was at the bottom of the stairs."

"That's awful."

"Yes," said Jez and presented the solicitor with a mug of tea.

"Thanks. Well, I'll get straight to the point. I have your mother's will and have been going through a few formalities this morning. If you can let me have the death certificate, I'll get it registered for you. Have you done anything about the funeral?"

"No, not yet. I haven't been able to think about it. The police were here earlier, but I've not heard anything more."

"Yes, there will need to be a post-mortem. Nothing to worry about, standard practice. Once that's been taken care of, the Coroner will release your mother's body for the funeral. Again, we can help with all the arrangements; your mother gave some instructions in her will. She doesn't want to be buried anywhere near your father. She was quite adamant about that.

My advice would be to go for a cremation; it will be a lot more straightforward."

"Yes, whatever you think," said Jez.

"Regarding the will, did your mother ever discuss her finances with you?"

"No, not really, she paid the household bills for the Hall from her investments, but she was always careful with money, I know that. I gave her rent and paid the electricity and internet bills."

"Hmm, well there're a few bequests, but otherwise, everything is left to you, including Deighton Hall. However, your mother's portfolio took a big hit in the banking crisis in 2008, and I'm afraid there's not a great deal of capital left. After payments, it's unlikely there will be enough to cover the Inheritance Tax liability."

"What are you saying?"

"Well, not to put too fine a point on it, you're going to have to sell Deighton Hall unless you can raise money from elsewhere."

Jez sat for a moment trying to register this information. "How much? Do you know?"

"Not off the top of my head; I'll need to speak to our tax specialists."

"How long will it be before I have to leave?"

"Oh, not for some time. It will take several months, maybe a year, to wind up the Estate."

Jez sat there with his head in his hands trying to process the information, but his brain was finding it difficult.

"Are you alright, Jeremy?"

Jez looked up. "Yes, I'm ok; it's all been a lot to take in."

"Would you like me to call in tomorrow?"

"Yes, if that's ok."

"Ok, I'll call in about the same time. In the meantime, I'll speak to the Coroner's office and see what's happening."

"Yes, thanks," said Jez and led the solicitor to the front door.

Jez watched the Audi as it slowly went down the drive. He checked his watch, five-thirty; Sarah would be catching her train now.

He went back into the kitchen and looked around; the place suddenly felt very empty, but he had things to do.

He went back upstairs and started up his computers. He ignored the many emails from clients chasing their laptop repairs and found Sarah's last email which he read again. He could feel the physical pain. 'Started seeing someone else', he read it again and again. Someone had turned her head, but who?

He hacked into Sarah's Facebook account, but there was nothing on there; she hadn't posted in some time. He checked LinkedIn for any recent additions. There was only one, Adam Fowler. Jez checked his background; he also worked at Huntsman's; a compliance manager, it said. He downloaded the profile picture, enlarged it as far as he could before the image was unrecognisable, and printed a copy. He read the narrative; hobbies included playing rugby with Meanwood RFC, travelling and sport. This could be the one, he thought, but he would need to investigate further. He suddenly had a purpose and focus; his mind became clearer and sharper; his motivation had returned.

He checked the other common social media sites. He couldn't find a Facebook profile, but there was something on Instagram, some pictures of a trip to Costa Rica a few months earlier, nothing more recent. There was one picture of Adam with a young lady who looked local judging by her complexion and hair colour. They were close; he had his arms around her; now, that was interesting. Maybe it wasn't him; perhaps it was just a coincidence. More research was going to be required.

By eight o'clock, he was starting to feel hungry; he'd hardly eaten anything all day. He went down to the kitchen, found the meal Mrs Dawson had left him and put it in the microwave. He consumed the food, and put the dishes in the dishwasher, then returned to his den.

The rest of the evening was spent on the Huntsman's Intranet website trying to get more details on Adam Fowler. He'd accessed Adam's internal account, but it was all business related, and there was nothing which would confirm his association with Sarah.

It was midnight before the need to sleep got the better of him.

Jez didn't sleep well after the initial exhaustion. By three a.m., he was wide awake again, consumed by jealousy, anger, resentment, hate; vicious emotions which were slowly driving him crazy. The house was empty, but somehow, he could sense his mother's presence. He could hear her words echoing around his room; *"told you so, told you so, she's nothing but a trollop; told you so,"* like the playground taunts of bullies. He put his hands to his ears to stop the mocking. He went to the window and opened the curtain. Rain spattered the windows as he stared out at the total blackness of the night.

He needed a plan. His priority was to get her back; she'd made a terrible mistake, she would soon realise that. If only he could make her see. Maybe if he could talk to her again, she would realise that what they had was special. Yes, he would convince her, but how to arrange such a meeting? He couldn't just turn up at her house; she would turn him away, and what if the 'someone else' was there? Jez buried his head in his hands.

There was only one thing for it; a trip to Leeds was going to be required.

It was ten o'clock on Tuesday morning, and Jez was eating cereal in the kitchen. His head was still heavy from lack of sleep. His mind was still on Sarah; she would be at work by now. He wondered if it was still as hectic.

He heard the door open, and Mrs Dawson walked in. "Hello, Jeremy," she called, expecting him to be upstairs She walked into the kitchen.

"Hello," he said as Mrs Dawson entered. She nearly jumped out of her skin.

"Oh, Jeremy, you gave me such a fright, you did. How are you?"

"Feeling much better today, thanks," he replied. "Here, let me help you with that." He picked up a bag of potatoes she was carrying.

"Did you get any sleep?"

"Yes, some."

"It'll be those tablets; the doctor said they would knock you out."

"Speaking of the doctor, can you ring the surgery for me and cancel the appointment. You can tell them I'm feeling much better, thanks. I need to pop into Leeds later."

"Yes, ok, if you're sure. What do you need to go all that way for?"

"Just some business, I'll be back this afternoon."

"Yes, ok, what time will you be going? I can do you some lunch."

"It's ok thanks. I'm leaving around eleven. I'll catch a train in, save driving."

"Good idea, you don't want to be driving too far after what you've been through. Have you thought about what you're going to do with your mother's things?"

"No, I haven't, as it happens."

"Well, I can take care of that for you if you like."

"Yes, ok. Help yourself to anything you want; it's no good to me."

"Oh, that's very kind of you. I'll tell you what; I'll get our Sophie over here tomorrow she can give me a hand. You don't mind, do you?"

"No, of course not. I don't think I've met Sophie."

"No, she used to come with me when she was off school sometimes, but that was before you came back. It's been some time. She's got a family of her own now, lives in a nice terrace in Skipton."

"Oh, right… Yes, that'll be fine," said Jez.

A few minutes later, Jessica, the Social Services counsellor arrived and was amazed to see Jez's recovery.

"You look so much better, Jeremy. How are you feeling?"

"Yes, good, thank you, and thank you for yesterday. Everything was a bit of a shock."

"Yes, I'm sure it was. What about the arrangements for the funeral?"

"My solicitor's going to deal with all that as soon as the Coroner's finished; it'll be a cremation. Don't know when."

"You must let me know," interrupted Mrs Dawson. "I'll want to be there."

"Yes, of course. Well, if you'll excuse me, things to do," said Jez.

"You've got my phone number if you need to contact me

anytime," said the social worker as Jez walked up the stairs.

Jez turned. "Yes, I have, but I'm fine now thanks."

Jessica looked at Mrs Dawson. "Well, I don't think I'm needed here. He seems to have made a remarkable recovery. I didn't like the look of him yesterday."

"I reckon it was those tablets the doctor gave him; our Sophie swears by them when she gets depressed," said Mrs Dawson as she escorted Jessica to the front door.

Jez meanwhile was focussed entirely on his latest mission; he needed to speak to Sarah. He clearly couldn't message her; she wasn't replying, but she usually popped out at lunchtime, he recalled from their conversations. He would wait for her and invite her for a coffee.

The identity of the 'someone else' was not, for the moment, a priority.

Just before eleven o'clock, Jez came down the stairs dressed in his leather jacket. He went into the kitchen to see Mrs Dawson.

"I'm off now, back around three, I expect."

"What if anyone calls?" asked the daily.

"Tell them to call back later."

He left the house and took the car into town; he would park at the station, then catch the train into Leeds for the thirty-five-minute journey.

The city was buzzing as he arrived at Leeds station; the shops and cafes packed with office workers on their lunchtime break. He walked towards the store and went inside. The doorman, Clarke, opened the door for him. Jez was in the cosmetic department; he would wait around pretending to view the items on sale; there was a good view of the lift.

Chapter Fourteen

After twenty minutes, Jez's behaviour in the cosmetics department was starting to attract attention. One of the security guards was keeping a watchful eye as Jez picked up merchandise while staring at the lift, then returned the item to the shelf. A couple of assistants had already asked him if he needed any help.

The elevator was busy with customers and staff exiting from the administrative floors. At just after twelve-thirty, the lift arrived, and among the group, there was a rugged-looking man with dark wavy hair and a semblance of a beard; he was smartly dressed in a suit with an open neck. Instead of heading outside, he waited by the lift; he looked familiar. Jez moved as close as he dared behind a perfume display, then squinted to get a better look. It was him, Adam Fowler; he was sure. The lift emptied another couple of times, and then Sarah appeared. She looked beautiful. Jez watched as she smiled at the man, a loving smile; they touched hands briefly. Jez almost slumped to his knees, but quickly recovered. One of the security guys approached him.

"Are you alright sir?" he said with a concerned look.

"Yes, sorry; I just need some air."

Jez pushed passed the security man and went out on to the street. He looked at the crowded precinct, left and right then left again, then he saw them disappear into a coffee shop. He didn't know what to do; he'd not considered this eventuality. The sight of Sarah with the man was like a blow below the midriff. It had taken the wind out of him. His hands were shaking, and he started to hyperventilate. One or two shoppers noticed him and started staring. He ignored them and walked towards the café. He had to be careful; he couldn't afford to be seen.

This part of the city was littered with coffee shops, and there was one on the other side of the pedestrianised area. He turned and put his collar up, then walked in that direction.

As with most eating places at this time of day, it was quite full, but he managed to get a coffee and a seat with a view of the café where Sarah and Adam were. He didn't take his eye off the place for one minute in case Sarah left.

His breathing gradually steadied, but his head was all over the place. The anger and hate he'd experienced the previous night had returned.

It was the helplessness, the total lack of control of the situation; his idea of talking Sarah into seeing sense had been blown out of the window. He had to do something.

For the next fifty minutes, he sat staring across at the café where Sarah and Adam were enjoying their lunch. Jez felt sick; every mouthful of coffee caused nausea; in the end, he left it.

Just before one-thirty, he noticed Sarah at the door of the café putting on her coat; her companion chivalrously helping her. Jez quickly left his coffee shop and moved closer to get a better view. There were too many people for Sarah to notice him. Jez wasn't prepared for what happened next. Sarah looked around, then leant up and kissed him.

That was just too much. Jez turned and walked back to the station, the pain almost unbearable.

Jez had no recollection of the journey back to Deighton; his mind was mush. He drove up to the Hall and was surprised to see a police car parked outside the main entrance.

He walked inside and was greeted by Mrs Dawson.

"Hello Jeremy, Sergeant Mayfield's here again. I said you wouldn't be long; he's in the sitting room; he said he would wait."

Jez was trying to get his head together. "Hello," he said walking into the sitting room. The officer, seated on one of the sofas, was looking at his notebook; a mug of tea had been placed on the coffee table next to him. He stood up as Jez entered.

"Hello Jeremy, I shan't keep you long. Hope you're feeling better today."

"Yes, much better, thanks," responded Jez, hoping the lie wouldn't show.

"I just wanted to let you know that we're not making any further investigations into your mother's death. We've advised the Coroner that as far as the police are concerned it was an accident and you'll be able to make the funeral arrangements."

"Oh, that's good news. I'll let the solicitor know; he's calling by later."

"There was one other thing. We've had a complaint about a laptop, one of my colleagues called yesterday about it."

"Really, I don't know why you've been involved. Is this Mr Lever?"

"Yes."

"Hmm, he's always complaining, thinks you can repair laptops just like that." Jez snapped his fingers.

"Mr Lever claims you threw a computer at him and then assaulted him."

"That's nonsense, I gave him the laptop, and he dropped it. Then I shut the door. I don't know why he would say I threw it at him."

"That's not what he's saying."

"Then I don't know what I can say. I'm sorry, but things have not been too good for me over the last couple of days. What do you want me to do?"

"Ok, nothing, for now, leave it with me."

"Thanks," said Jez.

The officer got up, and Jez escorted him to the front entrance and watched as he drove away.

"Would you like a cup of tea, Jeremy?" said Mrs Dawson, as Jez walked into the kitchen.

"Yes, please. Thank you."

"How did you're meeting go?"

"Eh, what? Oh, ok, you know. I'm going to my room."

"Ok, I'll bring your tea."

"Thanks," said Jez.

Jez switched on his computer. Having confirmed the identity of the 'someone else', the next question was, what he was going to do about it; he needed to do something. Somehow, he had to convince Sarah that she had made a big mistake.

He logged-on to Adam's social media sites again. He checked LinkedIn and accessed his profile; it seemed to have been updated fairly recently. 'A member of Meanwood RFC', he noticed. He went to the club's website and, sure enough, there were team pictures featuring Adam, some only a few weeks old. He clicked on the tabs for the various sections; fixtures, results, teams, social events. He checked the fixtures list; the next 'home' match was this coming Saturday; Jez made a note. Then he read the sports and social section; this Friday; 'Awards night and disco'. He had noticed there was a LinkedIn post saying that Adam would be there; Jez assumed Sarah would be as well. He started sweating again, but then calmed himself.

There was a knock on the door which caused Jez to jump.

"Jeremy, I've brought your tea." Mrs Dawson knocked again and entered Jez's den.

"Thanks," said Jez as the daily handed him the mug.

"I'll be off in a minute. Don't forget your solicitor will be here later. Oh, and I've done you a bit of tea, macaroni cheese; I know you like that. It's in the fridge; it just needs heating up."

"Ok, thanks."

"And, it's ok if I bring Sophie tomorrow to clear your Mum's stuff?"

"Yes, that's fine," said Jez, taking his first sip but hardly registering the question.

"Thank you so much. It's hard being a single mum these days. Boyfriend cleared off as soon as the baby was on the way. Still, you do what you can for them don't you?"

"Yes, I guess," said Jez and turned to his computer to continue his research.

Jez didn't notice Mrs Dawson leave, but he did hear the door chime at four forty-five when his solicitor arrived.

Jez answered the door and welcomed his guest who was carrying a smart leather briefcase. "Would you like a drink? Tea, coffee or anything."

The gesture seemed more in politeness than sincere, and the solicitor declined the offer.

"Thank you, no, I can't stop long; I just wanted to update you on a few things."

"Ok, thanks," said Jez and led the man to the sitting room.

"Right, down to business," said the solicitor and opened his briefcase. He produced the first piece of paper. "I've had a note from the Coroner's office, and they're issuing a death certificate tomorrow. That means you can go ahead with the funeral."

"Yes, the police were here earlier and told me. What do I do about an undertaker?"

"Don't worry we can see to all that. As her executors, we'll make sure everything is as she would have wanted." It wouldn't be a problem; the solicitors would be billing the estate by the hour. "What about a date?" asked the solicitor.

"I don't know; I've not thought about it." This was true, Jez had given no thought to his mother's demise.

"Shall we say, next week? I'll speak to the undertaker and see when he's free."

"Yes, ok, thank you," said Jez.

"Have you any questions for me?" asked the solicitor.

"No, I don't think so, you've covered everything."

"Right then, I'll let you get on," said the solicitor and he closed his briefcase. Jez escorted him out. "I'll be in touch when I have more details of the funeral. Let me know if you have any questions."

"Thank you; I will."

Jez returned to his den and logged-on to his computer to continue his research. He accessed Adam's LinkedIn profile again. Before his trip to Costa Rica, Adam was working for The Standard Bank of South America. There was no way of hacking into their computer system; that was way beyond even Jez's skill. He did, however, find some background on the bank. A major player in South America with branches in all the major countries including Costa Rica. There was nothing that would help him in his quest for retribution. The award-night on Friday seemed to offer the best possibilities; at least he knew where Adam would be. What he would do, he hadn't yet decided, but he was determined to win Sarah back, somehow. She needed to realise that the new suitor wasn't right for her.

He raised his head from his workstation and looked at

Sarah's picture; her Facebook profile image he had downloaded and enlarged; it was stuck on the wall in front of him. The Settle selfie still had pride of place. He could feel the tears welling inside him again. He could picture Adam touching her body, her breasts, between her legs. He let out a scream, like an old-fashioned whistling kettle.

He got up and walked to his aquarium. He stared at the fish meandering randomly among the weed. One appeared to have made its home in the sunken wreck and chased away interlopers. Their antics had a calming effect on Jez.

Jez was in the kitchen when Mrs Dawson let herself in on Wednesday morning. It was nine-fifteen.

"You're early," observed Jez.

"Yes, Sophie's here. They're just parking the van."

"Van?" said Jez.

"Yes, one of Sophie's friends, to help with your mum's stuff."

"Oh, yes, I see."

"It's still ok, isn't it? Only you said yesterday..."

"Yes, of course. Take what you want. Not the jewellery though, I may keep it. Some of it's quite valuable."

Mrs Dawson's expression was one of disappointment. "Yes, whatever you say. Let me see how they're getting on."

She left the kitchen then returned a few moments later accompanied by a woman in her late teens to early twenties and a scruffy-looking young man about the same age with tattoos down both arms.

"This is Sophie, my daughter, and this is Stanley; we call him Stan, he's one of Sophie's friends. It's his van."

Jez acknowledged the pair.

"Would you like another cup of tea?" asked Mrs Dawson, looking at Jez. "I'll just make these two a drink before we get on."

"No, thanks. I'll leave you to it."

Jez went back upstairs. With nothing further to do on the Adam Fowler front, he wanted to see if he could do some real work. The complaints and threats were beginning to cause more anxiety. When he opened his emails, there was one from Mr Lever, the laptop man. It wasn't very complimentary. "Disappointed the police would take no action, intend to pursue via the Small Claims Court…"

Jez couldn't handle it; he just sent a reply, apologising and explaining the bereavement. He then offered to replace the laptop to put an end to it.

A little later, he walked down the corridor to his mother's bedroom where there was frenetic activity. All the wardrobes and drawers had been cleared. Stan was taking an armful of clothes down the stairs. Garments were stacked up on the bed, and Sophie was sifting through them.

"Hello, Jeremy, we've nearly finished. What about this coat, Mrs S always said I could have it?"

She was holding a beautiful waist-length fur and leather jacket which Jez remembered cost over three-thousand pounds. As far as he could recall, his mother had only worn it once.

"Yes, that's fine. I have no use for it," said Jez.

Mrs Dawson took it downstairs before Jez could change his mind.

"I've left her jewellery box on the dressing table. There are some nice things in there," said the daily.

"Yes," said Jez. "Some of them belonged to my grandmother."

"Oh, right," said Mrs Dawson. She wasn't going to push it;

she knew she was onto a good thing.

"What Sophie can't use, we'll take to the charity shop; which do you prefer?"

"Whatever you think," said Jez. "Anyway, if you'll excuse me."

"Yes of course, would you like me to make a drink?"

"Just a coffee, thanks," said Jez and returned to his den.

Sarah was in her office drinking her mid-morning coffee. She checked her texts again for the third time that morning, and there was another message from Adam.

'You ok for lunch today?'

'Yes, 12.30, fine. Miss you xxx'.

'Miss you more xxx'.

She switched off her phone and sighed; she wished she was somewhere else, somewhere alone with Adam. The thought of what they could be doing distracted her, but it made her feel warm inside.

Her fantasies were interrupted by a knock on her door.

"Hi. Sarah?"

She looked up and saw a shock of red hair; proper red, not ginger.

"Yes."

"I'm Tilly, the new head of Sales and Marketing."

"Of course, yes. I heard you were starting today. Come in; have a seat, we need a chat."

She looked at her new colleague who was like no one else she had seen before. Pale skin, brown lipstick, what looked like a man's shirt, and a short skirt with red tights. She spoke with a strong accent. Here was someone making a statement, thought Sarah.

"Would you like a coffee?"

"Do they have soya milk?" asked Tilly.

"I don't know," said Sarah.

"I'll leave it, but thanks anyway."

"Where are you from? I can't place the accent; it sounds Australian."

"Originally? New Zealand, but I've lived in the UK for ten years."

Sarah and Tilly chatted for forty minutes, and mutual respect was soon established. Tilly definitely fell into the category of a 'breath of fresh air', and Sarah was looking forward to working with her.

At lunchtime, the conversation was dominated by the new arrival.

"I think she's very brave," said Adam.

"Oh, I don't know; she's tough, I'm sure she can look after herself. I think it's a great appointment. We really need to break a few moulds here," said Sarah.

"Yes, I couldn't agree more. Oh, by the way, I have a meeting at the rugby club tonight. Won't be back until about ten."

"Oh, ok. Will you call me when you get in?" She turned her head to make sure no one was listening. "We can Skype if you like."

"Mmm, I like the sound of that," said Adam.

Sarah reached across the table and held his hand. "Don't be too late or I'll start without you," she said and blew Adam a kiss.

Later that afternoon, Sarah received an internal call.

"Oh, hi Sarah, it's Cressida, Sir Basil's PA."

Sarah wanted to scream 'you moron', but propriety held her

back.

"Yes," she said abruptly.

"Sir Basil would like to see you at four-thirty."

"Ok. I'll put it in my diary," she said with more than a hint of sarcasm. Cressida dropped the call with no more formality. "How rude," said Sarah to her handset.

Just before the appointed time, Sarah made the stairs again to the chairman's office. It was becoming a well-trodden path.

"Take a seat; I'll let him know you're here," said Cressida.

Sarah didn't acknowledge her but sat on the waiting chair outside his door. There was a distinct frostiness between them. Jealousy thought Sarah; Cressida probably had designs on Adam.

Cressida's phone rang; she looked at Sarah. "Sir Basil will see you now," she said with a wry smile.

Sarah walked in.

"Ah, Sarah. Come in; take a seat. How are things?"

"Fine, thanks."

"And you've met the new Head of Sales?"

"Yes, we had a chat, this morning. I'm looking forward to working with her."

"Yes, I think you two will make a great team."

"Sarah," he looked at her, rather uncomfortably. "This is a bit sensitive, but, er, it's come to my attention you are in a relationship with the new compliance manager, Mr Fowler."

Sarah noticed that when referring to male colleagues, he always used the term 'Mr', but when he mentioned females, he called them by their first names.

"Well, I don't know where you've got that information from, but I can't see it's anyone's business what I do outside work."

"Yes, quite," said Sir Basil. "The thing is, we can't afford to have any distractions and, in my experience, over many years you understand, that's what happens in office relationships. Do you see what I'm trying to say?"

Sarah wanted to say something but waited for the chairman to finish.

"It's not when everything's going well, no, no; it's when it breaks down that it becomes very difficult. I've never allowed married couples to work in the same department, a recipe for disaster in my view."

"I don't know what to say, do you want me to resign?"

"No, no, no, good grief no, of course not. I'm just concerned that it might affect your work."

"It won't," said Sarah.

"Right, good, glad to hear it. We shall say no more about it then."

"Right, is that it?"

"Yes, thank you. I hope you didn't mind me mentioning it, but I can't afford my best people to take their eye off the ball."

"No, I understand," said Sarah. "Will you be speaking to Mr Fowler as well?"

"No, no, that won't be necessary; the matter's closed as far as I'm concerned."

"Ok," said Sarah and got up and left his office.

Sarah was livid; she gave Cressida a look that in Biblical times would have turned her to stone. Cressida looked down, ignoring the scowl.

She got back to her office and opened her phone.

'Hi, just had a lecture from Sir Basil on inter-company relationships!!! I'm so angry, I feel like resigning'.

The reply came back ten minutes later.

'Don't do that, I'll call you before I go out tonight we can

chat about it'.

    'Yes, ok, I'll be fine once I've calmed down'.

    'I can think of ways to relax you!'

    'Hmm, that's the kind of remedy I like. Chat later xxx'.

Sarah felt better for the interaction. There was a knock on her door.

"Have you got a minute?" It was Michelle with a business query. Sarah was back in the zone.

Wednesday evening, Jez was in his den. He'd finished the fish pie that Mrs Dawson had left him and was staring at his aquarium. He was back in deep despair; he'd tried doing some work on some of the outstanding computer repairs but lacked any motivation. He'd not taken any of the prescribed medication since the first occasion. His mood was uncontrolled, swinging back and forth from apathy to anger. His concentration levels were non-existent.

He'd managed to do more research on the 'someone else'. This, at least, had given him some purpose, some motivation. Adam Fowler had become a figure of pure hate. Jez had printed off pictures of him from the internet, including the Costa Rica one and poked out the eyes with a pencil and put it on his cork-board. It didn't improve his mindset.

He didn't have a clear idea what to do. One option he had considered was to leave early on Friday and check out the Rugby Club and wait for him to arrive. He took the knife from the drawer and looked at it. In former times, he had seen his mother carve many a Sunday joint with it, but now he thought it could serve a different purpose.

He looked up. He could see his mother stood in the doorway with that look; the one of hatred and disdain. He could hear her voice. *"She's nothing but a trollop. I told you so, I told you so."*

He put his hands to his ears again to shut out the sound, but there was no sound; the house was empty. It was as though it had lost its soul.

He put the knife back in the drawer. He couldn't really kill anyone; besides, he would get caught, then he would lose Sarah forever. He was smarter than that, something else, it had to be.

Something else had occurred to him.

He logged back onto Adam's Instagram picture with the girl in Costa Rica and stared at it for a few minutes. He copied it to his computer, then opened Adam's LinkedIn home page and posted it on his timeline with a note; *'Missing our wonderful times together xx'.* To any casual viewer, it would appear to be his own post.

That should set the hares racing, thought Jez. He had no idea how long it would be before Sarah saw the post, but he would love to be a fly on the wall.

Earlier, Sarah had arrived home at the usual time and after feeding the cat, called Adam.

"Hi, are you ok, now?" said Adam.

"Yes, I'm fine, but I'd swing for that Cressida Bolton, fucking busy-body. I'm sure it was her that said something to Sir Basil."

"Well, you know what they say, revenge is a dish best served cold."

"Yes, you're right. I'll have my day. What time are you going out?"

"The meeting starts at seven-thirty, so I'll have to leave about quarter-past. It's a social committee meeting, just finalising arrangements for Friday."

"Right, ok, I better let you go then. Text me when you get in, and I'll open Skype."

"Hmm, can't wait," said Adam. Sarah rang off and went to get something to eat.

Adam's meeting, as expected, lasted a couple of hours and he was back at his flat just before ten. All the arrangements were in place for Friday's award night.

His flat was one of six in a large converted Victorian terrace which were popular with commuters and the wealthier students. Adam's was on the top floor which was larger than the others and with a nice view of the park and beauty spot. He strode the three floors and opened his front door. It opened immediately into the lounge. Opposite, was a small corridor with two bedrooms and the bathroom, and to the left, the kitchen. He went to the refrigerator and poured himself a glass of milk, then returned to the lounge and opened up his laptop which was on his dining table. He was about to text Sarah when he noticed an alert on his LinkedIn App. He ignored it; he was always getting posts from people who had reached a career milestone, got promoted, or were celebrating some meaningless work anniversary, most merely serving to massage egos.

He sent a text to Sarah. *'Hi, I'm back; ready to Skype xx?'*

'Definitely!' came the immediate reply.

He logged into the video messaging service and waited for Sarah to do the same. The sound of the video request made him jump. He accepted the call and waited for the screen to buffer. Sarah appeared on screen dressed in a tee-shirt and shorts. She was holding a glass of red wine.

She blew him a kiss. "How was your meeting?"

"Fine, everything's ready for Friday, although I have to say

I'm not really interested in the disco. I'm just looking forward to seeing you again."

"Yes, me too," said Sarah.

"You look terrific," said Adam.

"So do you," said Sarah. "I've been thinking naughty thoughts about you."

"Really?"

"Yes, I've been trying to watch TV, but I couldn't concentrate, so I had a bath."

"Hmm, I wish I could have scrubbed your back."

"That would have been good."

"I like your outfit," said Adam.

"Ha, ha, really? It's just an old tee-shirt."

"And you fill it so well," said Adam.

"Hmm," said Sarah, lifting her tee-shirt over her shoulders and dropping it on the settee beside her.

"That better?" she added sitting there, topless.

"God, you are so beautiful. I can't wait to hold you again."

"I hope you'll do more than that," said Sarah and moved closer to the screen.

"Oh, definitely," replied Adam.

The sexually-charged chat continued for another twenty minutes before Sarah called a halt.

"I better go, meetings tomorrow, and I shan't sleep at this rate," she excused herself.

Adam logged off Skype and shut down his laptop, then checked his phone one last time before turning in. He noticed the LinkedIn alert was still there and he opened the App out of curiosity.

For a moment he just stared. *"What the…"*

He checked if he could see the originator, but there was none; it was as though he had posted it himself, but that was impossible. How on earth? He deleted the picture. Then he remembered the 'Instagram' photo; he'd forgotten all about that; he hadn't posted there since he came back from Costa Rica at the end of November. He opened Instagram, deleted all the pictures, then removed his account.

He thought about doing the same with LinkedIn but, given his position, people would expect him to have a presence there. He still couldn't work out how it had been posted. Then all sorts of thoughts went through his mind. Was it a warning? That was possible. He was extremely worried. Then he thought about Sarah. She obviously hadn't seen it; otherwise, questions would have been asked. At least that was something.

That night Adam lay in bed; he couldn't sleep thinking about the LinkedIn post. It was a message; it had to be. He thought back to Costa Rica; how on earth could he have let that happen. He shouldn't have got involved, but it was too late now.

Chapter Fifteen

It was over nine months ago, in early September; Adam would always remember 'that' phone call. He was seated at his desk in the Canary Wharf headquarters. Twenty-second floor with a spectacular view over the Thames, the long meander with the Millennium Dome, now a concert venue, in centre stage.

Adam Fowler, Senior Compliance Manager, Standard Bank of South America; a great job, great salary and a role in which he was excelling. 'A young man with potential', it had said on his last appraisal. There was huge responsibility within the role; ensuring compliance with Banking Regulations was a major challenge for all banks, particularly those with South American connections. The SBSA, pronounced 'Subsa' in banking circles, had a global presence. Primarily in South America, where it had branches in all the Latin American countries; it also had representation in the major financial centres; New York, London, Paris, Frankfurt, Singapore, Hong Kong and Tokyo. The London office was the biggest outside South America and one of the busiest.

Adam picked up the receiver.

"Señor Fowler?" A Spanish accent was not unusual; many of his calls were from countries with Hispanic origins.

"Yes, can I help you?"

"Si, yes, please. I, er, represent some people who have your... how can I say? Your interests at heart."

Adam was puzzled. "What do you mean?"

"I can explain more but not over the telephone, are you free this lunchtime?"

"I can be," said Adam.

"Muy Bien; let us say twelve-thirty? Meet me outside

Lacey's; I will book a table."

Adam was intrigued as much as anything and had no hesitation in accepting the lunch date.

Lacey's Restaurant was well-known in the area and a popular eatery among the banking set. It was expensive, even for the lunchtime 'specials'. You would need to book at least three weeks ahead if you wanted a table after five-thirty when it opened for the evening sittings.

At twenty-past twelve, Adam put on his suit jacket and headed for the lift. He pressed the '-1' button which would take him to the main underground concourse.

Much of the Canary Wharf area is below street level, and numerous shops and bars cater for the office fraternity, including the familiar designer outlets which do lucrative business at bonus time. Lacey's was at the end of one of the Malls and had an outlook over the dock.

Adam approached the restaurant, keeping a watchful eye for his lunchtime host. Then a tall, slim man, wearing a smart Trilby hat, spectacles and light-coloured raincoat, appeared from the side of the building. His behaviour seemed rather odd; his head was bowed, and his collar raised as if he was hiding his face from the myriad of closed-circuit cameras. "Señor Fowler?" he enquired.

Up close, Adam could see he was an older man, probably in his fifties with a grey goatee beard and moustache. His eye-glasses were rimmed with gold, but understated, so they weren't a defining feature of his face.

"Yes," replied Adam and the pair shook hands.

"Please, come," said the man and they went inside. The receptionist took the man's name and escorted the pair to a table by the window which overlooked the water.

"Nice view," said Adam, trying to make conversation.

"Si," said the man.

A waiter came and handed the pair the lunchtime menus. There was a three-course set-meal with several alternatives; the man chose a starter and main course. Adam did the same. There was no offer of alcohol, and the man poured a measure of the complimentary mineral water into one of the glasses. Adam did the same. He was starting to feel uncomfortable, and once the waiter had taken the order, Adam opened the conversation.

"So, you wanted to see me?"

"Si, yes, my name is Abel Eduardo Ramirez. I represent certain people... investors." Adam glanced him a quizzical look. "Yes, investors," he clarified.

His English was excellent but with a hint of a Spanish accent. He took a drink of his water. Adam watched him; his actions seemed deliberate and his speech slow and measured as if he every word was important.

"I am in a position to be of assistance to you, in a professional capacity, certainly, and personal capacity as well, I think. You have an important position at the bank, si?"

"Yes, I think so," replied Adam, still unsure of what was being offered.

The man's eyes narrowed. "You live in London. Black Heath, a small apartment, I think."

"How do you know that?"

"It is my business to know these things. It is very expensive, no?"

He was assertive in his delivery, clearly someone who meant business, but there was something else in his demeanour, an underlying menace. Adam was on the defensive.

"Yes, very," said Adam who was feeling uneasy with

this scrutiny. He was struggling financially, but how did this stranger know that?

"You have a student loan, I expect?"

"Yes," said Adam.

"Also expensive." This time it was an observation.

"Yes," said Adam who was wondering where this was going. He considered leaving the meeting but was unsure of the consequences.

Mr Ramirez looked at Adam; his expression changed, almost fatherly. "You deserve more reward for the responsibility I think."

Adam did not comment. The man picked up his glass again and took another sip; he seemed to savour the measure as if it was fine wine.

"Well, let me get straight to the point. I am in a position to provide some assistance, some help that could ease your financial worries significantly."

"Where's the catch?"

"The catch…? No, no catch," he replied as he wrestled with the colloquialism.

"But you will want something from me in return."

"Well, we do not want you to do anything."

"What, nothing?"

"That is exactly the case. Let me explain more. My associates have many business interests; much money is involved, and sometimes we need to move it around."

They were interrupted by a waitress bringing their first courses. The man took another drink, and Adam poured more water.

"I get it," said Adam. "You want me to endorse money transactions."

"Legitimate money transactions," he asserted. "From London to our bank in Costa Rica."

"I can't do that; I would lose my job."

"Well, that's what I mean about helping you professionally. You help us, and you will see your career move in a positive direction. We do have many contacts in the financial community. You will certainly not lose your job."

Adam reflected on this statement; someone else at the bank, or close to it, must be on the payroll, and at a senior level.

"And what about the F.C.A? You can't get around their audit."

"We know all about them, they will not investigate unless there is an enquiry, and they are too busy to check everything."

"You are well-informed," said Adam.

"It is my job, as I say," said the man.

"What will I have to do," asked Adam.

"Like I said, nothing. We want to send money to Costa Rica, two, sometimes three times a month. We just need you to er... what is the word? Endosar?"

"Endorse," corrected Adam.

"Si, endorse. Endorse the transfer."

"How much are the transactions?"

"That depends on the amount of business, but in dollars, ten sometimes twenty."

"Million?"

The man smiled for the first time. "Yes, millions."

"I'm not sure how I can help you, I can't authorise that much."

"What amount can you do?"

"That's confidential," said Adam, sharply.

"Si, ok, let me try another way. You can authorise five, yes?"

"Yes," said Adam.

"What about seven?"

"Hmm, yes," said Adam hesitantly.

"Eight?"

"No, I can't do eight."

"Ok, let's say we keep the transfers down to seven and a half."

"Hmm, I could probably do that," said Adam.

"Si, good, that is good. We may need to increase the…" He struggled to find the right word. "Regularity."

The first course was finished, and the waitress cleared the plates. "Are you ready for your next course?" she asked.

Adam looked at the man. "Yes, please bring it," said the Hispanic.

"You realise I could go to prison if I get caught?" said Adam.

"You will not get caught. Who will question your decision?"

This was true; as long as it was not discovered in an internal audit, the risk was relatively low. Adam was taken aback at the amount of knowledge of the bank's internal systems the man had.

"And for my help, I get what?" asked Adam.

"We will pay off your student debt and help with your living expenses, depending on the number of transactions we complete."

Adam was deep in thought; it was a very inviting proposition. "Hmm, now that is tempting. How will this work?"

"The transactions will originate here and be sent to an account in San José. La Compañía de Cinco Iluvias Inc. They will be referred to you as usual, and you will sign them off."

"Five Rivers?"

"Si, you speak Spanish?"

"A little; you pick it up," said Adam.

"That is good."

The waitress returned with the main courses.

There was silence as she handed out the meals, giving Adam time to consider the proposal. The money was attractive and a consideration which would drive his decision.

Adam enjoyed spending money and, being a social animal, he lived life to the full. The local rugby club tended to be the centre of his world; he was still playing most Saturdays, but the many clubs and bars in the vicinity were also a diversion. His appetite for girlfriends had become a standing joke among his friends. "You're only jealous," he would respond to the light-hearted jibes and, for the most part, he was probably right.

For transport, he used a ten-year-old Porsche 911; totally in keeping with his lifestyle; a present from his father when he left university with his 2:1. Unfortunately, it was expensive to run, and he didn't take it out unless he wanted to impress a date.

He earned a good living; his role at the bank attracted a high salary package by most standards, but he did not enjoy the hyper-bonuses of his contemporaries in the dealing rooms. Over recent months, he had only just managed to cover his rent and was often up to his overdraft limit. His recent holiday to Magaluf had added to his debt.

He weighed up the decision. He was, by nature, used to taking risks; as long as the odds were stacked in his favour. The man was right; although there was a great deal of scrutiny at the bank, as the final authority for sign-off, any indiscretions would need to be picked up by an internal audit which he knew were not as robust as they should be. It was worth a chance.

"What if I say no?" said Adam. The man's eyes narrowed again behind his spectacles.

"You can say no, of course, then this conversation did not take place. Nothing will happen, but my investors, they remember and value those people who assist them. Those that don't..." The man shrugged his shoulders.

Adam took a while, taking sips of water as if giving the matter serious consideration.

"Ok, I'm in. What happens next?"

"Excellent, excellent. I am sure it will be a profitable enterprise for both of us. There will be a transaction in the next few days. It will be for exactly seven and a half million. I will send you a text message to confirm. You will need to let me have your personal telephone number."

"My mobile?"

"Yes," replied the man. "Also, you may want to consider opening another bank account, somewhere away from your bank. We will send some money after the first three transactions have been sent. Let me have your new bank details."

"Yes, ok."

Things started happening quickly.

Adam opened the new bank account at one of the smaller foreign banks where he thought there would be less scrutiny and confirmed the details by text to the number Ramirez had given him. Three days later, an assistant handed Adam the daily transaction list for authorising. Mostly small amounts; the largest was for fifty-thousand dollars. Then he noticed the big one, seven and a half million dollars; originator, La Compañía de Cinco Iluvias Inc, to their account at Primera Banco de Costa Rica, San José, Costa Rica.

Adam felt a shiver of anxiety as he scrutinised the list, once he had committed to his next action; there would be no turning back.

"What about the large one?" asked Violetta, his attractive Portuguese assistant.

"Yes, it's fine. I know this company, they've been cleared to make this transaction."

His assistant showed no sign of surprise or sense of challenge. At the bottom of the page, there was a dotted line, below it the words; 'Authorised Signatory'. Adam signed the form, and his assistant left his office. There was no going back now.

The transactions became more regular than Adam had been led to believe, once-a-week at irregular intervals, occasionally twice. The amounts varied, partly not to attract suspicion, but also it was governed by cash-flow. As promised, after the third transaction, he received the twenty-five thousand pounds that would pay off his student loan. Further payments of seven and a half thousand dollars followed after each transaction, which represented about point-one percent of the bank transfer, a mere drop in the ocean and good value to those initiating the transfers.

La Compañía de Cinco Iluvias Inc was a substantial business; to hide their financial activities, various dummy companies had been set up across Europe and the United States. The money would also flow in from Asia, especially Thailand; in fact, anywhere where the drug trade was thriving. The activities attracted an enormous amount of cash; managing it was the major challenge for the drug barons. The law enforcement mantra was always, 'follow the money'. A labyrinth of exchanges took place, switching the money before it would eventually end up in London.

The London-Costa Rica link was the last in a long chain before the money arrived in San José where the cartel could easily access it. The money would be distributed among the 'investors' and used to finance the whole supply chain. It was an incredibly profitable and cash-rich enterprise.

Abel Eduardo Ramirez was an important member of the 'family', not least because his brother was the president of the Primera Bank in the Costa Rican capital. They lived lavish lives with huge mansions up in the hills outside the capital, complete with a small army of bodyguards. Other members of the cartel lived in Columbia and Nicaragua and were similarly rewarded by their venture. Security was tight and brutal; lives were cheap. Numerous murders had taken place, many of them were police and judiciary. The CIA was aware of the cartel, but they tended to leave them alone in a policy of 'containment'; it was a Costa Rican problem, and they had directives not to get involved.

At the end of October, about six weeks after that initial meeting, Adam's initial apprehension of the enterprise changed to one of enthusiasm. After a few weeks, he had cleared his student loan and his other debts, and he was starting to accumulate money. Christmas was looking good; even his friends had commented on his new-found wealth as he splashed his cash.

He was back at his desk in the Canary Wharf tower. It was a dismal autumn day, cold and wet; the falling leaves were creating havoc on the railways, and the commute seemed to take forever. He was drinking a coffee when he received a call to his mobile phone; 'number withheld', it said.

"Señor Fowler?" Adam recognised the voice immediately.

"It is Ramirez. I wanted to speak to you to say my investors have been very happy with your assistance in the matter of the transactions. You have received payment?"

"Yes, thank you," replied Adam.

"That is good. The reason I make this call to you; I want you to meet some of my investors here in San José; you come here for a holiday, maybe? You can stay in my apartment in town. We will buy your plane ticket. You will have a good time, I guarantee."

It sounded like an order rather than an invitation, but, since his involvement with Ramirez, he had taken an interest in Costa Rica; it was a place he was keen to visit.

"Yes, ok, when?"

"Next week, you come here for three weeks or one month, see the country, enjoy the sunshine."

"I don't know," said Adam. "It's a bit short notice. I'll have to talk to my boss."

"It will not be a problem, I think. I will introduce you to my brother; he is President of the Banco Primera de Costa Rica, a good connection for your bank."

"Yes, it would be."

"You tell your boss the President of the Banco Primera has invited you; it will be a business trip. You can discuss matters of… how do you say? Compliance?"

Adam was thinking this through. "Yes, ok, great."

"I will send you an invitation to a reception; you can show to your boss. It will be no problem. Si, it will make your visit official."

Sure enough, a three-week absence was not only sanctioned but encouraged by his manager who had taken an interest in Adam's visit to meet the bank's president. The email from the

Ramirez's brother was impressive, complete with a formal invitation via a PDF. His first-class tickets arrived with the message.

So, in early November, Adam was seated in the business-class lounge at Gatwick Airport, anxiously waiting for the long-haul trip to Costa Rica to be called, an almost eleven-hour journey. He considered how his life had changed since his involvement with Ramirez and his 'investors'.

Professionally, his career was also on the up and up. He had been singled out for a management development course at one of the prestigious training venues just outside London, with the possibility of attending another in Harvard in the United States as part of a bank-sponsored MBA programme.

His finances had definitely taken a turn for the better; with all his debts finally repaid, he finally traded in the ageing Porsche and bought himself his dream car.

The flight took off just before midday, arriving in San Jose mid-afternoon. There was a seven-hour time difference to which Adam would need to adjust.

Juan Santamaria Airport is located just twelve kilometres away from San José city; it is the second-busiest passenger airport in Central America. The main terminal building is a modern structure with a curved stainless-steel and glass roof making the whole ambience light and airy. Air-conditioning kept the internal temperature cool. Adam was impressed as he made his way through passport control; it was not what he was expecting. He retrieved his luggage from the carousel then followed the signs to the exit. He was travelling reasonably light, considering a three-week trip, just a modest suitcase and his cabin luggage; he was hoping to see more of the country and would back-pack if necessary.

Outside the arrivals area, there was the usual jostle of taxi-drivers and others holding signs welcoming their rides. Adam scanned the names, then saw his being held by a swarthy-looking man with an ill-fitting chauffeur's uniform and hat. He was in need of a shave, and his greasy black hair hung down below his hat. He was sweating.

Adam approached the man. "Hello, I'm Adam Fowler."

"Si, si, welcome Señor Fowler to Costa Rica. Please follow." His accent was strong with a smoker's rasp. He grabbed Adam's bags and headed for the exit. Adam tagged along behind. The automatic doors opened as they approached. As they exited the terminal building, to the right, Adam noticed a line of taxis waiting for customers, a mix of the municipal red cars and the orange airport taxis.

Outside, it was hot. The change in temperature was marked, particularly compared with London. Being a tropical climate meant there was little difference in the temperature across the year; averages vary by only two or three degrees with just two seasons, wet and dry. November is the start of the dry season.

Although San José is not a large place by international capital standards, it is spread out. Adam stopped and surveyed the scenery for a moment. He could see the skyline; it was hilly with high-rise buildings protruding at regular intervals from the muddle of dwellings. In the distance, mountains loomed large, casting a watchful eye over the city.

They walked for about a hundred metres towards a large, black, seven-series BMW which was parked in one of the VIP bays.

"Entrar, entrar. You, get in," said the driver urgently as he opened one of the rear doors. Adam complied, ignoring any unintended rudeness. The interior was spacious with luxurious white leather; it was mercifully cool, and Adam soon made himself comfortable.

As they drove into the city centre, there was no conversation. Adam took a great interest in his new surroundings. It was a lively and bustling place with traffic queueing and jostling for positions at junctions. There was a mixture of traditional and colonial architecture with parks and open spaces where the locals were socialising or just passing through. They passed a large, impressive building.

"What's that place?" Adam enquired.

"El Edificio del Gobierno... er... the government."

They entered a wealthy area; the buildings and pavements were well-maintained, trees lined the wide boulevard. After a couple of minutes, the driver turned onto a side road and drew up outside a small apartment block.

"Out, out," said the driver. Again, Adam complied.

The driver extracted the luggage from the boot and walked towards the building entrance; Adam followed. The man rather awkwardly pulled open the glass doors while trying to negotiate Adam's luggage at the same time. Adam followed the man inside. It was quite stark, but clean with ivory colour walls. It was noticeably cool; Adam was grateful that the air-conditioning was working. It was still warm outside in the heat of the late-afternoon sun.

In front of them, was a small lift which would just about hold two people. The man walked in dragging Adam's baggage, and Adam followed. It was cramped and not a comfortable environment. The driver smelt of stale cigarettes and body odour; it was oppressive, and Adam tried to hold his breath.

It was only two floors, but it seemed to take forever. The elevator juddered to a halt; the driver pulled the concertina metal gate apart, and they exited the lift. Adam exhaled.

It opened onto a short corridor, and in front of them, there was a door which the man unlocked. They entered; it was a spacious apartment. Adam looked around; it was larger and much better appointed than his flat in Blackheath. The man handed Adam the keys and paused before leaving.

Adam rummaged in his pocket and found a five-dollar bill which he handed it to the man. The driver grunted an acknowledgement and left. Adam would use dollars for everyday use; they were generally preferred, he had read. He did have a small supply of Colón, the local currency, for use in an emergency.

He spent a few minutes looking around and unpacking his stuff. There were two bedrooms, a modern kitchen, bathroom and well-furnished lounge, a real home-from-home. Before he settled down, he sent a message to his parents to say he had arrived safely, then put the phone on charge.

He'd been in the apartment for less than an hour when his phone rang; it was Ramirez.

"Señor Fowler?"

"Hello, yes."

"You like the apartment, si?"

"Yes, it's great, thanks."

"Ok, you should have everything you need; make yourself at home. Tomorrow, you rest, the day after someone will come for you at midday. You have a suit?"

"No, just a jacket."

"Si, a jacket will be ok. You will return later in the evening; you will have a good time."

Adam spent the next day relaxing from the journey and acclimatising to his new surroundings as Ramirez had suggested. By lunchtime, he was getting restless and decided to take a stroll to explore his locality. The weather was cloudy which had raised the humidity, but it was pleasantly warm. It was different to what he had expected; the tree-lined streets with their wide pavements were not as busy in this neighbourhood. He walked well over a mile before he entered a more urban environment with a few scattered shops and bars. Yellow buses passed him in both directions, and this looked to be the likely mode of transport to get around while he was in San José.

By mid-afternoon, Adam had returned to the apartment; he was feeling the effects of the journey and slept for a couple of hours. Later he walked in the opposite direction and found a small bar where he enjoyed a couple of beers before returning to the apartment. So far everything was going well.

The following day, a Saturday, Adam was ready for his reception. He was wearing the light-brown sports-jacket he had brought with him together with a pale-blue shirt, matching chinos and white shoes; smart-looking without being overdressed for the occasion.

Just before midday, he walked down to the entrance of the apartment block and waited for his lift. It was cloudy again but bright, and Adam immediately put on sunglasses to protect his eyes from the glare. It was almost quarter-past when a large Chevrolet Tahoe pulled up outside. It was a different driver from the airport run. As the driver exited the car, Adam felt some anxiety. The man looked more like a hitman with his large frame and close-cropped hair, resembling a Special

Forces operative. Adam could clearly see a gun holster beneath his jacket. His greeting was friendly enough.

"Señor Fowler? Welcome to San José, I will take you to Señor Ramírez. My name is Jacó. Please sit."

The man opened the rear passenger door.

"Can I sit in the front?" asked Adam pointing to the empty passenger seat next to the driver. The man shrugged his shoulders and opened the front passenger door.

They belted up, and the seven-seater eased away; it was almost like being on a bus with the panoramic windows giving a great view. They headed north out of town.

Once escaping the city-sprawl, the scenery was breath-taking, lush, green and mountainous. Just after the toll booth on the Ruta 32, the driver turned off the main highway, and they started to climb. After about three miles, there was another, less-noticeable turn, which Jacó negotiated easily. It was a winding road running parallel to a stream which had cut a course down the mountain. The fauna was thick forest with Guanacaste and palms lining the route and bright red heliconia adding colour. Adam found it awe-inspiring.

They came to a large gate surrounded by a ten-foot wall which stretched left and right as far as Adam could see. As the car approached, the gate slowly opened, and on the right-hand side, there was a small wooden hut. A man appeared carrying an assault rifle; he looked at the driver and Adam and waved them through. The track widened; it was brown compacted dirt, not a tarmac surface, and with the dry weather a trail of sandy-coloured dust followed the Chevvy.

After another two-hundred yards, a white mansion appeared surrounded by terraces and balustrades. Small palms and various other plants decorated the driveway which opened up in front of the main building into a courtyard. Several high-end cars were parked there, and armed men wandered around, looking menacing. Adam felt anxious once again.

The driver pulled up outside what appeared to be the front entrance; a large wooden door ornately carved with birds and flowers. Four wide steps led up to the entrance. The driver walked around to the passenger side and opened the door for Adam to alight.

"We are here. Señor Ramirez is waiting; please follow."

Adam exited the Chevvy, and Jacó led the way up the steps.

Adam was trying to take in the scenery; it was breath-taking. The mansion was on two floors and stretched in both directions; Adam couldn't see the ends from where he was standing.

Jacó was at the door and made a slow, deliberate double rap. Adam thought it might be a code of some sort. It was opened by another bodyguard also holding an assault rifle; two loaded bandoliers crisscrossed his body, sash-like. He resembled pictures of the Mexican General, Pancho Villa, famous for his bandoliers.

There was a brief discussion in Spanish; Adam heard his name mentioned. Then the bandit turned his head and shouted something which Adam didn't understand.

Moments later, Ramirez appeared.

"Adam, so good to see you, welcome to Castillo de Rosa."

"Thanks," said Adam. "Great place you have here."

"Si, yes, thank you; we like it. Come, come; you must meet the family and my guests. They are looking forward to meeting you."

Inside, the mansion was as magnificent as the exterior. It was an enormous ranch, very typical Latin American in style. There were wonderful paintings and tapestries, indoor water features and plants. Outside one of the side windows, Adam noticed one wall resembling the Hanging Gardens of Babylon, adorned in creeping plants with brilliant-coloured flowers. Hummingbirds flitted among the blooms, taking nectar then flying back out along a courtyard. Adam followed Ramirez through the house along a central corridor which led immediately to the rear of the property.

The doorway opened into a wide terrace and, on exiting the building, Adam found it difficult to take in the sight before him. Sweeping terraces in steps, each with an array of potted shrubs and flowers. There were three levels before the ground seemed to slope away gently with grass. Adam couldn't see how far down it went or what lay beyond. Several children were running around. But it was the view; 'awesome' was the only word that came to mind. The surrounding mountains rose way above them in the distance, far enough away to ensure there was no issue with sunlight. Everywhere was green and lush. It looked like what it was, a tropical paradise.

The first level terrace was big, probably over a hundred metres end-to-end, and about half that wide. To the right, was a covered area where a Mariachi band was playing; five portly Mexicans with guitars and trumpets, and enormous Sombreros. There was a barbecue in the corner, slightly away from the music, attended by three men in chef's attire. There were probably forty people milling about on the terrace being attended to by numerous waiting staff in white uniforms.

Suddenly Adam felt alone and a long way from home. Part of him wished he was still at his parents' cottage in Salisbury.

Chapter Sixteen

"Come, come. There are many people I want you to meet," said Ramirez.

Many of the guests appeared to be carrying small plates of food and were trying to balance champagne glasses as they nibbled away. Others were queued at the barbecue, waiting for their turn to be served. The women were dressed in their finery as you would see at Ladies' Day at Ascot. The men too were smartly dressed, mostly in white suits, but with the occasional blazer. Adam felt a little underdressed but would not be too bothered by any sartorial faux-pas; he had travelled light.

As they walked onto the terrace, a man approached them. Adam immediately recognised the family resemblance; it had to be Ramirez's brother.

"Ah, Adam I want to introduce you to my brother, Andrés, president of the Prima Banco de Costa Rica."

"Señor Fowler, it is a pleasure to meet you and to say thank you, personally, for everything you have done for us. It will not be forgotten," said Andrés.

The greeting seemed genuine, and Adam felt slightly overwhelmed. The man looked older than Abel Ramirez, but not much. He was dressed in a white suit, white shirt and red tie with a motif emblazoned in the weave - the crest of the bank.

"That's ok," said Adam, humbly, and accepted the vigorous hand-shake.

"Come, you must tell me all about the work you do. Compliance manager, si?"

"Yes," said Adam.

A waiter appeared and offered Adam a glass of champagne which he accepted without reservation. Ramirez junior excused himself and went to join other guests.

There was a lengthy discussion on banking matters which Adam enjoyed, and he started to relax for the first time since his arrival at the mansion.

"I was saying to your brother what a beautiful house you have here," said Adam at an appropriate moment.

"Si, yes, it is not mine; I have a place about one hour away. This one, it belongs to Abel, it once belonged to a coffee merchant. Coffee is very big here in Costa Rica, many of my important bank clients are in coffee; very rich," he said and laughed.

Adam could see Abel on the far side of the terrace talking to an attractive dark-haired woman in her mid-forties; they were joined by two young children about six and four. Abel picked up the younger child, a girl, and a made fuss of her. Andrés noticed Adam's interest.

"That is Abel's wife, Isabella, and their children. He is devoted to them."

"Yes, I can see," said Adam.

A young woman, probably in her twenties, approached them. Adam looked at her and was momentarily lost for words.

"Adam, let me introduce you to my daughter, Evelyn."

"Evelyn, this is Señor Fowler from England, the one I told you about." He spoke in English out of courtesy which Adam appreciated.

Evelyn was dressed in a pale-blue blouse buttoned down the front with cut-off sleeves, and light-grey tapered slacks, which seemed to emphasise her long legs. White, three-inch heels completed her outfit. Her dark hair was swept back and pinned off her face by a pair of sunglasses which were raised to her forehead. Adam was transfixed. There was an elegance about her, something inbred; it wasn't something you could manufacture.

"Hello," he managed to stammer. "It's Adam; you can call me Adam."

"Hi, Adam," said Evelyn, her voice low; an American-English accent with a wonderful Spanish inflexion. She held out her hand for the daintiest of handshakes.

Adam was suddenly oblivious to anyone or anything else. The surroundings, the people, they were all in soft focus; Evelyn had his complete attention. He hadn't noticed that Andrés had left to mingle with other guests.

"Have you had anything to eat?" said Evelyn.

"No," replied Adam. Food was not at the forefront of his mind.

"Come, I am hungry, and we can talk."

Evelyn led Adam to the barbecue. She spoke Spanish to the chef who put two pieces of spiced chicken on a plate and handed it to her.

"Same," said Adam. Evelyn translated, and a similar portion was handed over.

"Gracias," Adam replied in his best Spanish accent.

"Tu hablas Español?"

"Not really," said Adam.

"Your accent is perfect," said Evelyn.

"Thank you," said Adam and smiled.

They helped themselves to accompaniments. With food served, Adam followed Evelyn to the corner of the terrace next to a large palm. There was a table with two seats, set for dining.

"Here, we can sit; it is more private."

Adam would follow her anywhere.

"Yes, it's fine," said Adam and they both sat down.

"The view is magnificent," said Adam. "You are lucky to live here."

"Ah, yes, but I don't live here, not now. I have an apartment in town. It is easier for me."

"I see, so what do you do for a living, your work, I mean?"

"I do not work. I am at the University."

"Really? What are you studying?"

"International relations. I want to be a diplomat after I graduate."

Adam watched her tackle her food; even eating her chicken was completed with a certain finesse.

"Really? That's interesting; what made you want to do that?"

"I want to make a difference and being a diplomat will help me do that."

"You speak excellent English," Adam observed.

"Thank you, yes, I studied here at the English School in San José and then I spend two years in Miami after I finished High School."

This would explain her age; up close she was certainly older than his original estimate; closer to thirty, Adam guessed.

"That must have been an experience."

"Yes, it was. My father has business interests there, so I helped with the administration."

"So, you were helping run your father's business in Miami?"

"No, no, I was in charge; and it is more than one. My father has many interests, not just the banco, although that takes up most of his time."

"So, who's running the businesses while you're at University?"

"I have cousins who are involved; they are in charge."

Adam watched as Evelyn sipped, what looked like a punch, through a straw. She had finished her food and was looking across the valley with her legs resting on the balustrade in front of her. She had removed her shoes and Adam could see her red toenails wiggling in the afternoon sun, free from their constraints. Evelyn was not used to wearing formal footwear, he surmised.

She turned and looked at Adam.

"What are you doing, after today with your time?"

"I haven't worked anything out yet; nothing planned," he clarified. "I wanted to see what was available, but I do want to see more of the country."

"Si, you must," said Evelyn. She took another sip of her drink. "I have an idea. I have been thinking of travelling north. There are many beautiful beaches, surfing, great nightlife; but my father would insist I take one of the bodyguards with me. Not so much fun. I am sure if you would come with me he would be cool with that. What do you think?"

"Sounds fantastic," said Adam trying not to appear over-enthusiastic, but failing miserably.

"Muy Bien. Tomorrow we can ride the truck to Tamarindo."

"Yeah, sound's great, I've always wanted to see that place."

"Si, it is beautiful, wonderful beaches. Do you surf?"

"Not very well; it's been a while."

"That is cool; I will teach you. There are many coves I know which are not so busy. Tamarindo is very popular with the tourists. They come from everywhere, and the town gets very full, very busy."

She looked at Adam, dark eyes, wide and alluring. He was being drawn into her like a bug on a spider's web.

"When will we go?" asked Adam.

"I will speak with my father, but every day a delivery truck goes to Tamarindo. I will see if we can ride with it. There will be room for us, I think."

"Sounds perfect," said Adam.

"Si, it will be," she said, flashing her eyes again in Adam's direction.

They continued talking for a while, sharing family backgrounds and personal interests, before they were interrupted by Abel Ramirez.

"Ah, there you are, Adam. Come, I have some people who want to meet you."

Adam looked at Evelyn. "Duty calls," he said.

"I will speak to my father, and we can talk later," said Evelyn, and Adam got up and followed Ramirez. He glanced back and saw her still reclining on her seat with her legs on the wall, head back, eyes closed as if in a trance.

They approached a group of five men in close conversation to the left of the barbecue, near the steps that led down to the next terrace. Three of the men left as Adam and Ramirez joined them, the remaining two turned to Ramirez and smiled. They spoke in Spanish, and Adam felt momentarily excluded. The two men, on first appearance, looked like typical wealthy Latin American landowners. The white suits were on the generous side; they clearly had been living well. On closer inspection they looked tough; that was the only word that came into Adam's mind. The faces bore scars; the older man's was lined from years of smoking and stress, it would seem.

Ramirez turned to Adam. "Señor Fowler, please forgive the discourtesy, my business associates do not speak much English."

"That's ok, no problem."

"Let me introduce you. Señor Fowler, this is Señor Camacho; he's from Colombia, and he is a senior partner in our venture."

Ramirez spoke to the man in Spanish, and he shook hands warmly with Adam. Then spoke to Ramirez in Spanish.

Ramirez translated. "He says you are a special friend and will always be remembered for your help to our venture here. He says if there is anything he can do for you, he is in your debt."

Adam had no idea of the significance of this statement. Ramirez added. "Señor Camacho has many, many contacts, not just here in Costa Rica but in Colombia, Nicaragua and America. If you have any trouble while you are here you can call him; he will solve it." The man handed Adam a business card and addressed him in Spanish.

Ramirez translated. "You are very privileged; he has given you his personal contact details, a sign of trust. You should not share this with anyone," he added and gave Adam a serious look.

"Gracias, muchas gracias," said Adam and the man gave a broad grin and nodded. Adam looked at the card then secured it in his jacket pocket.

Ramirez turned to the next man. Adam tried to weigh him up. He was a good ten years younger than the first with long wavy black hair and dark eyes; he looked incredibly fit. He reminded Adam of some of the guys at the rugby club gym who had become obsessive with weight-training; the body profile greatly exaggerated.

"And this gentleman is Señor Gabriel Gonzales; he is from Nicaragua and runs our business there."

"Encantado de conocerte," said Adam, attempting to try out his limited Spanish.

The man replied in a tirade of words that Adam had no comprehension. Ramirez was on hand to spare his blushes.

"Señor Gonzales thanks you and says how much he appreciates your assistance." Adam nodded to the man.

Ramirez put his arm around Adam's shoulder. "Come, let's go inside; it is cooler, and we can talk and enjoy some food, si?"

"Yes, ok," said Adam, and Ramirez guided him up the steps and into the house. They turned right into a magnificent drawing room with a large picture window overlooking the valley.

The two associates followed.

"Please sit," said Ramirez. There were two long settees either side of an ornately carved wooden coffee table, probably measuring six feet by four feet. Adam took in the opulence for a moment. Marble floor, Persian rugs, ornaments; there was a large porcelain Chinese dog either side of the main wall. A large oil painting of a mountain landscape was the centrepiece. Adam sat down with Ramirez next to him but without invading his private space; the other two made themselves comfortable on the settee opposite.

Within seconds, two young waiters, possibly Mexican, joined them and started distributing drinks. Another followed pushing a trolley. It was covered with a white tablecloth and an array of canapés and tapas. The men were handed a plate each.

The food was duly served, and some nibbles were left on the table; the waiters exited the room and closed the door. There was a short silence as the snacks were being consumed; Ramirez opened the conversation. Adam was drinking a local beer in an ice-cold glass. Condensation dribbled down the side and dropped onto the floor.

"My associates here would like to offer you a proposition.

Adam was immediately on his guard.

"What kind of proposition?" said Adam rather anxiously.

"As I said earlier, we have been very pleased with your assistance in our financial arrangements, and we would like to bring more business to your bank."

"I don't know about that," said Adam quickly; his body-language was defensive which Ramirez immediately detected.

"Before you say 'no', please let me say how you can help; there will be no risk to you."

He said something to his two associates in Spanish.

"We want to extend, the transactions through your bank. Let me explain; my associates here have other business interests in Colombia and Nicaragua" Adam looked at him, he could see where this was going. "And in America," added Ramirez.

"I can't get involved in any transactions through the States. If you know anything about our banking system, you will know they are closely monitored by their own financial authorities."

"Si, si, this I know." He spoke to his associates again.

"No, we will be using the banco here but just more regularity, two, maybe three times a week."

"That's impossible; it's bound to be spotted."

"Si, I know, I know, so we make the payments smaller; they will not be a million dollars even. We will use different accounts. I have a list here."

Ramirez handed Adam a list of names, ten, maybe twelve; Adam had difficulty focussing.

"These payments will start one week after you return to London. We will pay you one percent of each transaction."

Adam looked up; this was serious money.

"Can I think about it?" asked Adam.

This was a ridiculous question; he was in too deep, and he

wasn't sure that if he declined, he would make it out of the hacienda alive, but he wanted to at least give the impression he retained some control.

"Si, si, of course. So, what do you think of my country so far?" said Ramirez changing the subject. The other two were watching Adam while they nibbled at bits of food that had been left on the table.

"It is beautiful, really beautiful."

"And you will see more, I hope. Maybe Evelyn will be able to show you around?"

"Yes, I hope so; she has offered."

"Si, that is good, I hoped that you and she would get along."

Ramirez said something to the associates, and they laughed.

Adam took a drink of beer, trying to give an impression of calm consideration. He knew he was in a corner and had no wish to drag things out. Maybe he could do something when he got back to London; find some excuse for him not to get further involved, explain there had been increased scrutiny perhaps; change of job, even; that made more sense. So, Adam embarked on a stalling tactic.

"Yes, ok I have thought about your offer, and I would like to continue assisting you."

Ramirez got up, prompting Adam to do the same. Ramirez grabbed Adam in a hug,

"Excellent, excellent," he said and spoke to the others. They too approached Adam and hugged him. He could feel something hard against his chest as Gabriel completed his embrace of gratitude. He definitely had a gun in his pocket.

"Come, Adam, I want you to meet my family."

Ramirez led the way back onto the terrace. It was early afternoon; the mountain haze had now gone and was replaced by a cloudless sky and an increase in temperature. Adam was still wearing his jacket which was now getting uncomfortable. He noticed all the men were still wearing theirs so for the moment he would have to endure it.

Gonzales and Camacho left to join other family groups, and Adam watched them make a fuss of children. Their wives or girlfriends, he couldn't make out which, were considerably younger than their partners, he noticed.

"Adam, please let me introduce you to my wife, Isabella."

A stylish woman in her early forties, probably twenty years younger than Ramirez offered her hand. Adam looked at her; immaculate make-up, olive skin without a blemish, perfect eyes, teeth and hair, coiffured to perfection. She was wearing a white designer trouser-suit and a considerable amount of jewellery.

"Encantado de conocerte," said Adam, attempting his Spanish again.

"It is ok, I speak English," said the woman. "Pleased to meet you too, my husband, he has spoken much about you. You are a banker, si?"

"Yes, from London."

"Si; and you have been helping with our business, I think."

"Yes," said Adam.

"And it is your first time in Costa Rica; do you like it here?"

"Yes, it's beautiful. I love it."

A young girl aged about three or four approached them and tugged at the woman's trousers.

"Mamá, tengo hambre," she said and started to grizzle.

Isabella picked her up. "She is hungry; please excuse me, Señor Adam."

"Yes, of course. Nice to meet you."

Isabella walked towards the barbecue with her daughter, a young boy, a little older than the girl, joined them."

"That is Pedro, my son. I hope one day he will have all of this for his family."

Ramirez was clearly building a dynasty.

"He will be a lucky boy," said Adam.

"Si; we are blessed," said Ramirez.

Adam could see Evelyn down on the next terrace sitting on a chaise-longue looking out across the valley. Ramirez noticed the interest.

"Evelyn, she is there. You should talk to her, I think."

"Thank you, I will," said Adam and descended the steps and walked over to her. She looked beautiful, and totally in tune with the incredible scenery.

"Hello," said Adam. "You look deep in thought."

"Hola. Yes, I love looking at the mountains, they talk to me. Always, since I was a little girl, they talk to me."

"And what do they say?"

"They tell me things, things I should do; they say I should go to Tamarindo with you."

"Really?"

"Yes, they say that, but I already knew. I have spoken to papa, and he says it is fine; I can go with you. He will speak to you soon."

"That's fantastic."

"Si, we will leave tomorrow at eight-thirty in the morning. We will meet at the Parada de Buses De Sabana Cemeterio. It is where the buses go; the truck will meet us there. You can get a taxi, no? It is not far from my uncle's apartment."

"Yes, no problem."

They continued chatting and time seemed to fly. Adam

found they had much in common, particularly sport. Evelyn loved horses; her father owned several racehorses and had a working stable on the outskirts of the city. Evelyn spent much of her spare time there helping exercise them.

"Do you ride, Adam?"

"I've never had the opportunity," said Adam.

"Oh, it is wonderful; when we get to Tamarindo, we will get horses and go into the country."

"Sounds great, I can't wait," said Adam.

All thoughts of his wider mission had gone; he was mesmerised by Evelyn.

By five o'clock, the sun had set behind the mountains, and it was starting to get dark. Waiters placed lanterns on the tables to provide illumination which, if anything, enhanced the ambience. The temperature had dropped marginally, but it was still humid. Insects started to flit around the light-sources.

The Mariachi band had started to pack away their instruments; children were being rounded up, and farewells exchanged. Adam and Evelyn were still on the second terrace; it was so peaceful. They were seated together on the chaise-longue over-looking the valley and, with most of the guests on the top terrace, they were not disturbed. The conversation had continued for most of the afternoon; drinks had been brought to them on a regular basis; Adam stuck to beers while Evelyn was drinking the homemade punch. A couple of times Adam had to answer the call of nature and waved to Ramirez who was playing the ever-attentive host with his guests.

"What are you doing this evening?" asked Evelyn. The glow from the lantern highlighted Evelyn's face; the atmosphere was almost ethereal.

"I have nothing planned. I wasn't sure what time the

reception finished."

"Si, I understand. I will go back to my apartment soon. You can ride with me if you like; my father won't mind."

"Yes, that will be good, thanks," said Adam. She touched his arm, then held his hand.

"Come, let me find my father and I will tell him what we are doing."

They got up, Evelyn was still holding Adam's hand as they walked up to the top terrace. It was much quieter now; many of the guests seemed to have left. Ramirez was stood in the corner chatting to the two men Adam had met earlier. Two women and assorted children were waiting patiently by the door. One of them shouted something in Spanish, and a young man shouted back. The caller immediately turned and went back inside.

Andrés was standing with Isabella and another woman; he noticed Evelyn and Adam approach.

"Ah, Evelyn," he said in English. "You have had a good time with Adam, si?"

"Si, papa."

The conversation continued in Spanish, which Adam couldn't translate but Andrés was nodding and smiling.

Evelyn turned to Adam. "Si, it is settled. Jacó will take us back to the apartment, and the truck will take us to Tamarindo in the morning. I have to take my phone with me; my papa, he worries."

"Glad that he does," said Adam and Andrés smiled.

"You both have a good time in Tamarindo and you, Adam, look after my lovely daughter, si?" said Andrés.

"Yes, of course," said Adam. He gave Adam a fatherly hug. "Where is Abel? I will tell him you are leaving."

Ramirez junior was spotted, and Andrés beckoned him over.

"They are leaving now," Andrés said as his brother approached.

"Adam, I hope you have enjoyed your time as my guest. Evelyn, I think, has been your host, she has looked after you, si?"

"Yes, very well, thank you."

Adam looked at Evelyn and smiled.

"And you are going exploring, I hear, to Tamarindo?"

"Yes, tomorrow," replied Adam.

"Bueno, that is good. What you don't need to take with you, you can leave in the apartment; it will be quite safe. I will not be needing it until you return to London."

"Thank you, that's very good of you," said Adam.

"Now, where is Isabella? She was seeing to the children I think."

A moment later, his wife appeared from the back entrance.

"Ah, Isabella, Adam is just leaving."

She approached Adam. "Very pleased to meet you, Señor Adam, off to Tamarindo, si?"

"Yes, Evelyn has promised to teach me how to ride a horse."

"Bueno, that is good. Evelyn is a champion."

After further lengthy farewells, Evelyn and Adam finally made it to the car. It was the Chevvy that had transported Adam earlier.

Jacó opened the rear door, and they both climbed in. This time, Adam did not want to sit next to the driver.

As they headed down the dirt road out of the estate, it was pitch black with not a hint of light anywhere, and Adam found it quite spooky. Evelyn held his hand.

It took nearly an hour to reach Adam's apartment; the journey was mostly silent; words seemed superfluous as the couple grew closer. The street lights of the capital were a welcome relief after the eeriness of the mountain roads. Adam recognised one or two landmarks as they approached his neighbourhood. They were a few minutes away; Adam turned to Evelyn and leaned towards her. The kiss was slow and passionate and was only disturbed by Jacó announcing their arrival at Adam's apartment.

Evelyn said something to the driver in Spanish.

"I come with you to get your things then we go to my apartment, si? It will be easier tomorrow."

"Really? Yes, ok, I won't be long," said Adam

"Si, it is ok; Jacó will wait."

They got out of the car and went into the apartment block. As they rode the elevator, the kissing continued. Evelyn was breathing heavily.

The lift made its customary judder to a halt, and the pair exited. Adam opened the door to the apartment, and they went inside.

"Please, you collect your things; I need the bathroom," said Evelyn.

Adam went to the closet, took out the items he would need, and put them in the rucksack he had used on the journey to Costa Rica from England. He would travel light; two pairs of shorts, a spare pair of jeans, tee-shirts, underwear, sandals and trainers. He changed out of his formal gear and put on a pair of black jeans, trainers and a khaki-coloured tee-shirt.

Adam heard the toilet flush and moments later Evelyn appeared.

"Nearly finished," said Adam, as he walked out of the bedroom carrying his rucksack.

"Muy Bien, we can go to my apartment; it is not far."

Adam wanted to hold her again but played it cool.

"One minute," said Adam, and went into the bathroom; he returned holding his wash-bag.

He had one more check around. He saw the business card on the table which he'd removed from his jacket and put it in the pocket of his jeans; he had no idea why.

Evelyn looked at him as he entered the room. "You look good."

"Thanks," Adam replied. "Ok, let's go."

He turned out the lights and locked the door. Evelyn had called the elevator, and they watched the floor indicator as it made the tedious journey up from the ground floor. It arrived, and Adam opened the door and waited for Evelyn to enter, then followed carrying his rucksack. The kissing resumed; Adam could taste lipstick and smell the heady scent of her perfume.

Jacó was waiting by the car, texting on his phone, as the couple exited the apartment block. He immediately put away his phone and took Adam's rucksack, then opened the rear door. Adam and Evelyn got in while the driver stowed the luggage.

"It is not far," said Evelyn and she squeezed Adam's hand. The anticipation was almost unbearable; Adam had an aching feeling in the pit of his stomach, and his mouth was dry. He noticed a plastic bottle of water in the door compartment. He let go of Evelyn's hand and reached for it. He unscrewed the cap and took a gulp then handed it to Evelyn who did the same.

As Evelyn had said, it was only another five minutes until Jacó pulled up outside another apartment block. There were fewer streetlights, so it was difficult to see in detail, but it resembled Abel's apartment from the outside.

Jacó opened the door, and the pair got out; the driver passed Adam his baggage and spoke to Evelyn in Spanish. They watched as the Chevvy pulled away.

"Jacó will meet us in the morning and take us to the truck," she said taking Adam's hand and leading him inside the building.

It was three floors to the top, and again they used the elevator, but this one was much quicker.

"It is just here," said Evelyn as she opened the door in front of them.

"Wow. This is amazing," said Adam as he entered Evelyn's flat. It was in a totally different league to Abel's. That one was a bolt-hole to stay in when needed. Evelyn's was a home with all the trappings and accoutrements of a luxury apartment. It was much bigger, a large lounge with a panoramic window; the lights of the city stretched out before them. A beautiful suite with red scatter-cushions, carpet, tasteful pictures, a large TV on the wall. In the corner, was a drinks cabinet. Evelyn closed the drapes.

"There, that is better. You would like a drink, si?" said Evelyn. "Let me take your bag."

"Yes, thank you."

Adam was still trying to take in his new surroundings. Evelyn opened one of the doors and disappeared down a corridor. She returned a few moments later.

"I have put your bag in the bedroom. Now you must try the drink of Costa Rica; it is called Guaro; it is made from sugar cane."

She went to the drinks cabinet and took out a bottle; Cacique, it said on the label. She poured measures into two shot glasses and handed one to Adam. He watched as she warmed the glass in her hand and then tipped it back in one gulp. Adam did the same. It tasted a bit like vodka only sweeter; it wasn't unpleasant.

Evelyn looked at Adam.

"Now we fuck, si?"

"Si," said Adam.

Chapter Seventeen

At seven-thirty the following morning, Adam and Evelyn were in the kitchen eating muesli and fruit at the kitchen table. An Espresso machine was dispensing shots of caffeine. Adam was reflecting on the previous day; it was something he would never forget, the mansion, the scenery, and Evelyn. She had turned his world upside down.

The closeness of the sex was something he had never experienced before. His previous conquests had been about self-gratification, but with Evelyn, it was so different. He looked at her dressed in a vest and cut-off jeans. She wasn't wearing a bra, and the sides of her breasts were visible. She had no inhibitions at all. Adam had never met anyone like her.

"I am going to shower; you can have the bathroom after me. I will not be long," said Evelyn and kissed him.

"Ok, thanks," said Adam and continued eating his cereal. Evelyn left the kitchen leaving Adam with his thoughts.

He did have one big concern, of course, which he was trying to put to the back of his mind. The new 'arrangement' with the investors. Despite their assurances, the level of risk had significantly increased, and he was anxious. The number of transactions he had authorised so far was not too large and unlikely to raise any eyebrows but two or three a week could be a problem. He still didn't know what he should do.

After a few minutes, Evelyn called him to say the shower was free, and he went along the corridor to the bathroom.

"Leave the towels when you have finished. Juanita will see to them."

"Juanita?" said Adam.

"Si, she is the housekeeper."

"Ok," said Adam, and smiled; a housekeeper, of course.

By eight-fifteen, Adam and Evelyn had packed and were outside the apartment block waiting for their lift. Adam was wearing shorts, a tee-shirt and sandals for what was going to be a long journey. Evelyn was similarly dressed. Moments later, the familiar Chevvy appeared and pulled up at the roadside. Jacó was again driving and helped load their luggage into the back of the SUV.

They arrived at the bus station ten minutes later. As it was a Sunday, there was no rush hour, but it was still busy with buses dropping off passengers and reloading. Evelyn spotted the truck waiting in one of the bays.

"The truck is here," said Evelyn and the Chevvy parked alongside.

Adam and Evelyn exited the car and waited for Jacó to extract the baggage. Evelyn spoke to him in Spanish, and he returned to the Chevvy and drove off.

It was a medium-sized truck; Isuzu five-ton, with the distinctive "Compañía de Cinco Iluvias Inc" logo on the side. The driver climbed down from the cab, took the two rucksacks and threw them onto the front seat. Evelyn held the hand-rail and took the two steps to get aboard; Adam followed. The driver was speaking urgently to Evelyn in Spanish; she translated.

"He says we have to go quickly; he has a deadline to reach Tamarindo."

The man walked around to the driver's side and climbed in. There was a roar as he started the engine, followed by the hiss of the airbrakes. He looked left and right, then eased out of the bus station onto the main highway. The man seemed calmer once they were on the road and spoke to Evelyn again.

"He says his name is Ángel, and it will take five or six

hours."

The cab was roomy and surprisingly comfortable. The baggage had been stowed in the space behind the front seats which also doubled as a sleeping area for long-haul journeys. There was even a cool-box where bottles of water had been stashed and plenty of space for two people and the driver. There were two loose seat belts; Adam buckled up and encouraged Evelyn to do the same. Ángel saw them and laughed, then said something to Evelyn.

"He says we shouldn't be nervous; he is a good driver." Adam acknowledged the comment with a grin and 'thumbs-up' sign, then suddenly wondered if that was a rude gesture like in Brazil; the driver didn't seem to take offence.

From the bus station, they turned left; La Sabana, the large central park, was on their right. They soon joined Route 27, the Autopista Jose Maria Castro Madriz. As a motorway, it attracted tolls, and the driver would have to stop regularly at booths to pay. Once out of San José, they headed west through the mountains reaching the coast at Puerto Caldera, around seventy-five miles from where they had started. They had been on the road for the best part of two hours.

Just after Caldera, Adam noticed a service station sign; Ángel had spotted it too, and he pulled in for a break.

He turned to Evelyn. "Quince minutos," he said.

"Fifteen minutes," said Adam before Evelyn could translate, and they both laughed.

They made their way into the café and ordered coffee. The eating area was full of truckers taking the opportunity of a break before heading onwards.

"You must try one of those," said Evelyn pointing to an array of cakes. "Tres Leches; muchos delicious," she added and laughed again.

There had been a lot of laughter.

"Yes, go on then," said Adam, and they made their way to a spare table carrying their mid-morning snacks.

"You're right about these," said Adam. "You must give me the recipe. I'll send it to my mother."

Just after the truck stop, there was a major intersection where Route 27 crossed the Pan-American Highway, Route 1. Ángel eased the Isuzu onto the new road and turned to Adam.

"Pan-American Highway."

"Si," said Adam, acknowledging the road which stretches down from Alaska, along the West Coast of the States all the way to the bottom of Argentina, over thirty-thousand miles long, and the longest driveable road in the world.

The next landmark was Las Hermanas, the Three Sisters, where there was another truck stop and interchange. This time Adam and Evelyn were given thirty-minutes for their break. Here, the truck turned west again, onto Route 18. They continued chatting for most of the journey, Evelyn pointing out places of interest. Eventually, they reached a huge suspension bridge which had Adam's attention.

"Si, it is the Puente La Amistad de Taiwán, it was built by the Taiwan people, and it's called the 'friendship bridge'."

Adam took in the view as they crossed the wide Tempisque River. The driver spoke to Evelyn in Spanish.

"Next stop Tamarindo," translated Evelyn.

There was still another hour and a half of winding roads to negotiate.

"I wouldn't enjoy driving a truck here," said Adam. Evelyn translated for the driver, and he smiled a toothy grin.

It was mid-afternoon as the truck made its way through the narrow streets of Tamarindo.

"Where are we staying?" asked Adam. For some reason it hadn't been discussed; Adam had assumed Evelyn knew the area. He wasn't really surprised by the answer,

"We can use papa's apartment; he uses it when he has business here. Uncle Abel also uses it. Or you can go to a hostel," she said and smiled.

"No, I'm happy to go with you."

She spoke to the driver, and he continued further into town.

Adam was transfixed; the main street was alive with people, mostly in swimwear; some were carrying surfboards. Shops and stalls were selling beachwear and fishing gear. They drove by a taxi-stand on the main corner where two vehicles were waiting for fares, but with several more rough-looking men hanging around the office doorway. Evelyn noticed the interest.

"Los Colombianos; they control the drugs in Tamarindo."

"Really?" said Adam but decided not to pursue it.

They reached the beach road, the Calle Cardinal, and the truck turned left, parallel to the sea-line. The view to the right was amazing with the sun starting to move downwards towards the beckoning surf. The beach was not crowded, but the sea was, with surfers out in force. As they reached the end of the beach, the view was obscured by a headland. After a short distance, the truck turned right and drew up outside a large gated apartment complex. There was a security guard on duty, and he took an interest in the new arrivals.

The driver spoke to Evelyn.

"This is where we get out. The apartment is not far."

Adam and Evelyn said their farewells to Ángel. He was not quite at the end of his journey; his depot was at the other end of the town, Evelyn explained. Adam got out, and Evelyn passed down the baggage. They waved to the driver who pulled away in a cloud of exhaust fumes.

They walked up to the security gate, and Evelyn said something to the guard. He appeared to stand to attention, then waved the couple through. They walked past several impressive condos. The lawns surrounding them were trimmed, and large shrubs added further colour to the area. At the end of the block, they came to the boundary wall, and on the left, was the last apartment.

"We are here," said Evelyn.

There was a short driveway leading to an integral garage to the left the entrance. Evelyn opened her purse and took out a swipe card. There was a click as she presented the card to the reader on the side of the door frame.

She pushed the door open and went inside.

Like the other residencies, it was beautifully presented. A short entrance hall opened onto a large lounge. The property was on two floors, and there was a spiral staircase leading to the next level. Adam followed Evelyn.

"The bedrooms are here," she said and opened the first door on the right. Adam went through and took in the view. The beach was about two hundred yards away; below them, in the back garden, was a swimming pool.

"Wow," said Adam.

"Si, the view; it is perfect. We can use here for our stuff," she added opening the closet door and stowing her rucksack; Adam did the same. The room was white; the centre-piece, a large double bed. There was also an en-suite bathroom and shower. Adam went to Evelyn and held her.

"We shower, si?"

"Si," said Adam, and he watched as Evelyn discarded her tee-shirt and shorts and walked into the bathroom.

The shower was reviving in more ways than one, and Evelyn soon had Adam ready. She turned around, and as the water cascaded down, he entered her from behind. Evelyn almost fainted as she felt Adam pushing into her; then she climaxed. Adam followed, and for a moment they allowed the stream from the shower to wash over them.

"Bueno," said Evelyn. "It was wonderful," she added as she turned around and kissed Adam passionately. She turned off the shower and passed Adam a towel.

"Would you like something to eat?"

"Yes, please," said Adam.

"Ok; get dressed, and we can go into town. I will show you the place, and we can go to a bar and get some food."

Twenty minutes later, the pair left the apartment. Evelyn took out a fob from her purse and aimed it at the garage door. It slowly arose. Adam couldn't believe his eyes; an orange beach-buggy; complete with roll-bars.

"Wow, great car," said Adam.

"Si, you can drive if you like," and Evelyn handing him the keys.

They got in the car, and Adam could see two surfboards leaning against the wall.

"Tomorrow we go surfing," said Evelyn, noticing Adam looking at them.

"Great," said Adam. He started the car, and there was a throaty roar as the engine sprang into life.

He tentatively eased the car out of the garage and stopped. Evelyn turned around, aimed the fob at the garage door and watched it slowly descend.

Adam turned right towards the complex entrance, and the security guard raised the barrier as he saw the vehicle approach. With an open canopy, Evelyn had to shout directions, but it was straightforward enough; just a question of following the coast road for a couple of miles, then turning right into the main street where all the activity seemed to be.

"We can stop over there," said Evelyn pointing to a space in front of a row of private houses.

Adam parked up, and the couple got out.

"Over here," said Evelyn, and they walked hand-in-hand to a bar across the street. There was a wooden sign over the doorway "Las Estaciones". The bar was open at the front with four tables outside; there were more inside. Two of the tables were taken by sun-bronzed couples in beachwear. Evelyn was wearing a bikini top, cut-off jeans and flip-flops.

They sat down, and a man in his fifties appeared from inside, bringing them two menus.

"Qué le gustaría beber," he said.

They both ordered beers.

Adam took out his phone and took some pictures, then turned around and spoke to the couple at the adjacent table. He nodded at the phone indicating a picture.

"Yeah, sure," said the man in a broad American accent.

"Thanks," said Adam, and passed him the phone.

Adam sat next to Evelyn and looked at the camera. The man took two photos and handed the phone back. "Cheers," said Adam and opened the photo app to examine the picture.

"Hey, this looks really good," he said and passed the phone to Evelyn.

"Si, bueno," she said and returned the phone to Adam.

"I'll post it on Instagram; my rugby buddies will be so

envious."

The bar owner returned with the beers, and they chose food from the menu.

They spent nearly two hours at the bar; it was early evening and dark. The lights from the nightclubs and bars shone like beacons trying to attract customers. Loud disco music echoed around the streets which were packed with tourists looking for somewhere to eat. Las Estaciones was now full.

"We timed that well," said Adam watching the throng of tourists milling about in the street.

"Si. Let's go for a walk; I will show you some of the nightclubs here."

"Yeah, ok I want to look for a souvenir or two to take home for my parents."

"Si, si, there are many shops you will like."

They got up, and Evelyn went to the desk to pay the bill.

"My shout tomorrow," said Adam.

"It is ok; papa gave me money to pay for some food,"

"Well, that's very good of him; you must thank him for me."

"Si, si, I will do that. I will call him later and tell him we have arrived ok."

As they wandered around the packed streets, Adam was reflecting on recent events and couldn't remember being this content, despite the potential hazards ahead. He turned to Evelyn.

"I don't want this ever to end."

"Si," said Evelyn. "It is very special," and she squeezed his hand.

"Why don't you come back to the UK with me?"

"No; it is not possible. I am sorry; I wish it was different," she replied. Adam was unhappy with the knockback but would not give up that easily.

They turned and headed back down Main Street to pick up the buggy; after the day's journey, an early night was beckoning. They reached the taxi-rank on the corner. Four taxis were lined up; their drivers huddled in a group outside the office waiting for the phone to ring. One of the men started taking an interest in the couple. He followed the pair to the end of the drag until they reached the buggy. Then pulled out his mobile phone and talked animatedly into the handset.

The following day Adam woke up with Evelyn lying in his arms. The early night had turned out to be anything but relaxing; he had never experienced anything like it.

He kissed her on the forehead. "Mmm, what time is it," she said as she opened her eyes.

"Quarter-to-eight," replied Adam checking his smartphone.

"I need the bathroom," she said and slowly got out of bed.

The sun had been up for over two hours, and the room was bathed in daylight shining through the curtains. Evelyn returned to bed. "Do you want coffee?" she said snuggling up to Adam.

"Have you got tea?"

"Si, si, I think," she said. "I will make you some in a minute." Adam could feel Evelyn's fingers moving down his body, and she wrapped her hands around his sleeping penis. He was called into action again.

At the end of the corridor from the bedrooms, there was a set of glass doors which opened to a covered veranda with a table and four chairs. Forty-minutes later Adam and Evelyn were enjoying coffee, croissants and the amazing view of the ocean in the distance.

"Today, I will take you surfing, si?"

"Sounds excellent," said Adam. "You will have to show me what to do."

"Si, si, I will be a good teacher."

After breakfast, Adam and Evelyn loaded the buggy with two surfboards and some snacks to keep them going.

"I will drive," said Evelyn. "I know a place where nobody else goes."

They left the condo and turned left outside the security gates, heading south away from the town. They travelled about ten miles with the Pacific Ocean to their right. Adam caught glimpses of it when the tree-line and geography allowed.

They passed a couple of villages where roadside diners advertised "Desayuno todo el día"; all day breakfasts, Evelyn translated. Evelyn slowed down the buggy and made a right turn down a dirt track. The narrow, unmade road stretched on for almost two miles through overhanging palms and other tropical fauna.

Then, it was in front of them. Evelyn stopped the buggy, and for a moment they just looked.

"Wow," said Adam. "This is amazing."

They had arrived at the beach, not pebbly, like those nearer the town, but with fine, white sand. It was an inlet with sharp cliffs on either side; not tall, about thirty or forty feet, but enough to encase the ocean. Waves crashed onto the beach, then disappeared before repeating the process, a perpetual motion of water.

Evelyn parked the buggy under the shade of an overhanging palm tree, and the pair started unloading the buggy. Within minutes, they were in the crystal clear waters, paddling out to catch the waves. Adam was wearing his swim shorts, Evelyn, a bikini. Although rusty, Adam soon got the hang of balancing on the board, but he was nowhere near Evelyn's standard.

They spent a couple of hours surfing before returning to the beach. Evelyn had packed a couple of towels from the apartment, and they lay down next to each other. They had discarded their swimwear allowing the sun to dry their bodies naturally. It was Adam who made the first move, and they made love on the beach.

Afterwards, Evelyn produced a litre bottle of water from a cool-box, together with some savoury pastries and fruit; they enjoyed their picnic before re-engaging with the surf.

It was three o'clock before they started packing away their gear for the return journey.

Back in the condo, Adam was on the veranda reading a paperback. Evelyn had finished showering and brought two soft fruit juice drinks and sat down.

"What you said yesterday, about coming to London?"

This had Adam's attention.

"Yes," said Adam and looked at Evelyn. She took a drink.

"I do not think it will be possible right now. Papa wants me to finish my studies at the University."

"Yes, I understand," said Adam.

"But you could come here. Papa will find you a job in his banco; he likes you, I know that. I am sure it will be ok."

"Hmm, now that is a very tempting thought. I don't want to leave you." Adam grabbed Evelyn's hand and kissed it.

"I feel that too. I don't know what to do."

"Well, we have this time together, we can talk about it."

"Si," said Evelyn and leaned over and kissed Adam.

She changed the subject. "Tomorrow, we go riding the horses. There is a place where I go near the airport; it is beautiful, we can go into the jungle." Adam looked concerned.

"Do not worry, it will be ok, I will look after you. The horses are very gentle." She laughed.

"Yeah, ok; sounds great," said Adam.

That evening they took the buggy back into town. Adam parked in the same place as the previous day. The closeness between them continued to grow with every minute they were together. Adam found a souvenir shop and chose an ornament for his mother. At the same shop, while Evelyn was looking at some silk scarves, he bought a silver bracelet.

They returned to the bar for their evening dinner, and Adam presented it to her.

"For me?" she said as she took it out of the box. "It is beautiful, thank you. I will wear it for you always."

There were several cars parked across the road from Las Estaciones, including a taxi and, as the couple enjoyed their meal, the driver was taking an unusual interest in them.

The next day, as arranged, Evelyn drove the buggy north, through the town and out on the Avenue Las Palmas. Conversation was not easy in the open-top; wind noise was not conducive for discussion, so Adam took in the scenery instead. Evelyn turned left onto the Calle Sangria and headed north. The spattering of houses was replaced by forest. After two miles, the road widened, and, on the right, several wooden buildings appeared. There was a short track to what looked like an entrance with a sign over it, "Centro Equino", with a picture of a rampant stallion on its hind quarters.

"We are here," shouted Evelyn as she negotiated the buggy through a narrow portico into a quadrangle, surrounded by stables. The sandy ground was covered with horse droppings.

She parked out of the sun, and the pair exited. A groom approached them, and Evelyn hugged the girl warmly. She led her to Adam and introduced her.

"This is Sabrina; she looks after the horses here."

Adam shook her hand. She was younger than Evelyn, with a fresh face and dressed in riding gear.

She spoke to Evelyn in Spanish, who translated for Adam.

"She says she has some nice horses, very gentle."

"Thanks, I hope so," he replied and laughed.

While Evelyn and Adam waited by the buggy, Sabrina went through an alleyway in the wooden outbuildings and returned a few minutes later leading two mares.

She led the horses to the couple and handed them two helmets.

There was more conversation in Spanish between the two girls, punctuated with laughter. Adam was sure he was the butt of their levity, but he wasn't concerned.

Evelyn helped Adam with his hat, and then with Sabrina's help, managed to get Adam seated on the mare. Adam was holding the reins as tightly as he could.

"Where are the brakes?" he shouted, and Evelyn laughed and translated for Sabrina.

Evelyn tacked up and mounted her mare like a professional jockey.

"Come, I will teach you," she said, and led Adam around the courtyard for a few minutes until he felt more comfortable.

"How is it?" she shouted, after the fifth circuit.

"Yeah," said Adam. "Ok, I think."

"Bueno, we will go out and follow the jungle trail."

Adam negotiated the horse behind Evelyn's and trotted along gradually gaining in confidence. The first few minutes he spent focussing on holding on, but slowly he relaxed and started to take in some of the scenery. The trail was full of animal noises. Luckily, the horses didn't seem to be bothered, and the pair ambled through the greenery, following a well-trodden path. For Adam, it was a new experience, and one he was determined to enjoy to the full.

They eventually arrived at a small village. Most of the dwellings were constructed with wood, resembling an Indian settlement. Some young children were kicking a ball to each other; chickens were scurrying around; there was little sign of any motorised transport. Their presence had alerted the children, who started running alongside the horses shouting in Spanish. Evelyn led Adam to a small cantina.

"We can stop here and have a drink and something to eat," she said as she dismounted. A couple of children came over to them, their eyes wide and bright. Evelyn put her hand in her trouser pocket, pulled out some notes and handed them over. They went away looking very happy with their haul.

Adam tried to dismount but landed in a heap below his horse as his foot got caught in the stirrups. The children roared with laughter.

Evelyn was also in fits. "You will soon get used to it."

No damage was done, except to Adam's pride, but he could see the funny side. They tied up the horses next to a water trough to enable the mares to drink while Adam and Evelyn went to the cantina.

There were few people about; a woman of about fifty appeared from inside and walked towards them. Evelyn spoke to her and translated for Adam.

"She says she has some paella cooking which will be ready in about twenty minutes."

"Sounds good," said Adam who was walking up and down stretching his legs.

Evelyn went to him and held his hands. "You did very well. I am proud of you," she said and kissed him.

"It was all down to the coach," replied Adam and Evelyn smiled.

There were two small fold-up tables with accompanying chairs outside the cantina, and they both sat down. Adam took out his phone and started taking pictures.

Evelyn gave Adam some background. "This is the village of Santa Maria de las Vírgenes. The jungle we came through goes all the way to the Estero de Playa Grande. It's about six miles, but we will not go there with the horses. There are crocodiles there, very dangerous; some tourists get eaten."

"No, we'll definitely give those a miss," said Adam.

"It is all a nature reserve with many rare animals; the noises you could hear…" She mimicked the sound. "They are monkeys. Many monkeys live in the jungle."

Evelyn continued with the travelogue; Adam was amazed. The lady returned with a large bottle of water and two glasses. She spoke again to Evelyn.

"The paella will be ready soon," Evelyn translated.

While on the trail, Adam had been thinking a great deal about Evelyn's suggestion of moving to Costa Rica. In one way, it would solve his biggest dilemma. If he was working for the Costa Rican bank, he wouldn't be involved in the London end and the subsequent risks. He wasn't sure what Ramirez would say, but he would raise the question; he wanted to be with Evelyn forever.

He watched her sipping water. She was wearing a baggy vest top and black jeans; sensible attire for horse-riding. The woman eventually brought out a large bowl with the rice dish; steam was coming from the contents. She put it on the table and went back for two plates.

Evelyn dished up, and they tucked into their lunch. Adam was hungry after the fresh air and made short work of the first plateful. Luckily, there was plenty to satisfy their appetite.

They stayed in the village for over an hour, and Adam learned more about the local culture and the wildlife; the howling monkeys provided an eerie soundtrack to the scene. Evelyn settled the bill with a generous tip which had the woman thanking her animatedly.

The next challenge for Adam was to remount his horse.

"Do you want a hand?" asked Evelyn as they approached the mares.

"Let me watch you, and then I'll copy," replied Adam.

Evelyn put her left foot in the stirrup and gracefully eased herself up and over. Adam followed rather ungainly, but at least he was in the saddle again. Children had started to gather around them as they headed back to the trail. Evelyn shouted to them, and they waved. Adam watched her interact with the children; she was going to make a great ambassador. There was a humanity about her; her ability to connect was a gift with which not everyone was blessed.

He rode alongside Evelyn for a while, no more than a gentle walk. They had been riding for thirty minutes when they were passing a fallen tree. Nothing strange about that; there were hundreds lining the path. But Adam noticed something moving over the top of it. His horse also detected it and reared up, throwing Adam off-balance and crashing to the floor. The horse bolted down the track.

Evelyn was quickly off her mare and over to Adam.

"I'm fine," said Adam.

"Stay still," said Evelyn. Adam watched as a grey shape slithered off the tree and into the undergrowth on the other side.

"Are you ok?" said Evelyn.

"Yeah, I'm fine; the ground is soft here." Adam stood up, brushed himself down and did some stretches; no damage. "What was it.?"

"It was a snake; a Fer-De-Lance, the viper, very poisonous. They kill many people in Costa Rica every year, particularly in the villages, children mostly. It scared the horse. I will ride up the track; it won't have gone far, just out of danger."

"I'll walk with you," said Adam, and the pair continued up the trail for about a mile until they were out of the trees and into grassland. Sure enough, the errant mare was grazing about a hundred yards ahead.

Evelyn dismounted and slowly approached the horse, holding onto the reigns of her mount. "I don't want to scare her," she said. Adam watched as she went to the frightened mare and gently stroked its head. The other horse seemed to take an interest as well and appeared to be bonding with it.

"They are great friends," said Evelyn as Adam watched.

After a few minutes, Evelyn was still stroking the horse. "I think she will be ok now. Try getting on; I will hold her."

Adam complied and gingerly eased himself onto the horse, half-expecting it to go shooting off, but it remained calm, and Evelyn let go of the reins.

"She should be fine now," said Evelyn. "We will head to the road and go back to the centro; it is not too far."

They had travelled in a large loop and were now only two or three miles from the Equestrian Centre.

Forty minutes later, they were handing back the horses and

the gear to the groom, Sabrina. Evelyn explained what had happened; luckily the horse was showing no ill effects. She handed the girl some money and then went to the buggy.

The sun had moved, and the jeep was now in the direct glare. The seats were hot to the touch, and Adam shouted as the backs of his legs made contact with the seat. "Mind your legs; the seats are hot," said Adam as Evelyn got in.

"Ow, yes," said Evelyn as her flesh touched the plastic.

She leant across and kissed him. "Are you sure you're ok?"

"Yes, I'm fine thanks, a few bruises I expect."

"Hmm. I will have to check you over properly when we get back."

They returned to the condo, and Evelyn checked Adam over in the shower; she was pleased to report no ill-effects from the fall, apart from a stiff shoulder where he had landed. The soft ground had saved him from a more serious injury.

That evening they returned to their, now familiar, bar. The food was good, and they had begun to recognise one or two of the regulars who acknowledged their arrival; the atmosphere was relaxed and friendly.

They had eaten their meal and ordered a second round of drinks when Evelyn got up from her seat.

"Baño," she said, and Adam watched as she walked towards the bar entrance.

He noticed a man walk in after her but didn't think anything of it. People were walking in and out all the time.

After ten minutes, Adam checked his watch. He was starting to feel anxious for some reason; an inner voice was telling him something was wrong.

He left his seat and went into the bar. To the left, was the interior seating area where a few people were chatting and drinking; there was a thick fog of smoke hanging in the air, not all from tobacco. There was more than a hint of cannabis. To the right, were the kitchens and cash desk. The bar owner was checking receipts and ferrying orders to the chefs.

Further along the corridor was the toilet, just one mixed cubicle. The door was open.

"Evelyn, Evelyn?" called Adam.

Chapter Eighteen

Adam noticed an open door at the end of the corridor. He rushed towards it and looked outside left and right. It was just a backyard; there was a rusting carcass of an unidentifiable vehicle to the right of the door. To the left, there was nothing remarkable, just a white-dirt area. Adam kept shouting Evelyn's name; a couple of lads were playing football against a wall under a street light fifty yards or so away. A million bugs flitted around the light source.

Adam approached the boys. "Have you seen a girl from here?" he shouted at them, pointing at the back door.

The nearest boy looked at Adam and shrugged his shoulders. Adam went closer; he wrestled with the language. "Er… has visto… una chica… desde esa puerta?"

He pointed at the back entrance to the bar. The other boy joined his buddy, and they spoke in Spanish.

"Si; ella estaba con tres hombres en un coche."

Adam translated; three men and a car. "Un coche?"

"Si, un coche."

"Where did it go? Er… dónde?"

"Esa dirección," the lad shouted pointing away from the bar.

There was nothing to see now; they would be well away.

He went back through the bar to his seat outside and retrieved his phone from his pocket. He dialled a number.

"Señor Ramírez, it's Adam Fowler. I am in Tamarindo. Someone has taken Evelyn."

He explained what had happened.

"Ok, now stay where you are. What is the name of the bar?" said Ramirez.

Adam told him.

"Ok, I have people there, and I will ask them to meet you in a few minutes. They will introduce themselves. I will get a team from here to you as soon as I can; this time of night, about three or four hours, I think."

He rang off, and Adam just stared at his beer asking himself if he could have prevented it. Maybe he should have gone with her to the toilet, but there had been no hint of threat.

Ten minutes later, Adam noticed three heavy-duty men in suits walking up the street towards the bar. He was on alert. They stopped at the outside seating area and appeared to be looking around. One of them made eye-contact with Adam and walked over.

"Señor Fowler?"

"Yes," said Adam.

The man sat down on the chair vacated by Evelyn. The other two were behind him surveying the scene.

"My name is Sorenson; I work for Abel Ramirez; he has just called. Tell me what happened."

The man spoke with a strong American accent. Adam explained the course of events.

"Show me," said the man and Adam took him into the bar and down the corridor past the toilets.

"This door was open; I went outside. There were two boys playing football, and one of them told me that three men took Evelyn into a car and drove off."

"Where are the boys?"

"There; those two," said Adam pointing to the two lads who were still kicking a ball to each other. One of the other heavies joined them.

The men walked over to the boys who immediately stopped playing. Sorenson took out some money from his pocket and waved a note at the first lad. The new heavy spoke to them in Spanish. There was a great deal of pointing and gesturing.

Sorensen walked back to Adam.

"Yeah, just as you said. They took the girl and drove off in a black car."

"Oh God," said Adam.

"Yeah, these guys don't mess around; best case scenario, a kidnap for ransom; worse case, a show of power. If this is the case, we won't have long." He paused; Adam was horrified. "Have you noticed anything unusual since you've been here?"

"No, everything's been fine; everyone's been very generous and welcoming."

"What about routine; have you used this bar before?"

"Yes, every night."

"Hmm, that could be a problem."

"Did you notice anyone following you?"

"No, as I said, it's been fine."

"Think. It could be important."

"There was a taxi parked outside here last night. I remember thinking it was unusual it wasn't at the rank with the others. I thought he might have been waiting for someone."

"Did you see the driver?"

"Yes, but not clearly, it was dark."

"What kind of taxi was it?"

"Black. A Mercedes, I think; I didn't take a great deal of notice. I just remember it being parked there for a long time. It certainly didn't pick up any passengers."

Sorensen spoke to the two heavies in Spanish, and they left. Adam had his head in his hands.

"Stay here; I need to speak to the barman."

Sorensen got up and walked over to the bar entrance. Adam

watched Sorensen remonstrating fiercely with the proprietor. The heated exchange continued for a couple of minutes before the barman held up his hands in submission.

Sorensen returned.

"Anything?" said Adam.

"No, he says he doesn't know anything, but if he's lying, he's a dead man."

Adam had a feeling he wasn't joking.

Sorensen took his phone from his pocket and dialled a number. He spoke in Spanish, but Adam thought he was calling Ramirez.

He rang off and brought Adam up-to-date. "The team from San José are on their way; they should be here in three or four hours. You should go back to the condo."

"I can't get in, Evelyn has the key."

"That's ok, speak to the security guard, he will let you in."

"Yes, ok," said Adam.

"Ramirez is coming here too. He will meet you at the condo."

"Ok," said Adam.

"Give me your phone number in case I need to call you."

Adam complied and was just about to leave when one of the heavies returned and spoke to Sorensen.

He turned to Adam. "Come with me," he said and left the bar with Adam following. The other heavy was leading.

Adam was not someone who was ordinarily frightened; he got anxious occasionally, like when he visited the hacienda, but the emotion he felt now was on a different scale.

They reached the corner of the main street where the taxi-rank was situated. The third heavy stood on the corner monitoring movement.

"Los Colombianos," said Sorensen. "They are competitors. They cause trouble from time-to-time but usually we get on ok; there's plenty of business to go around," said the American. "Have a look at the dude in the white shirt by the office."

"Yeah," said Adam.

"He's got a black cab, Mercedes, just pulled up. Could he be the man you saw?"

Adam squinted. "I can't tell from this distance."

"Ok, let's go see," and Sorensen walked across the street with Adam and the other two heavies following.

As they reached the line of taxis, the man spotted the approaching men and said something to the chap at the office window, then started to run along the street away from them. He turned left down an alleyway about fifty yards down the drag. It was a stupid thing to do. Sorensen broke into a run and chased after him. Adam followed in the same direction, but well behind.

There was a gunshot and screams from passers-by. Adam reached the end of the alleyway and could see three men manhandling a fourth. Adam didn't move. The two heavies had the taxi driver by each arm and were dragging him towards Adam. Sorensen was leading.

"Is this him, the man you saw?" he said lifting up the man's head by his hair.

Adam looked at him. He had been shot in the shoulder and blood was oozing from the wound. The heavies lifted the man's head; his eyes were closed.

"I don't know; it could have been but, as I said, it was dark."

Sorensen spoke to the men in Spanish, and they began rummaging through the man's pockets. They found a wallet and passed it to Sorensen. He started pulling out papers and photographs.

"Tus niños, si?"

"Si, si," said the man hysterically; his eyes wide with fright.

"Están muertos," said Sorensen.

"No! No!" shouted the taxi driver. "Por favor… no."

"Speak to me; you know what we want."

"Si, si."

The man spoke quickly in Spanish and Adam couldn't understand. Sorensen translated.

"It's bad; the Escobar's have her."

"Pablo Escobar? I thought he was dead," said Adam.

"Yeah, years ago, but there are several families; Colombians, dangerous dudes."

Sorensen took out his phone and called again. He spoke in Spanish.

"Yeah, Ramirez is on the road, about three hours, maybe less. He says to go to the condo; he'll meet you there. We'll see to this."

He said something to the heavies; one of them took out his gun and shot the taxi-driver in the head causing blood to spurt out from the entrance hole; the body slumped to the ground.

Adam exhaled quickly several times and put his hands to his head. It was as if he were in a video game; only this was real. He wanted to be sick.

"You can get to the condo?" asked Sorensen.

"Yes," said Adam, still shaking with shock and trying to take in what he had just witnessed.

"Ok, you go there and wait, you'll be safe there. Ramirez will call you when he arrives."

Adam walked back to the buggy in a state of numbness; he had the keys in his pocket having driven to the bar. He couldn't stop thinking about Evelyn, he hoped against hope she would be safe.

He arrived at the condo and, as Sorensen had said, the security guard unlocked the door having recognised Adam.

Adam found it difficult to settle. He walked aimlessly around the apartment. Reminders of Evelyn were everywhere. What had been an idyllic trip of a lifetime, had turned into a nightmare. He thought about the taxi-man who wouldn't be seeing his children again. It didn't get much worse.

It was just over three hours later when Adam heard a rustling outside the door. Then a click as it opened. It was Ramirez, followed by Jacó who had acted as chauffeur. The noise had startled Adam who was on his guard.

"Señor Ramirez?" said Adam, as the man entered the apartment. He looked stern; worry and anger, mixed on his face.

"Si, yes, we are here. I have bought Jacó."

"Is there any news?"

"No, nothing, Sorensen is checking places where they might have taken her, but nothing yet."

Adam put his head in his hands. "If only I had gone with her to the toilet, but everything was so calm."

"Si, I know."

"What will happen?"

"I do not know, but, if it is the Escobars, then it will be war."

"What about your brother?" asked Adam.

"Si, he is not good; very angry. He will kill those who would hurt Evelyn."

"Is he coming here?"

"Si, maybe tomorrow, but he is needed with his family right now."

"Yes, I understand. Should I speak to him?"

"No, you should wait until we have some news."

Near Route 158 on the outskirts of Tamarindo, there is a small community called Villareal. Sorensen was driving towards a ranch just off the Calle Satellite. It was a long shot, but there was a rumour that there was a drug processing centre in one of the buildings; a place where cocaine and heroin were bagged, ready for onward shipment. It would be heavily guarded.

As they approached the ranch, Sorensen killed the lights and cruised the car to the outer gates. They could see lights in the ranch-house and surrounding outhouses. He was with the same men who had interrogated the taxi driver. He spoke to them in Spanish.

"Carlos, Mario, check out the outbuildings and report back to me. Do not shoot unless you are compromised. I will check the main building. Meet me back at that barn over there," he said, pointing to one of the closest outbuildings to the main house. "If you hear shooting come at once."

They went to the rear of the car and opened the boot. There was a supply of Kalashnikov automatic rifles and assorted handguns, enough to kit a small army. The men picked up what they needed and left holding the rifles and tucking handguns into the waistbands of their trousers. Sorensen walked up to the ranch-house. He heard several dogs barking and could see a large kennel in the corner of the grounds; black shapes appeared to be prowling around.

There were no curtains at the ranch windows, and Sorensen checked each one in turn. He could hear voices and cheering coming from a room at the back as if someone was watching a football match. He reached the source of the commotion and lifted his head above the mantel to see inside. It was a large bedroom with a four-poster bed in the centre. A woman was on the bed with her arms tied to two of the posts. She had been stripped from the waist down; her tee-shirt was pushed up to her neck. Five men were surrounding her, drinking from bottles, but Sorensen could not see clearly what they were doing; she was not moving. He waved to his compadres who saw his signal and quickly joined him.

"I think she is here in the back room; it's a bedroom. We will need to go through the house unless we can get in another way. Come."

They followed Sorensen back to the rear of the ranch. The bedroom window was about four feet from the ground, a comfortable height if you wanted to look into the room, but not so accommodating if you needed to break in. Sorensen had another peek.

"It doesn't look good," he whispered. "We need to move now."

"How do we get in?" asked Mario.

"Not through the window… There must be another way in."

The three skirted around the back of the ranch; halfway along the other side, there was a door.

"There," said Sorensen.

The three went to the entrance, and Sorensen gently turned the handle. There was a click as the door unlatched. He pushed forward. It was a kitchen and in darkness. The revelry was coming from the left.

They crept slowly down the corridor, weapons at the ready; there were more bedrooms left and right. They reached the end room, the master bedroom. The door was slightly open; the light from inside creating a shadow on the floor.

"When I give the signal we rush them," Sorensen whispered.

"Si," said Mario.

"Si," said Carlos.

He unlocked the automatic. "Now!"

It was like a scene from a 1930's gangster movie as they rushed in and opened fire on the unsuspecting men.

One of them had his trousers around his ankles. Sorensen peppered his body with bullets, and he dropped to the floor like a stone.

"Stop firing," said Sorensen. They surveyed the scene; it was total carnage. The bodies of the five men were riddled with bullets; blood splattered across the walls. Everywhere was covered with red.

They quickly untied the woman, and Sorensen flung her over his shoulder.

"Quick, let's get out of here," he said, and they hurried up the corridor to the front entrance.

They could hear shouting coming from the outbuildings, followed by gunfire. They ran down the drive as fast as they could, Sorensen still carrying the woman over his shoulder. Mario stopped and put down a barrage of fire, giving them enough time to reach the car. Carlos opened the rear door, and Sorensen lay the woman down on the back seat and got in next to her. Carlos got in behind the driving wheel and started up. Mario let off another burst of fire as they drove away.

"How is the girl?" asked Mario.

Sorensen turned on the interior light. He could see blood oozing from her chest. He covered her with his jacket to keep her warm.

"It's not good; we need to get her to the hospital."

There was no hospital in Tamarindo; the nearest was Hospital

Enrique Baltodano Briceño, almost an hour away. Carlos floored the accelerator, but it still took too long. Sorensen was pressing a handkerchief over the wound in her chest trying to stem the bleeding but with little effect. Just ten minutes away, he made an announcement. "She's stopped breathing. I think she's dead."

They pulled up outside the hospital, and Sorensen gently lifted Evelyn; the seat was covered with blood, he carried her into the reception area.

"Can we have some help here?" he shouted in Spanish.

A nurse approached. "What is the problem?" she asked.

"She has been shot; she's stopped breathing, I think."

"Quick, through here," said the nurse and led the men to an emergency ward. Sorensen lay her gently onto a bed, and a doctor joined them. He checked her pulse and vital signs, then confirmed Sorensen's diagnosis.

Sorensen took out his phone and made a call.

Ramirez was still in the condo with Jacó and Adam; there had been little talking. There was the sound of a ringtone and Ramirez took out his phone.

"Hello," he said and listened. His face confirmed the news.

"Nooo!" screamed Adam and put his head in his hands.

Ramirez dropped the call. "Evelyn is dead," he confirmed and told Adam Sorensen's version of events.

"I must tell Andrés," he said. "There will be much bloodshed over this."

It was an emotional call, and Ramirez was trying to maintain his composure after he'd finished speaking to his brother. He turned to Adam.

"It is best that you return to the UK. Jacó will drive you back to the apartment, and you should leave as soon as possible. It may be dangerous for you here."

"Yes, ok, whatever you say," said Adam. "When?"

"You go now; find the next flight to London and leave as soon as you can. Your life could depend on it."

Adam could understand why he might be in danger; he had just witnessed a brutal murder. If anything, he was an accomplice.

He went to the bedroom and packed his stuff into the rucksack. Evelyn's clothes were still in the wardrobe.

"What about Evelyn's clothes and things?" he said as he came back to the lounge.

"We shall see to it; you should go."

Adam walked up to Ramirez. "I am so sorry for your family's loss, I really am. She was a special person."

"Yes, she was," said Ramirez.

The pair shook hands but with little warmth. Jacó took the rucksack and headed out of the condo.

It took four hours to get back to San José; it was starting to get light as they entered the city just after five a.m. Adam had slept for some of the journey, but it was a fatigue sleep and not restful.

The Chevvy pulled up outside Ramirez's apartment. Jacó turned to Adam. "I wait; you go get things, then aeropuerto."

"Si," said Adam who was in no position to argue.

Adam went inside, and a few minutes later, returned with the rest of his belongings. He handed the keys to the driver.

Twenty minutes later, Adam was at the airport desk to find the next flight back to the UK. It was almost ten-to-six. The only direct flight to the UK left at two-thirty in the afternoon, but there was one via Frankfurt that left at eight-fifty. He found the airline ticket office and bought a business-class single.

The flight was over fourteen hours with the stop-over in Germany and landed at Heathrow at eleven o'clock, in the evening, Costa Rican time, six a.m. local time. Adam had managed to get some sleep during the flight, but his grief and anguished kept surfacing. He had no idea what he should do.

The journey to his apartment from the London airport was a nightmare; it was the middle of rush-hour and the Tube was packed. It took over two hours to reach Blackheath. He felt travel-weary and in desperate need of a shower. He had trouble remembering what day it was; his phone said Friday. He'd missed Thursday somewhere over the Atlantic.

He managed to freshen up before collapsing into bed and falling into a deep slumber.

He woke up around midday, totally disoriented. He was trying to make sense of the past week. He missed Evelyn. When he closed his eyes, he could see her lying next to him; he had never met anyone like her, but now he needed to think about the future.

He felt safer now he was back in the UK, but he had no idea if he was still in danger. He'd done nothing wrong, but he was still getting flashbacks of the taxi driver, his pitiful pleading and the ruthlessness of his dispatch. That would haunt him for a long time.

Then there was the bank.

He had been lucky so far; the transactions he had authorised for Five Rivers had not, to his knowledge, attracted any suspicion, and with the charges his bank had taken for making the transfer, they had done well from the activity too. It was a win-win in many ways, just illegal.

The big problem Adam had was the deal with the Hombres. He had had reservations about it from the start but went along with it just to get out of the situation. He knew that if he continued authorising the payments, it would be only a matter of time before he was discovered; the increase in high-value transfers to one bank was bound to attract attention.

He made himself a coffee and switched on his laptop. There was a website in Costa Rica that gave local news in English; he'd accessed it before his trip when he was doing some research. He keyed in the URL and opened the site. The front page was full of coverage of a recent election. The next page, though, contained details of the kidnap and shooting of 'the daughter of a prominent banker' in Tamarindo. Adam started to read the account but found it too painful. He shut down the webpage.

With the weekend to reflect, it was time to enact his plans. He would give in his notice to the bank and move away, somewhere new. It would mean he wouldn't have to deal with the Costa Rican transfers when they started coming through; that would be someone else's problem. He didn't want to work in the City any longer; he wanted no contact with the bank or anyone connected with it.

He started scanning the internet for possible jobs and, after a great deal of searching recruitment websites, he spotted one for a compliance manager for a major store in Leeds. The salary package was nowhere near his current one, but that wasn't an issue at the moment; the more he thought about it, the more he knew it would be ideal. There was an added bonus; one of his University rugby-playing friends lived in Leeds and Adam had kept in touch via social media. He would make a great contact.

Adam spent Saturday updating his CV and completed the online application form.

On Monday morning, Adam was officially still on holiday,

and he had no intention of going into the office. Any personal belongings he had there could stay. His work laptop was in his drawer; he could give his manager the access code; there was nothing private that should concern him.

He sent his boss an email, very brief and to the point.

'Please accept this email as my formal resignation from the Standard Bank of South America with immediate effect. This is due to personal reasons.'

Within minutes of sending it, his mobile phone sounded from his jacket pocket; he had a feeling who it might be. He decided to answer it.

"Hi Emil," Adam said, recognising the number.

"Adam, what are you doing back? And why the resignation?"

"I decided to come home early. I had a lot of time to think while I was away, and realised I need a new challenge."

"But why? Is it the money? I'm sure we can come to some arrangement, re-align your package in some way." His boss spoke quickly.

Why do people always assume it's about the money, thought Adam.

"No, it's not the money. I want a fresh start away from banking."

"But what about the courses we've lined up for you? We're talking senior management… within the next eighteen months or two years."

"I'll have to pass on that," replied Adam.

"And you're quite sure? There's nothing I can do to make you change your mind?"

"No, I'm sure, thanks, and for your support."

"Ok; if that's the way it is. You'll need to let me have your access codes."

"Yes, I'll text them."

"Right, well, good luck, then. I'll pass on your email to HR and get them to do the necessary."

There was a hint of anger in the voice; he was clearly not impressed at losing Adam.

Tuesday morning Adam received a phone call from the H.R. Manager of Huntsman and Darby.

"Hi, Adam, my name is Wendy Phillips, Head of HR, Huntsman and Darby in Leeds. I've been reviewing your application for our Compliance Manager's position, are you ok to answer a few questions?"

Adam was good at interviews; he had never failed one in his life. He was confident and articulate, plus of course, ideally qualified and experienced for the role.

The telephone interrogation lasted for just over forty minutes. Adam was pleased with the way it had gone and was promised a response within twenty-four hours.

Sure enough, the following day, Adam was asked to attend a final interview at the store. It would consist of meetings with the Head of Operations and the Chairman, Sir Basil Huntsman. He had never met a knight of the realm before and was looking forward to the prospect.

Thursday morning, Adam was on the train to Leeds for an eleven o'clock appointment at Huntsman's. During the journey, he made use of the free Wi-Fi and accessed the Costa Rica newspaper website. He couldn't believe what he was reading. There was a front-page banner headline, "Carnage in Tamarindo".

'There has been no let-up in the number of shootings in the Tamarindo and surrounding area, following the murder of

Evelyn Ramirez, with the discovery of two more bodies today, making a total of seven. Police are working on the theory that the murders are revenge killings. Some of the victims had been tortured, according to a police spokesman. As part of the investigation, officers, with support from army special forces, raided a ranch near Villareal and found a significant quantity of drugs and weapons. Four people have been taken into custody.'

Adam realised he had been incredibly naïve, and lucky. He had shut out the reality of the situation or the potential consequences for personal gain under the heading of 'adventure'. Only now, were the ramifications beginning to hit home. If he hadn't had got involved, Evelyn would still be alive; that was the truth of it. He strangely felt guilty about the poor taxi driver and the children who were now without a father. He put his head in his hands, but the pain was not going to leave him anytime soon.

He arrived in Leeds in good time and made his way to Huntsman and Darby; the up-market store he hoped would be a new beginning. He was greeted by Clarke, the concierge who doffed his top hat and opened the door for him to enter the store. The sight almost took Adam's breath away. It was heaving with Christmas shoppers; the whole of the ground floor was festooned in bunting, Father Christmas, trees, reindeers, anything to entice the hard-earned money from potential customers. There were queues at all the checkouts.

After a five-minute wait, his enquiry at the customer-service desk resulted in a further delay while the Head of H.R. took the lift to collect him. She led Adam to the sixth floor where Ryan Matthews, Head of Operations, was expecting him. One or two heads from the admin staff were watching as he walked through the department; there followed some sniggering. The interview lasted about an hour before Adam was escorted to the next floor to Cressida Bolton, the indomitable custodian of Sir Basil's diary. Cressida, exercised her power, making Adam wait on a chair outside Sir Basil's office until he received the 'royal' summons.

This time, Adam did feel slightly nervous as he waited, but once he had got into his stride, he soon relaxed. After about five minutes of introduction, Sir Basil asked him a question he wasn't expecting.

"I see you've recently returned from Costa Rica, a fascinating place. The family had interests there, you know, many years ago now; my great-great uncle, I think it was, had a coffee plantation in the eighteen hundreds; don't know what became of it."

Adam just listened as Sir Basil continued to share the exploits of various members of his family for what seemed an inordinate amount of time, probably over twenty-five minutes. Adam nodded politely. It was the easiest job interview he had ever had. After forty-five minutes, Sir Basil stood up and shook Adam's hand warmly.

"Good to meet you, old boy, I think you'll settle in here just fine."

That was it; Adam received confirmation of the job offer the following day. He would start a week on Monday.

This gave Adam enough time to arrange some temporary accommodation. He also contacted his rugby friend who promised an introduction at his club. His social life seemed assured.

The activity had helped Adam with his grief over Evelyn's death; keeping busy was the key. He'd heard nothing from Ramirez and preferred it that way; he had no idea what was happening or how they would react when they eventually discovered that he had left the bank. He was sure they would find out. He changed his mobile phone number and email address which would avoid any contact from them. Realistically, he knew there was no hiding place if someone really did want to find him. He would deal with that if it happened.

The following Sunday, on a cold and dreary winter's afternoon, Adam made the trip to Leeds in his newly-acquired M3. His friend had recommended a small hotel on the outskirts of the city which would act as a base until he had found something more permanent. It was early December; the Christmas lights shone brightly in the city as he drove through; just over two weeks earlier, things were so different. He did not feel remotely festive.

Chapter Nineteen

It was against this background that, just over three months later, Adam was wrestling with sleep after receiving Jez's message.

He had settled in well into his new career; thoughts of rogue transfers to South American countries were gradually fading. His rugby friend had made the introductions at Meanwood, and following a trial shortly after arriving in Leeds, he was soon playing regularly for the club. At the store, his new boss had been very complimentary about his work. He'd moved into his new flat and life seemed back on track.

Then there was Sarah.

Sarah had come out of the blue; she made him feel like he did with Evelyn.

Since arriving in Leeds, he had been out with several girls he had met through the Rugby Club; in fact, his capacity for attracting girls had become a standing joke among his team-mates. For Adam, girls had become trophies.

But that had changed when he met Sarah. She was funny, intelligent and attractive.

Thursday mid-morning, the day before the rugby club awards-night, he was in his office at the store when his mobile phone alerted him to a text message. It was from Sarah; he opened it.

'We need to talk.'

Earlier in Deighton, Jez was back on his computer; it would be an hour before Mrs Dawson was due. He'd accessed Adam's social media accounts, and noticed Adam had removed his Instagram profile, but the LinkedIn account was still there. The previous message he had posted had been deleted. "Hmm, you're not getting away with it that easily," said Jez to himself, and reposted the original message complete with picture.

He looked at the photograph for a moment and felt a pang of jealousy. He so wished it was him and Sarah, just the two of them in some exotic hideaway. The girl was very attractive; he couldn't understand why Adam would leave her and go out with anyone else. The way they were holding each other, so together; there was obviously a strong bond between them. A picture tells a thousand stories.

He checked the rugby club website again. The awards-night was still on, starting at seven-thirty. He began to feel anxious again. To give him focus, he started making a checklist of what he might need.

It was mid-morning at the store; Sarah had gone to the staff room to collect a coffee. She didn't want to go down to the store coffee shop; it was always busy. While she was waiting for the kettle to boil, she took out her phone and accessed her social media. There was a LinkedIn alert; one of her college friends had got a new job. Sarah sighed, then remembered she hadn't updated her profile to reflect her new position. She should do that. It was her turn to tell everyone else that she too was successful.

She opened the timeline, and there was a post from Adam which attracted her curiosity. She read the message, and her legs almost gave way. She felt nauseous.

"Are you ok, Sarah?" said one of the Admin team who was on a nearby seat devouring a chocolate profiterole.

"Yes," said Sarah and went back to her office.

She opened her phone again and expanded the picture; two people, clearly in love; then the message. "The bastard," she said out of earshot of anyone.

She sent Adam a message *'We need to talk'.*

'Lunchtime?' came the reply.

'Yes, 12.30'.

Adam guessed that Sarah must have seen the message. He had some explaining to do.

Adam was waiting for Sarah by the lift at twelve-thirty; she hardly acknowledged Adam as she exited the lift. She walked briskly out of the store with Adam following, not saying a word. They ordered their lunch separately and found a seat in the corner.

"Are you not eating?" said Adam, seeing she had only bought a coffee.

"I'm not hungry," she replied.

"I think I know what this is about," said Adam.

"Missing our times together?"

"My account has been hacked. I never posted that message; nor would I." He sounded upset.

"What do you mean?" said Sarah, her posture changing. She leant forward.

"The girl in the picture is dead."

Sarah's expression changed. "Dead?"

"Yes, she was murdered. I'll tell you everything. I've nothing to hide."

Sarah took a drink. "Ok," she said. "I'm listening."

"It was last November; I met her on my trip to Costa Rica, the one I told you about. She was back-packing too, and we teamed up. A few days later, we were in a bar, in the north, and she was kidnapped when she went to the toilet. She turned up dead the next day."

Adam's story had been embellished, but it was mostly true.

"God, how awful." Sarah's expression changed to one of sympathy.

"Yes, it was terrible. I went to the police, and they interviewed me all the next day. When they let me go, I got the hell away. She was a girl I met, that's all."

"You look close in the picture."

"Well you pose for these things, don't you? We had a good time for a couple of days, and then... well, you know the rest."

"But how did it get posted on your LinkedIn timeline?"

"That's the point; I have no idea. It just appeared this morning. It shook me up too, I can tell you."

"Yes, I can imagine," said Sarah.

"It must be someone with a grudge. I mean, the picture wasn't particularly private; it was on my Instagram page; I've not been on there since I came back; I'd forgotten all about it. I'm sorry if it's upset you."

"It's ok. I was furious at the time, but now you've explained, I'm ok."

Adam held her hand. "And we're still ok?"

"Yes, we're ok."

Inside, Sarah was beginning to realise the effect Adam was having on her. She accepted the explanation without question; mostly because she wanted to.

"I can't wait to be with you tomorrow," said Adam.

"No, me neither. Would you like to come over tonight? I could do with some serious TLC."

"Yeah, me too; what time?"

"Half-seven, eight o'clock?"

Adam leaned across the table and kissed her; he didn't care who had seen them.

She responded warmly and squeezed his hand.

That afternoon, Sarah found it difficult to focus on work; her mind was still on the girl in the picture and Adam's story. Something was nagging her; who might have a grudge against Adam strong enough to hack into his social media account, and have the skills to do it? A thought suddenly crossed her mind; Jez.

She hadn't heard from him in a while, and she preferred it that way; he had started to become creepy towards the end. He was into computers, and maybe he had the knowledge to hack into someone's account. Then she thought about her old boss, Pete, and the problems he had had from a hacker; Jez again? It was a scary thought, but possible. She didn't know why he would, or what to do about her suspicions at this moment.

That evening, Sarah was wearing a loose top and tracksuit bottoms when Adam knocked on the door. There was little conversation, just a frantic removal of clothes and urgent copulation on the settee, totally ignored by Moses, the cat, who was fast asleep in his basket. Sometimes, the best times are when passion takes over.

"God, I needed that," said Sarah as they relaxed in the 'cigarette moment'. Neither of them smoked, so it was just quiet reflexion and contentedness.

"Yes, me too," said Adam as he kissed Sarah.

Nothing more was said about the Costa Rica picture; Sarah had accepted Adam's version of events, and there was nothing to forgive.

As they lay there in each other's arms, Sarah realised that she had never been this close to anyone before; It was a new and exciting experience. For Adam, too, there was a realisation; he had finally exorcised Evelyn's ghost and could move on.

The moment was interrupted when Moses emerged from his basket, stretched, jumped up onto the settee and started to nuzzle up to Sarah. She pushed the cat back to the floor. "We don't need a threesome," she said, and they both laughed.

As they had to work the following day, Adam left around ten-thirty.

Back in Deighton, Jez was becoming more and more depressed. The solicitor had called about his mother's funeral arrangements, but he couldn't take in what he was saying. Mrs Dawson had made him some dinner, but he ended up throwing most of it into the garbage bin. His only solace was his aquarium; it was the only thing that gave him some tranquillity.

Later, he was at his desk just staring at his computer; his mind wasn't functioning. He would occasionally look up at the pictures of Sarah on his wall. Pride of place was the Settle-selfie which he had subsequently printed off on A3 glossy paper, and it now dominated the 'shrine'. He hacked back into Sarah's Facebook account, opened her photos and found another he liked. A holiday snap, probably taken in Scotland by her brother; she looked relaxed and vibrant. He copied it to his desktop and decided it would be his new screen-saver. He enhanced it with some software, giving it some soft focus, and printed it onto some A4 glossy photo paper, then pinned it on the wall next to his others.

His desk drawer contained far more sinister images, of Adam, mostly copied from his Instagram account before he closed it. Jez had added various embellishments; devil horns, women's breasts, a limp penis; it was an attempt at humiliation and control. All the pictures had had the eyes removed. Far from helping his mindset, he was becoming deranged. The more he pursued this activity, the more his thoughts turned to murder.

He hacked back into Adam's LinkedIn account and re-posted the picture. This time with a new message. *'Can't wait to see you soon, my darling. I miss you so much. All my love xxx'*.

There was nothing Adam could do about the message. It appeared to be his own post again so there was nobody he could block. He had changed his password and reported it to the administration people who said they would get back to him within forty-eight hours. Adam saw the new message when he returned from Sarah's and immediately called her.

"Sorry if I woke you. I've had another message," he said when she answered.

"It's ok; I was just reading. That's terrible. What did it say?" and Adam explained the new post.

"What are you going to do?"

"I'm closing my LinkedIn account for a while. I've got no choice. I don't use it that much, so it won't really be a problem, but it just feels like an intrusion."

"Yes, I can see that."

"Anyway, I just wanted you to know, I didn't want you to worry."

"No, that's ok; glad you did. Thanks for telling me. I love you," said Sarah.

The last three words had come unexpectedly, not least to Sarah.

"I love you too," said Adam.

On Friday morning, Jez had had very little sleep; his obsession with Sarah and his hatred for Adam had completely taken over his life. He had tried to hack back into Adam's LinkedIn account but found it had gone; he had obviously closed it. This gave Jez a small feeling of victory; he knew he was getting to Adam.

He had been considering his next move. He had already decided to stake out the rugby club but to what end? He wasn't entirely sure, but he felt he had to be doing something. If he could get away with it, killing Adam was a viable option, but he would take his time; he was in no hurry, a plan would evolve, he was certain. In the meantime, he would think about another hack, maybe involving Huntsman's. He would work on it.

Tonight would give him more information to help him formulate a strategy. He regretted using the pornographic images on Sarah's old boss; that was a mistake. It would have been more useful on Adam, but, if he did it now, Sarah would work out it was Jez, and that would be the end of that.

For Sarah, life couldn't be better; she felt on top of the world after the previous evening's encounter with Adam. It had been amazing, and she noticed herself smiling on her morning commute; even a ten-minute delay for signals could not destroy her mood. She couldn't wait to meet up with him again. Her assistant commented on it when she went in for the morning briefing.

"You seem happy this morning. Did you score last night or something?" she said and laughed.

"That would be telling," replied Sarah.

With back-to-back meetings, including one with Tilly, the new Head of Sales and Marketing, she was going to be busy which was how she preferred it.

Adam was still worried about the messages and their implications. He wondered about the Costa Ricans and his departure from the bank and whether they were seeking payback. He couldn't work out why they would bother to hack into his LinkedIn account; it didn't make sense. Drug barons were not known for their subtlety. Maybe it was someone else with a grudge, but he couldn't think who.

In between work commitments, he had time for some last-minute checks for the award-night at the rugby club. This was his first event since being voted Social Secretary the previous month, and his reputation for organising was on the line.

Back in Deighton, Jez was trying to complete some work for one of his few remaining clients, but his concentration levels were zero; it was as if he was on auto-pilot. He was working out what time he would need to leave to get to the rugby club. He was still driving the hired Nissan; he lacked the motivation to sort out all the forms for the insurance claim.

He knew the event started at seven-thirty; he would need to leave around six o'clock if he was going to be there to see the guests arrive. There was only one in which he was interested.

Sarah, too, would have to leave early. She needed to get home, feed Moses, have something to eat and get ready. She had arranged to meet Adam at the rugby club; she would be taking an overnight bag. For once, she didn't see Adam at lunchtime; she worked through to clear her work. She felt no guilt about leaving an hour early. She did, however, make a call to the lingerie department during her afternoon break; Adam was in for a treat.

She left the office at four-thirty to catch the train. On Friday nights, many other commuters had the same idea, and it was packed. Sarah didn't mind; she could only think of the evening ahead.

Moses provided the usual greeting when she arrived home, and she spent a few minutes making a fuss of the cat before fixing something to eat and taking a shower. Dinner would be quick, just beans on toast; that would keep the hunger pangs away.

By seven o'clock, Sarah was ready. She had one last check of her overnight case; she had everything she would need. Then a final look in the mirror; her hair and make-up were perfect. She picked up her car keys and went into the kitchen; there was more than enough food to keep Moses happy until the morning.

"Bye Moses," she shouted to the cat who was fast asleep in its box.

Jez had met his deadline and was heading out of the Estate towards his destination. As he had predicted, traffic was a nightmare, and it was after seven before he arrived at the rugby club. There was a sign indicating a left turn down a dirt track before it widened into a large white-gravel car park. Several cars were already parked, and Jez realised he had probably missed Adam's arrival. He scanned the cars that were positioned close to the entrance and wondered which one belonged to his nemesis. He noticed a new BMW; there was undoubtedly some money about.

It was a reasonably sized parking area, surrounded by trees. The rugby pitch was the other side of the clubhouse; Jez could see the tops of the goal posts above the building. He reversed the Nissan into the corner of the car park about fifty yards away from the building in the shadows, but with a good line of sight to club entrance.

He watched other cars arrive. He still had no idea why he was there; something would occur to him. He considered the visit as part of his planning process for some action, yet to be determined. By understanding his target's movements, a plan would emerge. It had become an obsession.

By seven-thirty, the car park was packed; some cars were having to park on the verges of the track from the main road, restricting its breadth to just one car's width. Jez could still see the club entrance. Then, about twenty-five to eight, he saw her. With the car park now at capacity, she must have parked along the lane and walked. Jez caught his breath; he started to hyperventilate. Seeing Sarah again had rekindled a myriad of thoughts and emotions. His hands were shaking, and he felt sick. He opened the car door for a moment to let in some air.

Adam had been supervising the event since six-thirty. It wasn't a large venue, by any means. There was a small dance area in front of the stage at the far end from the door, where the DJ was selecting suitable tunes behind some impressive audio equipment. On one side, under the windows, there was a table with an array of shields and trophies which would be handed out to worthy recipients later in the evening. Next to that, the caterers had set up trestle-tables ready for the food. To the left of the entrance corridor, was the bar, which, by seven-thirty was doing a roaring trade. There were eight volunteers tonight ready to serve the thirsty clientele.

Sarah entered the club and looked around for Adam. She spotted him near the trophy table chatting to an older man dressed in a blazer; Adam appeared to be giving him instructions. The man was nodding as Adam was talking.

Sarah walked past the melee at the bar and across the dance floor towards Adam. He turned around, a sixth-sense detecting her presence. He excused himself from his conversation, and the man smiled at Sarah as he walked past her towards the bar.

"Hi," said Adam. "You look amazing."

"Thank you," replied Sarah.

Sarah had made a significant effort considering the short time she had. She was wearing ass-hugging light-blue jeans, torn at the knees, white heels and a white top which buttoned down the front about half-way. A considerable amount of her chest and a lacy bra were visible.

Sarah looked around. "Wow, this is great; do all these people play rugby?"

"Ha, no, some of them wished they could. No, it's a mix, ex-players, supporters, members, oh, and some of the first team are here; one or two were busy, I'll introduce you in a minute. What would you like to drink?"

"Glass of red wine, please," replied Sarah, who continued to take in the surroundings.

She followed Adam through the crush towards the bar. Most people had been served and were standing and talking with their pints of beer, which had cluttered the area.

"Excuse me, excuse me," shouted Adam as he pushed through.

"Hi, Adam, what would you like?" asked a huge guy, at least six-feet-four with broad shoulders and a face that looked like it had been stamped on a few times.

"Pint of lager and a red wine, please Will."

Will turned and started dispensing the order.

"Will's our prop forward," said Adam. "A fantastic player; doesn't take any prisoners."

"No, I bet," said Sarah.

Will returned with the drinks and Adam paid.

"Let's move away from the bar," said Adam, and they jostled their way back through the scrum. Adam acknowledged several people as they negotiated their way to a vacant table.

As they sat down, they were approached by a smaller man about the same age as Adam escorting an extremely attractive young lady with long dark hair, heavy make-up, wearing distressed jeans, tee-shirt and leather jacket.

"Hi, Adam, how's it going?" said the man.

Adam turned to acknowledge the greeting.

"Oh, hi, Ben, Anita. Good, thanks, yeah," replied Adam.

"Do you mind if we join you? It's getting pretty crowded in here," said Ben.

"No, of course not. Ben, Anita, this is Sarah."

"Hi," said Ben and Anita almost in unison as they sat down.

Adam turned to Sarah. "Ben's our scrum-half; he's like a whippet," said Adam and laughed.

"Thanks for the build-up, Adam," said Ben.

Adam discussed rugby matters with Ben, with a view to the forth-coming match the following day. Sarah started chatting with Anita, exchanging career histories. Once the mention of Huntsman's came up, the topic quickly changed to clothes and fashion. Something in which Anita seemed to take a keen interest.

The atmosphere was convivial and, as the evening progressed, became more raucous. A group in the corner were starting to sing rugby songs but were soon drowned out when the disco started around nine o'clock.

The floor was quickly crowded with people moving up and down to the music; there was no space for dramatic expression.

At nine-thirty, waiters and waitresses appeared from the kitchen and started to bring out food and place the serving plates on the trestle-tables next to the trophies. A supply of paper plates and plastic utensils followed.

A few minutes later, the man who had been chatting to Adam earlier, approached the stage, took a microphone from the DJ and immediately blew in it. The music stopped, and he made an announcement.

"Hope everyone's having a great time, welcome to our annual awards evening," he shouted with due dramatic expression.

Roars of approval acknowledged the welcome. He continued. "We're about to start the formal proceedings, can you all take your seats please?"

One or two women were still on the dance-floor waiting for more music; there were looks of disapproval as they slunk back to their tables.

The M.C. continued in very authoritative terms. "Right, everyone, the moment you've all been waiting for, the announcement of this year's winners; don't worry, the food's coming, Matt," he said, addressing another particularly large man on a nearby table. There were hoots of laughter.

The trophies were duly presented with enthusiastic appreciation. There were various thank-yous to the caterers and volunteer bar-staff; Adam got a mention and a big cheer as the organiser. Sarah squeezed his hand in acknowledgement.

The DJ started playing some background music while everyone lined up for food. It was a simple spread; sandwiches, quiche, sausages on sticks, jacket potatoes. Judging by the urgency to get into line, it could have been mistaken for the last supper.

"What would you like?" asked Adam. "I'll get it… save you queuing."

"Oh, thanks," said Sarah. "Just a couple sandwiches and a slice of quiche will be great. I'm going to pop to the loo."

"I'll come with you," said Anita who was now best friends with Sarah.

"I'll watch the table," said Ben.

Adam headed to the queue for the food. As he reached the end of the line, there was a vibration in his pocket from his mobile phone. He took it out and opened it. 'Withheld', said the display.

There was some dialogue, but Adam couldn't hear over the sound of chatter.

"Hang on, I can't hear you," he shouted into the phone.

He walked out to the entrance lobby where it was much quieter.

"That's better, who is this?"

Adam's hands started to shake, and he went pale. "Yes, of course, straight away."

Adam left the club and stood at the entrance.

Jez was almost asleep in the Nissan; his concentration was waning by the minute. He was seriously questioning his judgement in staking out the rugby club; it had served no purpose whatsoever.

He checked his watch; it was ten-fifteen. He yawned which resulted in tears filling his eyes. He rubbed them to clear his vision then noticed someone appear at the front entrance. He looked familiar.

Jez cleared the windscreen with the back of his hand, squinted and rubbed his eyes again; there was no mistake, it was Adam.

Jez opened the car door and stood on the running-board, which gave him a better view above the other cars; he would not be visible in the shadow of the trees.

Adam appeared to be looking around; then, three men approached him. There was a brief discussion, and the four went around the side of the club. It was in darkness, away from the glare of the arc-lights which lit the front of the club. Jez could only see shapes, but arms were being raised, then lowered, and again, several times. Minutes later, the three men were walking away from the club and up the entrance lane.

Jez left the Nissan and squeezed by several cars, setting off one alarm and disturbing wing-mirrors on two more. He reached the clear space in front of the club; then went to the left, around the side in the direction Adam and the men had taken.

He couldn't believe what he was seeing. Adam was on the ground with blood pouring from his head; his skull appeared to be caved in; his brain was visible. Jez threw up against the club wall. He went closer; Adam's face was barely recognisable. He could see an object lying next to Adam, a crowbar or something similar. Jez bent down and instinctively picked it up.

"Adam?" he could hear someone calling from the front of the club. Jez immediately dropped the crowbar and skirted back to the Nissan; keeping in the shadows to make sure he wasn't seen.

He reached his car just as a couple of people went around the side of the club. There seemed to be a great deal of commotion.

Jez started up the Nissan and slowly eased the car out of

the car park and along the lane. He could see in the rear-view mirror that people were exiting the club and heading down the side of the building. One of them appeared to be carrying two chairs.

He accelerated away from the scene, his heart racing, his hands causing sweat-marks on the steering wheel. Then, in the light of the street-lights, he saw that it wasn't sweat; it was blood.

"Shit, shit, shit," he said.

He pushed the throttle harder; he needed to get back. In his distraught state, he crossed a set of traffic lights on red, narrowly missing another vehicle who managed to stop before there was a collision. Jez ignored the angry noise of a horn; he must get back. He would be safe.

It was a few minutes before Adam was missed. Sarah was at the mirror next to Anita; they were refreshing their make-up and chatting away like long-lost friends.

"So, how long have you been going out with Adam?" Anita asked as she was applying more lipstick.

"Not long," said Sarah. "A couple of weeks or so."

"Hmm, more than most; it must be serious," she laughed ironically. "I went out with him on a couple of dates," she added. "I can understand the attraction; he's a wild one, that one."

"Hmm," said Sarah. "No comment."

Anita put away her make-up and the pair left the toilets; Sarah, contemplative, now, and not in the mood for more chat. They reached the table to see Ben looking around.

"Have you seen Adam?" he said as they sat down.

"I thought he'd gone to get some food," said Sarah.

"Well, he's not in the queue. I'll go and see if I can find him."

Ben got up and went to the bar. "Have you seen Adam anywhere?" he asked Will, but the response was negative.

He went outside and called. He went to Adam's car to check; then, as he was returning to the club entrance, he noticed what looked like a tailor's dummy, lying on the ground, beside the club wall. An arm was just visible in the fluorescent lighting. Ben walked across to investigate.

"Oh my God," he shouted and bent over for a moment resting his hands on his knees, breathing heavily.

He staggered back into the club.

He went to the staff entrance of the bar and opened it. "Will, quick; it's urgent."

Will immediately left the bar and followed Ben to the side of the club. "Tell me I'm dreaming this," he said.

"Will looked at the figure."

"Fuck me," he said and retrieved his mobile phone from his pocket.

"Police and ambulance; quick, someone's been hurt."

"Ben, we need to close this up. Go inside and see if you can get everyone away… and find Jim."

Will's direction brought Ben back in focus, and he went back into the club and returned with the M.C. Will was examining the scene with the torch app on his phone; he had his hand to his mouth.

"Stay back. Adam's been beaten up. I think he's dead. There's nothing we can do. We must keep everyone away. This will be a crime scene. Can you set up a blanket or tablecloth or something, Jim, so people can't gawp?" said Will.

The M.C. and Ben went back inside and returned with a

tablecloth and a couple of chairs. They positioned the chairs and hung the tablecloth over them to obscure the view from prying eyes.

"What do I tell Sarah? She's inside and starting to get worried."

"I don't know, Ben, I really don't know," said Will. "But she's going to find out sooner or later."

Ben and the M.C., Jim, walked back into the club. Jim walked up to the stage through a crowd of dancers, raucously singing to one of the disco classics.

He walked up to the DJ. "Can you turn the music off and let me have the mic please?"

The DJ complied; there was a deathly hush, and some strange looks as the M.C. made the announcement.

"Can I have your attention, please. I'm very sorry, but I have to call a halt to proceedings."

There were cries of disappointment and derision, some heckling.

The M.C. put his hands up. "Yes, I know, I know, I'm sorry, but there has been an incident. The police are on their way. Now can you please leave in an orderly fashion and try not to make any noise; remember the neighbours."

There were curious looks among the crowd. "What's happened? What's happened?" was the question on everybody's lips.

Ben walked over to Sarah who was also wondering what was going on.

"Sarah, can we go somewhere quieter; we can go to the committee room."

"What's happened, where's Adam? Is everything alright?"

Ben ignored the questions and led Sarah to a room on the

left just past the staff entrance to the bar. Anita followed.

"Something's happened," said Sarah. "Tell me."

They entered the room; Ben turned the light on and closed the door.

"I'm sorry to be the one to tell you this, Sarah, but it looks like Adam's been attacked. I found him around the side of the club. I'm afraid he's dead. We're just waiting for the police and ambulance. I'm so sorry."

"Dead? No; he can't be. No. Who would want to attack him?"

"I don't know," said Ben "That's for the police to work out."

"Where is he? I want to see him."

"That's not possible; the police will want the scene protected for forensics. Nobody should go near him. We've put a blanket up."

It was twenty minutes before the sound of sirens could be heard in the distance. The car park was virtually empty. Will was still on guard in front of the tablecloth.

Chapter Twenty

Sirens echoed closer in the night sky as the first police car bounced its way down the pot-holed access lane. The arc-lights from the club cast an eerie glow as the yellow and blue squared squad-car pulled up outside the entrance. Two officers got out and walked towards Will who was still standing in front of the chairs, guarding the body.

"Will Summers?" asked the first officer.

"Yes," replied Will.

"P.C. Sanders; this is my colleague, W.P.C. Flynn. What seems to be the problem?"

"Someone's been attacked. He's dead."

"Ok; have we got a name?"

"Yes, it's Adam; Adam Fowler, he's one of our members."

Will moved out of the way. The officers walked towards Adam's lifeless body and surveyed the area; Sanders was holding a torch. He spoke into a walkie-talkie.

"Orange-two to control, over."

"Orange-two, go ahead."

"We're at Meanwood Rugby Club, off Roundhay Road. We have a body, believed to be that of an Adam Fowler. He's been badly beaten up. Request full back-up and forensics ASAP."

"Orange-two, messaged received, out."

The officer turned to Will. "Who discovered the body?"

"Ben Livingstone; he's inside with Adam's girlfriend."

"Georgie, can you go inside and see who's there?"

"They're in the committee room, on the left as you go in, past the bar entrance," directed Will.

The female officer entered the club. The door to the committee room was open. Sarah was seated at the long table in the centre of the room being comforted by Anita; Ben was talking to Jim.

"Hello," said the officer as she approached the group. Sarah was in tears, still trying to take everything in. Anita had her arm around her. Ben looked up.

"Hi."

"And you are?"

"Ben Livingstone."

The officer looked at the M.C.

"Jim Fairburn, club chairman."

She looked at the girls. "Anita Brown and this is Sarah; sorry I don't know your second name," said Anita turning to Sarah.

"Gooding," Sarah stammered in between sobs.

The officer took out a notebook.

"Mr Livingstone, I understand you discovered the body."

"Yes," said Ben.

"What time was that?"

Ben was thinking. "It would be about quarter-past or half-past ten. We were about to have food."

"Can you tell me what happened?"

Ben related the search for Adam. "I have no idea why he went outside; he never said he was going anywhere. He seemed to just disappear. One minute he was in the queue for the food, then he was gone. I never saw him leave."

"We were in the ladies," said Anita. "Sarah and me."

"You're his girlfriend?" said the W.P.C., looking at Sarah.

"Yes."

"How long have you known him?"

"Not long; we've only been going out for a couple of weeks."

"Can you think of anyone who might have done this; anyone who had a grudge against Adam?"

"No; nobody that would want to kill him."

Sarah thought of Jez but decided not to say anything; she needed to get her head straight.

Jez arrived back at the Hall; it had taken just forty minutes. He left the Nissan outside the house and went inside. He looked at his hands; they were covered in blood, so were his trousers and shirt where he'd touched them with his hands. He would need to dispose of his clothes.

He went upstairs; took a shower and changed. Adrenaline blocked his thought process and instinct took over. He put his clothes in a supermarket carrier bag from the kitchen and went outside. He went to the garage and grabbed the five-litre can of petrol which he kept there for emergencies. He walked across the big lawn to the edge of the wood and dropped the clothes on the floor.

It was pitch black and had been raining; it was also cold, but Jez felt nothing. He returned with a shovel from the gardener's hut. He picked up his clothes and look around for a suitable spot. His eyes had adjusted to the light; he had workable visibility.

He walked a few paces inside the canopy and started digging. The ground was soft and muddy; there was a layer of leaf-mould on top. He didn't need a big hole, just enough to contain his clothes. He piled the removed earth to the side and dropped the clothes into the cavity he had created. He poured petrol over the garments and set them alight. He watched the flames consume them and waited until they were reduced to ashes. He covered the remains with the earth and smoothed over the area, then sprinkled more leaf-mould over the spot. He would check again in the morning.

There was another job he would need to do. He was thinking about this on the journey back; he needed to get rid of the car in case it had been spotted. He decided the safest way would be to return it to the car-rental people and swap it for a different one.

He returned the items to their respective homes and then went back inside. His long-sleeve woodman's shirt was cold to the touch, and he shivered for the first time. He went to the kitchen cabinet and retrieved a bottle of whiskey.

He sat there staring into his whiskey tumbler trying to make sense of everything. Why did he go to the rugby club, it was a stupid mistake? He had no real reason to go. He berated himself, but it was done now.

The more he thought about it, the more he believed there was no reason for him to become a 'person of interest'; he didn't know him from Adam. He chuckled at the gallows humour, but he needed to cover his tracks, just in case. There was nothing to link him with Adam and no evidence he had been at the club.

Sarah couldn't remember getting home. It was very late by the time she had finished being interviewed by various police officers. The area around the murder scene had been cordoned off, and a tent erected over the body and the immediate surrounds. A team of forensic officers were examining the area in minute detail. What was assumed to be the murder weapon and various other items, were bagged and sent for analysis before Adam's body was released to the coroner for the post-mortem.

Detective Chief Inspector Hugh Garfield had taken over as the senior investigating officer. He had a team of five detectives at his disposal and had set up an incident room in police headquarters. He had personally interviewed Sarah and the others who were still at the club before letting them go home.

The following morning, Sarah felt rotten. She'd hardly slept; everything kept rolling around in her mind. She thought of Adam; why had this happened? They were so good together; she believed she had found her life-partner. She was in her bedroom emptying her over-night bag. She retrieved the lingerie, put it in a drawer and sighed.

A thought suddenly entered her head; what about work? She would need to speak to Adam's boss, Ryan Matthews. She had his mobile number and made the call around nine-thirty.

"Hello Ryan, it's Sarah. Sorry to bother you at home, but I thought you would want to know that Adam Fowler was killed last night. He was murdered at the rugby club. Can you let Sir Basil know? Thanks...yes, I'm sure it will be in the papers... yes, and all over the local news today. Ok, see you Monday."

As predicted, it was all over the news. Social media too had picked up on it. A condolences page had been set up on Facebook. Sarah was amazed at how popular Adam was; mostly females it seemed. The rugby match against Old Wintonians had been called off as a mark of respect.

There was another call Sarah needed to make; something had been bothering her all night. She picked up the business card from the table in the lounge and dialled the number. She was holding Moses for some comfort.

"D.C.I. Garfield, please," she waited. "Oh, hi; it' s Sarah Gooding, you asked me to contact you if I could think of anything that might help. Could you come over?"

Sarah gave the officer her address and went for a shower.

It was an hour later when Sarah spotted a car pulling up outside. Two people got out. She recognised the inspector; there was a woman with him, not in uniform. She went to open the door before they could knock.

"Hi Sarah, this is D.S. Beckenfield."

Sarah exchanged greetings. "I've just made a drink; would you like one?"

"Yes, ok, thanks," said the D.I. "Two coffees, thank you."

Sarah went into the kitchen and started a percolator. She caught herself in the mirror; drawn and haggard-looking; it was how she felt.

Moses was walking around the lounge, curious about the new arrivals. He started nuzzling against the legs of the D.S. who was stroking him. The cat was purring as Sarah brought in the coffees.

"What a lovely cat. What's its name?"

"Moses," said Sarah.

"Thanks for the drinks," said Garfield. He was keen that Sarah was as relaxed as possible which would help the interview process. "Mmm, nice coffee," he said, taking a sip. He put the mug back onto the coffee table. "You said on the phone that you might have some more information about the attack."

"Yes," said Sarah who now had Moses on her lap. She looked pensive, uncertain of what to say.

"Look, it may be nothing, and I don't want to get anyone into trouble, but Adam had some strange messages on his LinkedIn account recently."

"What sort of messages? Threatening?"

"No, not threatening, exactly; it was a picture of him and a girl he'd met in Costa Rica a few months ago with a message."

"Ok?" said the officer not sure of where it was leading.

"What sort of message?"

"'Missing you, can't wait to see you again', that sort of thing. The thing is, the girl was murdered out there. Adam thought his LinkedIn account had been hacked and someone was trying to cause a problem between us, him and me. I've been thinking about it, and it's possible it might be my ex."

"Go on," said the senior officer; the D.S. was taking notes. "What's his name?"

"Yes, his name is Jez, Jeremy. He lives at Deighton Hall; it's somewhere over Skipton way. He works with computers."

"Why do you think he may be involved?"

"Well, he was starting to become a bit weird towards the end, you know, clingy, and a bit obsessive, if I'm honest. That was the reason I ended it."

"Do you know his surname?"

Sarah had to think for a minute. "Steadman, I think."

Sarah outlined the other incidents involving her former boss. "I might be completely wrong; he's not been in touch with me since we split."

"Ok, so, how did you meet this man?"

"It was an online dating site."

"I see," said Garfield, but not in a judgemental way.

They continued talking for another hour, and as Sarah answered the officers' questions, she began to realise how little she knew about Adam.

"Did Adam mention any other past relationships at all?" asked D.S. Beckenfield.

"No, only the girl in Costa Rica, but even that wasn't much. He said they were backpacking, and she got killed, a mugging, I think."

The officers left, and the S.I.O. was speaking into a walkie-talkie; his tone sounded urgent.

Back in Deighton, Jez had a problem. His sleep-pattern was all over the place and having woken at five a.m.; he had fallen back into a deep slumber; it was now nine-thirty.

"Oh, no!" he shouted to himself as he checked the time on his phone. He quickly got dressed and left the house; his priority, he had to get rid of the Nissan.

He unlocked the car, got in and checked the driver's area. The steering column and sides of the seat were covered with bloodstains; he couldn't take it back in its present state. He went back to the house and returned to the car with a bucket of soapy water and a cloth. He wiped down the interior as best he could and tidied around until it was in a suitable condition. He decided he would drop it off then hire a new vehicle from a different franchise.

The exchange of cars was not as straightforward as he would have liked. Dropping off the Nissan proved particularly stressful, as he watched the assistant check the condition for what Jez deemed was longer than was necessary. Eventually, the forms were signed, and Jez had a twenty-minute walk to another car-rental firm. He chose a BMW three series; they were doing deals. Unfortunately, the paperwork took another forty-five minutes.

It was almost midday by the time Jez arrived back at the Hall. In his haste to leave, he hadn't bothered to close the external gate. As he approached the house, he could see two police vans, a car and movement.

"Shit, shit, shit," he said to himself, but it was too late; he had already been spotted. His first reaction was to turn and flee but, instead, he took a deep breath and decided to tough it out.

He pulled up in front of the house; he could see three officers rummaging about, looking through the windows of the Hall. One policeman had managed to open the garage and was having a good look around.

One of the officers, a female in plain-clothes, approached the BMW. "Jeremy Steadman?"

"Yes," said Jez. "What's the problem, officer?"

"My name's D.C.I. Florence Nicholas." She produced a warrant card and flashed it in Jez's direction. "We're investigating a serious assault in Leeds last night, and we believe you may be able to help us in our enquiries. Can we go inside?"

"Yes, of course," said Jez and opened the front door. He was cursing to himself; he wasn't sure how long he would be able to stall them. Perhaps, if he answered a few questions, they would leave him alone which would give him time to destroy the computer records.

Three of the officers followed Jez and the D.C.I. into the house. "Do you mind if my officers take a look around while we have a chat?" Jez was in a quandary but couldn't really refuse.

"Feel free," he replied. Two uniformed officers left and wandered off into the house.

Nicholas and a second officer walked into the kitchen and sat down. Jez went to the tap and poured himself a glass of water; his hands were shaking so much it was spilling down the sides. He ambled to the table, trying desperately to compose himself, and sat opposite them.

"This is my colleague, D.C. Walters." Jez nodded.

The D.S. looked around the kitchen; an investigator's eye. The range looked tired and in need of a good clean; wallpaper was peeling in the corners; there was an old-style deep sink with faded-silver taps.

"Nice kitchen," said the D.S. "Have you lived here long?"

"All my life, I was born here."

"And you live on your own?"

"Yes, my mother died very recently. I'm still trying to get used to her not being around. It seems strange," he said, trying to appear as relaxed as possible.

"Sorry to hear that," said Nicholas.

"Thanks," said Jez.

"Illness? Your mother?"

"Hmm, what? Oh, no, she had a fall… down the stairs."

"That's terrible; you must miss her."

"Yes," replied Jez.

The D.S. shuffled on her seat, getting comfortable; D.C. Walters was poised with a notebook.

"Ok, Jez. Does the name Adam Fowler mean anything to you?"

Jez gave the impression he was thinking. "Hmm, no. I can't say I recall the name; it's possible he's a client."

"A client? What is it you do for a living, exactly?" Walters was taking notes.

"I service laptops, websites, that sort of thing."

Jez took a slug of water.

"I see," said D.S. Nicholas. "How many clients do you have?"

"That's difficult say; over the years I've had hundreds," replied Jez.

"And, what? Mostly repairs, that sort of thing?"

"Mostly, yes, but data recovery, designing websites, networks; all sorts really."

She looked at him, deliberately making good eye-contact.

"Can I ask you where you were last night between, say, eight o'clock and eleven."

Jez was unable to hold the gaze and looked away momentarily. 'Shifty' was how Walters described him later.

"Here. I was working on a computer; it was an urgent job."

"And what time did you finish?"

"Hmm, I can't remember precisely, but it was quite late."

"Thank you," said Nicholas. "And you were on your own?"

"Yes, I told you; my mother's dead," he replied, sharper than he intended.

They were interrupted by one of the uniformed officers; he whispered something to the D.S.

"Do you mind coming with me a moment?"

"Why, what's the problem?"

"If you wouldn't mind, sir."

Nicholas and Walters both got up and followed the uniform out of the kitchen with Jez following anxiously behind. They went up the wide staircase; Jez had an idea where they were heading. For a second, Jez could see the form of his mother stood on the stairs mocking him. He could hear her voice; *"Told you so, told you so."*

They reached Jez's office. One of the officers was standing by the desk. The drawer was open, and the defaced photos of Adam were on top. Jez was starting to shake; he couldn't think properly.

Nicholas went to the drawer and put on a pair of forensic gloves. She examined the first picture.

"Can you explain these?"

"No. I don't recognise them."

"I'm sorry, sir, but I need you to come with me to the station."

Jez was taken to police headquarters in Leeds and questioned under caution. All his computer equipment was taken and bagged as evidence. He was remanded in custody, and a DNA swab was taken.

Several lines of enquiry were underway, but Jez was now the only suspect. One officer had the task of tracking down and interviewing all the guests at the awards night to find out if anyone had noticed anything.

Back at the Hall, one observant officer noticed that Jez's car was a rental; a phone call established that it was hired only that morning. The same officer rang other car-rental firms in the vicinity which resulted in the discovery of the Nissan. It had not been cleaned since its return and was impounded for examination.

Jez's computers were forensically examined, and the LinkedIn message discovered, but the clinching evidence was the trace of Jez's DNA on what was later confirmed as the murder weapon. The police had sufficient evidence to charge Jez with Adam's murder.

D.S. Nicholas set the recording device.

"For the record, this is Detective Sergeant Nicholas; I am with my colleague, D.C. Walters, Mr Jeremy Steadman and Hugo Burton, of Blunt Smythe, solicitors. Time is ten-thirty a.m."

D.C.I. Garfield was attentively watching the procedure in an adjacent room, behind a one-way glass. The decision to use a female interviewer was deliberate; it was concluded that Jez was likely to be more responsive.

Jez looked nervously at his solicitor.

The detective decided to use his preferred address.

"Jez, can you tell me where you were on the night of Friday 17th May between seven-thirty p.m. and eleven p.m.?"

"I was at home; I told you earlier," he said, looking at the D.S.

"So, if I were to tell you that your DNA has been found on an item that we believe was used in a fatal assault on Adam Fowler, how would you respond?"

"I have no idea how it got there." He twitched and touched the side of his face. He was beginning to shake.

"In an earlier conversation, you said that you had no knowledge of Adam Fowler. Is that correct?"

"Yes," said Jez.

"Then, if I were to mention that several pictures of Adam Fowler were found on your computer and in documents in the drawer of your desk; how would you respond?"

"I don't know," said Jez.

"I put it to you that you have been harassing Mr Fowler after he started a relationship with your former girlfriend, Sarah Gooding."

"No, no, no; not my former girlfriend. Sarah *is* my girlfriend. There's nobody else. She loves me; she told me."

Jez started crying uncontrollably.

"Would you like a glass of water?" asked the officer.

"No, no, I'm fine. I'm sorry. I will tell you everything."

He continued to sob.

"I did go to the rugby club; I wanted to see Sarah. I knew she was making a mistake with Fowler; he wasn't to be trusted. I wanted to warn her." This was the story he had worked out in his mind as a last resort.

"Ok, so tell me what happened on that night. What time did you arrive at the rugby club?"

Florence Nicholas was an experienced interviewer and was taking Jez gently through the process to build trust and get Jez to relax. It always produced results.

"It was after seven, about ten-past, something like that."

"And what did you do?"

"I just watched."

"For three and a half hours?"

"Yes."

"At any time during those hours, did you meet or see Adam Fowler?"

"Yes."

"Tell us what happened."

"He came out of the club; he was looking around as though he was waiting for someone."

"What time was that?"

"I can't remember; about ten, quarter-past, something like that, I guess."

"Ten o'clock?"

"Yes."

"And you approached him?"

"No, no, I was still in the car."

"This was a Nissan Primera, registration YE17 ETY?"

"It was a Nissan, but I don't know the registration; I rented it. I was waiting for the insurance company to pay up on my car." He looked at his solicitor. "I had an accident a few weeks ago."

"Oh, ok, so you were in the Nissan. Whereabouts in the car park were you parked?" The officer pulled out a to-scale drawing of the rugby club and its grounds. "Show me on here. For the record, I am showing Mr Steadman a scale map of Meanwood Rugby club and car park."

Jez pointed to the spot.

"That's quite a distance, and there were many cars in the car park."

"Yes, it was packed."

"So, how can you be certain it was Adam Fowler?"

"I would recognise him anywhere. I got out of the seat and stood on the running-board to see better. I was holding onto the door."

"I see; then you went over to him?"

"No, no, I went nowhere near him. I was just watching, and then I saw three men go up to him."

"Three men? Can you describe them?"

"No, they were facing away from me."

"Ok, then what happened?"

"They went around the side of the club."

"What happened next?"

"They seemed to be hitting him."

"Hitting him?"

"Yes, I couldn't see clearly; it was dark, and they were in shadow, but I could see their arms."

Jez demonstrated the movement.

"Ok, so what did you do?"

"After the men had gone, I walked over to see what had happened."

"Ok, then what?"

"He was on the floor; his head was all bashed in. There was a crowbar or something lying beside him, and I picked it up."

"Why did you do that?"

"I don't know; it was instinctive I suppose. Then I heard somebody calling, so I dropped the crowbar and ran."

"I see. So, why didn't you call an ambulance?"

"It would have been a waste of time his head was all bashed in; it was awful." Jez put his head in his hands.

"Why didn't you stay; you were a witness?"

"I don't know; I just panicked."

"So, these three men; what were they wearing can you remember?"

"No, not really, just dark clothes, I couldn't see very well because of the arc-lights. I told you, they were in shadow."

The officer looked at her colleague.

"Ok, we'll leave it there for now," said Nicholas. This was new information, and further enquiries were going to be necessary.

The officers got up and left the room; Jez was returned to the cells.

"So, what do you reckon, Guv?" asked Nicholas as the D.C.I. exited the adjacent room where he had been watching.

"Hmm, I don't buy it, but we need to check his story. Can you get some people down there to take another look; let's see if we can find anything."

"Yes, I'll get on it."

Further investigations at the site could find no evidence of the three men; there was no CCTV at the club, and, due to the activity around the crime scene, it was impossible to determine the nature of any individual footprints.

Two days later, after confirmation with the CPS, Jez was charged with the murder of Adam Fowler.

EPILOGUE

It was nearly four months before the trial of Jez Steadman was heard at Leeds Crown Court.

The evidence was overwhelming; the prosecution dismissed Jez's version of events; there was no evidence to support the 'three-men story'. Jez had a strong motive; the disfigured photographs were produced and computer records showing Jez's hacking into Adam's social media accounts. They also described Jez's treatment of Pete Draper, Sarah's former boss, and the impact that the malicious hacking had had on him.

Sarah was chief witness for the prosecution and described how Jez had become obsessed to the degree she was frightened of him, which was why she had ended the relationship. Later in the trial, a former girlfriend of Jez's, named Lucy, was called as a witness. She came up from London and described Jez's controlling behaviour around three years earlier; if anything, it was worse than Sarah's experience.

Jez was eventually found guilty of murder and sentenced to life imprisonment. He continued to protest his innocence and had to be restrained in the dock when the verdict was announced. He kept shouting. "It wasn't me. It wasn't me. I told you, it was those three men."

In a smart semi-detached house just off the ring-road, about a mile from the rugby club, Joy Cooper-Smith was in her kitchen-diner drinking a coffee; her partner Darren was opposite her.

"Did you read this?" said Joy

"Eh?" replied Darren, immersed in his phone.

"In the paper, the trial; that guy who killed poor Adam

Fowler."

"What about it?" said Darren, paying a little more attention.

"He's got life."

"Good," said Darren, still looking at his partner. "Adam was a great full-back, we've only won two games since he was murdered."

"Never mind rugby. It says here that the bloke who did it reckons he was framed, something about three men."

"So? They always say that. He's just trying to get off. I hope he rots in prison."

"Yes, but you remember that night, don't you? Those three men when we were leaving, they were walking down the lane. I remember you said they looked a bit shifty."

"Yeah, vaguely."

"So, do you think we should say something?"

"Too late now, the bloke's been found guilty."

"Yes, but what if was he was right; it's a bit of a coincidence, don't you think? I think we should call someone."

"Don't get involved. The trial's over."

"I know, but what if he didn't do it? I'm going to phone the police station."

An hour later, D.C. Chambers was hovering around D.C.I. Nicholas's desk; she was on the phone and ignoring his presence. Eventually, she dropped the call and turned to her colleague. She noticed a concerned look on his face. "What is it, Tom?"

"I've just had a call from a..." He checked his notes. "Joy Cooper-Smith. She was at the rugby club the night of the Adam Fowler murder with her partner."

"So?"

"Well, it seems the team never interviewed them; her and her partner left early, around ten. She claims that as they were driving up the lane from the car park, they saw three men walking towards them. Apparently, they were looking a bit 'shifty'; that's how she described them; they turned their heads as they went past. Thought they looked like illegal immigrants."

Nicholas stared at her blank computer monitor.

"Why has she just decided to say something?"

"I asked her that. She said she hadn't given it any thought until she read about the trial in the paper this morning and found out about Steadman's rant about the three men. What do you want to do?"

"Ignore it. We've got our man; no doubt in my mind."

"Ok, Guv."

Just after the trial, there was an announcement in the national business pages.

'Prestigious family-owned store calls in the administrators.'

The narrative followed.

'The Leeds-based upmarket store, Huntsman and Darby, have called in administrators. In a statement to the press, the chairman, Sir Basil Huntsman, blamed the decision on online shopping and the increase in out-of-town shopping centres, leading to poor trading conditions. The store employs two hundred and sixty-five people. The administrators, Smithson Andrews, are hopeful that a buyer will be found and that the store can survive. They could not rule out possible redundancies.'

Three days later, Sarah received her redundancy notice. Like many at the store, she had already started looking for a new position and had two interviews lined up already.

That evening, she was on her laptop; Moses was on the table

next to her, fascinated by the movement on the screen. Sarah had changed into an attractive top and had taken time with her make-up.

She logged into a website; LoveNet.com.

She clicked on the tab that said, 'Find Partners'. A woman's voice whispered seductively from Sarah's laptop speakers, soothing and deep; "Hello Sarah, this is Aphrodite, would you like to see your like-minded singles, selected just for you?"

THE END